MR CAMPION AND OTHERS

Margery Allingham took to writing naturally; in her family no other occupation was considered natural or indeed sane. Educated at the Perse School and Regent Street Polytechnic, she wrote her first novel while still in her teens. She began to leave a lasting mark on modern fiction in 1928 when, at the age of twenty-three, she wrote the first of her Albert Campion detective novels. Her early books, such as *The Crime at Black Dudley*, *Mystery Mile* and *Look to the Lady*, had to be written in spare time hard won from her film work. At that time her books were beloved by the few advanced spirits who enjoyed her gay and distinctive approach to the problems and pleasures of post-war youth. Since then her gentle detective and his strong-arm colleagues have become known and loved by readers of all ages all over the world. She also acquired a reputation as a more serious writer. In an *Observer* review of *The Fashion in Shrouds* Torquemada remarked that 'to Albert Campion has fallen the honour of being the first detective to feature in a story which is also by any standard a distinguished novel.' Her novels cover a broad field. They vary in treatment from the grave to the frankly satirical, yet each example contrives to conform to the basic rules of the good detective tale.

Margery Allingham was married to Philip Youngman Carter and lived for many years on the edge of the Essex Marshes. She died in 1966.

Mr Campion and Others

MARGERY ALLINGHAM

PENGUIN BOOKS
IN ASSOCIATION WITH
WILLIAM HEINEMANN LTD

PENGUIN BOOKS

Published by the Penguin Group
Penguin Books Ltd, 27 Wrights Lane, London W8 5TZ, England
Viking Penguin, a division of Penguin Books USA Inc.
375 Hudson Street, New York, New York 10014, USA
Penguin Books Australia Ltd, Ringwood, Victoria, Australia
Penguin Books Canada Ltd, 2801 John Street, Markham, Ontario, Canada L3R 1B4
Penguin Books (NZ) Ltd, 182–190 Wairau Road, Auckland 10, New Zealand

Penguin Books Ltd, Registered Offices: Harmondsworth, Middlesex, England

First published by William Heinemann Ltd 1939
Published in Penguin Books 1950
13 15 17 19 20 18 16 14 12

Copyright 1939 by P. and M. Youngman Carter Ltd
All rights reserved

Printed in England by Clays Ltd, St Ives plc
Set in Monotype Baskerville

CONTENTS

Grateful acknowledgements are due to the Editors
of *The Strand Magazine*, *The Daily Express*, *The
Evening Standard*, and the English and American
Harper's Bazaar.   M. A.

I

The Widow

THE second prettiest girl in Mayfair was thanking Superintendent Stanislaus Oates for the recovery of her diamond bracelet and the ring with the square-cut emerald in it, and Mr Campion, who had accompanied her to the ceremony, was admiring her technique.

She was doing it very charmingly; so charmingly, in fact, that the Superintendent's depressing little office had taken on an air of garden-party gaiety which it certainly did not possess in the ordinary way, while the Superintendent himself had undergone an even more sensational change.

His long dyspeptic face was transformed by a blush of smug satisfaction and he quite forgot the short lecture he had prepared for his visitor on The Carelessness Which Tempts the Criminal, or its blunter version, Stupidity Which Earns Its Own Reward.

It was altogether a most gratifying scene, and Mr Campion, seated in the visitor's chair, his long thin legs crossed and his pale eyes amused behind his horn-rimmed spectacles, enjoyed it to the full.

Miss Leonie Peterhouse-Vaughn raised her remarkable eyes to the Superintendent's slightly sheepish face and spoke with deep earnestness.

'I honestly think you're wonderful,' she said.

Realizing that too much butter can have a disastrous effect on any dish, and not being at all certain of his old friend's digestive capabilities, Mr Campion coughed.

'He has his failures too,' he ventured. 'He's not omnipotent, you know. Just an ordinary man.'

'Really?' said Miss Peterhouse-Vaughn with gratifying surprise.

'Oh, yes; well, we're only human, miss.' The Superintendent granted Mr Campion a reproachful look. 'Sometimes we have our little disappointments. Of course on those occasions we call in Mr Campion here,' he added with a flash of malice.

Leonie laughed prettily and Mr Oates's ruffled fur subsided like a wave.

'Sometimes even he can't help us,' he went on, encouraged, and, inspired no doubt by the theory that the greater the enemy the greater the honour, launched into an explanation perhaps not altogether discreet. 'Sometimes we come up against a man who slips through our fingers every time. There's a man in London to-day who's been responsible for more trouble than I can mention. We know him, we know where he lives, we could put our hands on him any moment of the day or night, but have we any proof against him? Could we hold him for ten minutes without getting into serious trouble for molesting a respectable citizen? Could we? Well, we couldn't.'

Miss Peterhouse-Vaughn's expression of mystified interest was very flattering.

'This is incredibly exciting,' she said. 'Who is he? – or mustn't you tell?'

The Superintendent shook his head.

'Entirely against the regulations,' he said regretfully, and then, on seeing her disappointment and feeling, no doubt, that his portentous declaration had fallen a little flat, he relented and made a compromise between his conscience and a latent vanity which Mr Campion had never before suspected. 'Well, I'll show you this,' he conceded. 'It's a very curious thing.'

With Leonie's fascinated eyes upon him, he opened a drawer in his desk and took out a single sheet torn from a week-old London evening paper. A small advertisement in the Situations Vacant column was ringed with blue pencil. Miss Peterhouse-Vaughn took it eagerly and Mr Campion got up lazily to read it over her shoulder.

WANTED: *Entertainer suitable for children's party. Good money offered to right man. Apply in person any evening. Widow, 13 Blakenham Gardens, W1.*

Leonie read the lines three times and looked up.

'But it seems quite ordinary,' she said.

The Superintendent nodded. 'That's what any member of the public would think,' he agreed, gracefully keeping all hint of condescension out of his tone. 'And it would have escaped our notice too except for one thing, and that's the name and address. You see, the man I was telling you about happens to live at 13 Blakenham Gardens.'

'Is his name Widow? How queer!'

'No, miss, it's not.' Oates looked uncomfortable, seeing the pitfall too late. 'I ought not to be telling you this,' he went on severely. 'This gentleman – and we've got nothing we can pin on him, remember – is known as "The Widow" to the criminal classes. That's why this paragraph interested us. As it stands it's an ad. for a crook, and the fellow has the impudence to use his own address! Doesn't even hide it under a box number.'

Mr Campion eyed his old friend. He seemed mildly interested.

'Did you send someone along to answer it?' he enquired.

'We did.' The Superintendent spoke heavily. 'Poor young Billings was kept there singing comic songs for three-quarters of an hour while W—— I mean this fellow – watched him without a smile. Then he told him he'd go down better at a police concert.'

Miss Peterhouse-Vaughn looked sympathetic.

'What a shame!' she said gravely, and Mr Campion never admired her more.

'We sent another man,' continued the Superintendent, 'but when he got there the servant told him the vacancy had been filled. We kept an eye on the place, too, but it wasn't easy. The whole crescent was a seething mass of would-be child entertainers.'

'So you haven't an idea what he's up to?' Mr Campion seemed amused.

'Not the faintest,' Oates admitted. 'We shall in the end, though; I'll lay my bottom dollar. He was the moving spirit in that cussed Featherstone case, you know, and we're pretty certain it was he who slipped through the police net in the Barking business.'

Mr Campion raised his eyebrows. 'Blackmail and smuggling?' he said. 'He seems to be a versatile soul, doesn't he?'

'He's up to anything,' Oates declared. 'Absolutely anything. I'd give a packet to get my hands on him. But what he wants with a kids' entertainer – if it is an entertainer he's after – I do not know.'

'Perhaps he just wants to give a children's party?' suggested Miss Peterhouse-Vaughn and while the policeman was considering this possibility, evidently the one explanation which had not crossed his mind, she took her leave.

'I must thank you once again, Mr Oates,' she said. 'I can't tell you how terribly, terribly clever I think you are, and how awfully grateful I am, and how frightfully careful I'll be in future not to give you any more dreadful trouble.'

It was a charming little speech in spite of her catastrophic adjectives and the Superintendent beamed.

'It's been a pleasure, miss,' he said.

As Mr Campion handed her into her mother's Daimler he regarded her coldly.

'A pretty performance,' he remarked. 'Tell me, what do you say when a spark of genuine gratitude warms your nasty little heart? My poor Oates!'

Miss Peterhouse-Vaughn grinned.

'I did do it well, didn't I?' she said complacently. 'He's rather a dear old goat.'

Mr Campion was shocked and said so.

'The Superintendent is a distinguished officer. I always knew that, of course, but this afternoon I discovered a broad streak of chivalry in him. In his place I think I might have permitted myself a few comments on the type of young woman who leaves a diamond bracelet and an emerald ring in the soap-dish at a public restaurant and then goes smiling to Scotland Yard to ask for it back. The wretched man had performed a miracle for you and you call him a dear old goat.'

Leonie was young enough to look abashed without losing her charm.

'Oh, but I am grateful,' she said. 'I think he's wonderful. But not so absolutely brilliant as somebody else.'

'That's very nice of you, my child.' Mr Campion prepared to unbend.

'Oh, not you, darling.' Leonie squeezed his arm. 'I was talking about the other man – The Widow. He's got real nerve, don't you think? – using his own address and making the detective sing and all that . . . So amusing!'

Her companion looked down at her severely.

'Don't make a hero out of *him*,' he said.

'Why not?'

'Because, my dear little hideous, he's a crook. It's only while he remains uncaught that he's faintly interesting. Sooner or later your elderly admirer, the Superintendent, is going to clap him under lock and key and then he'll just be an ordinary convict, who is anything but romantic, believe me.'

Miss Peterhouse-Vaughn shook her head.

'He won't get caught,' she said. 'Or if he does – forgive me, darling – it'll be by someone much cleverer than you or Mr Oates.'

Mr Campion's professional pride rebelled.

'What'll you bet?'

'Anything you like,' said Leonie. 'Up to two pounds,' she added prudently.

Campion laughed. 'The girl's learning caution at last!' he said. 'I may hold you to that.'

The conversation changed to the charity matinée of the day before, wherein Miss Peterhouse-Vaughn had appeared as Wisdom, and continued its easy course, gravitating naturally to the most important pending event in the Peterhouse-Vaughn family, the christening of Master Brian Desmond Peterhouse-Vaughn, nephew to Leonie, son to her elder brother, Desmond Brian, and godson to Mr Albert Campion.

It was his new responsibility as a godfather which led Mr Campion to take part in yet another elegant little ceremony some few days after the christening and nearly three weeks after Leonie's sensational conquest of Superintendent Oates's susceptible heart.

Mr Campion called to see Mr Thistledown in Cheese Street, EC, and they went reverently to the cellars together.

Mr Thistledown was a small man, elderly and dignified. His white hair was inclined to flow a little and his figure was more suited, perhaps, to his vocation than to his name. As head of the small but distinguished firm of Thistledown, Friend and Son, Wine Importers since 1798, he very seldom permitted himself a personal interview with any client under the age of sixty-five, for at that year he openly believed the genus *homo sapiens*, considered solely as a connoisseur of vintage wine, alone attained full maturity.

Mr Campion, however, was an exception. Mr Thistledown thought of him as a lad still, but a promising one. He took his client's errand with all the gravity he felt it to deserve.

'Twelve dozen of port to be laid down for Master Brian Desmond Peterhouse-Vaughn,' he said, rolling the words round his tongue as though they, too, had their flavour. 'Let me see, it is now the end of '36. It will have to be a '27 wine. Then by the time your godson is forty – he won't want to drink it before that age, surely? – there should be a very fine fifty-year-old vintage awaiting him.'

A long and somewhat heated discussion, or, rather, monologue, for Mr Campion was sufficiently experienced to offer no opinion, followed. The relative merits of Croft, Taylor, Da Silva, Noval and Fonseca were considered at length, and in the end Mr Campion followed his mentor through the sacred tunnels and personally affixed his seal upon a bin of Taylor, 1927.

Mr Thistledown was in favour of a stipulation to provide that Master Peterhouse-Vaughn should not attain full control over his vinous inheritance until he attained the age of thirty, whereas Mr Campion preferred the more conventional twenty-one. Finally a compromise of twenty-five was agreed upon and the two gentlemen retired to Mr Thistledown's consulting-room glowing with the conscious virtue of men who had conferred a benefit upon posterity.

The consulting-room was comfortable. It was really no more than an arbour of bottles constructed in the vault of the largest cellar and was furnished with a table and chairs of solid ship's timber. Mr Thistledown paused by the table and hesitated before speaking. There was clearly something on his mind and Campion, who had always considered him slightly inhuman, a sort of living port crust, was interested.

When at last the old gentleman unburdened himself it was to make a short speech.

'It takes an elderly man to judge a port or a claret,' he said, 'but spirits are definitely in another category. Some men may live to be a hundred without ever realizing the subtle differences of the finest rums. To judge a spirit one must be born with a certain kind of palate. Mr Campion, would you taste a brandy for me?'

His visitor was startled. Always a modest soul, he made no pretensions to connoisseurship and now he said so firmly.

'I don't know.' Mr Thistledown regarded him seriously. 'I have watched your taste for some years now and I am inclined to put you down as one of the few really knowledgeable younger men. Wait for me a moment.'

He went out, and through the arbour's doorway Campion saw him conferring with the oldest and most cobwebby of the troglodyte persons who lurked about the vaults.

Considerably flattered in spite of himself, he sat back and awaited developments. Presently one of the younger myrmidons, a mere youth of fifty or so, appeared with a tray and a small selection of balloon glasses. He was followed by an elder with two bottles, and at the rear of the procession came Mr Thistledown himself with something covered by a large silk handkerchief. Not until they were alone did he remove the veil. Then, whipping the handkerchief aside, he produced a partly full half-bottle with a

new cork and no label. He held it up to the light and Mr
Campion saw that the liquid within was of the true dark
amber.

Still with the ritualistic air, Mr Thistledown polished a
glass and poured a tablespoonful of the spirit, afterwards
handing it to his client.

Feeling like a man with his honour at stake, Campion
warmed the glass in his hand, sniffed at it intelligently, and
finally allowed a little of the stuff to touch his tongue.

Mr Thistledown watched him earnestly. Campion
tasted again and inhaled once more. Finally he set down
his glass and grinned.

'I may be wrong,' he said, 'but it tastes like the real
McKay.'

Mr Thistledown frowned at the vulgarism. He seemed
satisfied, however, and there was a curious mixture of
pleasure and discomfort on his face.

'I put it down as a Champagne Fine, 1835,' he said.
'It has not, perhaps, quite the superb caress of the true
Napoleon – but a brave, yes, a brave brandy! The third
best I have ever tasted in my life. And that, let me tell you,
Mr Campion, is a very extraordinary thing.'

He paused, looking like some old white cockatoo standing
at the end of the table.

'I wonder if I might take you into my confidence?' he
ventured at last. 'Ah – a great many people do take you
into their confidence, I believe? Forgive me for putting it
that way.'

Campion smiled. 'I'm as secret as the grave,' he said,
'and if there's anything I can do I shall be delighted.'

Mr Thistledown sighed with relief and became almost
human.

'This confounded bottle was sent to me some little time
ago,' he said. 'With it was a letter from a man called
Gervaise Papulous ; I don't suppose you've ever heard of
him, but he wrote a very fine monograph on brandies some
years ago which was greatly appreciated by connoisseurs.
I had an idea he lived a hermit's life somewhere in Scotland,

but that's neither here nor there. The fact remains that when I had this note from an address in Half Moon Street I recognized the name immediately. It was a very civil letter, asking me if I'd mind, as an expert, giving my opinion of the age and quality of the sample.'

He paused and smiled faintly.

'I was a little flattered, perhaps,' he said. 'After all, the man is a well-known authority himself. Anyway, I made the usual tests, tasted it and compared it with the oldest and finest stuff we have in stock. We have a few bottles of 1848 and one or two of the 1835. I made the most careful comparisons and at last I decided that the sample was a '35 brandy, but not the same blend as our own. I wrote him; I said I did not care to commit myself, but I gave him my opinion for what it was worth and I appended my reasons for forming it.'

Mr Thistledown's precise voice ceased and his colour heightened.

'By return I received a letter thanking me for mine and asking me whether I would care to consider an arrangement whereby I could buy the identical spirit in any quantity I cared to name at a hundred and twenty shillings a dozen, excluding duty – or, in other words, ten shillings per bottle.'

Mr Campion sat up. 'Ten shillings?' he said.

'Ten shillings,' repeated Mr Thistledown. 'The price of a wireless licence,' he added with contempt. 'Well, as you can imagine, Mr Campion, I thought there must be some mistake. Our own '35 is listed at sixty shillings a bottle and you cannot get finer value anywhere in London. The stuff is rare. In a year or two it will be priceless. I considered this sample again and reaffirmed my own first opinion. Then I re-read the letter and noticed the peculiar phrase – 'an arrangement whereby you will be able to purchase'. I thought about it all day and finally I put on my hat and went down to see the man.'

He glanced at his visitor almost timidly. Campion was reassuring.

'If it was genuine it was not a chance to be missed,' he murmured.

'Exactly.' Mr Thistledown smiled. 'Well, I saw him, a younger man than I had imagined but well informed, and I received quite a pleasant impression. I asked him frankly where he got the brandy and he came out with an extraordinary suggestion. He asked me first if I was satisfied with the sample, and I said I was or I should hardly have come to see him. Then he said the whole matter was a secret at the moment, but that he was asking certain well-informed persons to a private conference and something he called a scientific experiment. Finally he offered me an invitation. It is to take place next Monday evening in a little hotel on the Norfolk coast where Mr. Papulous says the ideal conditions for his experiment exist.'

Mr Campion's interest was thoroughly aroused.

'I should go,' he said.

Mr Thistledown spread out his hands.

'I had thought of it,' he admitted. 'As I came out of the flat at Half Moon Street I passed a man I knew on the stairs. I won't mention his name and I won't say his firm is exactly a rival of ours, but – well, you know how it is. Two or three old firms get the reputation for supplying certain rare vintages. Their names are equally good and naturally there is a certain competition between them. If this fellow has happened on a whole cellar full of this brandy I should like to have as good a chance of buying it as the next man, especially at the price. But in my opinion and in my experience that is too much to hope for, and that is why I have ventured to mention the matter to you.'

A light dawned upon his client.

'You want me to attend the conference and make certain everything's above-board?'

'I hardly dared to suggest it,' he said, 'but since you are such an excellent judge, and since your reputation as an investigator – if I may be forgiven the term – is so great, I admit the thought did go through my mind.'

Campion picked up his glass and sniffed its fragrance.

'My dear man, I'd jump at it,' he said. 'Do I pass myself off as a member of the firm?'

Mr Thistledown looked owlish.

'In the circumstances I think we might connive at that little inexactitude,' he murmured. 'Don't you?'

'I think we'll have to,' said Mr Campion.

When he saw the 'little hotel on the Norfolk coast' at half-past six on the following Monday afternoon the thought came to him that it was extremely fortunate for the proprietor that it should be so suitable for Mr Papulous's experiment, for it was certainly not designed to be of much interest to any ordinary winter visitor. It was a large country public-house, not old enough to be picturesque, standing by itself at the end of a lane some little distance from a cold and sleepy village. In the summer, no doubt, it provided a headquarters for a great many picnic parties, but in winter it was deserted.

Inside it was warm and comfortable enough, however, and Campion found a curious little company seated round the fire in the lounge. His host rose to greet him and he was aware at once of a considerable personality.

He saw a tall man with a shy ingratiating manner, whose clothes were elegant and whose face was remarkable. His deep-set eyes were dark and intelligent and his wide mouth could smile disarmingly, but the feature which was most distinctive was the way in which his iron-grey hair drew into a clean-cut peak in the centre of his high forehead, giving him an odd, Mephistophelean appearance.

'Mr Fellowes?' he said, using the alias Campion and Mr Thistledown had agreed upon. 'I heard from your firm this morning. Of course I'm very sorry not to have Mr Thistledown here. He says in his note that I am to regard you as his second self. You handle the French side, I understand?'

'Yes. It was only by chance that I was in England yesterday when Mr Thistledown asked me to come.'

'I see.' Mr Papulous seemed contented with the explanation. Campion looked a mild, inoffensive young man, even a little foolish.

He was introduced to the rest of the company round the fire and was interested to see that Mr Thistledown had been right in his guess. Half a dozen of the best-known smaller and older wine firms were represented, in most cases by their senior partners.

Conversation, however, was not as general as might have been expected among men of such similar interests. On the contrary, there was a distinct atmosphere of restraint, and it occurred to Mr Campion that they were all close rivals and each man had not expected to see the others.

Mr Papulous alone seemed happily unconscious of any discomfort. He stood behind his chair at the head of the group and glanced round him with satisfaction.

'It's really very kind of you all to have come,' he said in his deep musical voice. 'Very kind indeed. I felt we must have experts, the finest experts in the world, to test this thing, because it's revolutionary – absolutely revolutionary.'

A large old gentleman with a hint of superciliousness in his manner glanced up.

'When are we going to come to the horses, Mr Papulous?'

His host turned to him with a deprecatory smile.

'Not until after dinner, I'm afraid, Mr Jerome. I'm sorry to seem so secretive, but the whole nature of the discovery is so extraordinary that I want you to see the demonstration with your own eyes.'

Mr Jerome, whose name Campion recognized as belonging to the moving spirit of Bolitho Brothers, of St Mary Axe, seemed only partly mollified. He laughed.

'Is it the salubrious air of this particular hotel that you need for your experiment, may I ask?' he enquired.

'Oh no, my dear sir. It's the stillness.' Mr Papulous appeared to be completely oblivious of any suggestion of a sneer. 'It's the utter quiet. At night, round about ten o'clock, there is a lack of vibration here, so complete that you can almost feel it, if I may use such a contradiction in terms. Now, Mr Fellowes, dinner's at seven-thirty. Perhaps you'd care to see your room?'

Campion was puzzled. As he changed for the meal – a gesture which seemed to be expected of him – he surveyed the situation with growing curiosity. Papulous was no ordinary customer. He managed to convey an air of conspiracy and mystery while appearing himself as open and simple as the day. Whatever he was up to, he was certainly a good salesman.

The dinner was simple and well cooked and was served by Papulous's own man. There was no alcohol and the dishes were not highly seasoned, out of deference, their host explained, to the test that was to be put to their palates later on.

When it was over and the mahogany had been cleared of dessert, a glass of clear water was set before each guest and from the head of the table Mr Papulous addressed his guests. He made a very distinguished figure, leaning forward across the polished wood, the candle-light flickering on his deeply lined face and high heart-shaped forehead.

'First of all let me recapitulate,' he said. 'You all know my name and you have all been kind enough to say that you have read my little book. I mention this because I want you to realize that by asking you down here to witness a most extraordinary demonstration I am taking my reputation in my hands. Having made that point, let me remind you that you have, each of you, with the single exception of Mr Fellowes, been kind enough to give me your considered views on a sample of brandy which I sent you. In every case, I need hardly mention, opinion was the same – a Champagne Fine of 1835.'

A murmur of satisfaction not untinged with relief ran round the table and Mr Papulous smiled.

'Well,' he said, 'frankly that would have been my own opinion had I not known – mark you, I say "known" – that the brandy I sent you was a raw cognac of nearly a hundred years later – to be exact, of 1932.'

There was a moment of bewilderment, followed by an explosion from Mr Jerome.

'I hope you're not trying to make fools of us, sir,' he said severely. 'I'm not going to sit here, and –'

'One moment, one moment.' Papulous spoke soothingly. 'You really must forgive me. I know you all too well by repute to dare to make such a statement without following it immediately by the explanation to which you are entitled. As you're all aware, the doctoring of brandy is an old game. Such dreadful additions as vanilla and burnt sugar have all been used in their time and will, no doubt, be used again, but such crude deceptions are instantly detected by the cultured palate. This is something different.'

Mr Jerome began to seethe.

'Are you trying to interest us in a fake, sir?' he demanded. 'Because, if so, let me tell you I, for one, am not interested.'

There was a chorus of hasty assent in which Mr Campion virtuously joined.

Gervaise Papulous smiled faintly.

'But of course not,' he said. 'We are all experts. The true expert knows that no fake can be successful, even should we so far forget ourselves as to countenance its existence. I am bringing you a discovery – not a trick, not a clever fraud, but a genuine discovery which may revolutionize the whole market. As you know, time is the principal factor in the maturing of spirits. Until now time has been the one factor which could not be artificially replaced. An old brandy, therefore, is quite a different thing from a new one.'

Mr Campion blinked. A light was beginning to dawn upon him.

Mr Papulous continued. There seemed to be no stopping him. At the risk of boring his audience he displayed a great knowledge of technical detail and went through the life history of an old liqueur brandy from the time it was an unripe grapeskin on a vine outside Cognac.

When he had finished he paused dramatically, adding softly:

'What I hope to introduce to you to-night, gentlemen, is the latest discovery of science, a method of speeding up this long and wearisome process so that the whole business of maturing the spirit takes place in a few minutes instead of a hundred years. You have all examined the first-fruits of this method already and have been interested enough to come down here. Shall we go on?'

The effect of his announcement was naturally considerable. Everybody began to talk at once save Mr Campion, who sat silent and thoughtful. It occurred to him that his temporary colleagues were not only interested in making a great deal of money but very much alarmed at the prospect of losing a considerable quantity also.

'If it's true it'll upset the whole damned trade,' murmured his next-door neighbour, a little thin man with wispy straw-coloured hair.

Papulous rose. 'In the next room the inventor, M. Philippe Jessant, is waiting to demonstrate,' he said. 'He began work on the idea during the period of prohibition in America and his researches were assisted there by one of the richest men in the world, but when the country was restored to sanity his patron lost interest in the work and he was left to perfect it unassisted. You will find him a simple, uneducated, unbusiness-like man, like many inventors. He came to me for help because he had read my little book and I am doing what I can for him by introducing him to you. Conditions are now ideal. The house is perfectly still. Will you come with me?'

The sceptical but excited little company filed into the large 'commercial' room on the other side of the passage. The place had been stripped of furniture save for a half-circle of chairs and a large deal table. On the table was a curious contraption, vaguely resembling two or three of those complicated coffee percolators which seemed to be designed solely for the wedding-present trade.

An excitable little man in a long brown overall was standing behind the table. If not an impressive figure, he was certainly an odd one, with his longish hair and gold-rimmed pince-nez.

'Quiet, please. I must beg of you quiet,' he commanded,

holding up his hand as they appeared. 'We must have no vibration, no vibration at all, if I am to succeed.'

He had a harsh voice and a curious foreign accent, which Campion could not instantly trace, but his manner was authoritative and the experts tiptoed gently to their seats.

'Now,' said M. Jessant, his small eyes flashing, 'I leave all explanations to my friend here. For me, I am only interested in the demonstration. You understand?'

He glared at them and Papulous hastened to explain.

'M. Jessant does not mean the human voice, of course,' he murmured. 'It is vibration, sudden movement, of which he is afraid.'

'Quiet,' cut in the inventor impatiently. 'When a spirit matures in the ordinary way what does it have? – quiet, darkness, peace. These conditions are essential. Now we will begin, if you please.'

It was a simple business. A clear-glass decanter of brandy was produced and duly smelt and sampled by each guest. Papulous himself handed round the glasses and poured the liquid. By unanimous consent it was voted a raw spirit. The years 1932 and 1934 were both mentioned.

Then the same decanter was emptied into the contraption on the table and its progress watched through a system of glass tubes and a filter into a large retort-shaped vessel at the foot of the apparatus.

M. Jessant looked up.

'Now,' he said softly. 'You will come, one at a time, please, and examine my invention. Walk softly.'

The inspection was made and the man in the brown overall covered the retort with a hood composed of something that looked like black rubber. For a while he busied himself with thermometers and a little electric battery.

'It is going on now,' he explained, suppressed excitement in his voice. 'Every second roughly corresponds to a year – a long, dark, dismal year. Now – we shall see.'

The hood was removed, fresh glasses were brought, and the retort itself carefully detached from the rest of the apparatus.

Mr Jerome was the first to examine the liquid it contained and his expression was ludicrous in its astonishment.

'It's incredible!' he said at last. 'Incredible! I can't believe it ... There are certain tests I should like to make, of course, but I could swear this is an 1835 brandy.'

The others were of the same opinion and even Mr Campion was impressed. The inventor was persuaded to do his experiment again. To do him justice he complied willingly.

'It is the only disadvantage,' he said. 'So little can be treated at the one time. I tell my friend I should like to make my invention foolproof and sell the machines and the instructions to the public, but he tells me no.'

'No indeed!' ejaculated Mr Campion's neighbour. 'Good heavens! it would knock the bottom out of half my trade ...'

When at last the gathering broke up in excitement it was after midnight. Mr Papulous addressed his guests.

'It is late,' he said. 'Let us go to bed now and consider the whole matter in the morning when M. Jessant can explain the theory of his process. Meanwhile, I am sure you will agree with me that we all have something to think about.'

A somewhat subdued company trooped off upstairs. There was little conversation. A man does not discuss a revolutionary discovery with his nearest rival.

Campion came down in the morning to find Mr Jerome already up. He was pacing the lounge and turned on the young man almost angrily.

'I like to get up at six,' he said without preamble, 'but there were no servants in the place. A woman, her husband and a maid came along at seven. It seems Papulous made them sleep out. Afraid of vibration, I suppose. Well, it's an extraordinary discovery, isn't it? If I hadn't seen it with my own eyes I should never have believed it. I suppose one's got to be prepared for progress, but I can't say I like it. Never did.'

He lowered his voice and came closer.

'We shall have to get together and suppress it, you know,' he said. 'Only thing to do. We can't have a thing like this blurted out to the public and we can't have any single firm owning the secret. Anyway, that's my opinion.'

Campion murmured that he did not care to express his own without first consulting Mr Thistledown.

'Quite, quite. There'll be a good many conferences in the City this afternoon,' said Mr Jerome gloomily. 'And that's another thing. D'you know there isn't a telephone in this confounded pub?'

Campion's eyes narrowed.

'Is that so?' he said softly. 'That's very interesting.'

Mr Jerome shot him a suspicious glance.

'In my opinion . . .' he began heavily, but got no further. The door was thrust open and the small wispy-haired man, who had been Campion's neighbour at dinner, came bursting into the room.

'I say,' he said, 'a frightful thing! The little inventor chap has been attacked in the night. His machine is smashed and the plans and formula are stolen. Poor old Papulous is nearly off his head.'

Both Campion and Jerome started for the doorway and a moment later joined the startled group on the landing. Gervaise Papulous, an impressive figure in a long black dressing-gown, was standing with his back to the inventor's door.

'This is terrible, terrible!' he was saying. 'I beseech you all, go downstairs and wait until I see what is best to be done. My poor friend has only just regained consciousness.'

Jerome pushed his way through the group.

'But this is outrageous,' he began.

Papulous towered over him, his eyes dark and angry.

'It is just as you say, outrageous,' he said, and Mr Jerome quailed before the suppressed fury in his voice.

'Look here,' he began, 'you surely don't think . . . you're not insinuating . . .'

'I am only thinking of my poor friend,' said Mr Papulous.

Campion went quietly downstairs.

'What on earth does this mean?' demanded the small wispy-haired gentleman, who had remained in the lounge.

Campion grinned. 'I rather fancy we shall all find that out pretty clearly in about an hour,' he said.

He was right. Mr Gervaise Papulous put the whole matter to them in the bluntest possible way as they sat dejectedly looking at the remains of what had proved a very unsatisfactory breakfast.

M. Jessant, his head in bandages and his face pale with exhaustion, had told a heart-breaking story. He had awakened to find a pad of chloroform across his mouth and nose. It was dark and he could not see his assailant, who also struck him repeatedly. His efforts to give the alarm were futile and in the end the anaesthetic had overpowered him.

When at last he had come to himself his apparatus had been smashed and his precious black pocket-book, which held his calculations and which he always kept under his pillow, had gone.

At this point he had broken down completely and had been led away by Papulous's man. Mr Gervaise Papulous then took the floor. He looked pale and nervous and there was an underlying suggestion of righteous anger and indignation in his manner which was very impressive.

'I won't waste time by telling you how appalled I am by this monstrous attack,' he began, his fine voice trembling. 'I can only tell you the facts. We were alone in this house last night. Even my own man slept out in the village. I arranged this to ensure ideal conditions for the experiment. The landlady reports that the doors were locked this morning and the house had not been entered from the outside. Now you see what this means? Until last night only the inventor and I knew of the existence of a secret which is of such great importance to all of you here. Last night we told you, we took you into our confidence, and now . . .' he shrugged his shoulders. 'Well, we have been robbed and my friend assaulted. Need I say more?'

An excited babble of protest arose and Mr Jerome seemed in danger of apoplexy. Papulous remained calm and a little contemptuous.

'There is only one thing to do,' he said, 'but I hesitated before calling in the police, because, of course, only one of you can be guilty and the secret must still be in the house, whereas I know the publicity which cannot be avoided will be detrimental to you all. And not only to yourselves personally, but to the firms you represent.'

He paused and frowned.

'The Press is so ignorant,' he said. 'I am so afraid you may all be represented as having come here to see some sort of faking process – new brandy into old. It doesn't sound convincing, does it?'

His announcement burst like a bomb in the quiet room. Mr Jerome sat very still, his mouth partly open. Somebody began to speak, but thought better of it. A long unhappy silence supervened.

Gervaise Papulous cleared his throat.

'I am sorry,' he said. 'I must either have my friend's note-book back and full compensation, or I must send for the police. What else can I do?'

Mr Jerome pulled himself together.

'Wait,' he said in a smothered voice. 'Before you do anything rash we must have a conference. I've been thinking over this discovery of yours, Mr Papulous, and in my opinion it raises very serious considerations for the whole trade.'

There was a murmur of agreement in the room and he went on.

'The one thing none of us can afford is publicity. In the first place, even if the thing becomes generally known it certainly won't become generally believed. The public doesn't rely on its palate; it relies on our labels, and that puts us in a very awkward position. This final development precipitates everything. We must clear up this mystery in private and then decide what is best to be done.'

There was a vigorous chorus of assent, but Mr Papulous shook his head.

'I'm afraid I can't agree,' he said coldly. 'In the ordinary way M. Jessant and I would have been glad to meet you in any way, but this outrage alters everything. I insist on a public examination unless, of course,' he added deliberately, 'unless you care to take the whole matter out of our hands.'

'What do you mean?' Mr Jerome's voice was faint.

The tall man with the deeply lined face regarded him steadily.

'Unless you care to club together and buy us out,' said Mr Papulous. 'Then you can settle the matter as you like. The sum M. Jessant had in mind was fifteen thousand pounds, a very reasonable price for such a secret.'

There was silence after he had spoken.

'Blackmail,' said Mr Campion under his breath and at the same moment his glance lighted on Mr Papulous's most outstanding feature. His eyebrows rose and an expression of incredulity, followed by amazement, passed over his face. Then he kicked himself gently under the breakfast table. He rose.

'I must send a wire to my principal,' he said. 'You'll understand I'm in an impossible position and must get in touch with Mr Thistledown at once.'

Papulous regarded him.

'If you will write your message my man will despatch it from the village,' he said politely and there was no mistaking the implied threat.

Campion understood he was not to be allowed to make any private communication with the outside world. He looked blank.

'Thank you,' he said and took out a pencil and a loose-leaf note-book.

'Unexpected development,' he wrote. 'Come down immediately. Inform Charlie and George cannot lunch Tuesday. A. C. Fellowes.'

Papulous took the message, read it and went out with it, leaving a horrified group behind him.

Mr Thistledown received Mr Campion's wire at eleven o'clock and read it carefully. The signature particularly

interested him. Shutting himself in his private room, he
rang up Scotland Yard and was fortunate in discovering
Superintendent Oates at his desk. He dictated the wire
carefully and added with a depreciatory cough:

'Mr Campion told me to send on to you any message
from him signed with his own initials. I don't know if you
can make much of this. It seems very ordinary to me.'

'Leave all that to us, sir.' Oates sounded cheerful.
'Where is he, by the way?'

Mr Thistledown gave the address and hung up the
receiver. At the other end of the wire the superintendent
unlocked a drawer in his desk and took out a small red
manuscript book. Each page was ruled with double
columns and filled with Mr Campion's own elegant hand-
writing. Oates ran a forefinger down the left-hand column
on the third page.

'Carrie . . . Catherine . . . Charles . . .'

His eye ran across the page.

'Someone you want,' he read and looked on down the list.
The legend against the word 'George' was brief. 'Two',
it said simply.

Oates turned to the back of the book. There were
several messages under the useful word 'lunch'. 'Come to
lunch' meant 'Send two men'. 'Lunch with me' was
translated 'Send men armed', and 'Cannot lunch' was
'Come yourself'.

'Tuesday' was on another page. The superintendent
did not trouble to look it up. He knew its meaning. It was
'hurry'.

He wrote the whole message out on a pad.

'Unexpected developments. Come down immediately.
Someone you want (two). Come yourself. Hurry. Campion.'

He sighed. 'Energetic chap,' he commented and pressed
a bell for Sergeant Bloom.

As it happened, it was Mr Gervaise Papulous himself
who caught the first glimpse of the police car which pulled
up outside the lonely little hotel. He was standing by the
window in an upper room whose floor was so flimsily

constructed that he could listen with ease to the discussion taking place in the lounge below. There the unfortunate experts were still arguing. The only point on which they all agreed was the absolute necessity of avoiding a scandal.

As the car stopped and the superintendent sprang out and made for the door Papulous caught a glimpse of his official-looking figure. He swung round savagely to the forlorn little figure who sat hunched up on the bed.

'You peached, damn you!' he whispered.

'Me?' The man who had been calling himself 'Jessant' sat up in indignation. 'Me peach?' he repeated, his foreign accent fading into honest South London. 'Don't be silly. And you pay up, my lad. I'm fed up with this. First I do me stuff, then you chloroform me, then you bandage me, then you keep me shut up 'ere, and now you accuse me of splitting. What you playing at?'

'You're lying, you little rat.' Papulous's voice was dangerously soft and he strode swiftly across the room towards the man on the bed, who shrank back in sudden alarm.

'Here – that'll do, that'll do. What's going on here?'

It was Oates who spoke. Followed by Campion and the sergeant he strode across the room.

'Let the fellow go,' he commanded. 'Good heavens, man, you're choking him.'

Doubling his fist, he brought it up under the other man's wrists with a blow which not only loosed their hold but sent their owner staggering back across the room.

The man on the bed let out a howl and stumbled towards the door into the waiting arms of Sergeant Bloom, but Oates did not notice. His eyes were fixed upon the face of the tall man on the other side of the room.

'The Widow!' he ejaculated. 'Well I'll be damned!'

The other smiled.

'More than probably, my dear Inspector. Or have they promoted you?' he said. 'But at the moment I'm afraid you're trespassing.'

The superintendent glanced enquiringly at the mild and elegant figure at his side.

'False pretences is the charge,' murmured Mr Campion affably. 'There are certain rather unpleasant traces of blackmail in the matter, but false pretences will do. There are six witnesses and myself.'

The man whose alias was The Widow stared at his accuser.

'Who are you?' he demanded, and then, as the answer dawned upon him, he swore softly. 'Campion,' he said. 'Albert Campion ... I ought to have recognized you from your description.'

Campion grinned. 'That's where I had the advantage of you,' he said.

Mr Campion and the superintendent drove back to London together, leaving a very relieved company of experts to travel home in their own ways. Oates was jubilant.

'Got him,' he said. 'Got him at last. And a clear case. A pretty little swindle, too. Just like him. If you hadn't been there all those poor devils would have paid up something. They're the kind of people he goes for, folk whose business depends on their absolute integrity. They all represent small firms, you see, with old, conservative clients. When did you realize that he wasn't the real Gervaise Papulous?'

'As soon as I saw him I thought it unlikely.' Campion grinned as he spoke. 'Before I left town I rang up the publishers of the Papulous monograph. They had lost sight of him, they said, but from their publicity department I learned that Papulous was born in '72. So as soon as I saw our friend The Widow I realized that he was a good deal younger than the real man. However, like a fool I didn't get on to the swindle until this morning. It was when he was putting on that brilliant final act of his. I suddenly recognized him and, of course, the whole thing came to me in a flash.'

'Recognized him?' Oates looked blank. 'I never described him to you.'

Mr Campion looked modest. 'Do you remember showing off to a very pretty girl I brought up to your office, and so far forgetting yourself as to produce an advertisement from an evening paper?' he enquired.

'I remember the ad,' Oates said doggedly. 'The fellow advertised for a kids' entertainer. But I don't remember him including a photograph of himself.'

'He printed his name,' Campion persisted. 'It's a funny nickname. The significance didn't occur to me until I looked at him this morning, knowing that he was a crook. I realized that he was tricking us, but I couldn't see how. Then his face gave him away.'

'His face?'

'My dear fellow, you haven't spotted it yet. I'm glad of that. It didn't come to me for a bit. Consider that face. How do crooks get their names? How did Beaky Doyle get his name? Why was Cauliflower Edwards so called? Think of his forehead, man. Think of his hair.'

'Peak,' said the superintendent suddenly. 'Of course, a widow's peak! Funny I didn't think of that before. It's obvious when it comes to you. But even so,' he added more seriously, 'I wonder you cared to risk sending for me on that alone. Plenty of people have a widow's peak. You'd have looked silly if he'd been on the level.'

'Oh, but I had the advertisement as well,' Campion objected. 'Taken in conjunction, the two things are obvious. That demonstration last night was masterly. Young brandy went in at one end of the apparatus and old brandy came out at the other, and we saw, or thought we saw, the spirit the whole time. There was only one type of man who could have done it – a children's party entertainer.'

Oates shook his head.

'I'm only a poor demented policeman,' he said derisively. 'My mind doesn't work. I'll buy it.'

Campion turned to him. 'My good Oates, have you ever been to a children's party?'

'No.'

'Well, you've been a child, I suppose?'

'I seem to remember something like that.'

'Well, when you were a child what entertained you? Singing? Dancing? *The Wreck of the Hesperus?* No, my dear friend, there's only one kind of performer who goes down well with children and that is a member of the brotherhood of which Jessant is hardly an ornament. A magician, Oates. In other words, a conjurer. And a damned good trick he showed us all last night!'

He trod on the accelerator and the car rushed on again.

The superintendent sat silent for a long time. Then he glanced up.

'That *was* a pretty girl,' he said. 'Nice manners, too.'

'Leonie?' Campion nodded. 'That reminds me, I must phone her when we get back to town.'

'Oh?' The superintendent was interested. 'Nothing I can do for you, I suppose?' he enquired archly.

Campion smiled. 'Hardly,' he said. 'I want to tell her she owes me two pounds.'

II

The Name on the Wrapper

MR ALBERT CAMPION was one of those useful if at times exasperating people who remain interested in the world in general at three o'clock on a chilly winter's morning. When he saw the overturned car, dark and unattended by the grass verge, therefore, he pulled up his own saloon and climbed out on to the road, whose frosty surface was glistening like a thousand diamonds.

His lean figure wrapped in a dark overcoat was rendered slightly top-heavy by the fact that he wore over it a small travelling-rug arranged as a cape. This sartorial anachronism was not of his own devising. His dinner hostess, old Mrs Laverock, was notorious both for her strong will and her fear of throat infections, and when Mr Campion had at last detached himself from her husband's brandy and reminiscences she had appeared at the top of the Jacobean staircase, swaddled in pink velvet, with the rug in her arms.

'Either that young man wears this round his throat or he does not leave this house.'

The edict went forth with more authority than ever her husband had been able to dispense from the bench, and Mr Campion had gone out into the night for a fifty-mile run back to Piccadilly wearing the rug, with his silk hat perched precariously above it.

Now, its folds, which reached his nose, prevented him from seeing that part of the ground which lay directly at his feet, so that he kicked the ring and sent it wheeling down the moonlit road before he saw it. The coloured flash in the pale light caught his attention and he went after it. It lay in his hand a few minutes later, as unattractive a piece of jewellery as ever he had been called upon to consider. It was a circle of different-coloured stones mounted on heavy gold, and was certainly unusual, if not particularly beautiful or valuable. He thrust it absently into his coat pocket before he resumed his investigation of the abandoned car.

He had just decided that the departed driver had been either drunk or certifiably insane in the moment of disaster when the swift crackle of bicycle wheels on the frost behind him made him swing round, and he found himself confronted by another caped figure who came to a wobbling and suspicious halt at his elbow.

'Now, now, there's no use you putting up a fight. I ain't alone, and if I were I'm more'n a match for you.'

The effect of these two thundering lies uttered in a pleasant country voice rendered unnaturally high by what was, no doubt, excusable nervousness, delighted Mr Campion, but unfortunately the folds of his hostess's rug hid his disarming smile and the country policeman stood gripping his bicycle as if it were a weapon.

'You're caught!' he said, his East Anglian accent bringing the final word out in a roar of triumph not altogether justified. 'Take off your mask.'

'My what?' Mr Campion's startled question was muffled by his drapery, and he pulled it down to let his chin out.

'That's right,' said the constable with a return of confidence, as his prisoner appeared so tractable. 'Now, what have you been a-doing of? Answer up. It'll be best for you.'

'My good oaf' – Mr Campion's tone was forgiving – 'you're making an ass of yourself, and I should hold that bicycle still if I were you or you'll get the back wheel between your legs and fall over it.'

'Now then, no names, no names, if you please, sir.' The Law was showing signs of disquiet again, but the bicycle was straightened hastily. 'You'll have to come down to see the inspector.'

Mr Campion's astonishment began to grow visible and convincing, for, after all, the country bobby is not as a rule a night bird of prey.

'Look here,' he said patiently, 'this pathetic-looking mess here isn't *my* car.'

'No, I know that's not.' The triumphant note crept into the constable's voice again. 'I seen the number as soon as I come up.'

'Since you've observed so much,' continued Mr Campion politely, 'would it be tactless to inquire if you've noticed that?'

He swung round as he spoke and pointed to his own car, standing like a silver ghost a few yards down the road.

'Eh?' The Law was evidently taken by surprise. 'Oh, you ran into him, did you? Where is he?'

Campion sighed and embarked on the slow process of convincing his captor that the car ahead belonged to him, his licences were in order, and that he was properly and expensively insured. He also gave his own name and address, Colonel Laverock's name and address, and the time at which he had left the house. By way of full measure he also delivered a short lecture on 'Cars and How to Overturn Them', with special reference to the one on the verge, and was finally conducted to his own vehicle and grudgingly permitted to depart.

'I don't really know as how you oughtn't to have come along to find the inspector,' said the constable finally as he leaned on the low near-side door. 'You didn't ought to have been masked. I'll have to report it. That rug might have been to protect your throat, but then that might not.'

'That cape of yours may be buttoned up against the cold or it may be worn simply to disguise the fact that your tunic is loosened at the throat,' retorted Mr Campion, and, letting in the clutch, he drove away, leaving a startled countryman with the conviction that he had actually encountered a man with X-ray eyes at last.

*

On the by-pass Mr Campion ran into a police cordon, and once again was subjected to a searching inquiry concerning his licences. Having been, in his opinion, held up quite long enough while the police fooled about looking for stolen cars, he said nothing about the overturned one, but drove peacefully home to his flat in Bottle Street and went to bed. His ridiculous encounter with the excitable constable had driven all recollection of the ring from his head and he thought no more about it until it appeared on his breakfast table the following morning.

His man had discovered it in the coat pocket, and, deducing the conventional worst, had set it out with an air of commiseration not altogether tactful; anxious, no doubt, that his employer should remember first thing in the morning any lady who might have refused him on the night before.

Campion put aside *The Times* with regret and took up the ring. By morning light it was even less beautiful than it had appeared under the moon. It was a woman's size and was heavy in the baroque fashion that has returned after fifty or sixty years. Some of the stones, which ran all the way round the hoop, were very good and some were not; and as he sat looking at it his eyebrows rose. He was still admiring it as a curio rather than a work of art when his old friend Superintendent Stanislaus Oates rang up from Scotland Yard. He sounded heavily amused.

'So you've been running round the country in disguise, have you?' he said cheerfully. 'Like to come in for a chat this morning?'

'Not particularly. What for?'

'I want an explanation for a telephoned report which has come in this morning. We've been called in by the Colnewych police on a very interesting little case. I'm going over the stuff now. I'll expect you in half an hour.'

'All right.' Mr Campion did not sound enthusiastic. 'Shall I wear my mask?'

'Come with your head in a bag, if you like,' invited the superintendent vulgarly. 'Keep your throat wrapped up. There's nothing like an old sock, they say. Place the toe upon the windpipe and . . .'

Mr Campion rang off.

Half an hour later, however, he presented himself at the superintendent's office and sat, affable and exquisite, in the visitor's chair. Oates dismissed his secretary and leaned over the desk. His grey face, which was usually so lugubrious, had brightened considerably as Campion appeared and now he had some difficulty in hiding a grin of satisfaction.

'Driving round the country with a topper over your eyes and a blanket round your neck at three o'clock in the morning,' he said. 'You *must* have been lit. Still, I won't go into that. I'll be magnanimous. What do you know about this business?'

'I'm innocent,' announced his visitor flatly. 'Whatever it is, I haven't done it. I went to dinner with a wealthy and childless godparent. I mention this in case your mercenary soul may not be able to believe that any sober man will motor fifty miles into the wilds of East Anglia for a meal. When I left, my godparent's wife, who once had tonsillitis as a child and has never forgotten it, lent me a small rug. (It is sixty inches by sixty inches and is of a rather lurid tartan which I am not entitled to wear.) As she will tell you, if you ask her, she safety-pinned this firmly to the back of my neck. On my way home I passed a very interestingly overturned car, and while I was looking at it a large red-faced ape dressed up as a policeman attempted to arrest me. That's my story and I'm sticking to it.'

'Then you don't know anything about the crime?' The superintendent was disappointed but unabashed. 'I'll tell you. You never know, you might be useful.'

'It has happened,' murmured Mr Campion.

'It's a case of robbery,' went on Oates, ignoring the interruption. 'A real big haul. The assessors are on to it now but, roughly speaking, it's in the neighbourhood of twenty thousand pounds' worth of jewellery and little boxes.'

'Little boxes?'

'Snuff-boxes and patch-boxes, enamel things covered with diamonds and what-not.' Oates sounded contemptuous and Campion laughed.

'People of ostentatious tastes?' he ventured.

'No, it's a collection of antiques,' said Oates seriously, and looked up to find Campion grinning. 'You're a bit lah-di-blinking-dah to-day, aren't you?' he protested. 'What is it? The effects of your night on the tiles? Look here, you pay attention, my lad. You were found nosing round the wreckage of a car thought to have been driven by the thief or thieves, and the very least you can do is to try and make yourself useful. Last night there was a bit of a do at St Bede's Priory, about five miles away from your godpapa's place. It was a largish show, and the place, which seems to be about as big as the British Museum and rather like it, was full to bursting.'

Campion stared at him.

'You're talking about the Hunt Ball at old Allenbrough's private house, I take it?' he put in mildly.

'Then you do know about it?'

'I don't know about the robbery. I know about the Ball. It's an annual affair. Old Porky Allenbrough's ball is almost an institution, like the Lord Mayor's Show – it's very like that in general effect, too, now I come to think of it. I used to attend regularly when I was young.'

Oates sniffed.

'Well, anyway, there seem to have been close on five hundred people gathered together there,' he said. 'They were all over the house and grounds, cars going and coming all the time. A real party, the local Super says it was. All we know is that about two o'clock, just when the crowd was thinning a bit, her ladyship goes up to her room and finds her jewellery gone and her famous collection of antiques pinched out of the glass-fronted cupboard in the boudoir next door to her bedroom.

'All the servants were downstairs watching the fun, of course, and hadn't seen a thing. The local police decided it must have been a professional job and they flung a cordon round the whole district. They figured that a crook had taken advantage of the general excitement to burgle the place in the ordinary way. They were very smart on the job, but they didn't lay hands on a single "pro". In fact, the only suspicious character who showed up during the whole of the evening was a lad in a top hat with a plaid blanket—'

'What about that overturned car?' interrupted his visitor.

'I'm coming to that,' said Oates severely. 'Wait a minute. That car belonged to a very respectable couple who went to the dance and stayed at it. They were just going to leave when the alarm was given and it was then they discovered the car had been stolen. The gardeners who were acting as car-park attendants didn't remember it going, but then, as they said, cars were moving in and out all the evening. People would drive 'em off a little way to sit out in. It was a real old muddle by the sound of it. The Super told me on the phone that in his opinion every man-servant on the place was as tight as a lord the whole evening.'

'And every lord as tight as a drum, no doubt,' added Mr Campion cheerfully. 'Very likely. It sounds like the good old days before the Conferences. I see. Well, the suggestion is that the car was pinched by the burglar, who used it to escape in. What did he arrive in? A howdah?'

*

Oates sat back and scratched his chin.

'Yes,' he said. 'That's the trouble. The police are in a bit of a difficulty. You see, her ladyship is howling for the return of her valuables, but neither she nor her husband will admit for an instant that one of their guests might be the culprit. That was the awkward thing at the time. A watch was kept on those guests who left after the discovery of the theft, but no one was searched, of course.'

Mr Campion was silent for a moment.

'These shows are done in parties,' he remarked at last. 'People take a party to a ball like that. Porky and his missis would invite a hundred friends or so and ask them each to bring a party. It's a private affair, you see, not an ordinary Hunt Ball. Allenbrough calls it the Whippersfield Hunt Ball because he likes to see a pink coat or two about. He's M.F.H. and can do what he likes, and it's a wealthy hunt, anyway. Yes, I see the trouble. I don't envy the local super if he has to go round to all old Allenbrough's pals and say: "Excuse me, but did you include a professional jewel-thief in the party you took to the ball at St. Bede's on the twenty-third last?"'

'I know. That's what it amounts to.' Oates was gloomy. 'Got any ideas? You're our Society expert.'

'Am I? Well, in that capacity let me advise you that such a course would provoke endless correspondence both to the Chief Constable and the heavier daily Press. You're sure this was a professional job?'

'Yes. The jewellery was in a wall-safe which had been very neatly cracked and the show cupboard had been opened by an expert. Also there were no finger-prints.'

'No trade-marks, either, I expect?'

'No, it was a simple job for a "pro". It didn't call for anything sensational. It was simply far too neat for an amateur, that's all. We're rounding up all the likelies, of course, but with such a field to choose from the right man may easily slip the stuff before we can get round to him.'

Mr Campion rose.

'You have all my sympathy. It's not what you yourself would call a picnic, is it? Still, I'll ferret round a bit and let you have any great thoughts that may come to me. By the way, what do you think of that?'

He crossed the room as he spoke and laid the many-stoned ring on the desk.

'Not very much,' said Oates, turning it over with a dubious forefinger. 'Where did you get it?'

'I picked it up in the street,' said Mr Campion truthfully. 'I ought to take it to a police station, but I don't think I will. I'd rather like to give it back to the owner myself.'

'Do what you like with it, my lad.' Oates was mildly exasperated. 'Keep your mind on the important jewellery, because now Scotland Yard has taken over the case it means the Metropolitan area pays for the inquiry; don't forget that.'

Campion was still looking at the ring.

'Anyway, I showed it to you,' he said, and wandered towards the door.

'Don't waste your time over trifles,' Oates called after him. 'You can have that ring. If anybody asks you, say I said you could.'

*

It would have appeared that Mr Campion took the superintendent's final offer seriously, for he replaced the trinket carefully in his waistcoat pocket before turning into the nearest telephone booth, where he rang up that unfailing source of Society gossip, old Lady Laradine. After listening to her for a full two minutes, while she asked after every relative he had in the world, he put the question he had in mind.

'Who is Gina Gray? I've heard the name, but I can't place her. Gray. Gray with an A.'

'My dear boy! So pretty! Just the girl for you. Oh no, perhaps not. I've just remembered she's engaged. Announced last month. Still, she's very charming.' The old voice, which was strong enough to penetrate any first-night babel in London, rattled on, and Campion felt for another twopence.

'I know,' he shouted. 'I know she's lovely, or at least I guessed she was. But who, *who* is she? Also, of course, where?'

'What? Oh, *where* is she? With her aunt, of course. She's spending the winter there. She's so young, Albert. Straight down from the shires. The father owns a row of Welsh mountains or something equally romantic.'

'Who?' bellowed Mr Campion through the din. 'Who, my good gramophone, is the aunt?'

'What did you call me, Albert?' The famous voice was dangerously soft.

'Gramophone,' said Mr Campion, who was a great believer in the truth when the worst had come to the worst.

'Oh, I thought you said . . . never mind.' Lady Laradine, who had several grandchildren and regarded each new arrival as a personal insult, was mollified. 'I do talk very fast, I know, especially on the phone. It's my exuberant spirit. You want to know who the aunt is. Why, Dora Carrington. You know her.'

'I do,' said Campion with relief. 'I didn't realize she had a niece.'

'Oh, but she has; just out of the nest. Presented last year. A sweetly pretty child. Such a pity she's engaged. Tell me, have you any information about Wivenhoe's son? No? Then what about the Pritchards?'

She went on and on with the relentless energy of the very bored, and it was not until Mr Campion ran out of coppers that the monologue came to an end.

It was late in the morning, therefore, when Mr Campion presented himself at the charming Lowndes Square house which Dora Carrington had made her London home.

Miss Gina Gray only decided to see him after a considerable

pause, during which, he felt, old Pollard, the butler, must have worked hard vouching for his desirability.

*

She came into the lounge at last, looking much as he had thought she might, very young and startled, with frank, miserable eyes, but dark, curling hair instead of the sleek blonde he had somehow expected.

He introduced himself apologetically.

'It's rather odd turning up like this out of the blue,' he said, 'but you'll have to forgive me. Perhaps you could think of me as a sort of long-lost elderly relative. I might have been your uncle, of course, if Dora had taken it into her head to marry me instead of Tubby, not that the idea ever occurred to either of us at the time, of course. Don't get that into your head. I only say it might have happened so that you'll see the sort of reliable bird I am.'

He paused. The alarm had died out of her eyes and she even looked wanly amused. He was relieved. Idiotic conversation, although invaluable, was not a luxury which he often permitted himself now that the thirty-five-year-old landmark was passed.

'It's very nice of you to come,' she said in a polite, small voice. 'What can I do?'

'Nothing. I came to return something I think you've lost, that's all.' He fished in his pocket and drew out the ring. 'That's yours, isn't it?' he said gently.

He had expected some reaction, but not that it would be so violent. She stood trembling before him, every tinge of colour draining out of her face.

'Where did you get it?' she whispered, and then, pulling herself together with a desperate courage which he rather admired, she shook her head. 'It's not mine. I've never seen it before. I don't know who you are either, and I – I don't want to. Please go away.'

'Oh, Gina Gray!' said Mr Campion. 'Gina Gray, don't be silly. I'm the original old gentleman with the kind heart. Don't deny the irrefutable.'

'It's not mine.' To his horror he saw tears in her eyes. 'It's not mine. It's not. It's not. Go away.'

She turned and made for the door, her slender, brown-suited figure looking very small and fugitive as she ran.

Mr Campion was still debating his next move when Dora came in, a vision of fox-furs and smiles.

'My dear!' she said. 'You haven't been to see us for years and years and now you turn up when I'm due out to lunch in fifteen minutes. Where have you been?'

'About,' said Mr Campion truthfully, reflecting that it was all wrong that the people one never had time to visit were always one's oldest and closest friends.

They drank a cocktail together and were still reminiscing happily when Dora's luncheon escort arrived. In the end Mr Campion showed his hostess out of her own house and was standing rather forlornly on the pavement, waving after her departing car, when he observed a familiar figure stumping dejectedly down the steps which he had so recently descended himself.

'Jonathan!' he said. 'What are you doing here?'

Mr Jonathan Peters started violently, as if he had been caught sleep-walking, and looked up with only a faint smile on his gloomy young face.

'Hallo, Campion,' he said. 'I didn't see you. I've been kicking my heels in the breakfast-room. Hell! let's go and have a drink.'

In the end, after some half-hearted bickering, they went along to that home from home, the Junior Greys, and Mr Campion, who, in company with the rest of the world, considered himself to be the best listener on earth, persuaded his young acquaintance to unburden himself.

Jonathan was a younger brother of the two Peters who had been Campion's Cambridge companions, and in the ordinary way the ten years' difference in their ages would have raised an insurmountable barrier between them; but at the moment Jonathan was a man with a sorrow.

'It's Gina,' he said. 'We're engaged, you know.'

'Really?' Mr Campion was interested. 'What's the row?'

'Oh, I suppose it'll be all right in the end.' The young man sounded wistful and only partially convinced. 'I mean, I think she'll come round. Anyway, I hope so. What annoys me is that I'm the one with the grievance, and yet here I am dithering around as though it were all my fault.' He frowned and shook his head over the unreasonableness of life in general and love in particular.

*

'You were at Porky Allenbrough's show last night, I suppose?' Mr Campion put the question innocently and was rewarded.

'Yes, we both were. I didn't see you there. There was a tremendous crush and it might have been a really good bust if it hadn't been for one thing and another. I've got a genuine grouch, you know.' Mr Peters' young face was very earnest, and under the influence of half a pint of excellent Chablis he came out with the full story.

As far as Mr Campion could make out from his somewhat disjointed account the history was a simple one. Miss Gina Gray, while enjoying the London season, had yet not wished to give up all strenuous physical exercise and so had formed the habit of hunting with the Whippersfield five or six times a month. On these occasions she had been entertained by a relation of Dora Carrington's husband who lived in the district and had very kindly stabled her horses for her. Her custom had been to run down by car early in the morning, returning to London either at night or on the following day.

In view of all this hospitality, it had been arranged that she should go to the Priory Ball with her host and his party, while Jonathan should attend with another group of people from a different house. The arrangement between the couple had been, therefore, that, while Gina should arrive at the ball with her own crowd, Jonathan should have the privilege of driving her back before rejoining his own host and hostess.

'It was a bit thick,' he concluded resentfully. 'Gina

turned up with a crowd of people I didn't know, including a lad whom nobody seemed to have seen before. She danced with him most of the evening and finally he drove her home himself. He left me a message to say so, the little toot. I felt fed up and I imagine I may have got pretty tight, but anyway, when I arrived at the town house this morning ready to forgive and forget like a hero, she wouldn't even see me.'

'Infuriating,' agreed Mr Campion, his eyes thoughtful. 'Did you find out who this interloping tick happened to be?'

Jonathan shrugged his shoulders.

'I did hear his name ... Robertson, or something. Apparently he's been hunting fairly regularly this season and he came along with Gina's lot. That's all I know.'

'What did he look like?'

Jonathan screwed up his eyes in an effort of recollection.

'An ugly blighter,' he said at last. 'Ordinary height, I think. I don't remember much about him except that I disliked his face.'

It was not a very helpful description, but Mr Campion sat pondering over it for some time after the despondent Jonathan had wandered off to keep an afternoon appointment.

Suddenly he sat up, a new expression on his lean, good-humoured face.

'Rocks,' he said under his breath. 'Rocks Denver ...' and he made for the nearest telephone.

*

It was nine o'clock that evening when Superintendent Oates came striding into his office and, flinging his hat upon the desk, turned to survey the elegant, dinner-jacketed visitor who had been patiently awaiting his arrival for the best part of half an hour.

'Got him,' he said briefly. 'The lads shadowed him to Peachy Dale's club in Rosebery Avenue, and then, of course, we knew we were safe. Peachy may be a rotten fence, but he's the only man in London who would have handled those snuff-boxes, now I come to think of it. It was a lovely cop. We gave him time to get settled and then closed in on all five entrances. There he was with the stuff in a satchel. It was beautiful. I've never seen a man so astounded in my life.'

He paused and a reminiscent smile floated over his sad face.

'A little work of art, that's what that arrest was, a little work of art.'

'That's fine, then,' said his visitor, rising. 'I think I'll drift.'

'No you don't, my lad.' The superintendent was firm. 'You don't do conjuring tricks under my nose without an explanation. You come across.'

Mr Campion sighed.

'My dear good Enthusiast, what more can you possibly want?' he protested. 'You've got the man and you've got the swag. That's enough for a conviction – and Porky's blessing.'

'Very likely, but what about my dignity?' Oates was severe. 'It may be enough for the Bench, but it's not enough for me. Who do you think you are, the Home Office?'

'Heaven forbid,' said Mr Campion piously. 'I thought you might express your ingratitude in this revolting way. Look here, if I explain, my witness doesn't go into Court. Is that a bet?'

The superintendent held out his hand.

'May I be struck pink,' he said sincerely. 'I mean it.'

Since he knew from experience that this was an oath that Oates held peculiarly sacred, Mr Campion relented.

'Give me twenty minutes,' he said. 'I'll go and fetch her.'

Oates groaned. 'Another woman!' he exploded. 'You find 'em, don't you? All right, I'll wait.'

Miss Gina Gray looked so genuinely pathetic as she came into the office clinging to Mr Campion's arm a little over half an hour later that Oates, who had an unexpected weakness for youth and beauty, was inclined to be mollified. Campion observed the first signs of his heavily avuncular mood with relief.

'It's perfectly all right,' he said to the girl at his side. 'I've given you my word you'll be kept clean out of it. This solemn-looking person will be struck a fine hunting pink if he attempts to make me break it. That's written in the unchanging stars. Isn't that so, Superintendent?'

Oates regarded him with fishy eyes.

'You go and put on your mask,' he said. 'Now, what is all this? What's been going on?'

Gina Gray required a little gentle pumping, but beneath Campion's expert treatment she began to relax, and within ten minutes she was pouring out her story with all the energy of injured innocence behind it.

'I met the man I knew as Tony Roberts – you say his real name is Rocks Denver – in the hunting-field,' she said. 'He always seemed to be out when I was, and he talked to me as people do out hunting. I didn't know him, he wasn't a friend, but I got used to him being about. He rode very well and he helped me out of a mess once or twice. You know that sort of acquaintance, don't you?'

Oates nodded and shook his head. He was smiling.

'We do,' he said. 'And then what?'

'Then nothing,' declared Miss Gray innocently. 'Nothing at all until last night. We were all getting ready to go to the Priory in three or four cars when he phoned me at Major Carrington's, where I was staying, and said his car had broken down in the village and he'd got to leave it and would it be awful cheek of him to ask if one of us would give him a lift to the hall. I said of course, naturally, and when we met him trudging along, rather disconsolate in full kit, we stopped and picked him up.'

Oates glanced at Campion triumphantly.

'So that's how he got in?' he said. 'Neat, eh? I see, Miss Gray. And then when you got your acquaintance to the party you didn't like to leave him cold. Is that how it was?'

The girl blushed and her dark eyes were very frank.

'Well, he *was* rather out of everything and he *did* dance very well,' she admitted apologetically. 'He hadn't talked much about himself, and it was only then I realized he didn't live near and didn't know everybody else. His – his manners were all right.'

Oates laughed. 'Oh yes, Rocky's very presentable,' he agreed. 'He's one of the lads who let his old school down, I'm afraid. Well, and then what?'

*

She hesitated and turned to Campion.

'I've been so incredibly silly,' she murmured. It was a direct appeal, and the Superintendent was not unchivalrous.

'There's nothing new in that, Miss,' he observed kindly. 'We all make errors of judgement at times. You missed him for a bit, I suppose?'

'Yes, I danced with several people and I'd half forgotten him when he turned up at my elbow with a raincoat over his arm. He took me out on the terrace and put it over my shoulders and said – oh, a lot of silly things about being there alone without a soul to speak to. He said he'd found one man he knew, but that he was wrapped up with some woman or other, and suggested that we borrowed this friend's car and went for a run round. It was getting rather late and I was livid with Jonathan anyway, so I said all right.'

'Why were you livid with Jonathan?' Campion put the question curiously and Miss Gray met his eyes.

'He got jealous as soon as we arrived and drowned his sorrows rather too soon.'

'I see.' Campion smiled as he began to understand Mr Peters' astonishing magnanimity, which had hitherto seemed somewhat too saintly to be strictly in character.

'Well then . . .' Oates went back to the main story, '. . . off you went in the car. You drove around for quite a while.'

Gina took a deep breath.

'Yes,' she said steadily. 'We drove around for a bit, but not very far. The car wasn't his, you see, and he had trouble with it. It started all right, but it conked out down the lane and he was fooling about with it for a long time. He got so frightfully angry that I began to feel – well, rather uncomfortable. Also I was cold. He had taken the raincoat off my shoulders and flung it in the back seat, and I remembered that it was heavy and warm, so I turned to get it. Just then he closed the bonnet and came back. He snatched the coat and swore at me, and I began to get thoroughly frightened. I tried to persuade him to take me back, but he just drove on down the lane towards the main road. It was then that we passed the three policemen on motor-cycles racing towards the Priory. That seemed to unnerve him completely and he turned off towards Major Carrington's house, with the car limping and misfiring all the time. I didn't know what to do. I was far too frightened to make a row, you see, because I was a guest at the Major's, and – well, there was Jonathan and Aunt Dora to consider and – oh, you do understand, don't you?'

'I think so,' said Campion gravely. 'When did you take off your ring?'

She gaped at him.

'Why, at that moment,' she said. 'How did you know? It's a stupid trick I have when I'm nervous. It was rather loose, and I pulled it off and started to play with it. He looked down and saw me with it and seemed to lose his head. He snatched it out of my hand and demanded to know where I'd got it, and then, when he saw it clearly by the dashboard light, he suddenly pitched it out of the window in disgust. It was so utterly unexpected that I forgot where I was and made a leap for it across him. Then – then I'm afraid the car turned over.'

'Well, well,' said Oates inadequately. 'And so there you were, so to speak.'

She nodded gravely. 'I was so frightened,' she said. 'Fortunately we were quite near the house, but my dress was spoilt and I was shaken and bruised, and I just set off across the fields and let myself in by the stable gate. He came after me, and we had a dreadful sort of row in whispers, out in the drive. He wanted me to put him up for the night, and didn't seem to realize that I was a visitor and couldn't dream of doing such a thing. In the end I showed him where the saddle-room was, off the stable yard. There was a stove there and some rugs and things. Then I sneaked up to my own room and went to bed. This morning I pretended that I'd had a headache and got somebody to give me a lift home. He'd gone by then, of course.'

'Of course he had. Hopped on one of those country buses before the servants stirred,' Oates put in with satisfaction. 'He relied on you to hold your tongue for your own sake.'

'There wasn't much else he could do in the circumstances,' observed Campion mildly. 'Once he had the howling misfortune to pick a sick car all his original plans went to pieces. He used Miss Gray to get the stuff safely out of the house in the usual false pocket of the raincoat. Then his idea must have been to drive her a mile or two down the road and strand her, while he toddled off to Town alone. The breakdown delayed him and, once he saw the police were about, he knew the cordon would go round and that he was trapped, so he had to think out other tactics. That exercise seems to have unnerved him entirely. I can understand him wanting to get into the house. After all, it'd be a first-class hiding-place in the circumstances. Yes, well, that's fairly clear now, I hope, Superintendent. Here's your ring, Miss Gray.'

As Gina put out her hand for the trinket her eyes grew puzzled.

'You're a very frightening person,' she said. 'How on earth did you know it was mine?'

'Quite.' Oates was frankly suspicious. 'If you've never met this young lady before, I don't see how you guessed it belonged to her.'

Campion stood regarding the girl with genuine surprise.

'My dear child,' he said, 'surely you know yourself? Who had this ring made for you?'

'No one. It was left to me. My father's sister died about six months ago and told me in a letter always to wear it for luck. It doesn't seem to have brought me much.'

For a moment Campion seemed completely bewildered. After a while, however, he laughed.

'Your father's sister? Were you named after her?'

'Yes, I was.' Miss Gray's dark eyes were widening visibly. 'How do you know all this? You're frightening.'

*

Campion took the ring between his thumb and forefinger and turned it slowly round, while the stones winked and glittered in the hard electric light.

'It's such a simple trick I hardly like to explain and spoil the effect,' he said. 'About fifty years ago it was a fairly common conceit to give young ladies rings like this. You see, I knew this was Gina Gray's ring because it had her name on the wrapper, as it were. Look, start at the little gold star and what have you? Garnet, Indicolite – that's an indigo variety of tourmaline, Superintendent – Nephrite, Amethyst, then another smaller gold star and Garnet again, Rose Quartz, Agate and finally Yellow Sapphire. There you are. I thought you must know. G.I.N.A. G.R.A.Y., all done according to the best sentimental jewellery tradition. As soon as I came to consider the ring in cold blood it was obvious. Look at it, Oates. What man in his senses would put that collection of stones together if he didn't mean something by them?'

The superintendent did not answer immediately. He sat turning the ring round and round with an expression of grudging astonishment on his grey face. When at last he did look up he expressed himself unexpectedly.

'Fancy that,' he said. 'Dear me.'

When Miss Gray had departed in a taxicab, which, on Mr Campion's suggestion, a patient and sober Jonathan had kept ticking up outside on the Embankment during the whole of the short interview, he was more explicit.

'She had her name on it,' he said after a moment or two of purely decorative imagery. 'She had her dear little name on it! Very smart of you, Mr Campion. Don't let it go to your head. I don't know if I'm quite satisfied yet.

Who put you on to Rocky? Why Rocky? Why not any other of the fifty first-class jewel thieves in London?'

Campion grinned. It was not often that the Superintendent condescended to ask straight questions and he felt justifiably gratified by the phenomenon.

'You said he was a "pro",' he explained. 'That was the first step. Then young Jonathan Peters told me Gina had met the fellow hunting regularly, and so, putting two and two together, I arrived at Rocky. Rocky is an anachronism in the underworld; he can ride. How many jewel thieves do you know who can ride well enough to turn up at a hunt, pay their caps, and not make an exhibition of themselves? Hunting over strange country isn't trotting round the Row, you know.'

Oates shook his head sadly.

'You depress me,' he said. 'First you think of the obvious and then you go and say it, and then you're proved right. It's very irritating. The ring was a new one on me, though. D'you know, I wouldn't mind giving my wife one of those. It's a pretty idea. She'd like it. Besides,' he added seriously, it might come in useful some time. You never know.'

In the end Campion sat down and worked it out for him.

III

The Hat Trick

MR CAMPION received the hat as a sentimental tribute. Mrs Wynyard pressed it into his hand at her farewell party at the Braganza on the night before she sailed home to New York.

'I want you to have it,' she said, her curly white head held on one side and her plump hand resting lightly on the sleeve of his tail coat. 'It's ex-clusive. I got it from old Wolfgarten in one of those cute little streets off Bond

Street, and he gave me his solemn word by everything he feels to be holy that it's quite u-nique. There's not another one in the world, and I want you to keep it to remind you of me and Mr Honeyball and the grand times we've had this trip.'

Hubert Wynyard, who was so good-humoured that he let his wife call him anything, even 'Mr Honeyball', winked at Campion across his glass.

'So now you know,' he said. 'Don't worry about a speech of thanks. Time's short. Where's that confounded wine waiter?'

So Campion pocketed the hat, which was less than half an inch high and made of onyx, with a cunningly carved agate where the opening for the head should have been, and thought no more about it.

He found it again next time he put on full war paint, which was for the first night of Lorimer's *Carry Over* at the Sovereign Theatre. The occasion was so smart that he was beginning to feel that 'sticky' might be the term for it when the curtain descended on the second act and someone touched him on the shoulder. It turned out to be Peter Herrick, looking a trifle pink and disconcerted, which was unusual in one normally so very elegantly at ease.

'I say, old man, I need a spot of support,' he muttered. 'Can you come?'

There was a note of genuine supplication in the plea, and Campion excused himself from his party and joined him.

'What's up? Going to start a fight?'

His whisper was respectfully amused as they pressed their way through the noisy, perfumed crowd in the corridor.

'I hope not. As a matter of fact that's what I'm trying to avoid. It's social support I need.'

Peter had edged into a convenient corner between a gilt settee and an enormous basket of hydrangeas. He was a trifle red about the ears and his vivid blue eyes, which lent his young face most of its charm, were laughing but embarrassed.

'I suddenly caught sight of you,' he said, 'and I realized

you were probably the one man in the world of whom one could ask such a damn silly thing and not get cut for the rest of one's life. Come and back me up like a good bloke. You couldn't look like a duke or something, could you?'

'I don't see why not.' Mr Campion's lean face took on an even more vacant expression. 'What's the idea? Whom do I impress?'

'You'll see.' Peter was grim. 'I'm suspect, old boy. I'm not the thing. Not – er – quite *it*, don't you know. I think someone's spread it around that my old man's a bobby.'

Campion's eyebrows appeared above his horn-rimmed spectacles and he began to laugh. Major Herrick was well known to him as one of the Assistant Commissioners and one of the more poker-backed of his acquaintances, while Peter's worst enemy, if he had one, which seemed unlikely, could scarcely accuse him of being unpresentable. The whole situation seemed to Campion to have the elements of humour and he said so, delicately.

'But also very charming,' he added cheerfully. 'All olde worlde and young-man-what-are-your-intentions. Must you bother about the woman? There *is* a woman, I take it?'

Peter shot a revealing glance at him.

'Ah,' he said, 'but you wait until you see her. I met her on a boat and then I lost her. Now I've found her again at last, and there's this insane old father and the incredible tick of a fellow they're touting around with them. Come on, old boy, do your stuff. I'm out of my depth altogether. Prudence is embarrassed, and the other two have to be seen to be believed.'

A trifle under two minutes later Campion was inclined to agree with half the final statement. Old Mr Thomas K. Burns was not unbelievable, Norman Whitman was. As for Prudence Burns, he took one look at her slender red-headed loveliness and was prepared to sympathize with any enthusiasm which Peter might evince. The girl was a raving beauty of the modern type. She sat on her gold chair in Box B and smiled up at him with humour and intelligence as well as embarrassment in her brown eyes.

Her escorts were far less pleasant to meet. Old Mr Burns was a plain man in every sense of the word who had made an enormous amount of money in South Africa. He was in the midst of recounting these two obvious facts to Campion immediately after their introduction when a warning frown from the third member of his party silenced him as though a hand had been placed over his mouth, leaving him deflated and at sea. He turned helplessly, with an appealing flicker in his small grey eyes.

'This 'ere – I should say, this gentleman is Mr Norman Whitman,' he said, and paused for the name to take effect.

*

Entirely because he felt it was expected of him, Campion looked interested, while Norman Whitman favoured him with a supercilious stare. Campion was puzzled. He saw a plumpish, consequential little person with sleek hair and a pale face in which the eyeglass was a definite mistake. He was well dressed, not to say natty, and from the toes of his shoes to the highlight on his prominent white forehead he was polished until he shone. His voice, which was high, was so carefully modulated as to sound affected, and altogether he exuded an atmosphere of conceit and self-importance which was quite insufferable.

'I have not had the pleasure of meeting you before,' he said, making the announcement sound like an accusation. 'Not very good acting, is it? I'm afraid poor Emily is a sad disappointment.'

Campion had thought that Dame Emily Storm's performance was well up to its usual standard of polished perfection, and said so.

'She always says she's very nervous on first nights,' he added.

'Oh, do you know her?' There was real excitement and hero-worship in Prudence Burns's inquiry, and a quality of youthful *naïveté* in her eagerness which made Campion like her.

'My dear child, not the *stage!*' Norman Whitman shook

an admonishing finger at the girl and she stared at him
blankly, as did they all save old Mr Burns, who said somewhat hurriedly, 'I should think not. Not likely,' and
assumed a virtuous expression which was patently false and
ill suited to his round, red face.

The incredible Norman leant over the side of the box.

'Isn't that the Countess?' he exclaimed suddenly. 'Is
it? Why, of course. Yes, it is. You must all excuse me a
moment. I really must go and say "Hello". '

He bustled off and Mr Burns moved into his place and
looked down at the frothing pool of clothes and their
owners in the stalls below. There was something almost
pathetic in his interest, a quality of small-boyishness which
Campion found disarming. Peter was less sympathetic. He
looked scandalized and crossed over to the girl at once. It
seemed only charitable to give him a moment or so, and
Campion gallantly concentrated on the father.

Mr Burns glanced up at him and looked away again.

'He's not there yet,' he said and hesitated, adding
abruptly because of his embarrassment, 'do you see her?'

'Who?'

'The Countess,' said Mr Burns, lowering his voice to a
respectful whisper.

Campion became a little embarrassed also. His fingers
deep in his pockets found the onyx hat, and he began to
play with it, taking it out and letting it roll idly in his hand.
He was standing up in the box, a little behind the old man,
who seemed in danger of falling out altogether in his
eagerness.

'There he is.' Mr Burns's voice rose in his excitement.
'That's her, is it? You don't recognize her, do you?'

'No, I'm afraid I don't,' said Campion helplessly as he
glanced at the large lady in the crimson cloak who had
paused to speak to Norman Whitman in the crowd below.
Mr Burns nodded gloomily as though he had feared as
much, and Campion was aware that both he and Peter had
lost caste. Having stared his fill, the old man straightened
himself and stepped back.

'Better not let him catch us,' he remarked, and coughed explosively but a trifle too late to cover the ill-advised statement. For the first time he was able to give Campion his attention.

'You're in business, I suppose?' he inquired, regarding him morosely.

The tall thin man in the horn-rimmed spectacles grinned unhappily. The *bourgeois gentilhomme* is an age-old character who moves some people to laughter, but others are apt to find his wistful gaucherie a little dispiriting, and Campion was of the latter category. He was so anxious not to hurt in any way that he hesitated over his answer.

'Not exactly,' he said, casually, and flicked the little hat into the air, catching it again and rolling it over between his fingers. The gesture was so idle that he was scarcely aware that he had made it, so that Mr Burns's reaction came as a complete surprise to him.

All he saw at first was that the old man's eyes were positively bulging and that there were pale patches in the mottled crimson of his cheeks. The next moment Prudence's father's entire attitude towards his new acquaintance underwent a complete change. His depression vanished and he became more than merely friendly. Within two minutes he had offered Campion a cigar, told him his hotel, begged him to visit him, and imparted a tip for the Stock Exchange which his somewhat startled visitor happened to know was a good one. Even the young people, who were engrossed in themselves, were aware of the change in front. Indeed, Campion felt that the entire theatre must notice it. Old Mr Burns was not subtle.

In the midst of his expansiveness he glanced at Peter and, returning to Campion, jerked his head at the young man.

'Known him long?' he inquired with husky confiding.

'A great many years,' Campion assured him.

'Oh, he's all right then, is he?' The red face was very serious.

'He's one of my best friends.' Campion had no intention

of sounding severe, but the question was bewildering and
in spite of himself the words came coldly.

*

Mr Burns took the rebuke. 'That's all right then,' he
said, sighing. 'To tell you the honest truth, I'm not exactly
in my place yet. A bit out of touch.'

He glanced up shyly to see how this confidence had been
received and, noting that Campion remained affable if
blank, added in a conspiratorial whisper: 'You've no idea
what a weight off my mind that is.'

Campion began to feel that the weight on his own mind
was considerable, and he was on the point of launching out
into a minor campaign of discreet inquiry when the curtain
bell rang and he was forced to rejoin his own party. Mr
Burns let him go with great reluctance but consoled
himself a little when Peter accepted his invitation to remain.

Campion hurried down the corridor in a state of complete
mystification. He was used to being a success but not a riot,
and the single startled glance which Peter had turned upon
him at parting made him laugh whenever he thought of it,
but he was thankful he had not been pressed for an
explanation.

On the stairs he passed Norman Whitman. The little man
was bustling back to his seat and puffing consequentially
as he hurried. He glanced at Campion and nodded to him.

'She spared me a word, the dear thing,' he said, as if the
intelligence was good news of the highest importance, and
trotted on out of sight. Campion glanced after him and
somewhere in the far depths of his memory something
stirred only to be lost again immediately.

There are few things more irritating than an elusive
impression that one has seen someone or something before,
and as he went on down the staircase and re-entered the
now darkened auditorium Campion walked slowly, his
forehead wrinkled. Somewhere, some time had he seen that
plump little figure waddling along; but where and when
escaped him utterly. It was most tantalizing.

He did not see Peter again that evening, but the following morning the boy telephoned while Campion was still in bed.

'I say,' the young voice sounded enthusiastic over the wire, 'that was pretty sensational, wasn't it? How did you do it?'

'Did it last?' Campion inquired cautiously.

'Rather! We're all going off to the races this morning. I'm more than grateful to you. I knew you were remarkable in many ways but I wasn't prepared for a miracle. I'm still bewildered. Do you realize that I'd had the cold shoulder with icicles on it until you arrived? But now I'm the old man's white-headed boy. What did you say?'

With pardonable weakness, Campion was loth to cast down his laurels.

'Nothing much,' he said truthfully. 'I talked through my hat a bit, you know.'

'I have no doubt you did, old boy,' Peter agreed laughing, 'but what did you actually say? Hang it all, you've altered the man's entire attitude.'

'I scarcely spoke,' said Campion, regretting that this exactitude was hardly convincing. 'How about the "gentleman friend"? Did you cut much ice with him?'

'No,' Peter's tone carried unutterable contempt. 'I'm afraid I scarcely noticed the little twirp. I say, you might let me know how to work the oracle.'

Since he had no idea at all and could therefore hardly be helpful, Campion thought it best to change the subject.

'A very pretty girl,' he ventured.

Peter rose to the bait like a salmon to a fly.

'Amazing,' he said warmly. 'I don't mind telling you I'm not coherent on the subject.'

It was nearly ten minutes later when Campion was at last allowed to hang up the receiver and he re-settled himself, grinning. Peter had under-estimated himself.

Thinking over the entire incident, Campion was inclined to wash his hands of the whole affair, putting it down as one of those odd things that do sometimes occur. There are degrees of oddness, however, and the next time the onyx hat came under his serious consideration it was in circumstances which could hardly be disregarded.

*

The following Wednesday was the seventeenth and on the seventeenth of September, whenever he was in London, Campion took his Aunt Eva to dinner after the Dahlia Show. This was one of those family fixtures which begin as a graceful gesture in commemoration of past favours in the way of timely financial assistance in mid-term, and may very well end as awful responsibilities; but Aunt Eva might easily have been worse. She was a spry little old lady in brown velvet and bangles, and her mind was almost entirely devoted to horticulture, whereas, of course, it might easily have been Pekinese or other people's love affairs.

It was a time-honoured arrangement between them that she should choose the restaurant and, because of her preference for flower names, they sometimes dined well and sometimes appallingly, which was why Campion was not particularly astonished when he arrived at her hotel to find her all set, in garnets and gold galloon, to visit the Gillyflower.

'I warn you it may be expensive,' she said, settling herself in the taxi, 'but I remembered poor Marchant left you all that money in the spring, so I dare say you can afford it. Don't hesitate to mention it, my dear boy, if you'd rather not.'

'Darling, I can't think of a place in which I should enjoy seeing you more,' he assured her, and spoke with a certain amount of truth, for the Gillyflower was an exotic bloom and he was interested to see what she would make of it.

He had visited the place once himself about three months before, just after it opened, and had found it flashy, exorbitant and badly staffed, but there had been an air of ultra-smart sophistication about it which he thought might possibly strike a new note after the homely sobriety of the Manor House dining-room.

They found the place noisy but not crowded. It did not yet exude the cold depression of failure, but neither was there the cheerful blare of assured success. Aunt Eva was able to choose a table with an excellent view of the floral display round the band platform, although it gave her only an oblique angle on the cabaret. All the same the meal was not one of their triumphs. The staff still left much to be desired and the food, although quite extraordinarily pretentious, was certainly not cooked by a master.

The quality of the service began to irritate Campion about half-way through the meal. A dirty plate, a forgotten order, a leaking ice-pail, two delays, and impossibly cold coffee reduced him by slow stages to a state of politely repressed irritation, and he was relieved that Aunt Eva was too happily engrossed in her subject for the evening, which appeared to be the merits of ground bones as a fertilizer, to notice the many defects in the meal.

However, what with one thing and another it was a trying experience for Campion, and while he was waiting patiently for the second brew of coffee and the wine waiter his fingers encountered the onyx hat and he took it out and began to play with it, rolling it over and over upon the table-cloth.

The first thing that happened was that the waiter spilt the coffee. Campion drew back wearily and looked up to receive his second surprise. He was prepared for some sort of apology but not for abnegation. The unfortunate man was green. He grovelled. He all but wept, and from that moment the Gillyflower appeared to belong to Mr Campion.

The change was astounding. The head waiter appeared at his elbow in solicitous friendliness, myrmidons arrived on all sides showering little attentions like so many sallow amorelli, Aunt Eva received a bouquet of Lady Forteviot roses, and Campion was tempted with a Napoleon *fine* from a bottle which certainly looked as though it had seen Paris, if not the siege. There was no doubt at all about

their sudden rise to importance as guests of the Gillyflower
and Campion's eyes grew thoughtful behind his spectacles
as he turned the charm over and over.

'That's a nice little hat,' remarked Aunt Eva, smiling
over her roses.

'Isn't it?' said Campion. 'A smart little hat, not to say
clever.'

Just how clever it was, however, lay as yet unrevealed.
That surprise came later when the lady went off to collect
her old-fashioned sables and Campion glanced down at a
bill for three pounds, seventeen shillings and one penny.
On his nod of acceptance the waiter took the bill away.
There was no charge, of course, he said, and seemed hurt
that the guest should suggest it. 'But naturally,' no charge
at all.

Campion gaped at the man, who smiled at him with
bland satisfaction and expressed the pious hope that he had
enjoyed the meal. Campion was taking out his notecase in
stolid defiance when the *maitre d'hôtel*, round as a football
and sleek as a seal, appeared to corroborate the first man's
story.

'No charge, sir,' he said. 'No, no, no charge. If only you
had telephoned we should have been so happy to reserve
you a better table.'

Campion looked down at the onyx hat which sat, prim
and shining, on the edge of an ashtray. The man followed
his glance and beamed.

'You are satisfied?' he inquired.

Campion flicked the trinket with his forefinger and a
memory bringing enlightenment in its train blazed up
suddenly in his mind.

'That pays the waiter, does it?' he said.

And then they both laughed; but Campion laughed all
the way home.

*

It was over a fortnight later when he received a visit from
Peter Herrick. That young man was in an indignant mood.

'I say, I was glad you phoned,' he said, coming into the study in the Piccadilly flat like a small electric storm. 'I was just making up my mind to come down on you for another spot of help when you rang. Your success with old man Burns was so sensational that I was going to risk a second appeal. You wouldn't care to be the complete hero and have another go, would you?'

His host, who was mixing the drinks, looked round from the cocktail cabinet and grinned.

'My influence wore off, did it?' he said. 'I wondered if it might.'

Peter sat down. 'It weakened,' he admitted. 'It's that unspeakable little toot Whitman, you know. He's got an idiotic line in pseudo smart-set talk that gets the old boy all of a flutter. When we're alone he's perfectly happy, apart from the fact that he wants to talk about you still, which is curious – forgive me, but you know what I mean.'

He broke off to laugh at himself.

'I'm an ass,' he said. 'The whole truth of the matter – and you may be astounded to hear it, for I'm completely bewildered by it myself – the truth is that I'm nuts about Prudence, Campion, absolutely nuts. I want her to marry me, and she's dead keen on the idea, which is another staggering piece of luck, and, logically speaking, everything ought to be pretty good. However, the old boy is completely taken in by Whitman. Whitman sells him the most fantastic hints on etiquette and he falls for it every time.'

Campion looked sympathetic.

'Old Burns has an idea that Whitman is some sort of social capture, I take it?' he ventured.

'That's it, I'm afraid.' Peter was embarrassed. 'It's ludicrous, of course, and very uncomfortable, especially as the old lad himself is quite all right, really. Apart from this fantastic snob complex he's a darned interesting, shrewd old chap. Whitman is simply taking advantage of his pet weakness. Prudence says her old man has always had a touch of it, but it's got worse since he retired and settled down to enjoy his cash. Still, for Prudence's sake I'd put up with Whitman if it wasn't for this last piece of cheek. He's had the impudence to suggest that he might marry her himself.'

'Has he, by George?' said Campion. 'That's sailing near the wind, isn't it?'

'I thought so.' Peter spoke with feeling. 'Unfortunately the old man is half sold in the idea. He's anxious for Prudence to be happy, of course, for he's dead set on doing his duty and that sort of thing, but you can see that the idea of the socialite son-in-law is going over big. What is so infuriating is that he's being taken in. Whitman is about as bogus as they go. He's quite sincere, I expect, but look at him! What is he? A wretched little tuft-hunter with no more brains than that soda-water syphon. Wasn't that your impression?'

'Since you press me, no,' said Mr Campion judicially. 'No, old boy, I'm sorry, but it wasn't. I think you under-estimate him. However, that's beside the point. What does A do now? Have you anything in mind?'

'Well –' Peter was evidently leading up to a delicate subject with some trepidation. 'I may as well make a clean breast of it. Old Burns wants to take Prudence, Whitman and myself out to a meal to-night to "talk things over". It went through my mind that if I had the infernal cheek to ask you to join the party you might be able to do your celebrated heart-softening act once again. The old boy will be tickled to death, of course. He's worried my life out to get hold of you again. But I do see that it's a ghastly imposition from your point of view.' He paused unhappily. 'It's the limit,' he said. 'The ultimate outside edge. But she's grown so darned important to me that I'm forgetting the ordinary decencies.'

'My dear chap, not at all. I think it might be an extremely jolly gathering.' Campion sounded positively enthusiastic: 'There's only one thing, though,' he hurried on, while his visitor eyed him in astonishment, 'you don't think you could fix it so that we went either to the Gillyflower or the Maison Grecque?'

The other man sat up, his eyes wide with suspicion. 'Why on earth do you suggest that?'

Campion evaded his glance.

'They're the only two places in London at which one can eat, aren't they?' he murmured idiotically.

'Look here, Campion, what do you know about all this business?' Peter was scrambling out of his chair. 'You might have been imitating Whitman, except that he's got an extra half-dozen perfectly appalling places of the same type on his list.'

'Half a dozen others, has he?' Campion seemed impressed. 'What a thorough bird he is.'

'Thorough?' said Peter. 'I thought he was off his head.'

'Oh, dear me, no. He's an intelligent chap. I thought that the first time I saw him. You'll fix it then, will you? Either the Gillyflower or the Maison Grecque.'

The younger man stretched out his hand for the telephone.

'I'll get on to the old man this minute before you can change your mind,' he announced. 'Don't say I didn't warn you it might be a trying party. You're an astonishing chap, aren't you? I didn't know you'd ever seen Whitman before I introduced him. Where do you keep all this information?'

'Under my little hat,' said Campion innocently. 'All under my remarkable little hat.'

*

The first thirty-five minutes of Mr Thomas Burns's little dinner-party at the Maison Grecque amply justified Peter Herrick's worst fears. The restaurant itself was a trifle more pretentious than the Gillyflower, and on this occasion the service was even more ostentatiously attentive than that which had distinguished the latter half of Aunt Eva's night out. Mr Burns himself was considerably subdued by the fuss accorded him and frequently fingered his tight evening collar in a wistful fashion which made his desire to take it off as clear as if he had announced it in so many words.

Campion, glancing round the table, decided that Prudence was embarrassed by the avowed object of the gathering, but there was a line of determination in her firm mouth and an expression in her eyes when she glanced at Peter which made him like her.

Mr Herrick was frankly distrait and unhelpful, while Campion did his gallant best with the conversation.

The only person in the party who seemed both to experience no discomfort himself and to be capable of ignoring it in his fellows was Mr Norman Whitman. All through the over-elaborate meal he sat bored and superior, smiling superciliously at Campion's conversational efforts and only opening his own mouth to murmur an occasional comment on some celebrity whom he saw, or thought he saw, among the neighbouring diners.

Campion, who made a hobby of what he was pleased to call 'tick-fancying', could hardly refrain from the open gloat. The man was a collector's piece. His pallid shining forehead could express 'refaned distaste' with more downright vulgarity than seemed possible on a single surface and he revealed a line in 'host deflation' which had to be heard and seen to be believed.

It soon became clear to everybody that Mr Burns's hope of a 'little friendly chat about love and courtship' was doomed, and the young people were openly relieved. Mr Burns himself was depressed and Norman remained aloof but condescending.

Towards the end of the meal, however, the host brightened. A childlike gleam of anticipation came into his eyes, and Campion caught him glancing towards him once or twice with disarming eagerness. Moreover, every now and again he felt in his waistcoat pocket and at last, when coffee was served and Peter had carried Prudence off on to the dance floor, he could deny himself no longer but took a small onyx hat out of its hiding-place and let it roll over and over in his plump palm.

Norman Whitman frowned at him warningly, but the Burns blood was up and the old man ignored his mentor.

He was watching Campion with the same shy delight and triumph which is displayed by the child who suddenly produces a new toy as good as the other boy's.

Campion did not look at Norman Whitman. He stretched out his hand.

'That's very attractive, isn't it?' he said, and, taking up the charm, he turned it over.

The old man laughed. 'It's quite genuine,' he said. 'It's the real McCoy, isn't it?'

Still Campion did not glance at the third man, who was watching the incident with a face as innocent of expression as a ball of wool.

'I think so.' Campion spoke softly and frowned. It seemed such a shame.

'I think so, too.' The old man chuckled over the words. 'Waiter, bring my bill!'

It did not work.

After five minutes of such unbearable embarrassment and chagrin that Campion could have wept for him, Mr Burns had to face that indubitable fact.

He rolled the hat, he placed it black and shining in the midst of the white table-cloth, he waved it frantically beneath the waiter's nose, but the wooden face did not change and the man remained polite but immovable as a rock while the bill stayed folded on the table.

There came a moment – it was nicely timed – when both Mr Burns and Mr Campion looked at Norman Whitman. It was a steady inspection which lasted for some little time. The fat man did not change colour. His boiled eyes remained blank and his expression reserved. After a while, however, the silence became unendurable and he rose with a conciliatory laugh.

'I'll see the manager for you, Burns,' he murmured. 'You must forgive these fellows. They have to be very careful.'

If the implied insult was unmistakable it was also a master-stroke, and the old man, whose eyes had been slowly narrowing, permitted himself a gleam of hope.

All the same he did not speak. He and Campion sat in silence watching the consequential figure bustling across the room, to disappear finally behind the bank of flowers which masked the exit.

*

After allowing his host due time for meditation, Campion leaned back in his chair and took out his own onyx hat, which he placed on the table beside the other. They were identical; two little toppers exact in every detail.

'I had mine given me,' Campion observed.

Burns raised his eyes from the two trinkets and stared.

'Given you?' he said. 'Some gift. I thought I had a fair enough bank-roll, but I couldn't afford to give presents like that.'

The lean man in the horn-rimmed spectacles looked apologetic.

'A very charming American and her husband wanted to give me a little keepsake to remind me of their visit here,' he said. 'They bought this at Wolfgarten's in Cellini Street. He told them it was exclusive and unique, but then he has his own definition of the term. "Unique" to Wolfgarten means one for London and one for New York. He may have charged them about a fiver. I – er – I thought I'd better tell you.'

Mr Burns was sitting up stiffly, his face blank and his small eyes grown hard. Suddenly he swung round in his chair and gazed at the bank of flowers. Campion put out a gently restraining hand.

'Hold on,' he said. 'It's entirely up to you. I've taken the liberty of arranging it so that you can have him if you want him. At this moment, I imagine our Norman is in the manager's office asking why the devil the arrangement which he made here has been ignored. You see, three weeks ago he opened an account of twenty pounds each at quite a number of restaurants on the understanding that anyone who displayed a small onyx top hat, which he showed them, should be taken without question to be his personal representative. It was a curious request, but after all the personal token, the signet ring and so on, has served this sort of purpose from time immemorial, and the restaurants didn't stand to lose anything while they held his twenty pounds.'

Mr Burns swallowed. 'Go on,' he said.

'Well,' Campion was even more diffident, 'just now I'm afraid the manager may be explaining to Whitman that the particular twenty pounds which he invested here has been used up. Doubtless he is bringing bills to prove it. I've been eating here and at the Gillyflower until my little hat wouldn't do its trick any more, and I fear I must owe our Norman quite a considerable sum. However, that's beside the point. What is important is that the house detective is sitting in the manager's office. Now the story which he will hear from Mr Whitman is a perfectly innocent if eccentric one. But should he subsequently get a rather different tale from you – as he certainly has from me – well, it won't be toppers and tails and bogus countesses for our Norman for some time, will it? I'm so sorry to bring it out like this, but it seemed the only satisfactory and safe way if you should decide to prosecute.'

The old man sat perfectly still for some moments. He made a stolid, powerful figure, his shoulders bowed and his head, with its thatch of thick grey hair, thrust forward as his eyes dwelt upon the two hats. After a while he glanced up and caught Campion's eye. There was a moment of mutual understanding and then, to the youg man's intense relief, they both laughed.

Mr Burns laughed for rather a long time for one who has been suddenly confronted with unpleasant news, and Campion was growing a trifle apprehensive when the older man pulled himself together, and picked up his own hat.

'Five thousand pounds,' he said, looking at it. 'I thought it was a darned sight too cheap to be sound.'

'Too cheap for what?'

'Free food for life at all the best restaurants in London for as many guests up to six as I cared to bring,' said the old man calmly. 'Wait a minute. I'm not so daft as I look.

It was a good story. Norman's a smart fellow. He went to work very carefully. I'd known him about six weeks before he brought me in here one night, and I don't mind admitting that he impressed me with his way of doing things.'

He paused and looked at Campion shyly. 'I'm not what you might call a social swell,' he said. 'No, no, don't be nice about it; I'm a fool but not a damned fool. I came over here with plenty of money and plenty of time. I meant to get in with the right lot and learn all the tricks and the refinements that I'd read about, and I got just about what I was asking for. Norman looked all right to me. Obviously I was wrong. Anyway, he taught me one or two useful things about the clothes to wear and so on, and then we came in here and he did his act with his damn-fool hat.

'I was impressed. These stiffs of waiters always get me flustered, and when I saw it all go off so smoothly I was attracted. It seemed to be so easy, so dignified and gentlemanly. No money passing and so on. Well, I asked him about it, and he pretended he didn't want to tell me. But I'm a tenacious sort of chap, and presently out it came. It was a most ingenious spiel. This hat represented the Top Hat Club, he said, a club so exclusive that only the very best people in the land belonged to it ... royalty and so on. He also explained that, like all these very superior affairs, it was practically secret because the restaurant only entered into the arrangement if they were certain they were getting only the very best people.'

*

He broke off and grinned sheepishly.

'Well, you can guess the rest,' he said. 'It seemed quite reasonable the way he told it, and the business side of it was sound. If you can buy an annuity for life why shouldn't you buy a meal ticket, providing your honesty is guaranteed and they know you're not the sort of chap to make money on it by hiring it out? Oh, I'm the mug all right, but he had luck. I happened to see your hat, you see. I didn't mention

it to him, of course, because he didn't seem to like you and
I didn't want him getting jealous.'

'He was going to get you elected to this club, I take it?'

'That's about it, son. Five thousand quid entrance fee.
It seemed cheap. I'm fifty-six and I may go eating in
restaurants for another twenty years. But what about you?
When did you come into this?'

Campion told his story frankly. He felt it was the very
least he could do with those bright eyes watching him
suspiciously.

'I remember Norman,' he said. 'He came back to me.
It took me a tremendous time, but after my first free meal
at the Gillyflower the whole thing suddenly became as
clear as mud. I don't want to depress you, but I'm afraid
we've stumbled on the great forefather of all confidence
tricks. Years and years ago, just after I came down from
Cambridge, I went to Canada, and right out in the wilds
I came upon a fit-up company in an awful little one-eyed
town. They were real old barnstormers, the last in the world
I should think, and they gave a four-hour programme,
comprising a melodrama, a farce and a variety show all at
one sitting. The farce was one of those traditional country
tales which are handed down for generations and have no
set form. The actors invent the dialogue as they go along.
Well, the standard was frightful, of course, but there was one
fat young man who played villains who was at least funny.
He had a ridiculous walk, for one thing, and when I saw
Whitman bolting down the corridor to your box he
reminded me of something. Then of course when I saw the
top hat at the dinner table it all came roaring back to me ...
What's the matter?'

Mr Burns was gazing at him, an incredulous expression
growing in his eyes as recollection struggled to life.

'*Touch 'At Pays Waiter!*' he ejaculated, thumping the
table with an enormous fist. 'Good Lord! My old grandfather told me that story out in South Africa before I was
breeched. I remember it! "Touch 'At Pays Waiter", the
story of the poor silly bumpkin who was persuaded to

exchange his cow for a magic hat. Good Lord! Before I was breeched!'

Campion hesitated. 'What about Norman?' he suggested. 'What do you want to do? There may be a certain amount of publicity, you see, and –'

He broke off. The old man was not listening. He sat slumped in his chair, his eyes fixed on the far distance. Presently he began to laugh. He laughed so much that the tears ran down his face and he grew purple and breathless.

'Campion,' he began weakly, when he had regained comparative coherence, 'Campion, do you recall the end of that story?'

His guest frowned. 'No,' he said at last. 'No, I'm sorry, I'm afraid I don't. It's gone completely. What was it?'

Mr Burns struggled for air.

'The bumpkin didn't pay,' he gasped. 'The bumpkin ate the meal and didn't part with the cow. That is what I've done! This was the final try-out. I was parting with the cash to-night. I've got the cheque all ready made out here in my wallet. I haven't parted and you've eaten his forty quid.'

They were still looking at each other when the young people returned. Prudence regarded them with mild astonishment.

'You two seem to be making a lot of noise,' she remarked. 'What are you talking about?'

Mr Burns winked at his companion.

'What would you call it? The Hat Trick?' he suggested.

Campion hesitated. 'Hardly cricket,' he said.

IV

The Question Mark

WHEN Miss Chloe Pleyell became engaged to Sir Matthew Pearing, K.C., Mr Albert Campion crossed her name off his private list entitled 'Elegant Young Persons Whom I Ought to Take to Lunch' and wrote it in neatly at the foot of his 'People I Must Send Christmas Cards to' folder.

He made the exchange with a smile that was only partially regretful. There had been a time when Miss Pleyell had seemed to him to have a light-heartedness all her own, but once or twice lately it had occurred to him somewhat forcefully that light-headedness might be a more accurate description. Without the slightest trace of malice, therefore, he wished Sir Matthew, who was a monument of humourless pomposity, joy of his choice.

He was still wishing him every happiness, albeit a trifle dubiously, as he stood in the big old-fashioned office at the back of Julius Florian's Bond Street shop and watched the astute old silversmith persuading Chloe to decide whether Mr Campion should signify his goodwill on her marriage with the Adam candlesticks or the baroque epergne.

Chloe was in form. She sat on the edge of the walnut desk, her cocoa ermine coat slipping off her shoulders and her small yellow head on one side. Her eyes were narrowed, their vivid blue intensified by the tremendous mental effort involved in the choice.

Mr Florian appeared to find her wholly charming. He stood before her, his round dark face alight with an interest all the more remarkable since she had been in the shop for the best part of three-quarters of an hour already.

'The epergne is exquisitely fashionable now,' murmured Chloe, 'and I adore it. It's so magnificently *silly*. But the Adam things will be there always, won't they, like a family butler or something.'

Old Florian laughed.

'So truly put,' he observed, with a little nod to Mr Campion. 'Which shall it be, then? The fashion of the day or the pride of a lifetime?'

'I'll have the epergne, Mr Florian. And you're an angel to give it me, Albert. Every time I look across it at poor Matthew sitting at the other end of the table I shall think of you.'

'That'll be nice for both of us,' said Mr Campion cheerfully.

Chloe slid off the desk and drifted to the side-table where the epergne stood holding out its little silver baskets on slender curling arms. The silversmith trotted after her.

'A lovely thing,' he said. 'Fine early George the Third, eight sweetmeat baskets hand-pierced and chased, gadroon edges, ball feet. I can tell you its entire history. It was made for Lord Perowne and remained in that family for seventy-two years, when it was purchased by a Mr Andrew Chappell, who left it to his daughter who lived at Brighton and –'

Chloe's laugh interrupted him.

'How sweet!' she said. 'Like a dog. Having a pedigree, I mean. I shall call it Rover. All my furniture's going to have names, Albert.'

'When one buys a fine piece of silver one usually likes to know something of its history,' said Mr Florian stiffly.

Miss Pleyell's brain struggled with the information and came out on top.

'Oh, of course, in case it's stolen,' she said brightly. 'I never thought of that. How fascinating! Tell me, do you deal much in stolen stuff, Mr Florian? By accident, I mean,' she added belatedly, as the small man's face grew slowly red and then more slowly purple.

Campion hurried to the rescue.

'The police lists protect you from all disasters of that sort, don't they, Mr Florian?'

The silversmith regained his poise and even his smile.

'Ah yes,' he said graciously. 'The police lists are very interesting. I'll show you one.'

He touched a bell on his desk and went on talking in his slow, slightly affected voice.

'Whenever there has been a robbery the police circularize the trade with a list of the missing valuables. Then, if the thief or his agents are foolish enough to attempt to dispose of the haul to any reputable firm, they can be – ah – instantly apprehended.'

'How lovely!' said Chloe, with such emphasis that Campion glanced at her sharply, only to find her gazing at Mr Florian with an eager interest in her china-blue eyes which was utterly disarming.

The silversmith thawed visibly, and by the time his clerk reappeared with the folder he was beaming.

'I don't show these to everybody,' he said archly, his black eyes twinkling at Chloe. 'Here's a list of things taken from a mansion in Surrey. And here's another very curious thing. These are the valuables taken from the Hewes-Bellewe house in Manchester Square. No doubt you read of the burglary? I found it particularly interesting because I'm familiar with Lady Hewes-Bellewe's collection of silver. Most of these pieces have been through my hands from time to time for special cleaning and minor repairs.'

'Fascinating,' murmured Chloe, glancing down a column of technicalities with what was only too obviously an uncomprehending eye. 'What's an early silver muffineer with BG, LG?'

'A sugar sifter with a blue glass lining,' Mr Florian seemed delighted to explain, and it occurred to Mr Campion that a lot of beauty went a remarkably long way. 'That's a very interesting piece,' the silversmith went on. 'I had it here once when we gave a little loan exhibition of rare silver. It had a charming design of ivy leaves, hand-pierced, and on one of the leaves a little putto in a boat has been engraved. Engraving with hand-piercing is comparatively rare, and I told Lady Hewes-Bellewe that in my opinion the putto must have been the brilliant work of some eighteenth-century amateur. What a tragedy to think it's gone!'

'Frightful,' agreed Chloe, blank but game. 'But it all depends on how you look at it, doesn't it?'

Campion felt it time to be helpful.

'I remember that burglary,' he remarked. 'That was the Question Mark's last escapade, wasn't it? The fellow the newspapers call the "Crooked Crook".'

'That's the man.' The suave Mr Florian was almost

excited. 'The police can't put their hands on him, and I understand they think he's responsible for at least half a dozen London burglaries. I'm particularly interested in him because he has a mania for fine silver. He must be quite a connoisseur in his way. I can't bring myself to believe he has that beautiful stuff melted down. It must go abroad.'

Chloe smiled at the old man with ingratiating earnestness.

'This is wonderful,' she smiled. 'I feel I'm learning trade secrets. Why is he called the Question Mark and the Crooked Crook?'

'Because he walks with a stoop, my child,' explained Mr Campion. 'He's been seen once or twice, a thin bent figure lurking in dark passageways and on unlighted staircases. Frighten yourself to death with that vision, my poppet, and come along.'

'He's a cripple? How devastating!' Miss Pleyell was thinking rapidly, and the unaccustomed exercise brought most becoming spots of colour to her cheek-bones. 'Tell me, how does he get up drainpipes and do all the energetic things burglars do?'

Florian smiled, and Campion saw with relief that he had evidently decided to get into line with the rest of Chloe's acquaintances and consider her an adorable half-wit.

'Ah, but he's not a real crookback,' he said, lowering his voice as though he were speaking to a child. 'He was nearly captured on one occasion. A servant girl caught sight of him from an upper window and gave the alarm. He took to his heels and the woman told the police that he straightened up as he ran.'

'How very peculiar,' commented Chloe unexpectedly.

'Not really.' Florian's tone was still gently humorous. 'Most crooks have their little foibles, their little trade marks. It's a tradition. There's one man who always cuts a heart-shaped hole in the pane of a downstairs window and lifts the piece out carefully with a small rubber sucker so that he can get to the latch. There's another who

disguises himself as a milkman before he cracks a crib. This
fellow the Question Mark probably looks quite normal in
private life, but the police hunted for a long time for someone with a pronounced stoop.'

'Really?' said Chloe, her breathlessness a little overdone.

'Oh, yes. Dear me, yes. Crooks are extraordinary people.
Ask Mr Campion. He's the expert. Why, I remember when
I was a young man first in business there was a thief who
had our whole trade by the ears. We dreaded him. And he
used to do his work in a guardsman's uniform, red tunic,
moustachios, a swagger-cane, and all.'

Campion looked up with interest.

'That's a prize effort,' he said, laughing. 'I've never
heard of him.'

Florian shook his head.

'Ah well, it's thirty-five years ago at least. But he existed,
believe me. We were all very much relieved when he was
caught and gaoled. I don't know what happened to him
when he was released. Some of your older friends at Scotland Yard might remember him. They called him the
Shiner. Well, Miss Pleyell, you don't want to hear any more
of my reminiscences, I'm sure. I'll have the epergne dis-
patched to you immediately.'

Mr Campion carried Miss Pleyell away.

'It's sweet of you,' she said, thoughtfully eyeing him
across the little table in the crowded but fashionable lounge
where she had elected to take tea. 'I shall treasure Rover
always.'

'But not next to your heart,' murmured her host
absently. His thoughts had wandered to a curious little
notion which had come to him during the silversmith's
lecture on the crooks of the past. It was an odd little idea,
and presently he put it out of his mind as ridiculous.

He grinned at Chloe.

'I hope you didn't let old Florian bore you?' he said.

'Bore me? My dear, you know I'm never bored.' Chloe's
eyes were gently reproachful. 'Besides, the funny little

creature was quite amusing. As it happens, I'm frightfully interested in crime just now.'

'Oh?' Mr Campion's eyebrows rose apprehensively.

Chloe's smile was candid and confiding.

*

'Albert, my pet,' she said, 'I want your advice. I don't know if I've been frightfully clever or terribly childish.'

Her host resisted the impulse to cover his eyes with his hand.

'Criminal?' he inquired casually.

'Oh no!' Chloe was amused. 'Quite the reverse. I'm just employing a detective, that's all. It's really to oblige Gracie. Have you seen Gracie, my maid? She's the girl with little black eyes. She has Bulgarian blood, or something. She sews exquisitely. I couldn't lose her. She's invaluable.'

Her escort blinked.

'Perhaps I'm not quite right in the head,' he remarked affably. 'I don't get the hang of this at all. Is the detective keeping an eye on Gracie to see she doesn't wander off into the blue?'

'No, my dear.' Chloe was patient. 'The detective is engaged to Gracie – for the time being. It won't last. It never does. She's so temperamental. It's her Bulgarian blood. I'm simply giving him a job so she won't marry him and start a shop or something frightful. You don't follow me, do you? I'll explain it all most carefully because I'd like your advice. I think I've been rather bright.'

The tall man in the horn-rimmed spectacles sighed. 'Put the worst in words of one syllable,' he invited.

Chloe leant forward, her expression childlike and serious. 'First of all you must realize about Gracie,' she said earnestly. 'If I were cynical I should say that Gracie was the most important person in my life. Without Gracie my hair, my style, my clothes, my *entire personality* would simply go to pieces. Do you understand now?'

Mr Campion thought she looked very charming and he said so. Chloe looked almost worried.

'Yes, well, there you are,' she said. 'I'm not a fool. I give Gracie full credit for everything. I'm simply hopeless alone and I know it. I simply can't afford to lose her. Unfortunately she's frightfully susceptible. It's her Middle-European blood. It's always coming out. She's had nine serious love affairs in the past two years.'

'Dear me!' said Mr Campion. 'And now she's in love with a detective?'

'Ah yes. But he wasn't a detective to begin with,' explained Miss Pleyell, and went on airily: 'He was out of work, you see, and Gracie was passionately sorry for him. She gets all worked up on these occasions, urgently maternal and all that.'

'Her Bulgarian blood, no doubt,' put in Mr Campion soberly.

'Yes. She can't help it. She wanted to marry Herbert immediately and invest her savings in a shop so that she could settle down and make something of him. What are you thinking, Albert?'

'Thank heaven she can sew,' murmured her escort piously. 'When did you turn Herbert into a detective?'

'Oh, I didn't do it. It was entirely his idea. You see, when Gracie first told me about him I begged her to wait. A man must have the kind of work he really loves, mustn't he? Even I know that. I told her that she simply must make Herbert find out what his vocation was and then I'd see he got into it. Then we could both wait and see how it worked.'

She smiled brightly across the table.

'And Herbert thought he felt the call to become a "tec"?' Mr Campion's lean face split into a smile of pure amusement. 'How charming! What did you do? Bribe a private agency to take him on?'

'No, I didn't. I never thought of that. No, I simply employed him myself at two pounds a week. Gracie usually takes about six weeks to get over a passion, and I thought it would be the most inexpensive way of doing it.'

Her companion looked at her almost affectionately.

'You have a sort of flair, my child, haven't you?' he said. 'He just loafs around until Gracie's Bulgarian eye lights on another victim, I suppose?'

Chloe hesitated and evidently decided to make a clean breast.

'Well, no,' she said at last. 'Unfortunately he doesn't. In a way it's rather awkward. Herbert's devastatingly conscientious. He *will* work. He just insists on detecting all over the place. I put him on to Mother for the first week, but he found out that her cook was taking bribes from the tradesmen and had the idiocy to want the woman dismissed. Mother was furious, of course, as cooks are so scarce. I had a frightful time with the three of them. Now I've been rather clever, I think. I've told Herbert to keep an eye on Matthew. Matthew is the complete model of rectitude. He never forgets his dignity for an instant. I think Matthew will exhaust Herbert, don't you?'

*

Mr. Campion took off his spectacles, a sign with him of deep emotion. In his mind's eye he saw again the pompous young K.C., so correct and conventional that even his mother did not dare to use any diminutive of his Christian name.

'You astound me,' he said simply. 'You have my undying respect. How did you get Sir Matthew to stand for it?'

'I didn't,' she said at last. 'Herbert is very discreet, so I didn't think it necessary to mention it to Matthew at all. Do you think that was unwise?'

Mr Campion's face grew blank. 'My good girl,' he said flatly. 'My good insane girl.'

Miss Pleyell coloured and glanced down at her plate.

'It did just occur to me once or twice that it might not be such a good idea as it looked. That's why I mentioned it to you,' she murmured defensively. 'Matthew's ridiculously stiff in some ways, isn't he?'

Since he did not trust himself to speak, her host made no comment. She forced a smile.

'Still, he'll never notice Herbert,' she said. 'Herbert's such an ordinary, nondescript little man. Matthew never notices unimportant people.'

Mr Campion took himself in hand, and when he spoke his voice was almost gentle. He had a gift for lucidity when he chose to employ it, and his short lecture on the gentle art of blackmail and its perpetrators was clear and to the point. He also touched upon the more ethical side of the arrangement, with a direct reference to the dictates of good taste. His feelings carried him away, and he only came to an abrupt pause when Miss Pleyell's small face began to pucker dangerously.

'Oh, how awful!' she said, waving away his belated apology. 'I never looked at it like that. It never entered my head that Herbert might be dishonest. I do see it's dangerous and rather beastly; I do now. But before, it never occurred to me. I was simply thinking of not losing Gracie. What shall I do? Anything except tell Matthew. I daren't do that. I just daren't. He wouldn't see it in my way at all and I am terribly fond of him. What shall I do?'

She looked so small and pretty and woebegone that Mr Campion felt a brute.

'Call the watch-dog off,' he said cheerfully. 'Go round to Paul Fenner of the Efficiency Detective Bureau and tell him from me to give Herbert a temporary job at your expense. Then keep quiet. Don't tell the story to anybody.'

'No, of course I won't.' Miss Pleyell's relief was charming. 'You're a darling,' she said. 'A perfect dear. I'm terribly grateful to you, Albert. You're so frightfully clever. I'll do exactly what you say, and then everything will be all right, won't it? You don't think I'm a fool, though, do you? I couldn't bear that.'

Mr Campion surveyed her with great tolerance.

'I think you're fantastic, my child,' he said gravely.

*

He made a different and more forceful remark about her the following morning when her telephone call coincided with his early tea. She was tearfully incoherent at the other end of the wire.

'It's happened.' Her whisper reached him, shaken with tragic intensity. 'It's Herbert. What shall I do?'

'Herbert?' Mr Campion shook the sleep out of his head and strove to collect his thoughts. 'Oh yes, Herbert the amateur detective. What's he done?'

'Can I tell you on the 'phone?'

'Well, I hope so.' Mr Campion raised his eyebrows at the instrument. 'What's he going? Demanding money?'

'Oh no . . . no . . . worse than that. Albert, he's found out something about Matthew and he wants to go to the police. Herbert says he's got proof that Matthew's a crook.'

There was a long silence from Mr Campion's end of the wire.

'Can you hear me? What shall I do?'

Campion held the receiver an inch or so from his ear. 'Yes, I can hear,' he said dryly. 'My voice had left me, that was all. Well, my dear young friend, your course is clear. Tell Master Herbert to go to the police and make his accusation by all means. When he changes his tone and you get down to the vital question of the fiver he has in mind, threaten to *send* for the police.'

'Oh, I see.' Chloe sounded partially convinced. 'Then you think Herbert's simply lying about Matthew being a mysterious thief and all that? He's very convincing. Are you there, Albert? Listen, you don't think it's *true?* What's the matter with your voice? Why does it keep going like this?'

'It's a form of nervous paralysis,' explained Mr Campion gently, and rang off.

While he was dressing he thought of Chloe and shook his head over her. She was beautiful and she was charming and at heart a dear, he reflected, but unfortunately hardly safe out. He hoped most devoutly for her sake that the dignified Sir Matthew would never hear of Gracie's Herbert.

A morning at the Leicester Galleries and a protracted

luncheon kept him away from the Piccadilly flat until half-way through the afternoon. He let himself in with his key and was walking down the corridor to his study when an unexpected vision on the floor of his sitting-room caught his eye through the half-open doorway. He paused and stared at it.

Lying on the carpet was a battered portmanteau, while round it, spread out in dazzling array, was as choice a collection of unfamiliar silver as ever he had seen. Blinking a little, he pushed open the door and glanced round. A sturdy, respectable figure with a round face and a permanently injured expression rose stiffly from an upright chair.

Campion surveyed the man in astonishment. He was a perfect stranger and was neatly dressed in nondescript tweeds.

'Mr Campion?' he demanded in a brisk, high-pitched voice. 'Your man said I could wait 'ere for you.'

'Oh yes, quite.' Campion's gaze wandered back to the array upon the floor. 'You've brought your – luggage, I see.'

'My name's Boot,' said the visitor, ignoring the remark. 'Miss Pleyell said I was to see you before I went to the police. Come what might I was to see you first. That's what she said.'

A great light dawned slowly upon Mr Campion.

'You're not Herbert, by any chance?' he inquired.

Mr Boot blushed.

'My young lady calls me Herbert,' he admitted grudgingly. 'I'm a private inquiry agent in the employ of Miss Chloe Pleyell. She said she'd mentioned me to you. Is that right?'

'Oh, yes. Yes, she did. She did indeed. Won't you sit down?'

Mr Campion's pale eyes were narrowed behind his spectacles. Gracie's young man was not at all the type he had expected.

'I'd rather stand, if you don't mind,' said Herbert without impoliteness. 'Time's short. I've been here since noon. Notice anything about this lot?'

Mr Campion ran a thoughtful eye over the glistening treasure trove at his feet. One item in particular caught his special attention. It was a large Georgian sugar sifter lined with blue glass and decorated with a design of hand-pierced ivy leaves. The centre of one leaf was exquisitely engraved with the tiny likeness of a cupid in a boat.

'Dear me!' said Mr Campion.

'Seen the police lists lately, sir?' Herbert inquired, his aggrieved expression deepening. 'I have. Do you know what this collection represents? It's the proceeds of a robbery committed on the night of the fifteenth at a house in Manchester Square. Hewes-Bellewe was the family's name. In the papers the police were said to be looking for a person they're pleased to call the Question Mark. Now you see, sir, whatever you or Miss Pleyell may say, I *must* go to the police with this stuff. I *must*. It's my duty and, in a way, my privilege. I owe it to myself. I've found it. I've got to report it. I know there's a dangerous criminal masquerading as a gentleman of title, and although I'm very sorry for Miss Pleyell, I'm in a cleft stick. I've got to do my duty.'

Mr Campion felt a little giddy.

'Look here, Herbert,' he said at last, 'let me get this clear. You're not thinking of accusing Sir Matthew Pearing of being the Question Mark, are you?'

Herbert's bright brown eyes became belligerent.

'I'm telling the police all I know,' he said. 'Since he done it he ought to be made to pay for it.'

Mr Campion's mind grappled with the absurdities of the situation. 'Before we go along to the Yard I think you'd better tell me the full story.'

'Would that be *Scotland* Yard, sir?' Mr Boot's tone was suddenly respectful. 'I've always wanted to go there and see the big shots,' he added naïvely. 'I was afraid I'd have to take these along to a common police station and let some jack-in-office of a local inspector take most of the credit.'

'Oh, I'll take you to Scotland Yard all right,' said Mr Campion, feeling a little foolish. 'We'll go and have tea

with the superintendent, if you like. Where did you get
all this incriminating property?'

Mr Boot smiled. The mention of the name 'Scotland
Yard' seemed to have thawed him into childlike affability.
He sat down.

'I'll tell you,' he said. 'Out of the cloakroom at Charing
Cross. Fancy that.'

'Fancy indeed,' echoed Campion. 'Where did you get
the ticket?'

'Ah . . .' Herbert raised his head. 'Where do you think?
Out of one of his lordship's own blessed suits, and that's a
fact. I've got witnesses.'

It seemed to Mr Campion that ever since he had met
Chloe on the previous afternoon the very flavour of life
had been touched with the fantastic, a circumstance he
had attributed entirely to the influence of her personality,
but this was a frank absurdity, and he began to doubt his
ears.

Herbert beamed at his perplexity.

'I'll tell you the story,' he said. 'I can see you're a bit
took back and I don't blame you. I was myself when I first
opened this suitcase. I was put on to Sir Matthew Pearing
by Miss Pleyell, who got to know of me through my young
lady. "Just keep an eye on Sir Matthew," she said. Naturally I asked her in what way and she said she didn't know,
but she thought there was something definitely mysterious
about him. Those were her very words, sir; "definitely
mysterious".'

Campion groaned silently and Herbert continued.

'Well, I kept an eye on the gentleman,' he said, folding
his hands on his waistcoat. 'And what did I find? Nothing
at all for a long time. That Sir Matthew's a sly bird. For
weeks he went on living a most regular life with his servants
as solemn as he was. And then – chance took a 'and.'

He nodded complacently.

'Then I got a bit o' luck. There's a Mr Tuke who is Sir
Matthew's valet. I ingratiated myself with 'im. He's one
of these lazy, overpaid gent's gents, and I found out he 'ad

the sauce to send 'is master's suits down to the quick cleaners to save 'isself the trouble of doing the pressing. 'E paid for them out of 'is own money, I dare say, but it wasn't right. I said nothing, of course, and as it happened that little trick of Master Tuke's was lucky for me. This morning I was in the kitchen – I often go round there early – and Mr Tuke asked me if I'd do him a favour by slipping down to the cleaners and collecting a dinner-jacket outfit he'd left there last night. I went, and when the girl gave me the parcel she handed over a little black wallet that had been left in the pocket. I examined it in accordance with my duties and inside I found two penny stamps and a cloakroom ticket.'

'You hung on to the wallet?'

'I did.' Herbert spoke firmly. 'I examined it in front of the girl. I'm very careful. You have to be in this business. I made her make a note of the case, the stamps, and the number of the ticket. Then I came away. I gave the suit to Mr Tuke, who identified it, mind you, but I kept the wallet and I went down to Charing Cross. I gave up the ticket at the cloakroom. I got this suitcase in return *and I opened it before the attendant.* "Now, my lad," I said to him when I see what was inside, "I'm a detective. Take a good look at me. Here's my card," I said. "Take a look at this stuff," I said. "I'll need you as a witness." After that I gave 'im a signed receipt for the case and kept the cloak-room ticket. I took a copy of the receipt and I mentioned the number of the cloakroom ticket on each slip of paper.'

'Did you, though?' said Mr Campion, whose respect for Herbert was slowly mounting. 'Then you went to Miss Pleyell and she sent you on to me, I suppose?'

'Exactly,' his visitor agreed. 'And now, if you please, sir, I'd like to go to Scotland Yard.'

Mr Campion glanced at the silver at his feet.

'Yes,' he said slowly. 'Yes. Quite. I think you'd better. I'll come with you.'

*

A little over an hour later superintendent Stanislaus Oates sat behind his desk in his private office at the head-quarters of the Central Branch and stared at his friend Mr Albert Campion, a slightly bewildered expression in his bright blue eyes.

Herbert had retold his story once and was now obligingly doing so again to a sergeant in another room, while a cons-table wrote it all down. The two friends were alone.

'It's idiotic,' said Oates suddenly. 'We'll check up on Boot's story, of course, and it *may* be false, yet I'm open to bet it's the truth. I know his type – we've got plenty of 'em in the Force. What an extraordinary thing!'

Campion lit a cigarette and his eyes were thoughtful.

'Oh, our Herbert is honest,' he said. 'Herbert's as honest as the day. You're sure you can identify the stuff?'

'Certain.' Oates glanced towards the battered suitcase on the table in the corner. 'There's no doubt of that. You heard what Inspector Baker said. He's working on the case. He's seen photographs and studied descriptions. Besides, my dear chap, it's all there. That's the proceeds of the Question Mark's Manchester Square haul all right; no doubt about it. We'll check up on the cloakroom attend-ant and the girl at the cleaners', and if these are okay we'll have to interview Sir Matthew. There's no other way. We must find out where the ticket came from. He'll be able to give us an explanation all right, but we must have it.'

Campion thrust his hands into his pockets and his lean face was troubled.

'That's going to be infernally awkward, isn't it?' he ventured. 'You'll have to drag in Herbert to protect your-selves, and *he'll* have to mention Miss Pleyell to protect himself.'

Oates, one of the kindest and most sympathetic of men, spread out his stubby fingers in a gesture of regret.

'He's a lawyer,' he said. 'Her name will come out in the end. You can't suppress it. She's asked for it, you know.'

Campion nodded. 'Still, it seems a pity she should get it,' he said, and grimaced. 'Sir Matthew's obviously not the Question Mark himself, and it's a pity to drag him into it. He'll never forgive her. He's not that type.'

The superintendent did not smile. 'I know, I know, my lad,' he said. 'You needn't tell me. I'd like to do all I could for the girl. Indirectly she's put us on to a very important thing. But what other course is open to me? I ask you.'

The tall young man in the horn-rimmed spectacles was silent for some moments. The vague idea which had come to him on the previous afternoon when Mr Florian had been talking to Chloe, and which had been knocking at intervals on the door of his mind ever since, suddenly presented itself as a concrete thing. He looked up.

'What was the number of the ticket for the suit?' he demanded.

'The cloakroom ticket?'

'No, that was for the suitcase. What was the number of the cleaners' ticket that Tuke gave Herbert when he sent him down to claim Sir Matthew's dinner jacket?'

Oates regarded him silently.

'Wait a minute,' he said at last. 'I've got it here. Boot got it from the girl and gave her a receipt instead. He's a cautious lad, is Herbert. Here you are – one hundred and sixty-one.'

He pushed over a small square of magenta paper on which the figures were roughly printed beneath a single line of very small type announcing 'The Birch Road Quick-Cleaning Coy.' Campion folded the heading over carefully and turned the slip round before he gave it back.

'How about that if a girl was in a hurry?' he inquired.

The Superintendent's heavy eyebrows rose as he stared at it.

'That's an idea,' he said cautiously. 'A genuine idea.'

Campion leaned over the desk.

'Come down yourself to the cleaners' with me now and bring the wallet,' he said. 'I've got an idea.'

'Another?'

'I think so. It's a notion which has been fidgeting me all day. There's just a chance I may be on to the man you want. Those two descriptions of the Question Mark which you had – one from a postman in the Clarges Street show and one from the nurse in the earlier business – both agreed that he was a stooping, sinister figure, didn't they?'

'Yes, but the other woman who saw him running said he straightened up when he was on the move,' Oates objected.

'Ah, but she saw him from above,' said Mr Campion. 'Will you come down to the cleaners' with me?'

The superintendent rose, grumbling.

'I don't mind you working yourself to death for your friends,' he said, 'but I resent it when I'm expected to do the same. All right, we'll take Herbert and a sergeant. I hope you have got something up your sleeve.'

'So do I,' murmured Mr Campion fervently. 'I should hate to have to take back that epergne.'

The Birch Road Quick-Cleaning Company's establishment was not a large affair. It was situated in a back street some way behind the magnificent block in which Sir Matthew Pearing had his super-flat. Herbert and the sergeant remained in the taxicab some little distance down the road, while Campion and the Superintendent interviewed the harassed but by no means unintelligent young woman in charge.

She left the steaming press in the window and listened carefully to their questions.

She remembered Herbert's visit perfectly, and readily produced his receipt for the suit and the wallet. Moreover, she remembered Mr Tuke, who was a regular customer, bringing in the dinner jacket on the previous evening. She also identified her own official ticket.

'One hundred and sixty-one,' she said. 'I remember it.'

Campion turned the magenta slip round.

'How about one hundred and ninety-one? It's an easy slip if you look at it quickly,' he suggested.

She glanced up at him with shrewd Cockney eyes.

'It could 'ave 'appened,' she admitted. 'But it didn't. I remember the suit.'

'Very likely, Miss.' Oates beamed upon her in his most avuncular fashion. 'But that's not the point. It's the wallet we're interested in. What happens when something is left in the pocket of a coat which comes in to be cleaned?'

The girl's face cleared.

'That's about it,' she said suddenly. 'Just a minute.'

As she crossed the shop to the inner room Oates glanced at Campion.

'She's sharp,' he said. 'We're lucky.'

'George,' shouted the girl, 'come here, will you?'

A tall thin man, clad in bedraggled trousers and a singlet came out of the steam chamber, wiping his face and arms with a towel.

'This is my brother George,' the girl explained. 'He does the suits. He'd know what you want.'

George stared at the black wallet which the superintendent showed him for some little time before he committed himself.

'That's right,' he said at last. 'I found it in an inside pocket in a waistcoat. It was very nearly empty when I saw it – a couple of stamps and a ticket.'

'That's right. It's of no value. But what did you do with it?'

'Put it in here, like I always do when I come across things.'

George pulled open a drawer in the cash desk, where several odds and ends were stacked neatly, each with a slip of paper attached.

'See?' he said. 'I lay the article in here and I write the number of the suit I took it from on a bit of paper and lay it on top of the thing. When Sis gives the clothes back she just matches the numbers and returns the property.'

Campion sighed with relief.

'Then it would have been possible to mistake the number one-six-one for one-nine-one, for instance?'

George hesitated. 'It might,' he said. 'I'll tell you one thing, if it's any help to you. I took that wallet from the inside waistcoat pocket of a brown tweed suit. I remember it distinctly – a brown tweed suit. What the number was I can't say.'

The girl pounced on the ledger and ran her finger down a column of hieroglyphics.

'You're right,' she said, grinning at Campion. 'That's how it happened. I took George's writing the wrong way up. One-nine-one was a brown tweed suit. The fellow came in for it half an hour ago.'

A muffled exclamation escaped the Superintendent, but Campion interrupted him.

'Just a minute,' he said. 'Was he by any chance a very tall, well-set-up man, about fifty-five to sixty? Grey hair, perhaps.'

'Yes, he was.' The girl seemed surprised. 'I didn't see his hair because he had a hat on, but he wasn't young. I noticed him particularly, being so tall. He was a bit hasty too. He said his landlady had taken the suit to be cleaned without his knowing – seemed quite shirty about it. He didn't ask about the wallet.'

'No, he wouldn't,' said Campion. 'He wouldn't want to call your attention to it.'

'He'll come back,' put in Oates suddenly. 'When he gets that parcel undone and finds he's lost the wallet he'll come back, if he doesn't see us first. We must clear out. Now look here, my dear, here's the wallet. It's got two stamps and a ticket in it. When he comes, give it to him, and whatever you do don't act in any way that may make him suspicious. Can I rely on you?'

She nodded and stretched out a firm, capable hand for the black folder.

The Superintendent hurried his friend from the shop, and the waiting sergeant in the taxi received his instructions.

'Right you are, sir,' he said, touching his felt hat. 'I'll lay for him and I'll tail him. He won't get away from me.'

Oates nodded and thrust Campion into the cab.

'The Yard first to get the stuff, and then Charing Cross,' he said briefly. 'Is that how you were figuring it out, Campion?'

The younger man leaned back in the cab.

'Perfect,' he said contentedly. 'There's nothing like a fair cop.'

Herbert, who had watched the proceedings with his little ferret's eyes glistening with excitement, ventured a question.

'Are we going to see Sir Matthew now, sir?'

Campion glanced at Oates.

'No,' he said. 'Sorry to disappoint you, Herbert, but no. For the time being the aristocracy is out of it. But we're going to meet a celebrity, I fancy, and when we see him we're going to take his fingerprints.'

The superintendent regarded his friend with eyes that were bright and suspicious.

'I want a word or two with you, my lad,' he said. 'What do you know about this chap we're after? When did you see him?'

'I haven't,' said Mr Campion.

'What about that description you gave the girl?'

'That was rather good, wasn't it?' Campion agreed grinning. 'I made that up.'

Oates opened his mouth to speak but caught sight of Herbert's fascinated gaze and thought better of it.

'Wait till I get you on your own,' he murmured, and rapped on the window to urge the driver to hurry.

The next fifteen minutes did not give anybody much opportunity for conversation. The cab paused for a moment at the Yard to take on board two plain-clothes men and the bag of silver, and afterwards swung round to speed back to Charing Cross Station.

'If I know the type we shan't have long to wait,' said Oates as he and Campion took up their positions in a convenient doorway, which afforded them a good view of the cloakroom window. 'As soon as he gets his hands on that ticket he'll beetle down here and make sure that the stuff is safe. I'm trusting that girl.'

Campion glanced casually across the station to where two inconspicuous plain-clothes figures were lounging by the bookstall.

'The clerk's giving them the sign, is he?'

Oates nodded. 'Yes, they understand one another. He's a good man, that clerk. The way he corroborated Herbert Boot's story was intelligent and convincing. My fellows have got to rely on him. They haven't the least idea who they're waiting for, see?'

Campion coughed.

'I don't think they'll miss him,' he murmured. 'He's a distinctive sort of chap, you know.'

Oates swung round on him. 'Damn it, Campion, what do you know about this business?' he demanded. 'This tale about the tall elderly man: where did you get it from?'

'Wait.' Campion laid a restraining hand on his friend's arm and nodded towards a figure which had come striding in through the crowd. The man was striking and even distinguished. Well over six feet four, he was very erect, with a clean-shaven, sharp-featured face which must, in youth, have been remarkably handsome.

Oates stiffened, a startled expression creeping into his eyes.

'Recognize him?' murmured Campion.

'Yes, I think so.' The Superintendent's voice was wondering, and he stepped forward at the same moment as the two Yard men darted out into the open and closed in on either side of the stranger as he took the heavy, battered suitcase from the cloakroom counter. There was only a very brief struggle.

The tall man glanced shrewdly at his adversaries.

'I guess I'm too old for a scrap, boys,' he said. 'I'll come quietly. It's all there in the bag – oh, you know that, do you?'

*

As Mr Campion and the Superintendent drove quietly back to the Yard together Oates was still thoughtful.

'It must be nearly thirty years ago,' he said at last. 'I was a sergeant at the Thames Court Police Station, I remember, and we had that fellow in the cells there for a couple of days. I can't think of his name, but as soon as I set eyes on him this afternoon I recognized him. He looks much older, of course, but you can't mistake that height or that face. What was his name, now?'

Mr Campion hesitated. 'Does "The Shiner" convey anything to you?' he said diffidently.

'The Shiner! That's it, The Shiner!' The superintendent's voice rose with excitement. 'By George, it's the same lark, too – old silver shipped to a fence in Amsterdam. That's him. Good heavens, Campion, how did you know?'

The younger man looked pleased.

'Oh, it occurred to me, you know,' he asid modestly. 'I was in old Florian's shop yesterday, talking about these burglaries, and he got reminiscing about crooks who had specialized in old silver in the past. He mentioned this chap, The Shiner, and said he hadn't been heard of since he came out of jail. Florian also said that The Shiner used to do his early burglaries in full guardsman's uniform.'

'That's right,' said Oates. 'So he did. Amazing vanity these fellows have. A guardsman before the war was a picturesque figure, and there were a lot of them about in London.'

Campion ignored the interruption.

'The fancy dress appealed to me,' he said, 'and I was thinking about it, and also your mysterious Question Mark, when the astonishing points of similarity between the two occurred to me. I didn't see how it worked out, of course, until I'd heard Herbert's contribution and put things together a bit.'

Oates shook his head.

'I'll buy it,' he said. 'I don't see any similarity between the Question Mark and The Shiner. One was a bent, sinister figure straightening up to run, and the other made himself conspicuous in a red tunic. They both pinched silver, I know, but if you can see any other likeness between the two you're a cleverer man than I am, or off your head.'

'It's imagination you lack, guv'nor.' Mr Campion regarded his friend regretfully. 'Think of the fellow. See him in your mind's eye. What is his one inescapable and most damning characteristic? His height. Think of it! What was he to do?'

'Good Lord!' The Superintendent sat up.

'You're right,' he said slowly. 'Of course. It didn't occur to me at once. The uniform disguised him when he was young, it didn't make him conspicuous. Everyone expected to see a tall soldier in a scarlet tunic. A shorter man would have looked peculiar. When he came back and started up again he had to think of something else, I suppose, so he counterfeited a stoop for the actual job, only straightening up when he made a dash for it. Wait a minute, though; he was seen running. The witness didn't mention his height.'

'Because she didn't see it,' Campion protested. 'She only saw him from above. It was that that strengthened my first suspicion. By the way, there'll be no need to interview Sir Matthew now, I take it?'

'No, it's a fair cop.' Oates spoke with satisfaction. 'We caught him with the stuff. That's good enough. You're saved again, Campion, or your girl friend is. Give her my regards and tell her she doesn't know how lucky she is to have a lucky pal.'

Mr Campion opened his mouth to protest but thought better of it. In his experience it was far more comfortable to be considered lucky than clever by any policeman. He was silent for some time and sat looking out of the window, a faint smile playing round his lips.

The superintendent glanced at him.

'What are you thinking of now?' he inquired suspiciously.

'I was wondering,' said Mr Campion truthfully, 'I was just wondering who young Gracie was going to get engaged to next.'

V

The Old Man in the Window

NEWLY appointed Superintendent Stanislaus Oates was by no means intoxicated, but he was cheerful, as became a man celebrating an important advance in a distinguished career, and Mr Campion, who sat opposite him at the small table in the corner of the chop-house, surveyed the change in his usually taciturn friend with interest.

'This promotion puts me into the memoir class when I retire, you know,' observed the ex-Inspector suddenly with uncharacteristic ingenuousness. 'I could write a first-rate book if someone put it down for me. We professionals get to know all kinds of things, interesting stuff a lot of it, that you amateurs never come across; things you'd never consider worth noticing. I struck something very curious to-day. Big business is extraordinary, Campion. Amazing inducements to crime in it. Let me tell you something about company law.'

Mr Campion grinned. 'Tell the world as well,' he suggested affably, for the Superintendent's voice had risen. 'I thought you said this place was deserted in the evening,' he went on, stretching his long thin legs under the table and adjusting his horn-rimmed spectacles. 'It seems to me to be pretty well crowded with youth and – er – passion.'

The ex-Inspector's innate caution reasserted itself and as he glanced about him his long face took on its natural melancholy expression.

'Must have suddenly become fashionable,' he said gloomily. 'That's the trouble with these places. The word goes round that So-and-so's is good, quiet and cheap, and what happens? Before you know where you are a great bunch of goggle-eyed sweethearts swoop down on it and up go the prices while the food goes to pieces. There's a lad over there out with someone he doesn't intend to take home to meet the family.'

Mr Campion, glancing casually over his thin shoulder, caught a glimpse of a heavily jowled face beneath a domed head prematurely bald, and beyond it the dark curls and crimson lips of a girl in a grey hat. He looked away again hastily.

'The name is March,' said Oates, whose spirits were reviving. 'Member of the big theatrical machinery firm. Funny we should see him. It reminds me of what I was going to tell you. They're in low water again, you know.'

His voice promised to carry across the small print-hung room and Mr Campion protested.

'Does alcohol always make you shout?' he enquired gently. 'Don't bellow. I know the fellow quite well by sight. We're members of the same club.'

'Really? I heard the clubs were having a thin time,' said Oates more quietly but unabashed. 'Still, I didn't know they had to let anyone in.'

Mr Campion looked hurt. 'He's a valued and respected member as far as I know,' he said, 'and may very well be out with his wife.'

'Don't you believe it,' said Oates cheerfully. 'That little kid is on at the Frivolity, or was until the show closed last week. And what's more, my lad, Mr Arthur March is due to marry someone else in less than a month. A good policeman studies everything, even the gossip columns, and that bears out what I told you about you amateurs not being thorough. You don't collect sufficient out-of-the-way information. Take this company law, for instance . . .'

He broke off, a light of interest in his mournful grey eyes. From where they sat the view of the entrance was unobstructed and Campion, following his glance, saw two young people come in. Superintendent Stanislaus Oates grinned broadly.

'This is good,' he said. 'That's the girl March is engaged to – Denise Warren. She's out on the spree with a boy friend too. They've come here because they've heard it's quiet, I bet you. They haven't seen March yet.'

Mr Campion did not speak. He was looking at the girl. She was an unusual type, taller than the average and very fair, with wide-apart blue-grey eyes and a magnificent carriage.

Her companion was a square, solid young man only a few years her senior. He was not unhandsome and had an air of authority about him unusual in one of his age. They found a table and settled down in full view of Campion and his guest. Oates was frankly delighted.

'They'll see each other in a moment,' he said with schoolboy mischievousness. 'Who's the fellow with her? Do you know?'

Mr Campion was frowning. 'Yes, I do,' he said. 'That's Rupert Fielding, a surgeon. He's young but an absolute prodigy, they say. I hope he's not playing the fool. His is the one profession that still demands absolute conventionality.'

Oates grinned: 'Another member of the club?'

Campion echoed his smile. 'Yes, as it happens. Spends all his spare time there. Gives the older members a sense of security, I think.'

Oates glanced at the girl again. 'Oh well, she's keeping it in the family, isn't she? What is this famous club? Not Puffin's?'

'No. Quite as respectable if not so eminent. The Junior Greys, Pall Mall.'

Oates sat up with interest. 'Curiouser and curiouser,' he said. 'Isn't that the place where the old boy sits in the window all day?'

'Old Rosemary?'

'That's the man. One of the landmarks of London. Hasn't changed in fifty years. It's a funny thing, I was hearing of him to-day, as I was going to tell you. Is he as old as they say?'

'He's ninety some time this year.'

'Really?' The Superintendent was interested. 'I've seen him, of course, dozens of times. You can't very well miss him sitting there in that great window. He looks young enough from the street. Scraggy men like yourself wear well. What's he like close to?'

Mr Campion considered. He was eager to give serious attention to any subject which would divert his guest's embarrassing attention from his two fellow-members and their more intimate affairs.

'One doesn't get very close to him in the ordinary way,' he said at last. 'That bay window is his holy of holies. There's a draught screen round the back of his chair and a table between him and the rest of the room. I'm seldom there early enough to see him come in in the morning but I meet him tottering out at half-past six now and again.'

'He's frail then?' the Superintendent persisted. 'Frail but young-looking? I'm sorry to be so inquisitive,' he added, 'but I don't like freaks. How young does he actually look close to in a good light?'

Mr Campion hesitated. 'He's very well preserved,' he began at last. 'Had all kinds of things done to him.'

'Oh, facial stuff, rejuvenation, toupets, special teeth to take out the hollows – I know.' The superintendent spoke with contempt. 'That accounts for it. I hate that sort of thing. It's bad enough in old women but in old men it's revolting.'

He paused and, evidently thinking that he might have expressed himself ungraciously, added handsomely: 'Of course, when you remember he was a famous actor it doesn't seem so bad. He was one of the first of the stage knights, wasn't he?'

'I believe so. Sir Charles Rosemary, one of the great figures of the eighties. I believe he was magnificent.'

'And now he spends his days sitting in a window trying to look sixty,' the Superintendent murmured. 'Is it true he does it all day and every day?'

'An unbroken record of twenty years, I believe,' said Mr Campion, who was growing weary of the catechism. 'It's quite a legend. He comes up to the club at eleven o'clock and sits there until six-thirty.'

'My God!' said Oates expressively and added abruptly: 'Hullo, he's seen her!'

Mr Campion gave up the hope of diverting him. The superintendent's round dull eyes were alight with amusement.

'Look at March,' he said. 'He's wild. Isn't that typical of that sort of chap? Doesn't seem to realize he's in the same boat. Can you see him?'

'Yes, in the mirror behind you,' Campion admitted grudgingly. 'Rather awkward for his guest, isn't it?'

'She's used to it, I'd say,' said the ex-Inspector cheerfully. 'Look at him.'

Arthur March was angry and appeared to be indifferent about showing it. He sat upright in his chair, staring at his fiancée and her companion with white-faced indignation. The girl opposite in the grey hat did her best to look faintly amused, but her eyes were angry.

Campion looked at Miss Warren and caught her at the moment when curious glances from other tables directed her attention to the furious man on the other side of the room. She met his eyes for a moment and grew slowly crimson. Then she murmured something to the stolid young man at her side.

Oates was very interested.

'March is going over,' he said suddenly. 'No, he's changed his mind. He's sending a note.'

The waiter who bore the hastily scribbled message on the half-sheet torn from a memorandum book looked considerably embarrassed and he handed it to Miss Warren with a word of apology. She glanced at it, blushed even more deeply than before, and passed it on to Fielding.

The young surgeon's square, immobile face became a shade darker and, leaning towards the girl, he said something abruptly. She hesitated, looked up at him and nodded.

A moment later the waiter was off across the room again, a faint smile on his face. The superintendent frowned.

'What happened?' he demanded. 'I didn't see, did you? Wait a minute.'

Before Campion could stop him he had risen from his seat and sauntered off across the room, ostensibly to get a pipe out of the pocket of his overcoat which hung on a stand near the doorway. The somewhat circuitous route he chose led him directly behind March's chair at the moment when he received the return note from the waiter.

Oates came back smiling.

'I thought so,' he said triumphantly as he sat down. 'She wrapped her engagement ring in his own note and sent it back to him. Oh, very dignified and crushing, whatever he wrote! Look at him now . . . is he going to make a row?'

'I hope not,' said Mr Campion fervently.

'No, he's thought better of it. He's going.' The Superintendent seemed a little disappointed. 'He's livid, though. Look at his hands. He's shaking with fury. I say, Campion, I don't like the look of him; he's demented with rage.'

'Don't gawp at him then, poor chap,' his host protested. 'You were going to tell me something of unparalleled interest about company law.'

The Superintendent frowned, his eyes still on the retreating figures at the other side of the room.

'Was I? This little show has put it out of my head,' he said. 'Ah, they've gone and the other two are settling down again. Well, that's the end of that little romance. I enjoyed it.'

'Obviously,' said Mr Campion bitterly. 'It's probably cost me two perfectly good acquaintances, but what of that if you're happy? The whole incident would have been washed away with a few pretty tears in a day or so and might have been decently forgotten. Still, if you enjoyed it . . .'

The ex-Inspector regarded him owlishly.

'You're wrong,' he said. 'I'm not a man given to – er – soothsaying . . . what's the word?'

'Prophecy?' suggested Campion, laughing.

'Prophecy,' echoed Oates with success. 'But I tell you, Campion, that the incident we have just witnessed is going to have far-reaching consequences.'

'You're tight,' said his companion.

He was, of course, but it was a remarkable thing, as he himself pointed out afterwards, that he was unequivocally right at the same time.

The engagement between Miss Denise Warren and Mr Rupert Fielding, F.R.C.S., was announced at the end of August, a decent six weeks after the intimation that her marriage to Mr. Arthur March, son of the late Sir Joshua March, would not take place, and when Mr Campion walked down Pall Mall to the Junior Greys one morning in October the whole affair was ancient history.

It was a little before twelve and the sun was shining in at the great bay windows of the club, windows so large and frank that the decorous gentlemen within looked almost more like exhibits under glass than spectators of the procession of traffic in the street below.

As he approached the building Mr Campion was aware of a subtle sense of loss. It was not until he had stood for some seconds on the pavement surveying the broad façade of the left wing of the building that he realized where the difference lay. When he saw it he was shocked. The great chair in the centre window of the lounge was occupied not by the familiar aquiline figure of old Rosemary but by a short fattish old gentleman by the name of Briggs, a member of but ten or fifteen years' standing, a truculent tasteless person of little popularity.

Mr Campion entered beneath the Adam porch with a premonition of disaster and was confirmed in his suspicions a few moments later when he discovered Walters, the head steward, in tears. Since Walters was a portly sixty-five and possessed a dignity which was proverbial, the spectacle was both shocking and embarrassing. He blew his nose hastily when Mr Campion appeared and murmured a word of apology, after which he added baldly: 'He's gone, sir.'

'Not old – I mean Sir Charles Rosemary?' Mr Campion was shocked.

'Yes, sir.' Walters permitted himself a ghostly sniff. 'It happened this morning, sir. In his chair where he always sat, just as he would have liked. Mr March and one or two other gentlemen had a word with him when he first came in and then he dozed off. I saw him sleeping heavily but didn't think anything of it, him being so old, but when Mr Fielding came in about an hour ago he noticed at once that something was wrong and called me. We got the old gentleman into a taxi between us and Mr Fielding took him home. He died in the taxi. Mr Fielding has just come in and told us. He'd have been ninety in two days' time. It's been a great shock. Like the end of an era, sir. I remember the old Queen going but it didn't seem like this. I remember him when I came here forty years ago, you see.'

Mr Campion was surprised to find that he was a trifle shaken himself. There was a great deal in what Walters said. Old Rosemary had been an institution.

As he came into the lounge he caught sight of Fielding standing by the eastern fireplace with a small crowd round him. Mr Campion joined it.

Fielding's professional calm was standing him in good stead. He was giving information quietly and seriously, without capitalizing or even seeming conscious of the undue prominence into which chance had forced him. He nodded to Campion and went on with his story.

'He was breathing so stertorously that I went and had a look at him,' he was saying. 'He wasn't conscious then and didn't recover before the end, which came in the taxi, as you know.'

'He had a flat in Dover Street, hadn't he?' said someone.

Fielding nodded. 'Yes. Walters got me the address. He'd gone before we arrived and I knew I couldn't do anything, so I got hold of his man, who seems a very capable chap. We put him on to his bed and the servant told me that his regular doctor was Philipson, so I rang Harley Street and came away.'

'Sir Edgar was upset, I bet,' said a man Campion did not know. 'They knew each other well. Still, he was very old. I don't suppose he was surprised. The very old often die suddenly and peacefully like that.'

The crowd split up into smaller groups, which grew again as other members came in to lunch. Mr Brigg's behaviour in commandeering the favourite seat came in for a good deal of comment and the secretary received several complaints. A half-excited gloom, as at a major disaster, settled over the smoking-room, and the newspapers, who had already been notified by one of Walter's underlings, received quite a number of calls.

The awkward incident occurred just before lunch, however. Mr Campion witnessed it and was shocked by it, in company with nine-tenths of his fellow-members present. Arthur March came in and made a scene.

It began in the hall when he heard the news from Scroop, the porter. His high thin tones protesting disbelief reached the lounge before he appeared himself, pale and excitable, in the doorway. He sank into a chair, snapped at the wine steward, and, after mopping his brow a trifle ostentatiously, rose to his feet again and came across the room to where Fielding stood with Campion.

'This is ghastly,' he said without preamble. 'I was with the old man only this morning, you know. He was in one of his black moods but otherwise he seemed perfectly all right. You found him, didn't you? Was – was it peaceful?'

'Perfectly,' said Fielding shortly. He was obviously embarrassed and Campion found himself wondering if the two men had ever spoken since the little scene in the City chop-house earlier in the year.

'Thank God!' said March with nauseating fervour. 'Oh, thank God!'

He did not move away and the surgeon hesitated.

'Relation of yours?' he enquired abruptly.

March coloured. 'Practically,' he said. 'My grandfather and he were like brothers.'

The explanation evidently sounded a little lame, even

to himself, for he took refuge in wholly unwarrantable abuse.

'You wouldn't understand that sort of loyalty,' he muttered and turned on his heel.

Fielding stood looking after him, his eyebrows raised.

'That chap's in a funny mental state . . .' he was beginning when Mr Campion touched his sleeve.

'Lunch,' said Mr Campion.

It was after the meal, nearing the end of the hour of pleasant somnolence sacred to the gods of digestion, when the Junior Greys experienced its first real sensation since the suffragette outrage, of which no one ever speaks. Campion had been watching with lazy eyes the efforts of the bishop in the chair next his own to keep his attention on the pamphlet on his knee when he saw that divine sit upright in his chair, the healthy colour draining rapidly from his plump cheeks.

At the same moment, on the other side of the room, Major-General Stukely Wivenhoe's cigar dropped from his mouth and rolled on the carpet.

A communal intake of breath, like the sigh of a great animal, sounded all over the room and in a far corner somebody knocked over a coffee-cup.

Mr Campion hoisted himself on one elbow and looked round. He remained arrested in that uncomfortable position for some seconds.

Old Rosemary, immaculate and jaunty as ever, was coming slowly across the room. There was a red carnation in his buttonhole, his flowing white hair glistened, and his curiously unwrinkled face wore its customary faint smile.

Behind him, portly and efficient, strode Sir Edgar Philipson, the Harley Street man.

It was a petrifying moment and one which demanded every ounce of the Junior Grey's celebrated aplomb.

Half-way across the room the newcomers were met by a page hurrying in with the early editions. Confronted by the spectacle of old Rosemary himself the boy lost his head completely. He thrust an *Evening Wire* at the old man.

'They – they say you're dead, sir,' he blurted out idiotically.

Rosemary took the paper and peered at it while the stupified room waited in silence.

'Greatly exaggerated,' he said in the unmistakable clipped tone they all knew so well. 'Take it away.'

He moved on to his chair. No one saw Briggs leave it. Some insist that he crawled out behind the screen on all fours; and others, more imaginative, that he dived out of the window and was afterwards found gibbering in the basement. But at all events, his departure was silent and immediate.

Old Rosemary sat down, and beckoning to a paralysed servant, ordered a whisky and soda.

Meanwhile, Sir Edgar Philipson stood looking round the room, and Fielding, pale and incredulous, rose to meet him. The elder man was not kind.

'That's the trouble with you younger men, Fielding,' he said in a rumbling undertone that was yet loud enough to be heard. 'Overhasty in your diagnosis. Make sure before you act, my boy. Make sure.'

He walked away, a handsome old man very pleased with himself.

Fielding glanced helplessly round the room, but no one met his eyes. Mr Campion, who alone was sympathetic, was looking at old Rosemary, noting the healthy brilliance of his eyes and the colour in his cheeks.

Fielding walked out of the room in silence.

Mr Campion dined alone that evening and was writing a brief report on his own share in the Case of the Yellow Shoes, which had just come to a satisfactory conclusion, when the young surgeon called. Fielding was embarrassed and said so. He stood awkwardly in the middle of the study in the flat in Bottle Street and made a hesitating apology.

'I'm terribly sorry to presume on an acquaintance like this, Campion,' he said, 'but I'm in such a devil of a mess. That chap Rosemary, you know, he was dead as mutton this morning.'

Mr Campion produced a decanter.

'I should sit down,' he said. 'It soothes the nerves and rests the feet. I suppose this affair is going to be – er – bad for business?'

Fielding looked relieved and a faint smile appeared for an instant on his square, solemn face.

'Frightfully,' he said, accepting the glass Campion handed him. 'It makes such a darned good story, you see. Rupert Fielding is such a brilliant surgeon that he doesn't know when he's beaten and the patient is dead – it's all over the place already. I shall be ruined. Incompetence is bad enough in any profession, but in mine it's unforgivable. And,' he added helplessly, 'he was dead, or at least I thought so. His heart had stopped and when I got him home I tried the mirror test. Of course, miracles do happen nowadays, but not under old Philipson. At least, I wouldn't have said so yesterday. It's funny, isn't it?'

'Odd, certainly,' Mr Campion agreed slowly. 'When you talk of these modern miracles, what are they exactly?'

'Oh, electrical treatment and that sort of thing.' Fielding spoke vaguely. 'You see,' he added frankly, 'I'm not a physician; I'm a surgeon. I've done a certain amount of medicine, of course, but I don't set up to be a G.P. Drugs are not in my line.'

Mr Campion glanced up and his pale eyes behind his spectacles were inquisitive.

'You're wondering if the old boy couldn't have taken something that produced a pretty good simulation of death?' he suggested.

The younger man regarded him steadily. 'It sounds far-fetched, I know,' he said, 'but it's the only explanation I can think of, although what on earth the stuff can have been I can't imagine. You see, the dreadful thing is that I didn't do anything. I just made up my mind he was dead and, realizing the whole was hopeless, I simply rang up Philipson in accordance with medical etiquette.'

'I see,' Mr Campion spoke gravely. 'What do you want me to do?'

Fielding hesitated. 'If you could find out what actually happened you'd save my reason, anyway,' he said so simply that the words were robbed of any hint of melodrama. 'Nothing can save my career – at least for a few years, I'm afraid. But I tell you, Campion, I must know if I'm losing my grip or if my mind's going. I must know how I came to make such an incredible mistake.'

Mr Campion glanced at the dignified youngster and noted that he betrayed no hint of the nervous strain he was undergoing. He felt his sympathy aroused and, at the same time, his curiosity. Before he could speak, however, Fielding went on.

'There are other complications too,' he said awkwardly. 'I'm engaged to old Rosemary's grandchild, you know, and when I tell you she's his principal heir you'll see how infernally awkward it all is.'

Mr Campion whistled. 'I say, that's very unfortunate.'

'It is,' said Fielding grimly. 'And it's not all. I'm afraid she broke off her engagement with Arthur March on my account and he had the impudence to phone her about this business almost as soon as it happened. I saw him this evening and frankly I don't understand the fellow. My mistake is an appalling one, I know. Old Rosemary's perfectly entitled to sue me. But March has taken the business as a personal insult. He blew me up as if I was a schoolboy, and, after all, he's only the grandson of a friend of the family. There's no blood tie at all. I couldn't say much to him; I'm so hopelessly in the wrong.'

Mr Campion considered. 'I noticed the old man when he came in this afternoon,' he said. 'He was looking remarkably well.'

Fielding smiled wryly. 'If you'd gone close to him you'd have been amazed,' he said. 'I was when I got him into the cab. It's vanity, I suppose, but the amount of time he must spend while his man gets him ready for the day must be considerable. It's gone on for so many years, I suppose, that the little additions and adjustments have mounted up, but what began presumably as a toupet is now damned nearly a wig, I can tell you. I don't think you'd have seen any ill effects of a drug, even if there were any. Still, I've talked too much. Will you have a shot at it?'

Mr Campion would not commit himself. 'I'll have a look round,' he said. 'I can't promise anything. It sounds like conjury to me.'

All the same, the following morning found him at the Junior Greys much earlier than usual. He sought out Walters and cornered him in the deserted smoking-room. The steward was in expansive mood.

'A dreadful thing, sir,' he agreed. 'Quite a scandal in its way. One gets to trust doctors, if I may say so. Still, I'd rather a dozen scandals than lose Sir Charles. Yes, he's here already, right on his usual time and in one of his good moods.'

Mr Campion smiled. 'His bad moods were pretty sensational, weren't they?'

'Well, he's old, sir.' Walters spoke indulgently. 'There are days when he snaps everybody's head off and sits sulking over his paper without speaking to a soul, but I don't take any notice because I know that to-morrow he'll be quite different, quite his old charming self with a nod and a smile to everyone. I always know which mood it's to be. As soon as he comes in he calls for a whisky. If it's a good day it's whisky and water and if he's upset it's whisky and soda, so I have plenty of warning, you see.'

Mr Campion thanked him and wandered away. He had suddenly become very grave and the expression in his eyes behind his horn-rimmed spectacles was one of alarm.

He went down to the telephone and called Oates. Less than twenty minutes later he and the Superintendent were in a taxi speeding towards Fleet Street. Stanislaus Oates was his customary sombre self. The somewhat elephantine gaiety which he had displayed at the chop-house was gone as if it had never been. This morning he was a trifle irritable.

'I hope this isn't a wild-goose chase, Campion,' he protested as the cab lurched down the Embankment. 'I'm not an idle man, you know, and I've got no business careering off on a purely private jaunt like this.'

Campion turned to him and the elder man was surprised by the gravity of his expression.

'Somehow, I don't think even you could keep this business private if you wanted to,' said Mr Campion. 'Here we are. Wait for me.'

The cab had pulled up outside a dingy building in a narrow court and the Superintendent, peering out after his departing guide, saw him disappear into the offices of the *Curtain*, a well-known stage weekly, famous for its theatrical cards and intimate gossip.

He was gone for some little time, but seemed pleased with himself when he reappeared. He gave an address in Streatham to the man and clambered back beside his friend.

'I've got it,' he said briefly. 'We shan't be too late to interfere, although of course the main mischief is done. Why? That's what I don't understand. It couldn't have been merely to discredit Fielding; that was taking far too long a chance.'

'I wish you'd explain and not talk like the wrong end of a telephone,' said Oates testily. 'What have you got from the benighted hole we've just left?'

Campion looked at him as though he had only just remembered his existence.

'The address, of course,' he said briefly.

The cab drew up at last in a wide suburban street where each pair of houses was exactly like the next – red brick, white stucco and solid chocolate paint.

Mr Campion led the way up a short tiled path to a neat front door and Oates, who had taken one look at the windows with their drawn blinds, followed him hastily, his irritation vanishing.

A little woman in a dark overall, her grey hair scraped into a tight knot at the back of her head, opened the door to them. Her face was mottled and her eyes red.

'Mr Nowell?' she echoed in response to Campion's question, and then, fishing hastily for her handkerchief, she began to cry.

Mr Campion was very gentle with her.

'I'm sorry,' he said. 'I shouldn't have asked for him like that. He's dead, isn't he?'

She looked up at him sharply. 'Oh, you're from the police, are you?' she said unexpectedly. 'The doctor told me there'd have to be an inquest, as the death was so sudden. It's been such a shock. He lodged here so long.'

She made way for them and they crowded into the little hall. The superintendent realized they were entering by false pretences, but there seemed to be no point in going into explanations just then.

'When did you find him?' Campion enquired cautiously.

'Not until this morning when I took up his tea.' The old woman was anxious to talk. 'He must have died last night, so the doctor says. He put me through it very carefully. "Well, he was alive at ten o'clock," I said, "because I spoke to him." I always go to bed at a quarter to ten and if Mr Nowell was later he didn't like me to sit up for him. He had his own key and there was always someone to help him up.'

She paused for breath and Campion nodded encouragingly.

'Well,' she went on, 'last night I had just turned out my bedroom light when I heard a motor stop and then the door went. "Is that you, Mr Nowell?" I called. "Yes, Mrs Bell," he said. "Good night." A little while afterwards I heard the car drive away.'

Oates interrupted her. 'Did the chauffeur come in with him?'

Mrs Bell turned to him. 'I don't know if it was the chauffeur, sir, but somebody did. He was nearly eighty, you know, and it was nothing for the gentleman who brought him home to help him up to his room.'

'Can we see him, please?' said Mr Campion softly.

Mrs Bell began to weep again, but afterwards, when they stood bareheaded in the big front bedroom and looked down at the gaunt still figure on the bed, she began to speak quietly and with pride.

'You're not seeing him as he was at all,' she said. 'He was wonderfully handsome with his white hair, his cane and his buttonhole. He used to take a great pride in his appearance. Spend hours and hours and pounds and pounds over it, he would. There was something he used to do with his cheeks to make them stand out more; I don't know what it was.'

Campion bent towards her and murmured something. She shook her head dubiously.

'A photograph, sir?' she repeated. 'No, that's a thing I don't think I 'ave got. He was extraordinarily touchy about having his photograph took, which was funny when he thought so much of himself, if I can say such a thing without meaning to be unkind. Wait a minute, though. I do believe I've got a little snapshot I took of him in the garden one day when he didn't know. I'll go and get it.'

As soon as they were alone Campion bent over the man on the bed and raised an eyelid very gently.

'Yes, I think so,' he said softly. 'Fielding couldn't be blamed for not noticing that. It would look like a perfectly normal death to him, thinking he knew the fellow's age. If we can get your people on to this at once and get 'em to test for morphia sulphate I fancy they'll get results if they hurry.'

The Superintendent's question was cut short by the return of Mrs Bell with a faded snapshot and they adjourned to a little light room at the back of the house.

'There he is,' she said proudly. 'I was lucky to find him. That was taken last summer. He wasn't going up to town so often then.'

'What did he do in London?' inquired Mr Campion, holding the photograph down, to the annoyance of the superintendent.

Mrs Bell looked uncomfortable. 'I hardly know,' she said. 'He used to tell me he spent his time in his nephew's office keeping an eye on things, but I think myself he was in a sort of high-class library and was one of those people who sit about making the place look respectable. "Dressing the house," we used to call it in my stage days.'

Oates smiled. 'That's a funny idea,' he said. 'I've never heard of it being done in a library.'

'Well, a very expensive tailor's, then,' she persisted. 'I know I thought I saw him sitting in a window in a est End street once. He wasn't doing anything; only sitting there and looking very nice. I asked him about it, of course, but he got very angry and made me promise never to speak of it again.'

The front-door bell interrupted her and she hurried out with a word of excuse.

Oates turned to Campion. 'I'm in a fog,' he said. 'You'll have to explain.'

The younger man gave him the snapshot and he stared at the little photograph of a tall, thin, distinguished figure walking down the gravelled path of the tiny garden.

'Old Rosemary!' ejaculated the Superintendent and raised a bewildered face to his friend's. 'Good Lord, Campion, who was that chap in the next room?'

'John Nowell, Sir Charles Rosemary's understudy at the Thespian Theatre thirty years ago – and ever since, apparently.'

Mr Campion spoke calmly.

'I admit the idea didn't seem credible when I first thought of it,' he went on, 'but afterwards, when I looked into it, it became obvious. Nowell got his job nearly sixty years ago because he resembled Rosemary; that was when he was twenty. Rosemary was nearly ten years older, but they were the same type and very much alike in feature. Since then Nowell has spent his life in imitating the greater actor. He copied his walk and his mannerisms, and as the two men grew older the simulation became easier. Rosemary resorted to artificial aids to keep young-looking, and Nowell, to the same aids to look like Rosemary.'

'Yes, yes, I get that,' said the Superintendent testily. 'But in the name of heaven, why?'

Mr Campion shrugged his shoulders.

'Vanity takes a lot of explaining,' he said. 'But Rosemary was a rich man and I think it was worth his while to employ a fellow, already a pensioner of his perhaps, to sit in the Greys and keep the legend of his perennial health alive. If ever Rosemary was prevented from going to the club Nowell took his place. When you think of it, Rosemary's record at the Greys, all day and every day for twenty years, is much more hard to swallow than this explanation of it.'

Oates continued to stare at the photograph.

'I grant the looks,' he said suddenly, 'now that I've seen the chap in the next room, but what happened if he had to talk?'

'He didn't,' said Campion. 'At least, hardly at all. For the last few years Rosemary's been having moods. On his good days he was his old self. On his bad days he was very nearly speechless with sulkiness. It was these moods that put me on to Nowell, as a matter of fact. Walters told me this morning that on his good days Rosemary drank whisky and water and on his bad ones whisky and soda. I have met men who'd drink whisky and soup at a pinch, but never one who hadn't a definite preference in the water or soda controversy when he was in a position to choose. It occurred to me, therefore, that there must be two men, and an understudy naturally came into my mind because the imitation had to be so perfect. So I called at the *Curtain* offices and was lucky to catch Bellew, who does the old-timers' gossip. I asked him if Rosemary ever had a regular understudy and he coughed up the name and address immediately.'

'Neat,' admitted the Superintendent slowly. 'Very neat. But what are we doing here and where's the crime?'

'Well, it's murder, you know,' said Mr Campion diffidently. 'Yesterday morning someone gave that poor chap in there a shot of something in his whisky and soda under the impression that he was giving it to Rosemary. Nowell dropped into a coma at the club and young Fielding the surgeon, seeing that he was pretty far gone, took him home. In the cab he died. Morphia sulphate produces very much the same symptoms as the sudden cardiac collapse of the aged, and Fielding, thinking it was a clear case, left the body with Rosemary's man at the Dover Street flat,

phoned Sir Edgar Philipson and went away like a polite
little medico. When Philipson got there, of course, he saw
Rosemary himself, who was perfectly fit. I imagine Nowell's
body remained at Dover Street all day and in the evening,
when Mrs Bell was thought likely to be in bed, the valet,
probably aided by Rosemary's chauffeur, brought it down
here. They took it up to his room, as they'd often done
before, and went away.'

'But the voice?' protested the Superintendent. 'He
spoke to the landlady; she said so.'

Campion glanced at him. 'I think,' he said slowly, 'old
Rosemary must have come down here, too, just in case.
After copying him so long, Nowell's voice was a replica of
Rosemary's, you see.'

'At ninety?' exclaimed the Superintendent. 'A nerve
like that at ninety?'

'I don't know,' said Mr Campion. 'It takes a bit of
nerve to get to ninety, I should say.'

Oates glanced towards the door. 'She's a long time,' he
said. 'I wonder if that was the coroner's officer . . .'

He went out on to the narrow landing with Campion
behind him and appeared just as Mrs Bell opened the door
of the front bedroom and showed a white-faced man out.

'I can't tell you any more, sir,' she was saying stiffly.
'Perhaps you'll ask the police gentlemen here?'

She got no further. With an inarticulate cry the stranger
swung round and the light from the landing window fell
upon his face. It was Arthur March. He stood staring at
Campion, his eyes narrowed and the knotted veins standing
out on his temples.

'You – you interfering swine!' he said suddenly and
sprang.

Campion only just met the attack in time. As the man's
fingers closed round his throat he jerked his knee upward
and caught his opponent in the wind. March collapsed
against the flimsy balustrade, which gave beneath the
sudden weight and sent him sprawling on to the stairs
below, Campion after him.

A vigorous pounding on the hall door announcing the arrival of the coroner's officer added to the general confusion, and the superintendent, with an energy surprising in one of his somewhat dyspeptic appearance, pounced down upon the two scuffling on the stairs.

It was nearly three hours later when Mr Campion sat in the Superintendent's office at Scotland Yard and expostulated mildly.

'It's all very well to arrest him on the assault charge,' he was saying, 'but you can't hold him. You cannot prove the attempted murder of Rosemary or the actual murder of Nowell.'

Stanislaus Oates sat at his desk, his hands crossed on his waistcoat. He was very pleased.

'Think not?' he enquired.

'Well,' said Mr Campion judicially, 'I hate to dampen your enthusiasm, but what have you got? Walters can swear that March met him in the lounge yesterday morning and persuaded him to let him take the old man's refresher over to him, as he wanted an excuse to have a word with the old boy, who was in a bad humour. There's opportunity there, I know, but that's not much in court. Then you can show that March spotted his error and, by much the same process of reasoning as mine, arrived at Nowell's. And you can prove that he attacked me. But that's your whole case. He'll go scot-free. After all, why should March want to kill Rosemary? Because the old boy's granddaughter wouldn't marry him?'

'That's not so absurd as you think, my boy,' Oates was avuncular. 'As a matter of fact, if Denise Warren had married Arthur March, Rosemary would never have been attacked.'

Mr Campion stared at him and the superintendent continued contentedly:

'Do you remember a meal we had together at Benjamin's chop-house to celebrate my promotion?'

'Perfectly. You were very tight and made an exhibition of us.'

'Not at all.' Oates was scandalized. 'I was observant and informative. I observed Miss Warren break off her engagement with the grandson of Rosemary's old friend, Sir Joshua March, and I tried to inform you of certain facts and you wouldn't listen to me. Do you remember me telling you that you amateurs don't collect enough data? Do you remember me telling you about company law?'

'It comes back to me,' admitted Mr Campion.

The Superintendent was mollified.

'Did you know it's a common practice among small companies to raise money on large life insurances taken out on behalf of a member of the firm for the express purpose of such money-raising?'

'Yes, I had heard of it. But it's usually a partner who insures his life, isn't it?'

'Not always. That's the point.' Oates was beaming. 'If the partners are none of them particularly good risks they often insure a junior member of the firm, or sometimes an outside person altogether who happens to be "a good risk", as they call it. Now look here, Campion . . .' Oates leant across the desk. 'When Allan March and Son – the first Sir Joshua was the son in those days – were in low water sixty-odd years ago they wanted to take out a sixty-thousand-pound policy in order to borrow upon it. Allan March was an old man and Joshua was a heart subject. They needed someone who was a good risk, you see, because the sum was so large that it was necessary to get the premium as low as possible. Rosemary and Joshua were friends and in those days Rosemary was something of a marvel. His constitution was wonderful, his habits were temperate, and also he had a strong publicity value.'

He paused and Campion nodded.

'Go on. I'm following.'

'Well, March and Son approached the Mutual Ordered Life Endowment, which was a young firm then, one of the first of the flashy, advertising insurance companies, and they agreed to take the risk at an extremely low premium because of the publicity and because, of course, the fellow

was a pretty good life. Rosemary agreed to stand for his
part in the business; that is, he agreed to have himself
insured for friendship's sake and because the Marches were
in a bad way. But as a sort of gesture he made a stipulation.
"If I live to ninety," he said, "the policy reverts to me."
It was a joke at the time, because the heavier Victorians
didn't usually reach anywhere near that age, and, anyway,
it was the immediate loan which interested everyone.
However, they agreed to it and it was all duly signed and
sealed.'

'Had March and Son kept up the insurance?'

'Oh yes.' The superintendent was watching Campion's
face as he spoke. 'I don't suppose it's been convenient for
them to repay the sum they'd borrowed on that policy, or
that, since the premium was so low, they could have
bought a loan more cheaply. But you see the situation now.
I'd have told you all this back in the summer if you'd
listened. It's a clear case, isn't it?'

Mr Campion blinked. 'If old Rosemary died before his
ninetieth birthday, then,' he said at last, 'the residue of
the sixty thousand went to March and Son; but if he lives
until after to-morrow it will pass into his own estate and go
to Denise Warren.'

'To-morrow's the ninetieth birthday, is it?' said Oates.
'March was cutting it pretty fine. I suppose he hoped the
girl would come back to him and he'd get the cash through
her. Well, my lad, what have you got to say now?'

'Nothing,' said Mr Campion affably. 'Nothing, except
that it wasn't company law, was it? It sounds more like
insurance to me.'

Oates shrugged his shoulders. 'You may be right,' he
said airily. 'I'm not a dictionary and I didn't go to a night
school. Still,' he added with a chuckle, 'we like to feel we
do a little, you know, we professionals. You amateurs have
your uses now and again, but when it comes to the ground-
work we've got you licked every time.'

Mr Campion grinned at him.

'I really think you believe that, you old sinner,' he said.

VI

The White Elephant

MR CAMPION, piloting his companion through the crowded courtyard at Burlington House, became aware of the old lady in the Daimler, partly because her chauffeur almost ran over him and partly because she gave him a stare of such vigorous and personal disapproval that he felt she must either know him very well indeed or have mistaken him for someone else entirely.

Juliet Fysher-Sprigge, who was leaning on his arm with all the weariness of a two-hour trek round the Academy's Summer Exhibition, enlightened him.

'We were *not* amused, were we?' she said. 'Old-fashioned people have minds that are just too prurient, my dear. After all, I have known you for years, haven't I, and I'm not even married to Philip. Besides, the Academy is so respectable. It isn't as though she'd seen me sneaking out of the National Gallery.'

Mr Campion handed her into a taxicab.

'Who was she?' he enquired, hoisting his lank form in after her.

Juliet laughed. Her laughter was one of her most charming attributes, for it wiped the sophistication from her débutante's face and left her the schoolgirl he had known three years before.

'My dear, didn't you recognize her? That would have been the last straw for the poor darling! That's Florence, Dowager Countess of Marle. Philip's Auntie Flo.'

Mr Campion's pale blue eyes grew momentarily more intelligent behind his horn-rimmed spectacles.

'Ah, hence the disgust,' he said. 'You'll have to explain me away. The police are always doing it.'

Juliet turned to him with the wide-eyed ingenuousness of one who perceives a long-awaited opening.

'You still dabble in police and detection and things, then?' she said breathlessly and not very tactfully, since his reputation as a criminologist was considerable. 'Do tell me, what is the low-down on these terribly exciting burglaries? Are the police really beaten or are they being bribed? No one talks of anything else these days. I just had to see you and find out.'

Her companion leant back in the leathery depths of the cab and sighed regretfully.

'When you phoned me and demanded to be taken to this execrable exhibition I was vain enough to think it was my companionship you were after,' he said. 'Now it turns out to be merely a vulgar pursuit of the material for gossip. Well, my girl, you're going to be disappointed. The clever gentleman doesn't know a thing and, what's more, he doesn't care. Have you lost anything yourself?'

'Me?' Juliet's gratification at the implied compliment all but outweighed her disappointment. 'Of course I haven't. It's only the really worth-while collections that have gone. That's why it's so interesting. The De Breuil diamonds went first. Then the Denver woman lost her emeralds and the glorious Napoleon necklace. Josephine Pharaoh had her house burgled and just lost her tiara, which was the one really good thing she had, and now poor old Mrs Dacre has had her diamonds and rubies pinched, including the famous dog collar. Forty-two diamonds, my dear! – each one quite as big as a pea. They say it's a cat burglar and the police know him quite well, but they can't find him – at least, that's one story. The other one is that it's all being done for the insurance and the police are in it. What do you think?'

Mr Campion glanced at her affectionately and noted that the gold hair under her small black hat curled as naturally as ever.

'Both stories are equally good,' he announced placidly. 'Come and have some tea, or has Philip's Auntie Flo got spies everywhere?'

Miss Fysher-Sprigge blushed. 'I don't care if she has,' she said. 'I've quarrelled with Philip, anyway.'

It took Mr Campion several minutes – until they were seated at a table on the edge of the Hotel Monde's smaller dance-floor, in fact – before he fully digested this piece of information. Juliet was leaning back in her chair, her eyes roving over the gathering in a frank search for old acquaintances, when he spoke again.

'Seriously?' he enquired.

Juliet met his eyes and again he saw her sophistication vanish.

'I hope not,' she said soberly. 'I've been rather an ass. Can I tell you about it?'

Mr Campion smiled ruefully. It was a sign of the end of the thirties, he supposed, when one submitted cheerfully to the indignity of taking a young woman out only to hear about her hopes and fears concerning a younger man. Juliet went on blissfully, lowering her voice so that the heart-searchings of the balalaika orchestra across the floor concealed it from adjoining tables.

'Philip is a dear, but he has to be so filthily careful about the stupidest things,' she said, accepting a rhumbaba. 'The F.O. casts a sort of white light over people, have you noticed? His relations are like it, too, only worse. You can't talk of anything without getting warned off. The aunt we saw to-day bit my head off the other evening for merely mentioning these cat burglaries, which, after all, are terribly exciting. "My child," she said, "we can't afford to know about such things," and went on talking about her old White Elephant until I nearly wept.'

'White Elephant?' Mr Campion looked blank. 'The charity?'

Juliet nodded. '"Send your white elephant to Florence, Countess of Marle, and she will find it a home where it will be the pet of the family,"' she quoted. 'It's quite an important affair, patronized by royalty and blessed by every archbishop in the world. I pointed out it was only a glorified jumble sale and she nearly had a fit. She works

herself to death for it. I go and help pack up parcels sometimes – or I did before this row with Philip. I've been rather
silly. I've done something infuriating. Philip's livid with me
now and I don't know what's going to happen when he
finds out everything. I must tell somebody. Can I tell you?'

A faint smile passed over Mr Campion's thin face.

'You're quite a nice girl,' he said, 'but you won't stay
twenty-one for ever. Stop treating me as though I was a
maiden uncle.'

'You must be thirty-six at least,' said Miss Fysher-Sprigge
brutally, 'and I'm rather glad, because presumably you're
sensible. Look here, if a man has a criminal record it
doesn't mean he's always going to be stealing things, does
it? Not if he promises to go straight?'

Her companion frowned. 'I don't quite follow,' he said.
'Age is stopping the brain from functioning. I thought we
were talking about Philip Graysby, Auntie Flo's nephew?'

'So we are,' said Juliet. 'He hasn't got the record, of
course, but Henry Swan has. Henry Swan is – or, rather,
was – Philip's man. He'd been with Philip for eighteen
months and been perfectly good, and then this came out
about him. Philip said he was awfully sorry, but he'd have
to go. Philip couldn't help it, I suppose – I do see that now
– but at the time I was furious. It seemed so unfair, and we
had a quarrel. I said some beastly things and so did he,
but he wouldn't give in and Swan went.'

She paused and eyed her companion dubiously. Mr
Campion shrugged his shoulders.

'It doesn't seem very serious,' he said.

Juliet accepted the cigarette he offered her and seemed
engrossed in the tip of it.

'No,' she agreed. 'That part isn't. But you see, I'm a
very impulsive person and I was stupidly cross at the time
and so when I had a wonderful idea for getting my own
back I acted on it. I got Swan a job with the most respectable person I knew and, in order to do it, I gave him a
reference. To make it a good reference I didn't say anything about the record. How's that?'

'Not so good,' he admitted. 'Who's the most respectable person harbouring this human bomb?'

Juliet avoided his eyes. 'Philip's Auntie Flo,' she said. 'She's the stiffest, thorniest, most conventional of them all. Philip doesn't go there often, so he hasn't seen Swan yet, but when he does and makes enquiries and hears about me – well, it's going to be awkward. D'you think he'll ever forgive me? He stands to get a fortune from Auntie Flo if he doesn't annoy her. It was a silly thing of me to do, wasn't it?'

'Not bright,' agreed Mr Campion. 'Are you in love with Philip?'

'Horribly,' said Juliet Fysher-Sprigge and looked away across the dance-floor.

Mr Campion had spent some time expounding a wise course of action, in which a clean breast to all concerned figured largely, when he became aware that he was not being heard. Juliet was still staring across the room, her eyes puzzled.

'I say,' she said unexpectedly, 'this place is wildly expensive, isn't it?'

'I hope not,' said Mr Campion mildly.

Juliet did not smile. Her cheeks were faintly flushed and her eyes questioning.

'Don't be a fool. You know what I mean. This is probably the most expensive place in London, isn't it? How queer! It looks as though Auntie Flo really has got her spies everywhere. That's her manicurist over there, having tea alone.'

He glanced casually across the room.

'The woman sitting directly under the orchestra?' he enquired. 'The one who looks like a little bull in a navy hat? She's an interesting type, isn't she? Not very nice.'

Juliet's eyes were still thoughtful.

'That's her. Miss Matisse. A visiting manicurist,' she said. 'She goes to dozens of people I know. I believe she's very good. How funny for her to come to tea alone, here of all places . . .'

Mr Campion's casual interest in the small square figure

who managed somehow to look flamboyant in spite of her
sober clothes showed signs of waning.

'She may be waiting for someone,' he suggested.

'But she's ordered her tea and started it.'

'Oh well, perhaps she just felt like eating.'

'Rubbish!' said Juliet. 'You pay ten and sixpence just to
sit in this room because you can dance if you want to.'

Her host laughed. 'Auntie Flo has a pretty turn of speed
if she tracked us down here and then whipped round and
set her manicuring bloodhound on us, all in half an hour,'
he said.

Juliet ignored him. Her attention had wandered once
again.

'I say,' she murmured, 'can you see through that mirror
over there? See that man eating alone? I thought at first he
was watching Miss Matisse, but I believe it's you he's
most interested in.'

Her companion turned his head and his eyes widened.

'Apologies,' he said. 'I under-estimated you. That's
Detective-Sergeant Blower, one of the best men in the
public-school and night-club tradition. I wonder whom
he's tailing. Don't watch him – it's unkind.'

Juliet laughed. 'You're a most exciting person to have
tea with,' she said. 'I do believe . . .'

The remainder of her remark was lost as, in common
with all but one visitor in the room she was silenced by what
was, for the Hotel Monde, a rather extraordinary incident.

The balalaika orchestra had ceased to play for a moment
or so and the dance floor was practically deserted when,
as though taking advantage of the lull, the woman in the
navy hat rose from her chair and shouted down the whole
length of the long room, in an effort, apparently, to attract
the attention of a second woman who had just entered.

'Mrs Gregory!' Her voice was powerful and well
articulated. 'Mrs Gregory! Mrs Gregory!'

The newcomer halted as all eyes were turned upon her,
and her escort expostulated angrily to the excited *maître
d'hôtel* who hurried forward.

Miss Matisse sat down, and in the silence Mr Campion heard her explaining in a curiously flat voice to the waiter who came up to her:

'I am sorry. I thought I recognized a friend. I was mistaken. Bring me my bill, please.'

Juliet stared across the table, her young face shocked.

'What a very extraordinary thing to do,' she said.

Mr Campion did not reply. From this place of vantage he could see in the mirror that Detective-Sergeant Blower had also called for his bill and was preparing to leave.

Some little time later, when Mr Campion deposited Juliet on her Mount Street doorstep, she was in a more cheerful mood.

'Then you think if I go to Philip and tell him the worst and say that I'm sorry he'll forgive me?' she said as they parted.

'If he's human he'll forgive you anything,' Mr Campion assured her gallantly.

Juliet sighed. 'Age does improve the manners,' she said unnecessarily. 'I'll forgive you for disappointing me about the burglaries. I really had hoped to get all the dirt. Good-bye.'

'Damn the burglaries!' said Mr Campion and took a taxi home.

Three days later he said the same thing again, but for a different reason. This reason arrived by post. It came in a fragrant green box designed to contain a large flask of familiar perfume and it lay upon his breakfast table winking at him with evil amusement. It was Mrs Dacre's ruby-and-diamond dog collar and it was not alone. In a nest of cotton wool beneath it were five diamond rings of considerable value, a pair of exquisite ruby ear-clips, and a small hooped bracelet set with large alternate stones.

Mr Campion, who was familiar with the 'stolen' list which the police send round to their local stations and circularize to the jewellers and pawnbrokers of the kingdom, had no difficulty in recognizing the collection as the haul of the last cat burglary.

The sender of so dubious a gift might have been harder to identify had it not been for the familiarity of the perfume and the presence of a small card on which was printed, in shaky, ill-disguised characters, a simple request and a specious promise:

Get these back where they belong and I'll love you for ever, darling.

Mr Campion had a considerable respect for the Law, but he spent some time that morning in acquiring a box of similar design but different and more powerful perfume, and it was not until the jewellery was freshly housed and the card burned that he carried his responsibility to Scotland Yard and laid it with a sigh of relief on the desk of Chief Detective-Inspector Stanislaus Oates, his friend and partner in many adventures.

The original wrappings he decided to retain. Its ill-written address might have been scrawled by anyone, and the fact that it was grossly overfranked showed that it had been dropped into a public box and not passed over a post-office counter.

He let the chief, who was a tall, disconsolate personage with a grey face and dyspepsia, recover from his first transports of mingled relief and suspicion before regretting his inability to help him further. Oates regarded him.

'It's my duty to warn you that you're under suspicion,' he said with the portentous solemnity which passed with him for wit.

Campion laughed. 'My cat-burglary days are over,' he said. 'Or am I the fence?'

'That's more like it.' The chief passed his cigarette case. 'I can't tell you how glad I am to see this lot. But it doesn't help us very much unless we know where it came from. These "cat" jobs are done by The Sparrow. We knew that as soon as we saw the first one. You remember him, Campion? — a sleek, handsome chap with an insufferable manner. These jobs have his trade-marks all over them. Pane cut out with a diamond and the glass removed with a sucker — no finger-prints, no noise, no mistakes.' He paused and caressed his ear sadly. 'It's getting on my nerves,' he said. 'The Commissioner is sarcastic and the papers are just libellous. It's hard on us. We know who and where the fellow is, but we can't get him. We've held him as long as we dared, three separate times this summer, but we haven't got a thing we can fix on him. I've been trusting the stuff would turn up somewhere so that we could work back on him from that angle, but, frankly, this is the first scrap of it I've seen. Where's all the early swag? This was only pinched five days ago.'

Mr Campion remained unhelpful. 'I got it this morning,' he said. 'It just came out of the air. Ask the postman.'

'Oh, I know . . .' The chief waved the suggestion aside. 'You'll help us just as much as you can, which means as much as you care to. Some society bit is mixed up in this somewhere, I'm sure of it. Look here, I'll tell you what I'll do. I'll put my cards on the table. This isn't official; this is the truth. Edward Borringer, alias The Sparrow, is living with his wife in digs in Kilburn. They're very respectable at the moment, just a quiet hard-working couple. He takes classes in the local gym and she does visiting manicure work.'

'Under the name of Matisse?'

'Exactly!' The Inspector was jubilant. 'Now you've given yourself away, my lad. What do you know about Margot Matisse?'

'Not much,' his visitor confessed affably. 'She was pointed out to me as a manicurist at a *thé dansant* at the Hotel Monde on Tuesday. Looking round, I saw Blower on her trail, so naturally when you mentioned manicurists I put two and two together.'

'Who pointed her out to you?'

'A lady who had seen her at work in a relation's house.'

'All right.' The policeman became depressed again. 'Well, there you are. It's quite obvious how they're working it. She goes round to the big houses and spots the stuff and the lie of the land, and then he calls one night and does the job. It's the old game worked very neatly. Too neatly, if you ask me. What we can't fathom is how they're disposing of the stuff. They certainly haven't got it about them, and their acquaintance just now is so respectable, not to say aristocratic, that we can barely approach it. Besides, to make this big stuff worth the risk they must be using an expert. Most of these stones are so well known that they must go to a first-class fellow to be recut.'

Mr Campion hesitated. 'I seem to remember that Edward Borringer was once associated with our old friend Bertrand Meyer and his *ménage*,' he ventured. 'Are they still functioning?'

'Not in England.' The chief was emphatic. 'And if these two are getting their stuff out of the country I'll eat my hat. The customs are co-operating with us. We thought a maid in one of the houses which the Matisse woman visits might be in it and so, if you've heard a squawk from your society pals about severity at the ports, that's our work. I don't mind telling you it's all very difficult. You can see for yourself. These are the Matisse clients.'

Mr Campion scanned the typewritten page and his sympathy for his friend deepened.

'Oh yes, Caesar's wives,' he agreed. 'Every one of 'em. Servants been in the families for years, I suppose?'

'Unto the third and fourth generations,' said the chief bitterly.

His visitor considered the situation.

'I suppose they've got alibis fixed up for the nights of the crimes?' he enquired.

'Fixed up?' The chief's tone was eloquent. 'The alibis are so good that we ought to be able to arrest 'em on suspicion alone. An alibi these days doesn't mean anything except that the fellow knows his job. Borringer does, too, and so does his wife. We've had them both on the carpet for hours without getting a glimmer from them. No, it's no use, Campion; we've got to spot the middleman and then the fence, and pin it on them that way. Personally, I think the woman actually passes the stuff, but we've had Blower on her for weeks and he swears she doesn't speak to a soul

except these superior clients of hers. Also, of course, neither
of them post anything. We thought we'd got something once
and got the Postal authorities to help us, but all we got for
our trouble was a p.c. to a viscountess about an appointment
for chiropody.'

Mr Campion was silent for some time.

'It was funny, her shouting out like that in the Hotel
Monde,' he said at last.

The chief grunted. 'Mrs Gregory,' he said. 'Yes, I
heard about that. A little show for Blower's benefit, if you
ask me. Thought she'd give him something to think about.
The Borringers are like that, cocky as hell.'

Once again there was thoughtful silence in the light airy
office and this time it was Stanislaus Oates who spoke first.

'Look here, Campion,' he said, 'you and I know one
another. Let this be a word of friendly warning. If you
suspect anyone you know of getting mixed up in this – for
a bit of fun, perhaps – see that she's careful. If The Sparrow
and his wife are still tied up with the Meyer lot – and they
very well may be – the Meyer crowd aren't a pretty bunch.
In fact, you know as well as I do, they're dirty and they're
dangerous.'

His visitor picked up the list again. Philip Graysby's
aunt's name headed the second column. He made up his
mind.

'I don't know anything,' he said. 'I'm speaking entirely
from guesswork and I rely on you to go into this in stock-
inged feet with your discretion wrapping you like a blanket.
But if I were you I should have a little chat with one Henry
Swan, employed by Florence, Dowager Countess of Marle.'

'Ah,' said the chief with relief, 'that's where the wind
blows, does it? I thought you'd come across.'

'I don't promise anything,' Campion protested.

'Who does?' said Stanislaus Oates and pulled a pad
towards him . . .

Mr Campion kept late hours. He was sitting up by the
open window of his flat in Bottle Street, the cul-de-sac off
Piccadilly, when the Chief Detective-Inspector called upon

him just after midnight on the evening of his visit to Scotland Yard. The policeman was unusually fidgety. He accepted a drink and sat down before mentioning the purpose of his visit, which was, in fact, to gossip.

Campion, who knew him, let him take his time.

'We pulled that chap Swan in this afternoon,' he volunteered at last. 'He's a poor weedy little beggar who did a stretch for larceny in twenty-three and seems to have gone straight since. We had quite a time with him. He wouldn't open his mouth at first. Fainted when he thought we were going to jug him. Finally, of course, out it came, and a very funny story it was. Know anything about the White Elephant Society, Campion?'

His host blinked. 'Nothing against it,' he admitted. 'Ordinary charity stunt. Very decently run, I believe. The dowager does it herself.'

'I know.' There was a note of mystification in the chief's voice. 'See this?'

From his wallet he took a small green stick-on label. It was an ornate product embellished with a design of angels in the worst artistic taste. Across the top was a printed heading:

This is a gift from the White Elephant Society (Secy, Florence, Countess of Marle) and contains – A blank space had been filled up with the legend: *Two Pairs of Fancy Woollen Gloves* in ink. The address, which was also in ink, was that of a well-known orphanage and the addressee was the matron.

'That's how they send the white elephants out,' Oates explained. 'There's a word or two inside in the countess's own handwriting. This is a specimen label. See what it means? It's as good as a diplomatic pass with that old woman's name on it.'

'Whom to?' demanded Mr Campion dubiously.

'Anyone,' declared the chief triumphantly. 'Especially the poor chap in the customs office who's tired of opening parcels. Even if he does open 'em he's not going to examine 'em. Now here's Swan's story. He admits he found the jewellery, which he passed on to a friend whose name he will not divulge. That friend must have sent it to you. It sounds like a woman to me, but I'm not interested in her at the moment.'

'Thank God for that,' murmured his host devoutly. 'Go on. Where did he find the stuff?'

'In a woollen duck inside one of these White Elephant parcels,' said the chief unexpectedly. 'We've got the duck; home-made toy with little chamois pockets under its wings. The odd thing is that Swan swears the old lady gave the parcel to him herself, told him to post it, and made such a fuss about it that he became suspicious and opened it up.'

'Do you believe that?' Mr Campion was grinning and Oates frowned.

'I do,' he said slowly. 'Curiously enough I do, in the main. In the first place, this chap honestly wants to go straight. One dose of clink has put him in terror of it for life. Secondly, if he was in on the theft why give the whole game away? Why produce the duck? What I do think is that he recognized the address. He says he can't remember anything about it except that it was somewhere abroad, but that's just what he would say if he recognized it and thought it was dangerous and was keeping quiet for fear of reprisals. Anyway, I believed him sufficiently to go down and interview the old lady.'

'Did you, By Jove!' murmured Mr Campion with respect.

Stanislaus Oates smiled wryly and ran his finger round the inside of his collar.

'Not a homely woman,' he observed. 'Ever met someone who made you feel you wanted a haircut, Campion? I was very careful, of course. Kid gloves all the way. Had to. I tell you one funny thing, though: she was rattled.'

Mr Campion sat up. He knew his friend to be one of the soberest judges of humanity in the police force, where humanity is deeply studied.

'Sure?' he demanded incredulously.

'Take my dying oath on it,' said the chief. 'Scared blue, if you ask me.'

The young man in the horn-rimmed spectacles made polite but depreciating noises. The chief shook his head.

'It's the truth. I gave her the facts – well, most of them. I didn't explain how we came to open the parcel, since that part of the business wasn't strictly orthodox. But I gave her the rest of the story just as I've given it to you, and instead of being helpful she tried to send me about my business with a flea in my ear. She insisted that she had directed each outgoing parcel during the last four weeks herself and swore that the Matisse woman could never have had access to any of them. Also, which is significant, she would not give me a definite reply about the duck. She was not sure if she'd ever seen it before. I ask you – a badly made yellow duck in a blue pullover. Anyone 'd know it again.'

Mr Campion grinned. 'What was the upshot of this embarrassing interview?' he enquired.

The chief coughed. 'When she started talking about her son in the Upper House I came away,' he said briefly. 'I thought I'd let it rest for a day or two. Meanwhile, we shall keep a wary eye on Swan and the Borringers, although if those three are working together I'll resign.'

He was silent for a moment.

'She certainly was rattled,' he repeated at last. 'I'd swear it. Under the magnificent manner of hers she was scared. She had that set look about the eyes. You can't mistake it. What d'you make of that, my lad?'

'I don't,' said Campion discreetly. 'It's absurd.'

Oates sighed. 'Of course it is,' he agreed. 'And so what?'

'Sleep on it,' his host suggested and the chief took the hint...

It was unfortunate for everyone concerned that Mr Campion should have gone into the country early the following morning on a purely personal matter concerning a horse which he was thinking of buying and should not have returned to his flat until the evening. When he did get back he found Juliet and the dark, good-looking Philip Graysby, with whom she had presumably made up her differences, waiting for him. To Mr Campion they both seemed very young and very distressed. Juliet appeared to have been crying and it was she who broke the news.

'It's Auntie Flo,' she said in a small tragic voice. 'She's bunked, Albert.'

It took Mr Campion some seconds to assimilate this interesting development, and by that time young Graysby had launched into hurried explanations.

'That's putting it very crudely,' he said. 'My aunt caught the Paris plane this morning. Certainly she travelled alone, which was unusual, but that may not mean anything. Unfortunately, she did not leave an address, and although we've got into touch with the Crillon she doesn't seem to have arrived there.'

He hesitated and his dark face became suddenly ingenuous.

'It's so ridiculously awkward, her going off like this without telling anyone just after Detective-Inspector Oates called on her last night. I don't know what the interview was about, of course – nobody does – but there's an absurd feeling in the household that it wasn't very pleasant. Anyway, the inspector was very interested to hear that she had gone away when he called round this afternoon. It was embarrassing not being able to give him any real information about her return, and precious little about her departure. You see, we shouldn't have known she'd taken the plane if the chauffeur hadn't driven her to Croydon. She simply walked out of the house this morning and ordered the car. She didn't even take a suit-case, which looks as though she meant to come back to-night, and, of course, there's every possibility that she will.'

Mr Campion perched himself on the table and his eyes were grave.

'Tell me,' he said quietly, 'had Lady Florence an appointment with her manicurist to-day?'

'Miss Matisse?' Juliet looked up. 'Why, yes, she had, as a matter of fact. I went round there quite early this morning. Swan phoned me and told me Aunt had left rather hurriedly, so I – er – I went to see him.'

She shot an appealing glance at Philip, who grimaced at her, and she hurried on.

'While I was there Miss Matisse arrived and Bennett – Aunt's maid – told her all the gossip before I could stop her. Oh my dear, you don't think . . . ?'

Instead of replying Mr Campion reached for the telephone and dialled a famous Whitehall number. Chief Detective-Inspector Oates was glad to hear his voice. He said so. He was also interested to know if Mr Campion had heard of the recent developments in The Sparrow case.

'No,' he said in reply to Mr Campion's sharp question. 'The two Borringers are behaving just as usual. Blower's had the girl under his eye all day . . . No, she hasn't communicated with anyone . . . What? . . . Wait a minute. I've got notes on Blower's telephoned report here. Here we are. "On leaving the Dowager Countess of Marle's house Miss Matisse went to the Venetian Cinema in Regent Street for the luncheon programme." Nothing happened there except that she pulled Blower's leg again.'

'Did she shout to someone?' Mr Campion's tone was urgent.

'Yes. Called to a woman named Mattie, who she said she thought was in the circle. Same silly stunt as last time. What's the matter?'

Campion checked his exasperation. He was desperately in earnest and his face as he bent over the instrument was frighteningly grave.

'Oates,' he said quietly, 'I'm going to ring you again in ten minutes and then you've got to get busy. Remember our little talk about the Meyers? This may be life or death.'

'Good . . .' began the chief and was cut off.

Mr Campion hustled his visitors out of the flat.

'We're going down to see Swan,' he said, 'and the quicker we get there the better.'

Henry Swan proved to be a small frightened man who was inclined to be more than diffident until he had had matters explained to him very thoroughly. Then he was almost pathetically anxious to help.

'The address on the duck parcel, sir?' he said, echoing Mr Campion's question nervously. 'I daren't tell the police that. It might have been more than my life was worth. But if you think her ladyship—'

'Let's have it,' cut in Graysby irritably.

'Please,' murmured Juliet.

Mr Swan came across. 'Nineteen A, Rue Robespierre, Lyons, France,' he blurted out. 'I've burned the label, but I remember the address. In fact, to tell you the truth, it was because of the address I opened the box in the first place. I never had such a fright in all my life, sir, really.'

'I see. Whom was the parcel sent to?' Mr Campion's manner was comfortingly reassuring.

Henry Swan hesitated. 'Maurice Bonnet,' he said at last, 'and I once met a man who called himself that.'

Mr Campion's eyes flickered. 'On those occasions when he wasn't calling himself Meyer, I suppose?' he remarked.

The small man turned a shade or so paler and dropped his eyes.

'I shouldn't like to say, sir,' he murmured.

'Very wise,' Campion agreed. 'But you've got nothing to worry about now. We've got the address and that's all that matters. You run along. Graysby, you and I have got to hurry. I'll just have a word with Oates on the phone and then we'll nip down to Croydon and charter a plane.'

Juliet caught his arm. 'You don't mean Philip's aunt might be in *danger?*' she said.

Mr Campion smiled down at her. 'Some people do resent interference so, my dear,' he said, 'especially when they have quite a considerable amount to lose . . .'

The Rue Robespierre is not in the most affluent quarter of Lyons and just before midnight on a warm spring evening it is not seen at its best. There silent figures loll in the dark doorways of houses which have come down in the world, and the night life has nothing to do with gaiety.

From Scotland Yard the wires had been busy and Campion and Graysby were not alone as they hurried down the centre of the wide street. A military little capitaine and four gendarmes accompanied them, but even so they were not overstaffed.

As their small company came to a stop before the crumbling façade of number nineteen A an upper window was thrown open and a shot spat down upon them. The capitaine drew his own gun and fired back, while the others put their shoulders to the door.

As they pitched into the dark musty hall a rain of fire met them from the staircase. A bullet took Mr Campion's hat from his head, and one of the gendarmes stepped back swearing, his left hand clasping a shattered right elbow.

The raiding party defended itself. For three minutes the darkness was streaked with fire, while the air became heavy with the smell of cordite.

The end came suddenly. There was a scream from the landing and a figure pitched over the balustrade on to the flags below, dragging another with it in its flight, while pattering footsteps flying up to the top storey testified to the presence of a fugitive.

Mr Campion plunged forward, the others at his heels. They found Florence, Dowager Countess of Marle, at last in a locked bedroom on the third floor. She had defended herself and had suffered for it. Her black silk was torn and dusty and her coiffure dishevelled. But her spirit was unbroken and the French police listened to her tirade with a respect all the more remarkable since they could not understand one word of it.

Graysby took his aunt back to her hotel in a police car and Mr Campion remained to assist in the cleaning up.

Bertrand Meyer himself actually succeeded in getting out on to the roof, but he was brought back finally and the little capitaine had the satisfaction of putting the handcuffs on him.

One of the gang had been killed outright when his head had met the flagstones of the hall, and the remaining member was hurried off to a prison hospital with a broken thigh.

Mr Campion looked at Meyer with interest. He was an oldish man, square and powerful, with strong sensitive hands and the hot angry eyes of a fanatic. His workroom revealed many treasures. A jeweller's bench, exquisitely fitted with all the latest appliances, contained also a drawer which revealed the dismembered fragments of the proceeds of the first three London burglaries, together with some French stones in particular request by the *Sûreté*.

Campion looked round him. 'Ah,' he said with satisfaction, 'and there's the wireless set. I wondered when some of you fellows were going to make use of the outside broadcasting programmes. How did you work it? Had someone listening to the first part of the first programme to be broadcast from a London public place each day, I suppose? It really is amazing how clearly those asides come, her voice quite fearless and yet so natural that it wasn't until some time afterwards that I realized she had been standing just below the orchestra's live microphone.'

Meyer did not answer. His face was sullen and his eyes were fixed on the stones which the Frenchmen were turning out of little chamois leather bags on to the baize surface of the bench . . .

It was some days later, back in the flat in Bottle Street, when Chief Detective-Inspector Oates sipped a whisky and soda and beamed upon his friend.

'I take off my hat to the old girl,' he said disrespectfully. 'She's got courage and a great sense of justice. She says she'll go into the witness-box if we need her and she apologized handsomely to me for taking the law into her own hands.'

'Good,' said Mr Campion. 'You've got the Borringers, of course?'

The chief grinned. 'We've got 'em as safe as a couple of ferrets in a box,' he declared. 'The man's an expert, but the woman's a genius. The story she told the old lady, for instance. That was more than brains. After she'd got her ladyship interested in her she broke down one day and told a pretty little yarn about her cruel husband in France

who had framed a divorce and got the custody of the kid.
She told a harrowing story about the little presents she
had made for it herself and had had sent back to her
pronto. It didn't take her long to get the old woman to offer
to send them as though they'd come from the White
Elephant Society. Every woman has a streak of senti-
mentality in her somewhere. So all the Borringer – alias
Matisse – girl had to do was to bring along the toys in her
manicure case from time to time and have 'em despatched
free, gratis, with a label which almost guaranteed 'em a
free pass. Very nice, eh?'

'Very,' Campion agreed. 'Almost simple.'

The chief nodded. 'She did it well,' he said; 'so well that
even after I'd given the old lady the facts she didn't trust
me. She believed so strongly in this fictitious kid that she
went roaring over to Lyons to find out the truth for herself
before she gave the girl away. Unfortunately, the Borringers had that means of wireless communication with Meyer
and so when she arrived the gang was ready for her. It's a
good thing you got there, Campion. They're a hot lot. I
wonder what they'd have done with her.'

'Neat,' muttered Mr Campion. 'That wireless stunt, I
mean.'

'It was.' Oates was still impressed. 'The use of the names
made it sound so natural. What was the code exactly? Do
you know?'

His host pulled a dictionary from a shelf at his side and
turned over the leaves until he came to a small section at
the end.

'It's childish,' he said. 'Funny how these people never
do any inventing if they can help it. Look it all up.'

The chief took the book and read the heading aloud.

'*The More Common British Christian Names and Their
Meanings.*'

He ran his eyes down the columns.

'*Gregory*,' he read. '*A watcher*. Good Lord, that was
to tell 'em Blower was on their track, I suppose. And
Mattie . . . what's Mattie?'

He paused. ' "*Diminutive of Matilda*",' he said at last. ' "*Mighty Battle Maid*". I don't get that.'

'Dangerous, indignant and female,' translated Mr Campion. 'It rather sums up Philip Graysby's Auntie Flo, don't you think?'

It was after the chief had gone and he was alone that Juliet phoned. She was jubilant and her clear voice bubbled over the wire.

'I can't thank you,' she said. 'I don't know what to say. Aunt Florence is perfectly marvellous about everything. And I say, Albert...'

'Yes?'

'Philip says we can keep Swan if we have him at the country house. We're going to be married quite soon, you know. Our reconciliation rather hurried things along ... Oh, what did you say?'

Mr Campion smiled. 'I said I'll have to send you a wedding present, then,' he lied.

There was a fraction of silence at the other end of the wire.

'Well, darling ... it would be just too terribly sweet if you really *wanted* to,' said Miss Fysher-Sprigge.

VII

The Frenchman's Gloves

MR ALBERT CAMPION was considering the hundred and fifteenth unintelligible oil painting under the muslin-shaded lights of the Excelsior Gallery's stuffiest room, and wondered if it was honest reaction or merely age which made him yearn for an occasional pair of gluey-eyed, human-faced dogs by old Mr Landseer. A pathetic sigh at his shoulder recalled him to his duty as a nursemaid. He glanced at Felicity apologetically.

'Do you like this?'

'Tremendously,' said Miss Felicity Carrington stoutly, adding, with a touch of candour induced by sheer physical exhaustion, 'if you do.'

A memory of his own youth returned to Mr Campion enlighteningly.

'My dear child,' he said, 'my *dear* child, you're not enduring this for my sake, are you?'

Felicity blushed, bringing it home to her escort that the fashion in nineteen-year-olds had changed. He felt kindly disposed towards 'Alice's girl', who had been handed over to him to amuse for the afternoon. She was certainly extraordinarily pretty. The first time he had seen her, he remembered, she had been bald, toothless and crimson in the face at a christening party, and he was gratified to see what Time could do.

'Let's get this straight,' he suggested. 'I thought you told me you wanted to go to a picture gallery to see something modern? I trust you didn't do that to put me at my ease?'

'Well,' Felicity's large grey eyes were honest, 'Mother did hint that you were frightfully clever, and it occurred to me that you might take a bit of living up to. A picture gallery seemed the only safe bet. Don't be annoyed. I only wanted to put you into a good mood.'

Mr Campion's lean face split into a smile.

'That's a mistake,' he said, piloting her towards the door. 'That's mistake number one in the art of being taken out. Never try to please the man beside you. It gives him a sense of superiority, and superiority breeds discontent. What would you really like to do? Eat ice-cream?'

The girl regarded him seriously. It appeared she was giving the question earnest thought, so that he found her final pronouncement surprising.

'What I'd like most, more than anything else in the world,' she said at last, 'is to go to the Hotel Balsamic and have some tea.'

'The Balsamic?' he echoed blankly. 'You've got the names muddled. You mean the Berkeley.'

'No, I haven't. I mean the Balsamic. I'd rather go there to tea than anywhere else on earth.'

'You're not only original, my girl; you're unique, I should think,' said her escort, obediently handing her into a cab. 'Ever been there before?'

'No, I'm afraid I haven't. I know it's not very gay.'

'Gay?' Mr Campion considered. 'No,' he said at last. 'The Balsamic is respectable, comfortable, worthy, florid, English, unutterably decent, but gay – no. I hear they've met the changing mode with a small unsprung dance-floor and a string band, but if it's food you're after, the French pastries should be excellent. Do you still want to go there?'

'Yes, please,' said Felicity, adding abruptly: 'Tell me about your mysteries. You're terribly clever at clearing them up, aren't you?'

Mr Campion leant back in a corner of the taxi and stretched his long legs.

'I'm brilliant,' he said, regarding her soberly from behind his horn-rimmed spectacles. 'Positively uncanny. I can't hide it. My best friends are always telling me. Don't run away with the suspicion that I'm vain, either. I simply happen to have X-ray eyes and all sorts of staggering personal gadgets of that sort. Nor am I proud. I'll show you my methods. For instance, I deduce from certain phenomena, obviously invisible to you but stunningly clear to me, that you, young woman, have been buttering me up all the afternoon with intent to convert my power to possible use in the near future. I deduce, further, that you have a small private mystery that you'd like cleared up, and that that mystery is connected with the venerable old Balsamic. Am I right?'

*

Felicity sat in her corner, silent and reproachful. She was at the small-cat stage, with enormous eyes, a pointed chin, and a little delicate neck rising up out of a scarlet choker.

'I'm so sorry.' Mr Campion was contrite. 'When I get

a chance to do my trick I can't resist it. Any opening goes to my head like wine. What's up? Lost something?'

Felicity's triangular mouth opened hesitantly.

'*I* haven't,' she began. 'But . . .'

'Not A Friend?' said Mr Campion firmly. 'I'm sorry, but as part of your educational system I cannot pass that. This is Rule Two. Avoid A Friend. He or she is a Mrs Harris whom no one likes. A Friend is dead. A Friend is a myth who never ought to have existed. As an alibi he's worse than being caught with the silver in a sack.'

The girl sat up.

'You think you're clever, don't you?' she said with sudden spirit. 'Do you know what I think of you? I think you're bogus. A silly, oldish fraud.'

Her companion sighed and settled down.

'That's fine,' he said. 'I knew the ice must break if only the pressure was great enough. Now that we understand one another, what's the trouble? Who has lost what?'

Felicity was mollified.

'I'm not taking anything back yet,' she said warningly, 'but I admit I did have a purpose in trying to put you in a useful frame of mind. It's Madeleine. Madeleine was at school with me, at Paddledean, and we're still great friends. She's living over here with some English god-parents down in Cornwall, but of course they haven't any authority at all. I mean, her father is the real court of appeal. So when she got engaged and the wretched Roundels became so difficult she had to write to him and . . .'

'Wait,' said Mr Campion hastily. 'Wait. My trick doesn't seem to be working. Let's do it again. Begin with Madeleine. Madeleine who?'

'Madeleine Gerard.'

'I see. She's living in Cornwall with some English god-parents. She's a Frenchwoman?'

'Well, of course!'

Mr Campion looked hurt.

'There's no "of course" about it,' he said firmly. 'That's

the worst of you amateurs. You take my astounding gifts for granted after the first performance. Well now, Madeleine Gerard, French, young, educated at Paddledean, and living with English people in Cornwall, has got herself engaged. So far, that's all right. Then we come to someone called Roundel. There can hardly be two families in Cornwall with that all-embracing name, so I take it you mean Sir Nigel Roundel and his good lady? They have, I seem to remember, about seventeen daughters and one small male lamb and heir called Henry, who must be about twenty. Madeleine, I take it, has got engaged to Henry? Unofficially, no doubt.'

Felicity laughed.

'I do take it back. You're not bad,' she said. 'You're right, even down to the part about it being unofficial. The Roundels are hopelessly old-fashioned and County in the worst sense of the word. Also they've got it in their heads that Henry is the most important thing on earth. The trouble is that both Henry and Madeleine are under age, and whereas the Roundels don't exactly say, or even think, that Madeleine isn't perfectly suitable, they want to make sure. You do see, don't you?'

'I do indeed.' Campion, who had met Sir Nigel and had a vivid memory of that sturdy old gentleman, spoke with understanding. 'So Madeleine wrote to her papa. Where does he live, by the way?'

'In Vaux.' Felicity was warming up to her subject and he was glad to note that all trace of restraining respect had vanished from her manner. 'That was a blow. You see, he's old-fashioned, too, and apparently he had some other idea for Madeleine's future. He's pretty rich, I think. Anyway, he wrote back a very stiff letter to Madeleine and everything was rather awkward. Madeleine and Henry stuck to their guns, however, and finally, after a lot of excitement and polite letters in bad English to Sir Nigel, followed by rather rude ones in worse French to Monsieur Gerard, it's been arranged that there shall be a luncheon party at Claridge's to-morrow for the parents to meet and discuss things. M. Gerard is in London now, and the Roundels are coming up from Cornwall to-night.'

'Madeleine,' she continued, 'has been staying with us since the beginning of the week and the tension is pretty high. It's a dreadful set-out. Apparently Madeleine's father hadn't been to England for fifteen years and feels he's making an enormous concession in coming as far as London to see the Roundels, and the Roundels feel it's monstrous that they should have to come to London to see M. Gerard, whom they insist on regarding as illiterate and "in trade". The whole affair has been nearly ship-wrecked half a dozen times, but Madeleine and Henry are convinced that if only the meeting comes off it'll be perfectly all right. Everything hinges on the lunch, doesn't it?'

'Food sounds to me to be the only hope,' said Mr Campion dryly. 'Let us trust not a forlorn one. What has Madeleine lost? The meal ticket?'

Felicity did not reply immediately. The taxi had pulled up at the discreet entrance of the Balsamic Hotel, and not until that vast foyer had swallowed them up did she return to the subject.

*

As they settled themselves at one of the tea-tables in the gloomy Palm Garden and glanced round at the three other adventurous couples who had braved that dignified wilderness of napery, she spoke again.

'It doesn't look a – a fishy place, does it?' she said candidly.

'Fishy?' Mr Campion was startled. 'My dear child, nothing more questionable than a sly Episcopal pun in Greek can ever have enlivened these revolting tomato-and-ormolu walls. Look here, let's get back to Madeleine. She's beginning to worry me. What can the poor girl have lost here, of all unlikely places?'

Felicity raised her large eyes to his. 'Her father, of course, silly,' she said.

Campion blinked.

'Dear me, that's almost vital, isn't it? His patience with Sir Nigel as a correspondent gave out, I suppose. How very unfortunate for young love, though. Hasn't there been any word of explanation? Has Papa simply not turned up here?'

'Oh no, it's nothing ordinary like that.' There was an engaging directness in the young eyes. 'You see, he's lost *in* the hotel. He's staying here – at least, that's what the management says. But he didn't come to call for Madeleine as he promised on Tuesday night. She waited for him, feeling rather scared because she knew he was angry with her, and on Wednesday she called up this hotel, where he had booked rooms. They admitted he was staying here, but they said he'd gone out. She left a message, but he didn't answer it, and since then she hasn't heard a word. This morning she was so nervy that she called here. The people at the office place were awfully polite but not very helpful. They simply repeated what they'd said before.'

Felicity hesitated and added with sudden *naïveté*. 'Madeleine's very young and rather shy, so I don't suppose they thought she was very important. She asked Mother's advice, and Mother, she said, thought it was safest to leave him alone and just trust that he'll turn up at Claridge's. It's terribly unkind of him, though, isn't it? I mean, he must realize what the suspense is like for Madeleine.'

Her companion considered the case of the harsh French parent.

'Gerard,' he said at last. 'What sort of business had Père Gerard over here?'

'I don't know. He's very rich in that quiet French way and has something to do with precious stones, I think.'

Mr Campion bolted a small portion of buttered tea-cake and swallowed hard.

'We're not discussing Edmond Gerard by any chance, are we?' he said. '*The* Edmond Gerard?'

'Yes, that's the man. Do you know him?'

'I know of him.' Mr Campion was thoughtful. 'He's a very famous and distinguished person in an exclusive sort of way. I heard his name the other day. Oh yes, he's rumoured to have the governing interest in Bergère Frères, who are an enormous jewel firm with houses in London, Paris and Amsterdam, but he's far too magnificent to worry his head about business. Dear me, the bluff Sir Nigel must have put a large riding-boot right into it. "In trade" indeed! My hat, that's going to be a sensational luncheon!'

'If it comes off,' said Felicity gloomily. 'I don't care how important he is, he's been a pig to Madeleine. It's so odd, because he's very fond of her, although he's so strict, and she adores him. Her mother died when she was a child. That's why his behaviour is so unreasonable. What are you thinking?'

Mr Campion was frowning.

'It is unreasonable,' he said. 'Thunderingly unreasonable. Almost unlikely. The hotel people said quite definitely that he was staying here, you say?'

'Yes, they told Madeleine so this morning. He's been here since Tuesday. Can't you find out where he is and if he's going to turn up at Claridge's to-morrow?'

She looked very young and hopeful seated before him, natural colour in her cheeks, and in her eyes an engaging faith in his power to work small miracles. Campion was touched and, what was more, his curiosity was aroused.

'There is one way of finding out a little,' he said at last. 'I don't altogether approve of this as a method, but if one suspects the front door may be closed in one's face the intelligent caller slopes quietly round to the back.'

He took a card from his case as he spoke and, scribbling a few lines upon it, beckoned to a waiter.

'Is Ex-Inspector Bloomer still here?'

'Yes, sir. No trouble, I hope, sir?'

'I hope not too,' agreed Mr Campion affably. 'If it's convenient I'll meet him in the foyer in five minutes. Rule Number Three,' he continued, turning to his pupil as the man went off. 'Never forget an Old Face, especially if it's in the Force. Bloomer – don't be misled by his name – was quite an ornament in the City police some years ago.

I don't mean anything flashy, mind you. Bloomer was always something solid and good. When he retired he received the job of house detective here as a man in a different profession might receive a quiet country rectorship. He's the man for our money. I'll be back in ten minutes. You needn't save me an *éclair*.'

His time estimate proved entirely wrong, as it happened. To his surprise he found the ex-inspector not only ready but eager to discuss M. Edmond Gerard. Bloomer had aged and widened in his three years at the Balsamic, and his close-cropped hair was white, but he still possessed that blue-eyed innocence of expression which his visitor remembered so well.

'Come into my office,' he invited, as soon as Gerard's name was mentioned. 'It's a cosy little place; sound-proof door, too. You can't be too discreet in this house. To tell you the truth I'm glad someone's going to bring the subject up. Three days is a long time for an elderly bloke to wander about London, without his luggage, say what you like.'

Campion controlled his question until the sound-proof door closed behind them, but once there he put it with some force. 'Do you mean to say Edmond Gerard hasn't slept here since Tuesday?'

'He hasn't slept here at all,' said Bloomer cheerfully. 'The management tells me not to be fussy, but he was a respectable, oldish cove, you know; not at all the type to go off gallivanting. He came in early on Tuesday, took up his reservations, and went out without leaving a message. That's all we've seen of him. At five-fifteen a Hatton Garden firm called Bergère Brothers rang through and asked if he'd come in. The clerk told them no, but promised to phone when he did arrive. He didn't show up all night. In the morning, just when we were going to ring them, Bergère's phoned again. We said we were alarmed and they shut us up at once. They said he was a director of their firm and that they would take full responsibility for making inquiries at the hospitals and so on. They were very insistent that it wasn't necessary to call the police, and, between you and me, we weren't keen on that idea ourselves.'

He grinned. 'We're slightly la-di-dah here, you know. In our opinion the police are a very common lot.'

Campion sat on the edge of the table and digested this alarming information.

'Did M. Gerard get any other calls?'

'Oh yes, I was forgetting. A little girl phoned every two or three hours yesterday and to-day she came round. They put her off. She was very young, the clerk said, and she said she was Gerard's daughter, but he was a Frenchman, you see, and she was so obviously English – not a trace of accent. Somehow we didn't altogether believe her.'

Campion laughed abruptly.

'Poor child!' he said. 'That's one of the disadvantages of a really good education, Bloomer: no one allows for it. I say, this is very odd.'

'I don't like it.' The old man shook his head. 'But what can you do? If a guest books a suite in advance and leaves his luggage in it there's nothing to stop him. His firm hasn't found him yet because they keep phoning, but they still say it's okay for us to wait. We don't want a fuss. He may have three or four unofficial families to see over here, for all we know.'

'That's unlikely,' murmured Campion. 'I'd like to see those rooms of his. What about it?'

'Oh, I couldn't do that, sir! You didn't ought to ask me.' The old man was honestly scandalized, so that it was a tribute to his visitor's powers of persuasion that ten minutes later they entered the deserted suite together.

The two rooms with the adjoining bathroom showed no signs of occupation whatever, apart from the two neat hide cases standing on the luggage bench. Nothing was unpacked. The soap in the bathroom was still a fresh cake. Clearly the visitor had merely seen his luggage safely deposited before walking out again. Mr Campion regarded the suitcases wistfully.

'No, sir, we couldn't. It's more than my job and my pension are worth,' Bloomer sounded adamant this time, and his visitor sighed.

'You hold things up so,' he said. 'Think of that poor child waiting downstairs.'

*

It took him another five minutes' hard persuasion, and when he finally discovered that the cases were unlocked Bloomer was standing with his back against the door, listening for footsteps, with the sweat standing out on his forehead.

'Hurry, for Pete's sake,' he whispered huskily. 'You frighten me, you do. Found anything yet?'

'Cut-up corpse,' said his colleague, sepulchrally.

'No!' ejaculated Bloomer, deserting his post.

'No,' agreed Campion, turning over a pile of white shirts with deft fingers. 'No, not even a bundle of Government plans. Not even a dirty collar.'

He closed the second case and went over to the soiled-linen basket. Its yield seemed to interest him. It contained one pair of crumpled grey cotton gloves and no more.

He stood looking at the gloves, which he spread out side by side on the bed.

'That's very curious,' he said at last. 'Don't you think so?'

'Well, no, Mr Campion, I can't say I do, since you ask me.'

'This basket would have been cleared before M. Gerard took possession of the room?'

'I should hope so.'

'Well then, since this suite hasn't been occupied by anyone else, presumably he left these.'

'Very likely. Why not?'

'Nothing. Except that it's very odd that these should be *all* he left. Don't you see, Bloomer, the old boy didn't even change his shirt. Think of it: he's come from Paris, travelled all night, come up from Southampton on the early train, and yet he doesn't bath, doesn't shave, doesn't even change his collar. I admit there are men who are above such trifles as soot round the cuff-band, but this lad wasn't one of these. He's only over here for four days and yet he's brought three suits, eight shirts, and a neat little soiled-linen bag embroidered with his monogram, to say nothing of a nest of collars. Why didn't he change? And what, in the name of goodness, does he look like by this time?'

Bloomer frowned.

'Does seem funny when you put it like that,' he said. 'What about the gloves? They don't look like part of a smart gentleman's outfit to me. Grey cotton ... that's not very natty.'

'Not so much natty as necessary,' said Campion. 'On the Continent, that home of iniquity, my good Bloomer, the trains are so inclement that the intelligent native traveller always provides himself with a pair of these to keep his hands clean. That's what makes it all so infernally fishy. Apparently the eminent M. Gerard rushed up here, tore off his gloves and rushed down again. Besides, there's something curious about the gloves, don't you think?'

Bloomer looked at them steadily for a long time.

'They're dirty,' he said at last.

'So they are, indeed,' agreed Campion, and put them in his pocket. 'Don't worry about trifles,' he insisted, brushing aside the detective's protest. 'We've got to get a move on. I want a cab and my poor patient Felicity.'

Bloomer gaped at him.

'Here,' he said, 'you don't think there's something criminally serious up, do you?'

'I hope not,' said Campion.

He repeated the same sentiment five minutes later to Felicity as he helped her into a taxi. 'Now you know what you have to do?' he said, leaning in at the door. 'Mr Bloomer will be waiting here for you both. After that, go straight on to Scotland Yard and ask for Superintendent Stanislaus Oates.'

'All right.' Felicity was scared but game, and her round eyes were anxious. 'Madeleine's going to be frightfully nervous; I suppose you realize that? It's not only about the luncheons. She's terribly fond of her father. I haven't made that clear, I'm afraid.'

'I detected that,' said Campion, grinning at her cheerfully. 'Don't worry. Stick to the instructions on the bottle and we'll all go to the party. You take the high road and I'll take the low and I'll be on the Embankment before you. That's a bet.'

As he stepped back and nodded to the driver his smile faded, and by the time he had captured another taxi and was on his way to Hatton Garden he was frowning, yet he was as good as his word. When Miss Felicity Carrington and Mlle Madeleine Gerard were conducted up to Superintendent Stanislaus Oates's office a little over half an hour later he was there to introduce them.

The Superintendent rose as they appeared. His grey face was even more lugubrious than usual, but he brightened up a little at the sight of Felicity. Oates had an avuncular spot in his heart for what he privately described as 'a County blonde'.

* * *

Madeleine was a surprise to Mr Campion. He had imagined, for some reason or other, a little dark seventeen-year-old, so that the tall, willowy young woman with the sleek ash-blonde hair and the indescribable air of chic about her was unexpected. She was trembling with nervousness and her first remark explained much that had puzzled Campion.

'I ought not to come to the police. My father will be so angry. He hates any sort of interference. Yet nothing could have happened to him, could it?'

The Superintendent smiled disarmingly.

'Suppose we sit down,' he said. 'I think we can consider this an unofficial talk for the time being. We can get a bit forrader without Mr Gerard ever knowing anything about it, if it all turns out to be normal.'

'The signature wasn't normal,' cut in Felicity. 'We did what you said, Albert. We went to the hotel and Mr

Bloomer showed us the register. Madeleine was startled by the signature; it was so shaky.'

'It's my father's writing, but it's so unsteady,' murmured Madeleine. 'I'm so afraid he's been taken ill. What can we do?'

Oates glanced at Campion.

'According to Bloomer, Bergère Frères are taking care of that end,' he said. 'I think, somehow, we ought to have them represented at this little conference. You got nothing out of them, you say?'

Campion shrugged his shoulders.

'I was not exactly pitched out,' he admitted. 'But the visit was not productive. I never met people who were so anxious not to talk to me.'

'That was a change for you, wasn't it?' said Oates with relish. 'If I may say so, it's authority you lack, my lad.'

'Which is why I'm here, of course,' agreed Mr Campion cheerfully. 'With my brains and your authority what could we two not accomplish? I don't want to hurry you, Superintendent, but these offices in Hatton Garden sometimes shut. As it is, I very much doubt if you'll get anyone to come down here.'

Oates took the hint.

'I'll phone them from the other room,' he said, rising. 'We'll see what my not-so-celebrated charm will do.'

He returned in five minutes, grave but secretly pleased with himself.

'Mr Kenway will be with us,' he announced, eyeing Campion with a faint gleam in his eyes. 'He said you'd called. It seems he couldn't see you. He's the manager. Do you know him, Miss Gerard?'

'I? Oh no. I'm afraid I don't know anything about my father's affairs. I wish I did. Has this man seen Daddy?'

'Yes. Apparently he called on Tuesday afternoon. Since then they haven't heard from him.'

'But where is he? This is terrifying.' The girl was obviously frightened and the superintendent's manner became heavily kind.

'Don't worry too much, young lady,' he said. 'He's not in hospital. Mr Kenway seems to have made certain of that. As a matter of fact, I thought Bergère's were relieved to hear from me. I couldn't understand why they hadn't been here themselves, but apparently they have the same ideas about your father that you have yourself. He's a little autocratic, is he? Likes to go his own way?'

'He doesn't like interference at all,' murmured Madeleine Gerard, and sounded as though she knew what she was talking about.

Oates pulled a pad towards him.

'Could you give me a description of your father?' he inquired. 'Don't be alarmed. This is only routine. Now, what age would he be, please?'

Mr Campion read the pencilled note over the superintendent's grey-tweed shoulder.

Age: 61. Height: 5 ft. 7 in. approx.
Hair: Greyish white.
Weight: She doesn't know at all.
Fattish, Complexion, pale.
Eyes: Grey-blue. Clean-shaven.
Wears no rings. No distinguishing marks she can think
   of. Probably smartly dressed.

As the policeman finished writing he glanced up at Campion.

'Any comments?'

'I was wondering ...' The younger man's tone was diffident. 'Mademoiselle Gerard, what are your father's recreations? Is he keen on any sports?'

'No.' Madeleine looked puzzled and so, to do her justice, did the Superintendent. 'He spends all his time in his study and in the strong-room in the little château at Vaux. I don't think he has any recreation at all, unless you count his violin.'

'His violin?' There was an inflection in Campion's voice which made Oates stare at him. 'He still plays, you say?'

'Yes. Only to amuse himself, of course. He's a recluse, Mr Campion. He likes to be alone. He lives alone. He travels alone. He hates to give any account of himself and loathes any intrusion on his privacy. That's why I'm so afraid I ought not to be here. And yet I'm so frightened he may have been taken ill.'

There was a charming honesty in her manner which made Campion like her, and he made a mental note of the fact that young Henry Roundel was a lucky youngster.

'Don't get alarmed, Miss Gerard. There's no need for that.' Oates turned away from Campion, whom he had been watching with terrier-like curiosity, to make the reassurance. 'That's very interesting, but I'm afraid it's not going to help us much. Ah, here's the man we want.'

*

Richard Kenway came hurrying into the room, past the helmetless constable who had announced him, like a very small train shunting into a station. He was a short, plump person, dark in the hair and pale in the face and at the moment he was breathless and startled out of his wits. He shook hands with Oates, nodded coldly to Campion, and pounced on Madeleine with relief.

'I had no idea that M. Gerard had a daughter over here or I'd have got in touch with you at once,' he said earnestly. 'This is terrible. Haven't you seen your father at all? Didn't you meet him at the station?'

'Oh no, he'd never have forgiven me.' Madeleine spoke with deep conviction. 'He doesn't like what he calls being fussed. Don't you find that?'

Mr Kenway passed a plump white hand over his hair. He coughed.

'As a matter of fact,' he said, 'that was the private information which we received from our Paris house. That was how it all happened. Dear me, this is terrible! Our hands have been tied, and we've been sitting about doing nothing, while anything may have happened to him, anything!'

'Oh, I hope not, sir, I hope not.' Oates spoke firmly and raised his eyebrows at the visitor. 'Suppose you tell us about M. Gerard's visit to you? He called about half-past four in the afternoon, I understand?'

'Yes, he did.' Mr Kenway hesitated. 'I don't know if I'm doing the right thing. This is an impossible situation. I really think I'd better tell you the whole story. If it proves to be indiscreet I must take the consequences. First of all I must disclose a trade secret. Although the firm of Bergère Brothers is now virtually owned by M. Gerard, he doesn't bother himself with business; in fact, he affects to know little or nothing about it and is even celebrated for his casualness and unconventionality in these affairs. May I say that, mademoiselle?'

Madeleine nodded. 'I believe that is his reputation,' she said. 'I've heard he's rather terrifying. He wanders about with stones loose in his waistcoat pocket. That's the kind of thing you mean, isn't it, Mr Kenway?'

The jewel-broker wiped his forehead.

'That is the kind of thing,' he agreed dryly. 'Added to that there is this dislike of ceremony, any sort of inter-ference, or – er – any friendliness; I had almost said any ordinary business civility. Our Paris manager warned me, in so many words, not to ask him to lunch, or even to make any effort at conversation. Well, there we were on Tuesday morning, all very much aware that our principal was due at any moment. We had a very fine collection of unset rubies which we knew he was interested to see, and the whole staff was hanging about on tenterhooks, myself included, until four-thirty in the afternoon. We had almost given him up when he walked in, produced his credentials, and asked to see the rubies. It was just like that; as formal and peremptory as if he had nothing to do with the firm at all.'

He paused and shook his head over the experience.

'Frankly, I saw at a glance that he was not faintly interested in me, even as another human being, so I imitated his own manner. I studied his credentials, handed them back to him and opened the safe. He sat down at the table and began to examine the tray of stones which I set before him. After a while he glanced up and said in French: "Don't disturb me for half an hour." Naturally I left him. I waited in the outer office for nearly an hour. When at last I did go back the door from my room to the corridor was open and he had gone. I haven't seen him since. He had evidently finished his examination and not bothered to summon me. The lift-boy who had brought him up naturally took him down again and he walked out of the building.'

'I see. Not an easy gentleman to entertain,' said Oates in a valiant attempt at tact. 'Then you rang up the hotel?'

'Yes. Yes, I did.' Mr Kenway seemed to be struggling with himself. Finally his anxiety prevailed. 'There is one thing I haven't made clear,' he said huskily. 'When M. Gerard went out he took the rubies with him.'

*

Oates smothered an exclamation. 'And yet you didn't report the matter?' he demanded.

'My dear sir, how dared I?' Mr Kenway was almost weeping. 'They were his own stones. The whole firm belongs to him. I had express instructions from Paris, from M. Bergère himself, that M. Gerard was to be treated with the utmost care. He was to have anything he wanted. I was to do anything, absolutely anything he told me. M. Bergère himself is something of an autocrat. He does not tolerate failure in a subordinate. I have not dared to report the affair to him yet. I gave myself until to-night, hoping against hope that M. Gerard would return. Now I must phone Paris and, frankly, I might as well hand in my own resignation at the same time.'

'Don't be too hasty, sir.' The Superintendent sounded genuinely sorry for the little man. 'Give us a chance to do what we can. This was the first time you'd met Mr Gerard, was it?'

'Yes. No one on this side knows him. He hasn't been in

England for a great many years. He hardly ever leaves his home. The news of his visit was a great surprise to us.'

'I see. Here's Miss Gerard's description of her father. Can you add anything to it?'

Mr Kenway took the slip of paper and read it carefully. 'No,' he said at last. 'No, that's accurate as far as it goes. He wore a grey suit and a soft hat, ordinary but very good. He spoke French all the time. No, I don't think I noticed anything else.'

'Did he gesticulate when he talked?'

Mr Campion's mild question sounded a trifle silly and even Oates stared at him, while Mr Kenway chose to be irritated.

'He did not, sir,' he said. 'As far as I remember he was very quiet. He stood with his left hand in his pocket, and his glove and stick in the other most of the time I was with him.'

'Really?' Mr Campion's vacant expression had misled many a shrewder man than Mr Kenway; and when the angry little broker had turned away in disgust Campion wandered towards the door. 'I think I'll go down and see Pleyel, if you don't mind, Superintendent,' he said quietly. 'I'll call you on the house phone. I fancy we might have to hurry, don't you?'

Oates stood looking at the door for a moment, an expression of incredulity growing in his eyes. The mention of the name had started a train of thought in his mind which was enlightening.

Inspector Pleyel spent most of his days looking over the Rogues' Gallery, now that his more active career was past, and in that department he was known disrespectfully as The Elephant. Since he was a slender, somewhat shrivelled man the name seemed pointless until one had once seen him at work. After that, however, its appositeness was obvious. Inspector Pleyel and the great beasts had one important attribute in common: like them, he never forgot.

Oates was watching his secretary attending to the formalities of certain official statements when the buzzer on his desk vibrated and Campion's voice came up to him.

'The address is 39 Welkin Street, Soho,' it said, sounding thin and far-away as the instrument distorted it. 'Pleyel recognizes my description. The name is Marcel Lautrec. Do you know him? He's been out of jail for about three months and was last seen with Lefty Rowe and a fellow called Patsy Carver.'

'I know Rowe and Carver.' The Superintendent's tone was grim. 'What's this 39 Welkin Street?'

'Pleyel says it's a cheap eating-house with lodgings above. Carver's wife runs it and Rowe has been staying there. I think we ought to hurry.'

The policeman's grey face grew hard and his eyes were no longer kindly.

'You're right,' he said, and added with a sudden burst of exasperation, 'what a nerve, Campion! What a thundering nerve!'

*

The raid on 39 Welkin Street made Soho history, and that is no easy thing to do. The dark, shabby thoroughfare with its rows of dingy shops and sooty upstairs windows is not a favourite place for the patrolling policeman at any time, but in the evening, when the street lamps are yellow in the blue twilight, it is sometimes avoided by him altogether, and the inhabitants have come to regard it as a stronghold where any inquisitiveness is met with swift discouragement.

Two police cars swept down the narrow road and stopped with beautiful precision directly outside the entrance to the café with the steamy window and the cracked glass door.

At the same moment a third car halted in Fern Mews, that unattractive little cul-de-sac which runs along behind the houses in Welkin Street, and from all three vehicles there stepped a number of heavily built men, all distinguished by the same peculiarly purposeful manner.

Oates took the lead, with Campion close behind him, and it was he who first strode down the narrow aisle between the tables to the curtained doorway behind the counter where the coffee urn boiled.

The rustle which heralded their appearance turned into complete silence as their escort tramped in behind them, and the company in the little dining alcoves studied their plates or their papers with the complete absorption of those who have decided to withdraw in the spirit if not in the flesh.

It was the woman who gave the alarm. She confronted them in the narrow staircase, her untidy black-gowned body completely blocking the way.

'Now then, Missus – ' Oates got no further. She screamed and screamed, standing there with her head thrown back and her eyes closed. The noise was deafening. But behind it there were other sounds, swift, furtive movements on the floor above.

Campion bent his head and ducked under her arm. She hit out at him, but the blow was trifling, and her screams redoubled as a vast plain-clothes man gathered her up and carried her, kicking, into the kitchen.

Meanwhile Oates and Campion had reached the landing, which was in darkness. There they were met by an odour strange in that house. It swept down upon them from the floor above, the clean, and in the circumstances highly suspicious, odour of fresh air.

'The roof!' shouted Campion and sped on.

They caught Lefty Rowe half in and half out of the sky-light. Carver was brought in much later after a wearisome chase round the chimney-pots. But it was not in these old acquaintances that Oates and his companion were most interested. There were two locked rooms on the top floor of that ill-ventilated house, each of which contained a bed, and on each bed lay a man who was approximately five feet seven inches in height, fattish, grey-haired, and French.

There the likeness ended abruptly, for doubles are not easy to find, and although Messrs Rowe and Carver had been clever they had not been very lucky.

Marcel Lautrec gave himself up with the resignation of a man who has already spent the best part of his life in jail and sees no other prospect for the future. Nothing, however, prevented him from grumbling.

'It's my arm,' he said bitterly, regarding his stiff sleeve. 'I haven't got a chance. That's what happens to a man who loses his arm defending his fatherland.'

'In a street fight in Amiens in 1926,' interrupted a stolid plain-clothes man, who made no other observation throughout the entire proceedings.

Lautrec shrugged his shoulders.

'What does it matter?' he said. 'It's my arm that betrays me every time. If I had had both my arms should I have been locked up here?'

Oates's grin was sardonic.

'Since you've raised the subject,' he said, 'let me tell you something. You were locked up by your pals because you double-crossed them. They trusted you to do a job and you let them down. Once you'd got your hands on those rubies you weren't sharing them, were you?'

Lautrec's small eyes widened in sudden terror and he began to swear violently in a mixture of Gallic and honest Anglo-Saxon, giving as varied a performance as anyone present had ever heard, which was no mean feat.

Oates let him run on for a while.

'That'll do,' he said at last. 'Don't exhaust yourself. You've convinced me. Where are the stones? Tucked away in a railway cloakroom? Give the ticket to the boys. Take him along,' he added over his shoulder, and went into the other room where Campion was bending over the second plump Frenchman, who lay so silent upon the bed.

Campion straightened himself as Oates appeared.

'He'll do, I think,' he said. 'He's pretty tough, thank God. His pulse is fairly normal. I think they've kept him under with one of the barbituric group. When the doctor comes we'll get him back to the hotel.'

The Superintendent stood looking down at the elderly man who was only so very superficially like Marcel Lautrec. His expression was faintly bewildered.

'It's the infernal *impudence*,' he said. 'That's what startles me every time, old as I am. Who do these darned crooks think they are? They might have got away with it, you know; that's the exasperating thing.'

'That's the terrifying thing, old boy,' observed Campion soberly, and for once Oates did not correct him.

*

It was after midnight when the two of them finally left the Hotel Balsamic. The superintendent was in cheerful mood. He was so clearly determined to talk that Campion did not attempt to dissuade him and suggested that they should go back to his own Piccadilly flat for a drink. Oates agreed with alacrity, and a few minutes later settled himself by the open window looking down on to the traffic and raised his glass to his host.

'We deserve it,' he said magnificently. 'I don't want to take all the credit. You were very useful. That was quite a touching little scene between father and daughter at the hotel to-night, wasn't it? The old man's delighted with her, and well he might be. If it hadn't been for her he'd have stayed in that Welkin Street hovel until Rowe and Carver had bullied Lautrec into a sense of the realities of life.'

'He did double-cross them, did he?'

'He tried to.' Oates laughed. 'They were far too experienced to fall for that sort of game. Lautrec's a mug. Still, he did us a good turn. He held 'em up by playing the fool. Otherwise the stones would be out of the country by this time. As it is, we'll get 'em.'

Campion lay back in his chair.

'It was an ingenious swindle,' he remarked. 'Who is the brain there?'

'Rowe. He's an old con. man and he always fails by falling back on force when cornered. He's behind the whole thing. He found out that Gerard was coming to London and that no one at Bergère's knew him personally. There's a leakage in Gerard's secretarial staff somewhere, if you ask me. Anyway, Rowe bought that information from someone. He picked up the Frenchman on the train from Paris, boarded the boat with him, and located his cabin. The rest was elementary. Gerard is notoriously a bad sailor, it appears. Rowe went in to help the old man, who was seasick, and mixed him up a dose which made him dopy.

'When they arrived at Southampton the kindly Mr Rowe helped his new friend through the Customs, and, since he was so ill, gallantly offered to drive him to an hotel. Gerard was taken off his guard and accepted the offer. Meanwhile, Carver was waiting with the car, by arrangement. They put Gerard in the back, where he collapsed, and Rowe got in beside him, ready to give him another shot if he recovered too soon.'

'All this was at six o'clock in the morning, mind you, so there was no one much about to get inquisitive. Instead of going to a Southampton hotel Carver drove to London, and when Gerard recovered consciousness he was where we found him.'

He drew a deep breath and raised his glass again.

'There you are,' he said; 'it was impudence, sheer impudence. Gerard's reputation and temperament made the whole thing possible. He travelled alone, he wasn't known, he was doing the unusual thing.'

Campion nodded. 'It was neat,' he admitted. 'Lautrec was waiting for them in London, I suppose?'

'Oh yes. Rowe got hold of him some weeks ago. He had to use a Frenchman, you see, and someone who would conform at least to a verbal description of Gerard. Lautrec was ideal, save for his arm. His artificial arm is dangerous, but he's used to concealing it, so they took the risk. Having deposited Rowe and Gerard at Welkin Street, Carver drove to Victoria and carried Gerard's two suitcases and all his papers on to the station, where Lautrec was waiting for them. Once Lautrec had all the necessary information, hotel reservations and everything, he took a cab to the Balsamic. He had to do that, you see, in case Bergère's phoned through and found Gerard had not arrived. He signed the register, making such a clumsy attempt at Gerard's signature that the innocent Mademoiselle thought her father might have been ill when he wrote it. After that he went upstairs, where he left his cases and his travelling gloves, which he had worn for the benefit of the hotel folk. Then he walked out of the building, to hang about until he thought Bergère's were ready to receive him.'

'Neat,' said Campion again. 'It's a serious thought, Oates, but it ought to have come off. Lautrec's arm let them down.'

'Ye-es,' agreed the Superintendent dubiously and then, since his host was uncommunicative, added with sudden bluntness, 'how do you make that out?'

Campion thrust his hand into his jacket pocket and brought out a pair of crumpled grey cotton gloves. Oates waved them aside.

'You showed me those before,' he said, 'I don't want a lecture. I want to know how you got on to Lautrec. And, what's more,' he added complacently, 'I'm sitting here in this chair drinking your whisky until I do know.'

Campion took off his spectacles.

'It seemed so obvious to me,' he said apologetically. 'The kidnapping and impersonation notion flickered into my head as soon as I found that Gerard had neither bathed nor changed his linen after his journey. With that in mind I looked at the gloves and saw that while the right-hand one was fairly dirty, the left, although it was crumpled and had been worn, was perfectly clean. No ordinary man travels from Paris to London and arrives with one dirty hand and one clean one. There had to be a special reason for it. The obvious explanation was that the man, whoever he was, didn't use his left hand, presumably because it wasn't usable. In your office Madeleine Gerard told me that her father was a violinist. That settled it that the gloves were not his. You can do a lot of things with one hand, my good Oates, but playing the violin isn't one of them. Therefore I took it that the gloves belonged to the impersonator. It was blindingly clear, I thought.'

'Yes,' said Oates again. 'But even old Pleyel couldn't pick out the right man when all he had to go upon was an artificial arm.'

*

Campion sighed. 'That wasn't all,' he protested mildly. 'Madeleine had described the real M. Gerard, superficially I admit, but at least she gave us the general impression of the man. Richard Kenway read her description and found that it tallied with his impression of his visitor, yet he, mark you, had only seen the impersonator. I went to Pleyel and asked him if he knew of any confidence man who was (a) French, (b) fifty to sixty years old; (c) plumpish and (d) one-armed. He supplied Lautrec's name at once and the current intelligence files gave us the rest.'

Oates laughed. 'Of course,' he said. 'Funny how I missed that. Well, I think that we can congratulate ourselves, don't you?'

Campion did not answer. He did not seem to have heard. There was a scandalized expression in his eyes.

'I say,' he said, 'this is frightful! Oates, I've forgotten Felicity. I left her in your office.'

'The little blonde?' Oates was mildly interested. 'She's all right. I sent her home with a sergeant from the College. Ring her up in the morning.'

Campion took his advice, but Felicity was out. His afternoon call was more successful.

'My dear, don't be silly.' She sounded jubilant as she waived aside his apologies. 'It was thrilling. I loved it, every minute of it. You're going to get deluged with praise and bouquets from the Gerards. I'm going to be a bridesmaid.'

'Are you, indeed? The lunch was not so horrific after all, was it?'

'The lunch was a success,' said Felicity. 'Got any more rules for me?'

Campion grinned. 'Only one,' he said, 'and I'm afraid it's one for me. When you invite a young woman to spend the afternoon inspecting a gallery of modern art with you, don't get her taken home by a policeman.'

'Rubbish,' protested Felicity. 'She *liked* it.'

'That's the catch,' said Mr Campion.

VIII

The Longer View

ON the day that the entrancing Beatrix Lea married her famous leading man, Mr Albert Campion took Mr Lance Feering to re-visit the happy scenes of Mr Feering's youth.

The expedition was purely remedial. Throughout their long luncheon Lance had remained mildly depressed. After all, as he said, a broken heart takes at least twenty-four hours in which to mend without a seam and, while he was perfectly prepared to believe that life with a young woman of Miss Lea's uncontrolled and vituperative tongue might drive a man to suicide, he yet needed a day or two to get used to his merciful deliverance.

Campion, who had known Lance long before he had become one of the leading designers of stage *décor* in Europe, was ready to agree, but it occurred to him that a little gentle exercise, judiciously coupled with a rival sentimental regret, might possibly speed up the recovery.

He was rewarded. As they turned into the web of little streets which floats out like a dusty cap round the neck of the Museum, Lance began to brighten visibly.

'I used to live round here once,' he remarked casually. 'Four of us existed in a hovel on the top floor of a house in Duke's Row. We were all under twenty. Berry was there, and Jorkins, and old Salmon, the poster chap. We were all broke and completely happy. We used to slave away like lunatics, all striving and dreaming of the glorious future when our respective geniuses would be recognized, and we should be rich and eat three times a day. It's tragic, you know, Campion. Look at us now. All recognized, all successful, and all damned miserable. We've got the apple off the top of the tree and the cursed thing's sour.'

Campion experienced a sensation of relief. The man was becoming recognizable. Once Lance got going on his time-honoured 'futility of endeavour' the next stage, 'self-expression, the comforter', was close at hand, and after that it was but a step to that mood of light-hearted good temper laced with high excitement which was his normal state.

'What we all miss now is adventure,' Lance continued, absent-mindedly crossing the road to reach a familiar turning. 'When we lived down here it was an adventure to be alive at all. Here we are. That's the place. Wonderful architecture. Look at that porch and those windows. Look at them!'

Campion surveyed the row of dusty houses, but even the rose-coloured spectacles of Lance Feering's reawakening enthusiasm could not restore Duke's Row to any sort of splendour. The backwater was forlorn and shabby. Fine doors hung open under the ragged elegance of graceful porches, betraying glimpses of bare and dirty communal hallways within. It was a sad street of decayed mansions, whose rooms were now let out unfurnished at a few shillings a week. Lance strolled down the road.

'I haven't been here for ten years,' he said regretfully. 'All the old crowd must have gone, of course. No one stayed here long. It was a sort of half-way house. If you lived here you were either going up or coming down. I wonder who's got our old hovel now?'

He had paused before an open doorway as he spoke and, after a moment's contemplation, suddenly dived through it and hurried up the fine but unsteady flight of wooden stairs inside. Campion followed dubiously, catching up with him just as he was shamelessly engaged in trying the handle of the door on the top landing.

'I say, is this wise?' Campion put out a restraining hand, but the door swung open and Feering grinned.

'Empty, by George!' he said delightedly. 'This is an omen, Campion. Who knows, it may be the will of Providence that we take this place, and, turning our backs resolutely on the fleshpots, settle down to adventure and art for art's sake.'

Campion remained polite but unimpressed. The crumbling attic with the discoloured walls, the wobbling floorboards, and the one dusty window did not attract him. But Feering was his old volatile self again.

'It's a hole, Campion, I admit,' he said. 'It's a dirty little hole, twice as dark and half the size I thought it was. Yet we all worked in here and slept in this bedroom. Lord, look at it! It's a cupboard. Salmon, Berry, and I shared this.'

He had thrown open an inner door and they stepped gingerly into a tiny room in which there was nothing but a broken chair, a cup without a handle, and a portrait of a film star torn from one of the weekly illustrated magazines. Feering's enthusiasm sagged before this scene of desolation.

'I wouldn't like to see us trying it now,' he remarked. 'You haven't met old Salmon lately, have you? He's grown very pompous since his success, poor chap. We used to make Jorkins sleep in this cupboard over here. He was short enough to lie down in it.'

He was still laughing as he opened the small door in the wall. Campion did not follow him immediately. An empty cigarette carton on the window sill had caught his attention and he had gone across to look at it. He still had it in his hand when Feering's voice came sharply from the cupboard.

'I say, Campion, come here. Look at this.'

Campion put his head into the little cell and glanced round its dingy walls through his horn-rimmed spectacles. The place was less than six feet square and was lit by a small window in the roof. It was quite devoid of furnishing, but possessed one startling feature. All round the rough plaster walls, about a foot above the wainscot, ran a string of six-inch crimson letters. They made out the words with difficulty.

'*Let me out,*' they read. '*O let me out let me out let me out let me out let me out.*'

The writing was shaky and irregular, but there was no mistaking the message. It sprang out at them from the little den like a cry and sent an unaccustomed thrill down Campion's spine. On and on the message went, all round the tiny room. Sometimes it was in a double row. Sometimes it staggered up the wall.

'*Let me out o let me out let me out let me out.*'

Very low down on the back of the door was the single word '*Janey*' repeated half a dozen times.

The two men stared at each other for an instant and finally Feering laughed.

'It's mad, of course,' he said. 'Some sort of joke. It gave me a shock, though, almost a superstitious thrill. "Let me out" written in blood on the walls of a prison. As soon as one's mind works one realizes it's a false effect. If anyone had been imprisoned here he would have shouted the words, not scribbled them. How attractively absurd!'

Campion was silent. He was kneeling down on the floor, peering at the inscription. Presently he rubbed one of the letters with an inquisitive finger and the colour came off on his hand. He moved under the skylight to examine it.

'It's recent work, anyway,' he observed at last. 'Wait a minute. Get out of the light, can you, old boy? Stand in the doorway while I have a look round.'

Feering moved obligingly and stood watching.

'I like to see the veteran sleuth sleuthing,' he remarked cheerfully. 'It's very instructive. Look out for the trouser knees. Hullo, have you got something? What is it? The clue the great man knew was there?'

'The clue the great man hoped was there,' corrected Campion modestly. He prised something small and bright from beneath the wainscot board, and rose, holding the treasure in the palm of his hand. 'There you are,' he said. 'There's half the explanation of the blood-stained hand-writing. All done while you wait.'

'Lipstick!' Lance took the small gilt holder from which

practically all the cosmetic had been worn away, and
turned it over curiously. 'Sample size,' he commented.
'What's the little bit of green thread for? That's amateur
work.'

'I shouldn't pull it off.' Campion spoke hastily, an
urgency in his tone which made the other man glance at
him inquiringly.

'Taking it seriously?' he asked. 'It is a joke of some
sort, isn't it? Have we stumbled on a crime?' He almost
sounded hopeful, and Campion shrugged his shoulders.
He was laughing.

'My dear chap, I don't know,' he said. 'I admit it
doesn't seem likely, and even if we have it's hardly anything to do with us. Yet it's odd that any woman should
waste a whole lipstick writing "*let me out*" all round the
wainscot of an empty room.'

'Perhaps it wasn't empty then?'

'In that case it's curiouser and curiouser. Why should
she move the furniture away from the walls in order to
write behind it?'

'I say, there is that.' Lance Feering's black eyes were
growing sharper. 'Still, why write it? Why not shout it?'
he insisted. 'And anyway, why so low down?'

Campion hesitated. 'I don't want to be melodramatic,'
he said, 'but if she were lying on the floor she could just
reach as high as that, and I can imagine a frightened
woman writing like that if she was prevented from shouting.'

'Good Lord!' Feering was staring at the little cell in
blank astonishment. 'Gagged!' he ejaculated. 'Bound and
gagged.'

'Hardly. If she was bound she couldn't write, and if she
wasn't bound she'd hardly remain gagged. But she might
have been frightened. It's very curious.'

'It's incredible.' Lance was frankly excited. 'What shall
we do? Call a bobby?'

'Oh, no, I shouldn't do that.' Campion was firm. 'He
might not be amused. We've got to account for ourselves
being here at all, you see. We walked in off the street

without being asked. There isn't even a "To Let" sign anywhere. We're on enclosed premises. If you call the police we shall spend the rest of the day making statements. It's interesting, though. I should say it had been written within the last forty-eight hours. The stuff isn't dry, you see.'

Lance grimaced. 'I came up here on a silly sentimental impulse, hoping to recapture some of the old spirit of adventure,' he remarked. 'Now I seem to have found it, and hang it, Campion, it's a responsibility. Look at it. "*Let me out o let me out.*" It's pathetic, poignant. It must be answered. I don't see what we're going to do, though, apart from making discreet inquiries from the people downstairs.'

'Wait a moment.' Campion was examining the lipstick holder. 'All in good time. Let's do the thing in proper academic style. First we learn all we can from the scene. Then we take the statements. I'll tell you something, young sir. This is not ordinary lipstick. Not only is it a sample but it has an inscription. Look. "*Prince Pierrot, Inc. 'Maiden Voyage'.*" What does that tell you? Nothing, I suppose. However, the experienced sleuth deduces instantly that Prince Pierrot is an American firm of high-class cosmetic manufacturers; American because he's "Inc." and not "and Co." and high-class because the smell of the stuff is not offensive but rather pleasing. Moreover, it's a nice expensive-looking colour. The "Maiden Voyage" provokes a longer shot, I admit, but there has been a pretty important maiden voyage from the U.S. just lately.'

'The *Eire!*' Lance swung round. 'I say, that's about it. That boat is the last word in floating hotels and I believe the advertising tie-ups were incredible. Probably these Pierrot people control the beauty parlours on board and ran off a few special samples with the complimentary name. There you are. This poor girl Janey—her name must be Janey—came over on the *Eire*. We're on to something highly peculiar. They were all first-class passengers on that trip. What's an American socialite doing in a dive like this less than a week after she lands in England? We must find her. Hang it, it's up to us!'

Campion smiled, but his eyes were still serious.

'Don't be disappointed,' he said warningly.

'Disappointed?' Lance was hurt. 'My dear chap, I'm not a ghoul. I only hope it is a joke. I don't want any beautiful young woman to have had a beastly time. What are you laughing at?'

'I was wondering if she was beautiful and if she was young,' murmured Campion. 'There's absolutely no guarantee of that.'

Lance grinned. 'Poor, ugly little beast, then,' he said. 'I don't care. I've got my adventure. Her name is Janey and I am her knight-errant. We've got all eternity before us. Where do we go from here?'

*

Their preliminary investigations were unexpectedly profitable. To Feering's delight he discovered that the old charwoman who had lived in the basement in the days of his youth was still in occupation. After a glorious reunion, which could not have been more hearty had he been her long-lost son, she told them all she knew of the ex-tenants of the top floor. This was not a great deal, but the story had points of interest.

There had been two of them, she said, 'flash boys, a little too smart to be trusted'. They had been living there for the best part of a month, and had seemed to her experienced eyes to be none too flush with money, even according to the standards of the neighbourhood. However, two days before there had come a change. The tenants of the attic had received visitors of an unusual kind. The strangers had arrived late one night. Out of her basement window she had caught a glimpse of their limousine, and afterwards had heard the sound of trampling feet on the uncarpeted stairs. The following evening the car had called again, and this time every one had gone off in it, carrying bundles and packages.

The old lady suspected a moonlight flit but had been surprised in the morning to discover one of the tenants still in possession. Even more to her astonishment, he had fetched in a junk dealer and disposed of the entire furnishings for a few shillings. Then, after leaving a week's rent for the landlord, he had walked out quietly into the blue.

That was all Mrs Sadd had to report, and she hardly liked to take the treasury note which Feering pressed upon her, but she came running after them to tell them that one of the 'flash boys' had spoken with an American accent.

'No girl,' Lance remarked dubiously, as he followed Campion into a cab. 'No mention of a girl at all. No screams. Nothing. The only corroboration we have is that one of the tenants had an American accent.'

'He liked American cigarettes too,' Campion observed. 'There was an empty "Camel" carton on the mantelshelf. They're expensive over here. Perhaps the visitors brought him a packet. It may be a wild-goose chase, but I think we'll try the shipping office.'

'Janey,' said Feering, leaning back in the cab. 'I see her as a dazzling blonde with dark eyes.'

Since Beatrix was a brunette with blue eyes, Campion took the observation to be a favourable sign.

Lance waited in the cab while Campion negotiated the somewhat delicate line of inquiry in the shipping office. It was a long vigil, but he was rewarded. The tall man in the horn-rimmed spectacles came striding out of the impressive doorway wearing that vacant expression which indicated that he was on the track of something interesting. He directed the taxi-man to the offices of one of the newspapers and climbed in beside his friend.

'Miss Janey Lobbet, travelling with her mother, Mrs Fran Lobbet, of Boston, Mass.,' he said briefly. 'That's all I can find out about her. Passenger lists aren't very communicative. But she was the only Janey on the boat, so far as I can find out. There's one other point. You were perfectly right. Messrs Prince Pierrot Inc. had the monopoly of the beauty trade on the ship and they did run a special line in "Maiden Voyage" samples, exclusive to the trip. How's that?'

Lance whistled. 'What an extraordinary thing!' he said at last. '"*Let me out o let me out*" ... what on earth does it mean? There's been nothing in the papers. What's happened, Campion?'

'I don't know.' The other man spoke with a seriousness unusual in him. 'I don't know at all, but I don't like the feel of it and I rather think it's something I ought to find out.'

At the newspaper office Campion's call was on Miss Dorothea Azores, well known as the most industrious gossip-writer of the day. The lady herself was out, unfortunately, but her secretary was able to give them at least the bare bones of the information they sought. Mrs Fran Lobbet was the widow of Carl Lobbet, the paper magnate, and she and her only daughter, Janey, were staying at the Aragon Hotel, overlooking the Park. The secretary apologized that she had no photographs and so little information about the pair, but explained gently that there were a great many Americans in London.

'Well, what do we do?' inquired Lance as they came out through the bronze-and-glass doors into Fleet Street again. 'Do we barge in on these good ladies and ask if either of them has spent a bad half-hour in Duke's Row?'

Campion hesitated. 'No,' he said, the anxious expression still lingering behind his spectacles. 'No, hardly that. But we might dine at the Aragon to-night if you're not doing anything. I think I shall go myself, in any case.'

'No, you don't,' said Lance firmly. 'No poaching. This is my adventure. I found it and I'm sticking to it. The dinner's mine. I'll meet you in the restaurant at a quarter to eight. Don't look so dubious. This is going to be good.'

'I hope so.' But Campion did not sound sanguine.

*

The Aragon was fashionable that year, and the big dining-room with the fine windows opening on to the Park

was crowded with the usual noisy, well-dressed crowd when
Lance arrived. He found Campion already installed at a
table at the far end of the room, on the edge of the little
dais which was part of the orchestra platform. It was a
most advantageous position, giving him a clear view of the
entire gathering.

'Any luck?'

'It all depends.' Campion was cautious. 'I'm not sure.
I've been talking to Baptiste. He's the *maître d'hôtel* here. I
cultivate a line in *maîtres d'hôtel*. He's an old friend. The
Lobbets are here all right, or rather Madame is. Mademoiselle is away for a few days, staying with friends. That's
the table, the little one down there by the window. She's
expected any moment now.'

'Staying with friends?' Lance repeated, his eyebrows
rising. 'That's suggestive, isn't it? This is damned silly and
exciting. Don't be so blasé – or is this an everyday affair
for you?'

'I'm not blasé.' Campion resented the accusation. 'I
don't like the look of the thing. If I'm on the right track,
and I'm afraid I may be, I'm appalled by it. Hello, here
she is.'

Feering followed his glance across the room to where the
portly Baptiste was settling a newcomer at the little table
by the window.

'It's Janey.' Lance turned to Campion. 'What did I
tell you? A dazzling blonde with dark eyes. I'm the seventh
child of a seventh child: I've got prophetic vision. She looks
a little pale, a little sad, doesn't she? Momma has been very
trying and she doesn't know anybody in London. By George,
she's lovely! Look at her.'

Campion was looking at her. He saw a pale slender girl
of twenty-eight or so, with ash-blonde hair and enormous
dark eyes, the shadows beneath them enhancing their
sombre loveliness. She was delightfully dressed, and from
the clasp on her shoulder came the unmistakable watery
gleam of real diamonds, yet he thought he had never seen
anyone who looked so forlorn and miserably unhappy in

his life. Lance drew a card from his wallet and began to scribble on it.

'One can only be snubbed,' he observed philosophically. '"Faint heart", "nothing venture", likewise "fain would I climb". Give me that lipstick-holder. The green thread may touch a chord.'

He pushed the card across the table so that Campion could read the message.

'*I think this is yours. May I tell you where I found it and how I know? It's a good story.*'

'Yes, that'll do, I think.' Campion produced the lipstick-holder as he spoke. 'I wonder, though,' he went on. 'It's not fair to spring it on her like this unless – '

His voice trailed away. Lance was no longer listening to him. He had signalled a waiter and was dispatching his message.

Together the two friends watched the man cross the room. He paused before the table in the window, and said something to the girl. She looked surprised and almost, it seemed to Lance, a little frightened, but she glanced across at him and took the card as the waiter placed the holder on the white table-cloth beside her plate. The card fluttered from her hand as she caught sight of it and even from that distance they saw all trace of colour creep slowly from her face. She grew paler and paler and her eyelids drooped. Campion rose.

'Look out, she's going to faint,' he said.

He was too late. The girl swayed sideways and crumpled to the ground.

Instantly there was commotion all round her, and the two men on the other side of the room had the uncomfortable experience of seeing her assisted to the door, Baptiste fluttering behind the procession like a scandalized duenna.

Lance turned to Campion. In any other circumstances the bewildered regret upon his face would have been comic.

'Ghastly,' he said. 'How did that happen? Was it coincidence or the sight of that confounded thing?'

Campion put his napkin on the table. 'We're going to find out,' he said briefly.

Baptiste, solemn and reproachful, was bearing down upon them. He paused before the table and gave the message in a tone in which respectful deference was subtly mingled with deep disapproval.

'Mrs Lobbet will be glad to see the two gentlemen who sent her the card in her private sitting-room.'

*

It was not so much an invitation as a royal command, and Lance said afterwards that he followed Campion to the suite on the first floor feeling as if he were bound for the headmaster's study. At any rate, five minutes later they stood side by side, looking helplessly at the pale, unsmiling woman who waited to receive them with courage and dignity as well as terror in her dark eyes.

As the door closed behind the servant who had conducted them she spoke. Her voice was unexpectedly deep, and its trace of New England accent made it very attractive.

'Well?' she said. 'Has the price gone up again? Or couldn't you wait until to-morrow?'

They gaped at her and Lance tugged at his collar uncomfortably.

'I'm afraid there's some mistake,' he began awkwardly. 'You see, we had no idea that you were Mrs Lobbet. We – that is, I – was looking for Janey.'

The name was too much for the woman. She remained for a moment struggling to master herself and then, with a gesture of complete helplessness, collapsed into a chair and hid her face.

'Don't,' she whispered. 'Oh, please don't. I've told you I'll meet any demands you like to make, but don't torture us like this. Is she all right? Please, please tell me. Don't you understand, she's my baby? Is she all right?'

Lance glanced sharply at Campion and met the other man's eyes.

'A child!' he said huskily. 'Good lord, I never guessed.'

Campion did not reply to him. His mouth was grim as he went across the room and looked down at the woman.

'Mrs Lobbet, you should have gone to the police,' he said quietly. 'When did you miss your daughter?'

The young widow sprang up. Before she had been broken-hearted; now she was terrified.

'Who are you?' she demanded. 'I tell you I don't know anything. I – I don't want to discuss anything with you. Please go away.'

He shook his head.

'You're making a great mistake,' he said gently. 'This is England, you know. Conditions are rather different over here. I know when someone dear is kidnapped in America it is often safest not to go to the authorities for fear of reprisals, but over here, believe me, it's not the same.'

The girl did not speak. There was a light of pure desperation in her eyes and her lips remained obstinately closed. He stood watching her for a little while and finally shrugged his shoulders.

'I'm sorry,' he said. 'You could have trusted us.'

He had reached the door before she called him back.

'If only I knew what to do,' she said brokenly. 'If only I knew what to do.'

Lance went suddenly across the room and took her hand. He looked young for his years and very handsome as he peered down into her face.

'We are both reputable people, my dear girl,' he said. 'We'll give you our credentials if you'll let us. We found that holder in such very odd circumstances that it made us curious, and quite by chance we were able to trace it to you. Won't you tell us all about it? We'll help you if we can.'

It was a sincere little speech and gradually the tenseness round her mouth slackened, although her eyes were still afraid.

'Where did you get it?' she whispered. 'Did you see her? Do you know where she is?'

It took them the best part of an hour to convince her that they were genuinely disinterested parties in the affair. Lance left the description of the scribbled message, which had now taken on such a new and pathetic significance, to Campion, who managed it very tactfully, without frightening the young mother unduly.

'So you see,' he finished at last, 'we were curious and just a little apprehensive. How old is Janey?'

'Only six.' Fran Lobbet's voice quivered. 'She's just a baby. I've never let her out of my sight before, but this new nurse seemed so sensible and trustworthy that I let them both go out into the Park. When they didn't return I was paralysed with fear. Then the telephone message from these – these people came.'

'Oh, they phoned you, did they? What did they say?'

'The usual thing. I nearly fainted when I heard the warning. I've read about the same sort of thing in our newspapers. I wasn't to tell anyone or – or I'd never see her again. I was to go to Oxborough Racecourse and put ten thousand dollars to win on a certain horse with a certain bookmaker. Then they promised she'd be returned to me.'

'Did you do it?'

'Oh, yes, of course. That was the day before yesterday. I did everything they told me, but there was no sign of her when I got back here. I waited by the telephone all day and this morning, when I was half out of my mind, they rang again. They swore that she was safe but they made another demand. They may be playing with me. She may be dead. But what can I do? What *can* I do?'

The appeal was too much for Lance.

'My poor, dear, good girl,' he said, forgetting himself completely, 'ring up the police instantly. This is frightful. You poor child, you must be in agony. See to it, Campion. Get on the telephone.'

'No, no, please don't! Please. They'll kill her if I do that. I know they will. They so often do. There are hundreds of cases of it back home.' She was clutching his coat imploringly, and Campion intervened.

'You're not back home now,' he said. 'Look here, it's not as bad as you think, or at least I think not, thank God. This is a smaller country and the law is tighter, but I think you may be right about not calling in the police at this juncture. Tell me, did the man you spoke to on the phone have an American accent?'

'Yes, a slight one.'

'I see. Then that's what's happened. Probably the whole thing's engineered from the other side, with confederates in this country. The nurse is in it, of course. When did you engage her?'

'Just before we sailed. She came to me with wonderful references and she seemed so placid and sensible that I never dreamed – '

Mrs Lobbet's voice trembled and she broke off, fighting with her tears.

'I'm alone,' she said. 'I daren't trust anyone. Even now I don't know about you. Forgive me, but you come to me out of the air with something that Janey had with her. How can I trust you? I oughtn't to talk. Oh, my God, I oughtn't to talk!'

'Wait a minute,' said Lance, who was still puzzled. 'What was a child of six doing with a lipstick?'

In spite of her anxiety a faint smile passed over Fran Lobbet's beautiful face.

'It belonged to her doll,' she said. 'Janey has a very grand French doll with a green belt, and on the boat, when they were giving away those little samples, she got hold of one because it was a doll's size. I tied it on to the belt for her with a piece of green thread. That's how I recognized it. Look, the thread's still there.'

'I see. And when she was too scared to shout she used it to write her name on the door. She's a clever kid for six.' Lance's black eyes had grown bleak. 'They're swine,' he said softly. 'They deserve what's coming to them. Now look here, Mrs Lobbet, you've got to allow us to manage this. We'll get her back, I promise you. We'll get her back safely if it's the last thing we do. You can rely on us.'

Campion did not echo the impulsive promise. Long experience of criminals had made him cautious. But there was a rare spark of anger in the shadows behind his eyes.

'Suppose you tell us about this latest demand,' he said quietly.

Mrs Lobbet glanced from one to the other of the two men. She seemed pathetically young and tragic and, to Lance at any rate, one of the loveliest women he had ever seen.

'It's so impressed on us back home that complete silence is the only hope,' she said, 'but I can't help it. They've lied to me once and they may go on doing it. I feel I'm taking her life in my hands, but I'll tell you, and please God I'm doing the right thing. This is what they've told me to do.'

As Campion listened to the instructions his opinion of the organizing powers of the gang increased. It was a pretty little plan, evidently devised by someone with a proper appreciation of English laws and police procedure. Janey's captors required her mother to attend Thursday's Oxborough meeting alone. She was to seek out a bookie called Fred Fitz, whose stand would be among the others, but she was not to speak to him until the second race was actually being run. Then she was to walk over and place two thousand pounds in one-pound notes on *Flyaway* to win the two-thirty.

The simplicity of the scheme was exquisite. Here was no clumsy passing of notes in narrow lanes, no leaving of mysterious boxes on churchyard walls. A bookmaker is the only man on earth who can receive large sums of money for nothing from perfect strangers in the open light of day without occasioning suspicion or even interest. Moreover, in the event of a police trap what man could have a better story? Any tale which she might tell about mysterious telephone messages could always come as a complete surprise to him, and who could argue? No charge could be preferred against him, for he had done nothing to offend.

'I've got the money ready and I shall do exactly what they say.' The girl spoke stiffly, as if her lips were set. 'You mustn't come with me. I mustn't jeopardize her chances in any way. I daren't. I just daren't.'

'Mrs Lobbet is right,' said Campion hastily before Lance could interrupt. 'For her own peace of mind she must keep her bargain with the crooks. She must go to the meeting and pay the ransom money alone.'

'But we shall be there,' Lance insisted.

Campion cocked an eye at him. 'Oh, dear me, yes,' he said and his precise voice was almost caressing. 'We shall be there.'

*

They *were* there. Lance Feering in chauffeur's uniform drove Fran Lobbet to the meeting in his own car.

Campion went racing alone. Apart from an hour's intensive telephoning in the morning, his day might have borne the scrutiny of the most suspicious of shadowing crooks. He had an early lunch at the celebrated White Hart Hotel in Oxborough Wool Market and drove gently down to the car park as though he had no care in the world. He watched the first race from the stand, won a little money, and afterwards wandered down to the bookies' ring to collect it and place another trifling stake.

He did not bet with Fred Fitz. Indeed, he scarcely looked at the wizened little man who was shouting so lustily. He did not recognize his face and did not expect to. The morning's careful inquiries had identified him as a small man of no reputation, nor of sufficient importance to be of any great interest to the police. After discussing him on the telephone with Superintendent Stanislaus Oates of Scotland Yard, Campion had been moved once more to admire the organizing abilities of the men who had engineered the kidnapping of the little American girl. Fitz was one of those men who float round the edge of the underworld, doing odd jobs for larger and more whole-hearted crooks. Since nothing definite was known against him the police were bound to treat him as an honest man, whatever their private opinions might be.

The man who was acting as his clerk, however, was a different person altogether. As soon as Campion set eyes upon that sharp white face his own expression became an amiable blank and he never glanced again in his direction. There was no mistaking Fingers Hawkins. Once seen never forgotten, and Campion had not only seen but had dealt before with that little crook, whose reputation was not admired even by his own kind.

He returned to the stand in thoughtful mood. If Fingers was a typical member of the gang with whom he had to deal, things could hardly be more unpromising.

He took up his position and reviewed the scene through his glasses. The meeting was not a very popular one and the crowds were not enormous, although there were enough people to make the gathering interesting. The racecourse is just outside the town, which lies in a hollow, and beyond the red rooftops the rolling green hills, dotted with country houses, rise up to the skyline. It was a sunny day, and as Campion's powerful glasses swept the country they brought him little intimate glimpses of manors and farms and villas nestling in their surrounding greenery. He spent some time apparently lost in the beauties of the scene, and dragged his attention back to the course almost with reluctance.

Just before the second race started, when the stand was full and the crowd was moving steadily towards the rails, he caught sight of Fran Lobbet. She was wearing the red hat on which they had agreed, and was quite alone, he was relieved to notice. Through his glasses he watched her edging her way towards the ring, clutching an enormous white handbag with both hands. She made a very small and pathetic figure in her loneliness, and his indignation rose to boiling-point. He did not notice the horses coming up to the start, and it was not until the roar from the crowd told him that they were off that he was ever aware of their existence.

As the crowd swept past Fran in a last-minute rush, the bookies and their stands were temporarily deserted, and Campion saw her walk resolutely forward. His glasses left the girl and focused upon the ignoble features of Fingers Hawkins. The little crook appeared to be employed in something which looked at first like amateur tic-tac work. His arms rose above his head and dropped again. Then Fran came into the circle. A package passed and she received her slip. Still Campion did not follow her. Fingers made his entry and then, stepping up on the box, raised his arms once again. Afterwards he too raised glasses and looked steadfastly out across the course.

Campion remained where he was for a few seconds and for a while appeared to watch the race, but he did not stay to see the finish. At the very moment when the horses passed the post he was forcing his way out through the excited throng, and two minutes later climbed into a solid-looking black car containing five expressionless men, all of whom appeared to favour the same particular type of nondescript raincoat.

'Over there, on the brown hill,' he said briefly to the man at the wheel. 'A modern white villa with a flat roof. Take the London road and branch off by a church with a spire.'

*

The short fat man with the American accent, who was known to the Federal Police as Louis Greener, was still standing on the flat roof of the white villa, his glasses trained on the racecourse which lay, a patterned ribbon of colour, in the valley below him, when one police car, followed by another, swung quietly up the steep drive and debouched its swarming cargo before it reached a standstill.

Mr Greener was engrossed in his vigil and was not disturbed from it until a shout from the room below him, followed by a volley of revolver shots, brought him back to present emergencies with a rush. He dropped his glasses and fled to the stairhead just as a lean figure appeared through the hatchway, an automatic in its hand.

'I should come very quietly if I were you,' said Campion.

Twenty minutes later the villa was calm and peaceful again, and the drive was empty. Fingers Hawkins drove up in a small car, a tremendous smile on his unbeautiful face, and a suspicious bulkiness about his coat pockets. He was not alone. Two men accompanied him, each betraying a certain careful solicitude for his safety which could hardly be accounted for by mere affection. Fingers was jaunty. He sounded the horn two or three times.

'You come be'ind me,' he said to his bodyguard. 'I deserve a committee of welcome for this lot. Now let's see how his American Nibs treats a bloke who's done 'alf his work for him.'

He strolled up to the front door and kicked it open.

'Anyone at 'ome?' he shouted as he passed into the hall. 'No 'anging about, if you please. Oi! Shop!'

His companions followed him, and as soon as they came into the hall the door closed quietly behind them. The little click which the latch made as it shot home brought them all round, the hair bristling on their necks. There was a moment of uncomfortable silence and the police closed in on them.

Meanwhile, in a private sitting-room at the White Hart, Fran Lobbet sat in an arm-chair clasping a grubby little bundle, while tears of pure relief streamed down her face. From the other side of the room Lance Feering beamed at her.

'She's all right,' he said. 'I believe she enjoyed it.'

'No, I didn't.' Janey Lobbet's bright eyes peered at him from a tangle of hair. 'Sometimes I was frightened. After Nurse left me I was frightened.'

'But you're not frightened now, are you, darling?' Fran put the question anxiously and the child chuckled.

'No,' she said. 'Not now. I'm *tough*.'

They laughed and Fran smiled at the man.

'I'll never be able to thank you.'

'Don't thank me. Campion worked the oracle.' Feering nodded towards the fourth occupant of the room, who sat on the edge of a table, an expression of mild satisfaction on his thin face. 'I don't see now how you spotted the house. What was it? Second sight?'

'In a way, yes. I did it with my little binoculars,' said

Campion modestly. 'Fingers takes full credit for the rest. As soon as I saw his little weasel snout quivering pinkly through the undergrowth I thought, "Hullo, my lad, you're not handling two thousand pounds of anybody's money without a pretty close watch being kept on you, I'll bet." I saw he had two attendants in the background, but neither of them looked exactly like the foreman of the sort of outfit we had been led to expect. I was completely in the dark until I noticed Fingers signal to someone apparently in the middle of the course. Then he put his glasses up and I saw he wasn't watching the race. Since he was taking a longer view, naturally I did the same myself and caught sight of a person whom I now know to be a most unpleasant bird called Louis Greener, standing on a flat roof and waving his arms about in reply.

'That was really quite enough in the circumstances. The police were waiting, as they had promised, so off we went and there was the gang and there was Janey. She and I came away and we left the boys waiting for Fingers and the loot. There should be a happy family party down at the police station by this time.'

His voice died away. Neither Fran nor Lance was listening to him. He watched them for some seconds, but they appeared to be having a satisfactory, if wordless, conversation of their own, so presently he wandered off to find the Inspector in charge of the raid. That good-tempered man was comforting.

'Fingers has been talking about you, sir,' he said cheerfully as Campion appeared. 'I've had it all took down. I'm thinking you might like a copy. Coming from him it's a regular testimonial. If it wasn't so highly coloured that some might think it vulgar, you could almost have it framed.'

IX

Safe as Houses

MR ALBERT CAMPION came gingerly down the steep staircase of the White Lion Inn at Little Chittering in Sussex with two important queries occupying his mind. One was the comparatively simple question, where was the bar, and the other a more philosophical matter concerning the Blood Tie, or how much need the average man endure for his relations before he is entitled to sneak quietly home to London and go to earth in his club?

He had just set foot upon the uneven floor of the narrow passage and had caught a welcome glimpse of a promising oak-and-pewter interior a step or so ahead, when there was a rustle at the top of the stairs behind him and a muffled voice inquired pathetically:

'Any luck with her, my boy?'

The thin man with the horn-rimmed spectacles swung round guiltily and glanced up. At the top of the staircase stood a sad and somewhat fantastic figure. He was a small man approaching sixty, who wore at the moment a long tweed coat which descended almost to his shoes, and an old school muffler which bound up his head so thoroughly that only a triangular patch of worried face and a tuft or two of bedraggled pepper-and-salt moustache showed among its brightly-coloured folds. One eye, too, was visible, a watery, red-rimmed affair with a depressed glaze. Mr Campion felt a twinge of pity for him and resented the emotion. Things were bad enough without adding Second Cousin Monmouth's troubles to them.

'I did have a word or two with Great Aunt Charlotte,' he admitted cautiously, 'but I'm afraid she still clings to the idea that this is the place to operate from.'

The unhappy figure at the top of the stairs groaned.

'It's this infernal head of mine, you know,' he complained

wretchedly, 'as I made it quite clear to everybody at the time. I knew the drive down here in that draughty old car of Mother's would give me neuralgia, and so it has. I've been lying on my bed, and I don't mind telling you it's as hard as a board and probably damp. Still, you can't expect any sympathy for that. That's Mother all over. If she'd made up her mind to stay in a mission hut at the South Pole there we'd all remain if I'd got pneumonia and you were crippled with rheumatism.'

'Well, come down into the bar,' said Campion, softening, against his better judgement, for Second Cousin Monmouth was not a beautiful personality with whom to drink. 'It must open eventually. All these things happen in time.'

'That's an idea.' The old man brightened visibly through the swathing folds of his scarf, but he changed his mind again almost immediately. 'Better not,' he said regretfully. 'This head of mine is playing me up, don't you know. Besides, if Mother gets it into her mind that I've been drinking there'll be the devil to pay. I don't suppose she'll keep such a tight rein on you, my boy, but I should certainly look out. She's a very determined woman.'

He spoke wistfully and shuffled back towards his room, leaving Campion ashamed for his Great Aunt.

'The whole thing is pure tommy rot, anyway. You realize that, don't you? That at least is obvious. I saw that before we left home.'

Second Cousin Monmouth put his head out of the door to fire the Parthian shot.

'It's probably some sort of joke,' he shouted. 'As I tell Mother, people do play jokes.'

'Not on me!' The retort, coming unexpectedly as it did from the door between them, silenced the older man, who disappeared like a shadow into his room, and stopped Campion in his tracks.

Lady Charlotte Lawn came out on to the little landing and caught him before he could escape.

'Well, Albert,' she said briskly, 'have you made those inquiries?'

'Not yet, Aunt. I –'

'Good heavens, boy, don't talk to me from the bottom of the stairs as if I were a builder's labourer on a ladder. Come up here at once.'

Campion pocketed most of his thirty-eight years and went up meekly. He offered the old lady his arm and conducted her back to the sitting-room which she had just commandeered from a reluctant management.

As usual, he found her terrifying. She was small and wiry, with a sharp nose and eyes like a bird's. He knew for a fact that she must be almost eighty, although there was no indication from her manner or appearance that she was within twenty years of that age.

'I've sent Dorothy down to the kitchen,' she said briskly. 'We shall have to eat here and probably spend the night, and I do like to know that my food is prepared in clean cooking utensils. I've told her to look at everything.'

'That should make us all very popular,' murmured Campion affably.

'Not at all.' Great Aunt Charlotte picked him up immediately. 'Dorothy has been in my service for over forty years and during that time she has acquired some of my tact. We very seldom give offence. Now then, how far have you got on? Have you discovered the house?'

'No, I'm afraid I haven't. Not yet. As a matter of fact I had hardly got downstairs from talking to you before.'

'That comes of gossiping with poor Monmouth,' said the old lady frankly. 'You young men will waste time. I've noticed it over and over again. From the moment you open your eyes in the morning to the instant you close them at night you dawdle and idle through life like children unless someone comes running behind you the whole time. Of course with poor Monmouth laziness is a disease. You've only got to think of his attitude towards this extraordinary business to see that. He thinks it may be a joke. He'd rather be burnt in his bed than stir himself for an instant.'

'Burnt in his bed?' said Campion, taken off his guard.

'Well, why not?' Great Aunt Charlotte's stare did not

flicker. 'A serious burglary may easily lead to a fire. It doesn't take much imagination to see that. They tell me you're very good at finding out things, but upon my word I can't say I'm very impressed by your performance so far. You arrived at my house at ten o'clock last night but only after I had sent you five telegrams in succession. I've spent most of the night explaining the extraordinary thing that has happened, and then, early this morning, we motored a hundred and forty miles over here and what have you found out? Precisely nothing.'

Campion felt himself wince.

'I've been thinking, though,' he said sternly, 'and quite frankly, Aunt, if I didn't know you I should certainly begin to wonder what you were playing at.'

'Perhaps you would care to explain just exactly what you mean by that?'

Campion was not intimidated. It had been a long and tiring morning and his patience was not inexhaustible.

'Nothing was stolen, you see,' he said. 'That's always fishy. I am making no vulgar accusations at the moment, but believe me the police always look with deep distrust at the householder whose premises are burgled but not robbed.'

Great Aunt Charlotte smiled.

'Naturally,' she said placidly. 'That was why I didn't send for the police. That was why I sent for you. Now would you like me to go all over it again?'

'No,' said Campion hastily. 'No, darling, I think I've got it all as clear as it'll ever be. Let me see, you returned yesterday after being away for a fortnight – '

'Yes. At Tunbridge Wells. Dorothy has been with me, and Monmouth spent the last week there, coming on from his sister's place in Bedfordshire.'

Once Great Aunt Charlotte was started there was no stopping her. As in certain old musical boxes her tunes always had to be heard to the end.

'I let my other two maids, Phyllis and Betty, go home on board wages,' she said. 'We locked the house, and the gardeners, of course, are not in the grounds after five at night.'

Campion nodded. 'It's an old house,' he said thoughtfully 'Very easy to burgle.'

'Waverley is a remarkable house,' said the old lady. 'Some of the beams in it must be nearly six hundred years old. That was one of the reasons why I bought it. I remember Monmouth was almost excited by it when we first discovered it over twelve years ago. Still, it's no use talking about its age. That's not the point. The fact remains that as soon as I went into the drawing-room last night I knew at once that it had been used while I was away.'

She paused, as she always did at this part of her story, for dramatic effect, but Campion was no longer the perfect audience.

'That's all very well, darling,' he said, 'but you know it is possible to imagine a thing like that very easily.'

'Not about my drawing-room.' The old lady was decided. 'You see, no one is allowed in it but me. Even Dorothy never dares to clean it unless I'm there. I keep my Spode there and my father's decorations. It's a most sacred room. Of course I could tell if it had been used.'

'You're sure it had?'

'Absolutely certain.' Lady Charlotte Lawn shut her mouth as if it had possessed a zip-fastener, and a brief silence ensued. 'There was the mark of a glass on my walnut lowboy,' she said at last, her voice dropping at the enormity of the crime. 'An odious white ring; I saw it at once. Then there was the cigarette ash in the coal scuttle and of course the notepaper – surely you're not going to ignore the notepaper?'

Campion hesitated. Yes, of course, she was right. There was the notepaper. The notepaper was the mystery, and even now, at high noon, with an exasperating morning behind him and an impossible evening ahead, he was forced to admit that the notepaper and its unexplained presence in Great Aunt Charlotte's walnut escritoire was still mysterious.

He took out his pocket-book and extracted from it the half-dozen sheets of pale blue bond which he had carried away from the Waverley drawing-room. He looked again at the embossed address which had brought Aunt Charlotte herself steaming out of Kent into Sussex with her son and her grand-nephew in tow. There it was, clear and bald and ugly in semi-Old English script.

> *Grey Peacocks*
> *Little Chittering*
> *near Horsham*
> *Sussex.*

'Burglary or not,' said Great Aunt Charlotte, 'someone sat down at my writing-desk and wrote a note there on his or her own notepaper. I want to meet the person who did that. Here we all are at the place. It should be very simple for you to find the house.'

The thin man glanced across the room at her and his wide mouth twisted helplessly as he laughed.

'Well, the Post Office hasn't heard of such a house,' he said regretfully. 'The postmistress says she's been here fifteen years and has never heard of any Peacock, let alone a grey one.'

'Then we've come to the wrong village.'

'Well, I thought that myself at first, naturally, but I'm afraid we've drawn a blank there too. There is only one Little Chittering in Sussex and this is it.' He hesitated. 'You see, Aunt,' he went on at last, 'I do hope you'll forgive me for saying so, but the entire thing is absolutely nuts. The more I think of it the more inclined I am to agree with Monmouth, that it's some sort of misguided effort at the humorous. Don't stationers sometimes send round samples of notepaper stamped with fictitious addresses?'

'They may, young man, but not by the half-dozen quires.' Aunt Charlotte was not troubling to conceal her contempt. 'That notepaper was put in my writing-table by someone who intended to write letters there. I've got the evidence of my own eyes. If this village is Little Chittering, Sussex, then you can depend upon it that a house called Grey Peacocks is somewhere near at hand. Go and find it.

And when you have done so come back in the car and drive
me over to make a call on the owners, for I have something
to say to them. I know exactly what I want to do, and I do
not intend to leave this place until I have done it.'

She dismissed him with a bright little nod and he went
downstairs again, irritated by a problem which he felt must
obviously have some very simple explanation but which
was as yet entirely beyond him.

He found the bar open at last, and stood leaning on the
scored oak, looking into his glass with a gloomy and introspective eye. It did not make sense. The picture of any sane
criminal breaking into an unoccupied house for the sole
purpose of leaving a stack of falsely stamped notepaper in
the drawing-room writing-table did not appeal to him as in
any way convincing.

The landlord of the Lion was sympathetic, but neither he
nor his wife was helpful. They had only been in the place
fifteen years, they said apologetically, but in all their time
there had been no house called Grey Peacocks in Little Chittering or in any other village nearby.

Regretfully Campion gave it up. He was just formulating
an elaborate plan to get Aunt Charlotte temporarily interested in something else while he made a dignified escape
back to town when something happened.

First there was the sound of a car braking sharply on the
dusty road outside, and then one of the prettiest girls he had
ever seen in a long and by no means misspent youth put her
head round the door of the bar and said distinctly:

'Excuse me, but could anyone direct me to Grey Peacocks?'

Instantly there was one of those long silences which in-
evitably follow a direct question delivered to a room full of
acquaintances. Campion felt his scalp rising, and he shot a
suspicious glance at his glass before looking at the girl again.
She was still there, however, and, meeting his eye, repeated
the house name obligingly.

'Grey Peacocks.'

No one answered her immediately. There was a general

exchange of blank glances and several breathy denials, and then somebody cackled behind the window curtain.

The entire company appeared to resent this insult to so attractive a stranger, and a red-faced old man in a dilapidated bowler and collarless pink shirt was hustled out of his shelter there without ceremony.

'Come on, come on, Mr Richart.' The landlord was gently reproving. 'Say what you've got to say. Do you know where the house is?'

Mr Richart began to laugh again. He had a face like something seen among the embers of a dying wood fire. A fluffy ash-grey beard and moustache flowed from his flaming cheeks.

'Don't act silly,' said a dour man beside him. 'Tell the lady if you know, and if you don't, stop making a fool of yourself.'

Mr Richart's grin died in anger, and he turned on the girl and directed her in a high-pitched sing-song which sounded frankly vindictive.

'Half a mile down the road you come to a pair o' white gates. Don't goo in they but keep straight on till you come to a mill. Branch off by the side o' that, goo through the woods, and you'll come to some owd stone pillars. Goo between they and very likely you'll come to Grey Peacocks. That's where that stood when I were last in they gates.'

'Oh, thank you so much. I'm so sorry to have troubled you.' The girl flashed a set of glistening teeth at him and was gone, leaving a general sense of gratified chivalry behind her.

Old Mr Richart scrambled into the window again.

'Piled high wi' luggage,' he gloated deliriously. 'A great Lunnon car piled high wi' luggage.' The sight seemed to be too much for him altogether, for he lay back on the settle and laughed until he choked and had to be thumped on the back.

'Seems to have been took funny,' remarked the landlord to Campion as he let himself out from behind the bar. 'Wasn't that the house you wanted, sir? Here, Mr Richart, you don't want to carry on like that. You'll give yourself veins. Come and talk to the gentleman. He's looking for that house you was telling the lady about.'

This last intelligence proved too much for Mr Richart altogether. He lay panting against the bar with streaming eyes and a mouth like the mask of comedy, emitting faint high-pitched crows of laughter. However, he recovered himself when the landlord got angry, and finally agreed to drive down to the address with Campion to show him the way.

He turned out to be a very silent passenger who was either deaf or contemptuous towards his host's efforts at conversation. He sat bolt upright in the front of the car, his face glowing and imperturbable, yet every now and again his whole body shook with some deep inward convulsion.

Campion drove quietly, hoping to see the joke.

They passed the white gates and turned by the mill, found the wood and drove for some time through a tunnel of trees until, at a croak from his companion, Campion pulled up before a dark gap in the greenery where two ancient stone posts could just be seen among the tall grasses.

'Here?' inquired Campion dubiously.

'Ah,' said Mr Richart, his voice shaking with suppressed excitement. 'This is Grey Peacocks. Scratch away the moss on they stones and you'll see the pictures of the birds theirselves. Goo on, turn into drive.'

Campion was edging the car slowly round the gatepost when the other car met him as it swooped out and they pulled up with a flurry of brakes, and the bonnets not two inches apart. Peering through his own windscreen, Campion saw a yellow-haired fury backed by a pile of luggage which rose in tiers behind her. She was white with indignation, and her large dark eyes were smouldering wickedly. She backed her overladen car with spiteful deliberation and came slowly alongside until she was level with Campion.

'I suppose you think you're terribly funny?' she said savagely, clipping the words so that they came out packed with venom. 'Let me tell you I think you're frankly disgusting and I hope you fall in and k-k-kill yourselves.'

The final quiver in her voice betrayed her, and at Campion's side Mr Richart let out a whoop of triumph. The girl flushed, included them both in a single glance of withering hatred, and then, letting in the clutch, swung round Campion's car at suicidal speed and disappeared back down the tree tunnel in a shower of dust and small stones.

Campion glanced after her with genuine regret. He didn't know when he had made such a bad impression on a woman at first bow. He turned to Mr Richart.

'What's the joke?' he demanded.

The old man roused himself with an effort from dazed delight and glowed at the prospect of further delectation.

'Drive on,' he commanded. 'Drive on.'

Campion steered his big car down a narrow overgrown chase where briars and laurels almost met across the mossy gravel. It was so overgrown that the midday light was pale green and uncertain. With Mr Richart palpitating at his side a sense of deep misgiving seized Campion.

'Don't you think you'd better explain?' he said ominously.

'No,' gasped his passenger, writhing with anticipation. 'Drive on.'

Campion did not reply. The chase turned abruptly, and he was some seconds negotiating a fallen branch which lay in his path. An instant later he trod sharply on the brakes and brought the great car up on her haunches.

Before them, lying at the end of the drive, in the place where a house might ordinarily be expected to stand, was a large rectangular hole, partly full of water and depressingly overgrown.

Campion looked coldly at Mr Richart, who, now that the cream of the jest was presented to him at last, had scarcely any stomach left for it, but who sat forward, his eyes glazed, a slightly sick expression overlaying his joy.

'Is this Grey Peacocks?' inquired Campion.

'This is where it were,' said Mr Richart. 'Noo it's gorn.'

'So I see. When did that happen?'

'When I were a youngish man. He sold that, the old owner did, to some American, and they pulled it down.

'Twere nothing but an old ruin when they bought it. That's twenty-five years ago, I should think.'

'Twenty-five years.' Campion repeated the words as if they constituted a barrier between himself and sanity. 'Was it called Grey Peacocks then?'

'No. That were called Playle's Farm, after the man 'oo farmed the land. But I remember years before that there was an old man pointed out the carving of the birds on the gatepost and he told me that one time the whole house was called Grey Peacocks. Then it were pulled down. That's what made me laugh outright when you and the lady came asking for it. You both wanted that and that was pulled down, see?'

'Very funny,' agreed Campion acidly. 'Perhaps you would like to laugh all the way home?'

To do Mr Richart justice he did not care. With five shillings of a foreigner's money in his pocket a walk of four miles or so was a pleasure. Campion left him swinging down the chase as happy as only a man with a sense of humour can be.

Campion in his fast car came up with the girl at the point where the road forked in the outskirts of the wood. The car was parked on the grass verge and the girl was sitting at the wheel apparently reading a book. Campion told himself that he was in credulous mood and that there was nothing at all extraordinary about the sight of a beautiful young woman, clearly in tears, reading a novel at the wheel of a car which contained the best part of her worldly goods, including bedding. He drew up, waiting for the storm.

It did not come. Instead he received a blow so unfair that it took all the wind out of his sails and left him gasping. She looked over at him, blinked away the worst of the rainstorm, and sniffed pathetically.

'Oh, don't tease me any more,' she said. 'I'm so tired and there's such a lot to do before they come. Where is the wretched place, for the love of Mike?'

Campion told his story, or part of it, with convincing exasperation.

'Our mutual friend, Mr Richart – that's the man with a

laugh – seems to be the only soul on earth who has even heard of it,' he finished plaintively, 'and he says that the house was pulled down some twenty-five years ago by some Americans who bought it as a ruin.'

'Oh, well, he's wrong about that, anyway,' said the girl casually, using her driving licence to mark the place in the book she had been reading. 'I do know that. I was there ten days ago.'

'What?'

She smiled at him. 'That's what makes the whole thing so infuriating,' she said confidingly. 'Mother and I came down to see the house on Friday night. It was a dark journey, of course, but we saw all over it, and then he brought us back again.'

'Who did?'

'Mr Grey. He brought us down from London. He owns the house.'

'Are you talking about Grey Peacocks?' Campion heard his own voice weakening.

'Well, naturally.' The girl clearly found him singularly unintelligent. 'That's the annoying thing. I've got the address, and I've even been to the place before, and yet I can't find it. Roads do look different at night, I know, and we came in a big closed car of Grey's, but still I was so certain I could manage that I told Mother I'd get the place ready on my own. I've got the servants coming down by train to-morrow. I expect there's a lot of work to be done because it must be in spotless order by the time Mother brings the others next week.'

'What others?' demanded Campion, giving up finesse.

'The Americans we've taken it for, of course,' said the girl. 'You don't think we could pay all that for a holiday house for ourselves, do you?'

The ground beneath Campion's feet reeled, shivered, and afterwards became rather horribly firm. He climbed out of the car and went towards her.

'I say,' he said, 'I don't want to be depressing, but I do hope you haven't parted with any cash yet?'

Her dark eyes, which were round and candid and discon-
certingly young, met his own, a slightly startled expression
in their depths.

'We paid Mr Grey a deposit,' she said. 'Half the amount.
Six weeks at seventeen guineas a week. Look here, I hope
there's nothing wrong, because it's their money, you see.
The Americans', I mean. Mother and I are frightfully hard
up. We could never afford –' She broke off, laughing. 'This
is absurd,' she said. 'You frightened me for a moment. Who
are you, anyway? Go away if you can't be helpful. It's
ridiculous, though, because – well – it's a famous house
isn't it? That's why we didn't have references and nor
did the agent. Look, it's all in here, address and everything.
I've been trying to work out the route, but it doesn't
give it.'

She handed him the book she had been reading and it fell
open where she had marked it. Campion took the volume
with interest. It was an oldish publication, printed about
1870, and was entitled, with engaging naïveté, 'Resting-
places in the Garden of England'. The make-up was simple.
Each chapter, of which there were several dozen, dealt with
a different country house, giving its features of interest,
something of its history, and a pen-and-ink drawing of some
part of its structure. Grey Peacocks, Little Chittering, near
Horsham, Sussex, had a long chapter to itself.

Campion stood looking at a somewhat over-careful sketch
of the panelled entrance-hall for some time.

'You say you went here last Friday night, Miss – ah – ?'

'Murphy,' supplied the girl cheerfully. 'Ann Murphy.
Yes, I did. Mother and I both went. Not last Friday, the
Friday before. As soon as the agent showed us this book we
both knew it would be just exactly what these Americans
would love, and so we phoned up the Cosmopolitan, where
Mr Grey was staying, and he asked us to go along to see
him. We had a chat with him and then he took us down to
see the house and very kindly lent us the book. It's a lovely
place. You see that little hound-gate at the foot of the
stairs? Well, it's still there. And that door leads into the

sweetest drawing-room.' She paused and sighed. 'It's ideal,' she said. 'Of course it is. And yet I'm rather sorry we took it.'

'Are you? Why?' Campion's interest was almost over-anxious.

The girl shrugged her shoulders. 'Oh, it's nothing. It's very silly of me to think of it at all. But Mother heard from an old school friend this morning saying that she'd like to let her place. It's a pity in a way, because it's really quite as antique, and it would be cheaper, which would have suited us, because Mother and I are doing the whole thing for a fixed sum, you see. Mother knew the American man years ago, and now he's a widower left with two grown-up sons who've come over for the shooting. Naturally she wants to impress them all and make them comfortable. I mean we don't want to look like a couple of unbusiness-like fools, do we? I really don't know why I'm telling you all this, but it is rather unnerving, isn't it, losing the house like this?'

Campion took another look at the sketch at the beginning of the chapter on Grey Peacocks before he returned the book to the girl, and there was a grim expression in his pale eyes.

'Tell me, did you pay this deposit to Mr Grey direct?' he inquired.

'Yes, yes, we did,' she said. 'He was going abroad, you see, and he pointed out that it would save everybody trouble if we did the little transaction, as he called it, there and then and let him see to the agent afterwards. He didn't bother about our references and we didn't ask for any from him because we could see the house. Hang it all, we were in it. So Mother gave him a cheque and he gave us a receipt on his notepaper stamped with the Grey Peacocks address. It seemed all right.'

Campion, who had become very thoughtful during the last ten minutes or so, held out his hand.

'Good-bye, Miss Murphy,' he said abruptly. 'The very best of luck in your search. Look here, just if by chance you can't find the place, the thing to do is to go back to the agent, you know. He'll always be able to find Mr Grey for you.'

She shook his hand and looked, he thought, a trifle injured by his ungallant desertion, which was certainly sudden. However, mentally consigning her to the care of three
stalwart Americans, he did not even look back.

He climbed into the car and drove away without so much
as a glance or a farewell wave.

Second Cousin Monmouth greeted him without enthusiasm. He had discarded his scarf and was sitting up in his
room in the cold, a small tray of drinks on his dressing-table.

'How much longer have we got to stay in this infernal
hole, Campion?' he demanded before the other man was
safely in the room. 'I shall catch my death, you know. I can
feel that. I've told mother we should never have come.'

'I shouldn't worry,' said Campion briefly. 'You're leaving
now.'

'Really?' The little man bounced off his chair and
picked up his scarf. 'Home, I suppose?'

'No. You're going to London. By the way, I hope you've
got that money still or you'll stay away from home rather
longer than ever before.'

Second Cousin Monmouth stopped in his tracks like a
shot bear.

'Eh?' he said cautiously. 'What money?'

'Six weeks at seventeen guineas a week, Mr Grey.'

There was a long and embarrassing pause.

'Well?' said Cousin Monmouth at last with an almost
creditable attempt at bluster. 'Well, my boy, what do you
know about that little peccadillo, eh?'

Campion's smile was not condoning.

'I know you let Aunt Charlotte's house, Waverly, to a
poor wretched mother and daughter, falsely representing to
them that it was an ancient structure called Grey Peacocks.
You drove them out to Kent, and in the dark they thought
they were coming to Sussex.'

'Not at all.' The little fat man shook his head. 'Get the
story right if you must be so blessed clever,' he said. 'Stick
to the facts. There was no false representation about it.
Waverly *is* Grey Peacocks. I've known that for years. Some

Americans bought it in 1914. They took it down brick by brick and beam by beam and packed it in numbered cases with the idea of putting it up again on the other side. There's nothing new in that. They're always doing it. However, in this case the War came and prevented transport, and after the War the original owner had died and his executors sold the thing cheap to a builder who put it up where it stands to-day. He thought Grey Peacocks was a silly name for a house and called it Waverly. I knew the place had been moved at some time, and the other day I was browsing among some old books in a friend's library and I recognized a sketch of our front hall in an article on the house.'

'So you pinched the book and launched out on to this jolly little swindle the moment Aunt was out of the house for a bit,' put in Campion. 'You stayed at the Cosmopolitan, saw the agent, hired a car and worked the whole thing while you were supposed to be staying with your sister, I take it?'

Second Cousin Monmouth rose to his feet.

'I may have borrowed the book,' he said with dignity. 'I admit that. But I resent the term "swindle". I tell you, Campion, I resent that bitterly.'

'Resent away,' said his cousin cheerfully. 'Get your coat on and find your cheque-book. We're going to the agent's.'

'To the agent's?' The old man was scandalized. 'Whatever for? That's the last place I should have thought of going.'

'We must pay the deposit back.' Campion spoke earnestly. 'Don't be a fool. It's that or jug or worse when Aunt Charlotte finds out.'

Cousin Monmouth spun round, his small eyes popping.

'Good lord, has Mother seen those people?' The little man hunched his shoulders and thrust his hands deep into his pockets. 'There'll be trouble when she does. I hadn't thought of that,' he said briefly and sat down on the edge of the table.

Campion was not the type to lecture anybody, much less a man nearly old enough to be his father, but he felt it behove him to say a few words on the unseemliness of robbing the widow and the orphan. Second Cousin Monmouth heard him out in owlish silence, and when it was over he rose to his feet.

'All right,' he said earnestly. 'All right. I'll pay up. I shouldn't have done it. I see that now. I've seen the light, my boy. The picture you've drawn of those two poor little women has made me regret my own hastiness. I've felt a fool all day sitting about with my face covered up, afraid lest one of them should come in. A fool and a knave, Campion, that's what I've been. It was a rotten trick. I am bitterly ashamed of myself. I ought not to have behaved like such an outsider.'

He paused in his flow of self-reproach, and Campion, who was entirely unprepared for the performance, eased his own collar uncomfortably.

Second Cousin Monmouth remained in contrite silence all through the drive to London until they actually neared the city. Then he shook his head.

'Every great criminal makes a fatal slip, Campion,' he said solemnly. 'Do you know what has been weighing on my conscience all this time? It's a very serious and upsetting thought. If I hadn't been such a fool as to forget I'd left that stamped notepaper in Mother's bureau, damn me, I'd have got clean away with it.'

X

The Definite Article

'My dear man,' said Old Lady Laradine, her remarkable voice penetrating the roar of the Bond Street traffic with easy mastery, 'don't think you're going to get away from me once I've settled down to a gossip. Come back here at once. Dorothea has got her girl safely engaged to Lord Pettering, I see. You know him, don't you? Tell me, do you approve?'

Mr Albert Campion bent his lean back once more and peered again into the tonneau of the elderly Daimler, where the redoubtable old lady sat enthroned.

His pale, somewhat vacant face, at which so many criminals had laughed too soon, wore a patient but harassed expression as his fifth attempt to escape was again frustrated.

'Forgive me, but you're holding up the traffic rather seriously, you know,' he ventured mildly. 'There's a bus having apoplexy just behind you, and I see a traffic policeman gazing over here with unhealthy interest. Does it matter?'

The old lady swung round to peer out of the window above her head with an agility which was typical of her.

'Yes, I dislike the police,' she said briskly. 'They have a mania for motor-cars. Get in.'

Mr Campion drew back involuntarily.

'Oh no, really,' he murmured. 'I – I'm late for an appointment now. Delightful seeing you. Good-bye.'

The car door swinging suddenly open on top of him silenced his excuses. 'Where is this appointment?' The old voice was commanding.

'Scotland Yard,' said Campion with what he took to be a flash of inspiration. 'Terribly important.'

'Get in then, idiot,' shouted the old lady. 'Bullard!' she screamed to the chauffeur. 'Scotland Yard! – and drive as fast as you like. It's official business.'

A moment later Mr Campion, who had no desire to go to the headquarters of the Criminal Investigation Department anyway, found himself sitting meekly beside his kidnapper as the big car slid quietly out into Piccadilly.

Lady Laradine regarded him with the affectionate pride of an angler for a landed fish.

'There,' she said. 'Now tell me! your friend Lord Pettering is hysterically in love with Dorothea's girl Roberta, isn't he? How did he get that abominable uncle of his to agree to the match?'

Mr Campion blinked.

'Tommy Pettering?' he repeated with irritating stupidity. 'Has he an uncle?'

Lady Laradine made a menacing noise in her throat.

'Don't you dare to take that line with me, young man,' she said, prodding his knee with a finger which felt as though it had a thimble upon it. 'You know as well as I do that Pettering's mother is determined he shall have a career in the Foreign Office and that old Braithwaite, her brother, who is in the Cabinet, is only willing to arrange everything if he's allowed to keep the whole family under his thumb. Young Master Thomas has to get his uncle's permission before he sells a plater, much less gets himself engaged. How did the boy talk his uncle round? You must know.'

Mr Campion was aware of her small faded brown eyes watching him with a shrewdness which was unnerving, and he stuck resolutely to his usual policy, saying nothing that could possibly be taken down and used against him.

'I imagine the request was purely formal,' he murmured cautiously. 'I don't know Miss Roberta Pendleton-Blake. There's nothing against her, is there?'

'Against Roberta? Of course not!' the old woman snapped at him. 'Dorothea is one of my best friends. But the money in that family did come from frozen meat in the last generation and everybody thought that the old uncle, Braithwaite, would put his stupid feet down on that account. So he would have done, of course, if there'd been any breath of scandal. The F.O. is so pristine, isn't it? But I suppose the meat is something they can bring themselves to forget and forgive. Still, I believe it was touch and go. Tell me, do you like Roberta? She's my godchild, but you can say what you like.'

Mr Campion patiently repeated his previous announcement that he had not met the Pendleton-Blakes. Lady Laradine was shocked.

'Oh, my dear, you must,' she said. 'I'll see you're invited to the dance Dorothea is giving for the girl next week. Mind you come. They're charming, all absolutely charming, even the husband – but he's dead, of course. Dorothea is a sweet creature. So original. She uses all the ideas I give her

for her parties. I've told her she must have the Psychometrist at the next dance. That's something new to amuse
people. It's so interesting, I think, to have something to do,
besides watching the younger people dance. It gives one
something to talk about afterwards. You really must meet
Dorothea. Oh, how disappointing, here we are.'

Her flow of chatter died abruptly as the Daimler turned
on to the Embankment, and her passenger sprang out with
uncharacteristic haste. He did not get clean away, however.

'I'll wait for you,' said Lady Laradine, her hand on his
coat. 'I want to hear all the news.'

Mr Campion, who had considered crossing the road,
picking up a cab and driving peacefully back to Bond
Street, was aghast.

'That would be too kind,' he said with earnest conviction.
'I'm afraid I may be hours, literally. Thank you so very
much. Good-bye.'

'Good-bye then,' said her ladyship regretfully. 'I shall
look out for you at Dorothea's next week.'

Mr Campion smiled a trifle wanly and walked towards
the entrance. Since there was nothing for it but a visit to his
old friend Superintendent Oates, or undignified conceal-
ment behind a gate pillar until the Daimler should elect
to depart, he sighed and, waving to the inquisitive figure in
the back of the car, he gave his name to the man on the door
and sent up his card.

The superintendent embarrassed him considerably by
receiving him at once, having taken his unheralded arrival
as a sign of great urgency.

'What's up?' he demanded. 'I've never known you blow
in here without making an appointment. Something
serious?'

Inwardly Mr Campion cursed all strong-minded old
ladies, and after a while he mentioned the fact aloud.

Oates began to laugh. He was a thin grey man with light
intelligent eyes and a certain natural mournfulness of
expression.

'That's fine,' he said with relish. 'This is just the place

for a nice rest in the middle of the morning. Put your feet up. Don't mind me.'

Mr Campion took a silver case from his pocket and drew out a cigarette, which he laid upon the desk with quiet dignity. 'Get this analysed for me, old boy, will you?' he said earnestly.

The policeman's smile faded and he prodded the cylinder gently with a broad forefinger. 'Which is it?' he demanded. 'Drugs or explosives?'

'Heaven knows,' said his visitor seriously.

'Really? Where did you get it?' Oates was as alert as a terrier.

Mr Campion surveyed him affectionately. 'I bought it in an open shop right in your own district. Think that over.'

Oates sniffed at the cigarette suspiciously. 'Righto,' he said, 'I'll send it down. What are your grounds for doubting it?'

'Three extra in a packet and they taste like hell,' explained his visitor affably. 'They're a new brand, advertised all over the place.'

The superintendent regarded him coldly for a moment or two and finally lit the exhibit, which he puffed contentedly.

'All right,' he said ominously, 'all right, my lad. If you're looking for something to employ your time I'll see what I can do for you. Sit down. I've got something in your line. This'll just about suit you. Somebody wants a miracle. I thought of you when I got the inquiry.'

His guest looked suitably chastened and would have drifted towards the door, but Oates's ferocious good humour increased.

'Sit down,' he repeated, taking up a sheaf of official papers. 'Here's the dope. This is what comes of persuading foreigners to say "Your police are wonderful". They're beginning to take it literally, the lunatics. This is an inquiry from the U.S. The Federal Police are looking for a Society blackmailer who, so they say, always spends October in England. They can't give us any more than that on him. They simply say they'd be obliged if we apprehended him. Obliged isn't the word. They mean staggered.'

Seated on the hard visitor's chair, Mr Campion did his best to look intelligent, and his pale eyes were amused and friendly behind his horn-rimmed spectacles.

'He's male, is he?' he said. 'That's a step. I mean it reduces it from all the population of America to half the population of America, doesn't it?'

Oates turned over the blue sheets in his hand.

'Yes, they seem fairly certain of that,' he said without smiling. 'But you see what I mean when I say the description is slight. This is the story, as far as I can make it out. Late last year there was a fatal accident to the young wife of one of those fabulously wealthy financial men they breed over there. She fell off the roof of a skyscraper, and no one seemed to know why. There was no suggestion of foul play, but the question of suicide was raised. The husband, poor chap, was far too broken up at first to go into the thing thoroughly, but afterwards he seems to have pulled himself together and made several interesting discoveries.

'The first thing he noticed was that the girl died without a halfpenny in her private account, and that there were records of large, ever-increasing sums withdrawn from it to explain this.

'This money had been paid out from the bank in cash and naturally he began to think of blackmail.'

He paused and Campion nodded.

'The girl,' Oates continued, 'was very young, not at all the type to have a dangerous secret, and the whole notion seemed incredible to the husband until he cross-questioned the coloured maid who had come up from his wife's home with her on her marriage. From her he got an interesting story.

'It appeared that the young wife had kept some letters, a sentimental memento of a boy-and-girl love affair which had fizzled out before the older man put in an appearance. The maid thought that someone had got hold of these and convinced the wife that her husband would read a great deal more into them than ever they had originally contained. To prevent this eventuality the poor wretched child ruined herself financially, worked herself into a state of nervous collapse, and finally threw herself off the roof. You know how these things sometimes happen, Campion.'

The elegant personage in the horn-rimmed spectacles did not speak at once. It was an ugly little story, and one which he had heard too often in his career to doubt. Like the superintendent, he knew only too well that the clever blackmailer who picks the right type of victim seldom has to find anything that is really reprehensible on which to base his threats.

'Too bad,' he said seriously. 'Didn't they get any line on the chap?'

Stanislaus Oates made a few vulgar and not altogether relevant remarks which seemed to relieve his feelings.

'I told you,' he said finally. 'Why don't you listen? They haven't got a sausage, not a whiff, not a faint delicate aroma floating out from the window of a passing car. They don't know anything. And they have the calm impudence to write and say "We hear your Force is wonderful. How about sending this lad along in a plain van?"'

'Yes, I know.' Mr Campion spoke soothingly. 'But they must have something to go on. Otherwise why apply to you? Why not go to the Chinese or to the Nevada Sheriff?'

Oates grunted.

'They think they've got two clues,' he admitted. 'They concede that they're slight. I like that word of theirs, "concede". They're both based on something the dead girl said to the maid. The first one is a remark she made late in the summer of last year, when she first showed signs of worry. "It'll be all right in October," she said. "He goes to England in October." She wouldn't explain herself and seemed to regret the admission of trouble as soon as she had made it. That's the first.

'The second is just demented. Apparently, on the morning of the "accident", she was sitting up in bed and she said to the maid, who seems to have been a reliable witness, "It's no good, Dorothy, it's no good. It's written in ink. He saw it in ink." And then she went out on the roof.'

He paused and shrugged his shoulders.

'There you are,' he said. 'There's the lot, and I hope, it means more to you than it does to me. Written in ink, indeed! What was written in ink? And why was it more important than if it had been written in pencil? Or cross-stitch, for that matter?'

Mr Campion sat looking thoughtfully at the toes of his shoes for some moments.

'This girl who died,' he inquired at last, 'what sort of life did she lead? Was she likely to come into contact with shady characters?'

'No, that's the odd part about it.' Oates studied the blue sheaf again. 'She was one of New York's pampered babies. Looked after as if she was royalty or something. She never went out unescorted and never visited anywhere but in the most exclusive circles. Whoever got hold of her must have had peculiar facilities for getting into the best houses. I think the whole story is scatty. I shall write and tell 'em so, in a nice way, of course, when you've broken a tooth or two on the problem.'

'Me?' Mr Campion seemed startled, and the superintendent was amused.

'I'll tell 'em I've put a Society expert on the job,' he said, grinning. 'That'll please 'em and keep 'em quiet for a bit. There you are. You came in here looking for something to do and now you've got it. There's a little miracle for you. Pull that off. Written in ink my foot!'

'In ink?' repeated Mr Campion with sudden interest as a chance remark he had heard earlier that morning returned to him with sudden significance. 'I wonder . . .'

Oates regarded him sympathetically.

'You're getting swell-headed,' he said kindly. 'It often happens to amateurs. You're beginning to think you're gifted with supernatural powers. This'll do you good. It's impossible. If you had all the luck in the world it'd still be impossible.'

Mr Campion collected his hat and gloves and wandered to the door.

'I'll let you know if I spot him,' he said.

'Do,' said Oates cheerfully. 'And send me a wreath at the same time. I'll need it.'

His visitor looked pained. 'Do I get a reward if I bring him in?' he inquired.

'You get an illuminated address of five thousand words, written in my own hand and coloured,' said the superintendent heartily.

Mr Campion seemed both pleased and surprised.

'I shall like that,' he said.

*

He went quietly out of the building, and that evening did what was in the circumstances a very extraordinary thing. After certain elementary researches he wrote a careful and slightly effusive note to old Lady Laradine and begged her not to forget her promise to get him an invitation to the dance in honour of Miss Roberta Pendleton-Blake.

He paid for this fit of apparent lunacy a few days later when he sat beside that paralysing old lady in the corner of a ballroom which was not so much decorated as obliterated with heavily scented flowers and watched a vast throng of young people moving in mass formation on a glistening floor.

Lady Laradine was at the top of her form. She had spent the earlier part of the evening in a black velvet tent in an ante-room of the big Clarges Street house consulting the latest Society entertainer, and was bursting with her experiences.

'My dear,' she was saying happily, 'my dear, the creature is too astonishing. Dorothea was *inspired* to engage him. I told her she would be. Look at Roberta and young Pettering dancing together over there ... aren't they charming? I'm so glad the uncle was reasonable. Dorothea tells me she cried with relief when she heard that the wretched man had consented. Dear me, let me see, where was I?'

Mr Campion had not the faintest idea and was on the verge of forgetting himself sufficiently to say so when she recollected unassisted.

'Of course,' she said, 'the fortune-teller. Quite an astounding person. A psychometrist. Fortunately I'm never indiscreet, but really some of the things he told me about people I know . . .'

Her resonant voice rose and fell, and it occurred to her patient audience that she must have told the seer quite as much as ever he told her. Her flow of chatter was quite remarkable.

'He took my ring and put it in an envelope,' she hurried on. 'I put the envelope under the crystal and then he looked in and told me the most astonishing things about my mother. Wasn't that amazing?'

'A ring?' inquired Mr Campion, pricking up his ears.

The old lady looked at him as if she thought he were deficient.

'I don't believe you've been listening,' she said unjustly. 'I've been explaining to you for the last half hour that Cagliostro is amazing. You give him something that belonged to someone dead, or elsewhere anyway, and he tells you all about them.'

'Cagliostro?' repeated Mr Campion, temporarily out of his depth.

Lady Laradine threw up her small yellow hands in exasperation.

'Bless the man, he's delirious!' she said. 'Cagliostro the Second is the fortune-teller, animal. The psychometrist. The man I've been telling you about. He's in a black velvet tent somewhere in the house. Go and see him yourself. I can't be bothered with you if you don't use your mind at all. All you young men ought to take up Yoga. It clears the brain. Come and see me and I'll put you on to a very good man.'

Mr Campion rose. His ears were singing, but his eyes were alert and interested. 'I'll go and find him at once,' he said. 'I like fortune-tellers.'

The suddenness of his dash for freedom routed the old lady, and he was half-way down the room and out of earshot before she collected sufficient breath to call him back.

Mr Campion went off on his quest with that hidden, almost absent-minded, purposefulness which was his most misleading characteristic. He paused in the doorway to exchange a word with Tommy Pettering and be presented to the entirely delightful Roberta, chatted carelessly with two or three acquaintances, put himself in the good graces of his hostess with a few intelligent compliments, and wandered out into the main body of the house practically by accident.

It took him some time to find the psychometrist and his velvet tent, indeed he became definitely lost in the house at one period before that and came to a full stop in a dark corridor on the floor below the ballroom.

He was standing on the threshold of a small room furnished as a woman's study. The place was dimly lighted and the slender walnut furniture made graceful shadows on the silk-panelled walls. But it was not at these that the tall man with the diffident manner remained to stare with speculative interest.

Kneeling before a bureau on the other side of the room was a girl in a green chiffon dress. The first thing Campion noticed about her was her extreme youth, and the second the astonishing fact that she was forcing the catch of a drawer with a brass paper-knife.

He then saw that her hair was curled on the top of a small and shapely head and that her green dress floated about a slender, childish figure.

As he watched her she slid the drawer open an inch or so and inserted a little inquiring hand.

Mr Campion, deeming that the moment had come, coughed apologetically.

The girl in the green dress stiffened and there was a moment of painful silence. Campion had some experience of the hardened criminal and he thought he had never witnessed such an exhibition of calm nerve. Before she even looked round she opened the drawer a little further and, with a nonchalance that had guilt stamped all over it, drew out a small flat packet which she wrapped in her georgette handkerchief. Then she turned and rose quietly to her feet.

Mr Campion found himself looking into a small, intelligent face which would blossom into radiant beauty in a year or so. At the moment he judged her to be seventeen at most. She was very red and her grey-green eyes were angry and alarmed, but her dignity was tremendous.

Her remark was as bald as it was unexpected, and it had a strong element of truth in it which silenced him altogether.

'It's nothing to do with you,' she said and darted past him before he could stop her, leaving him staring in blank astonishment at her tiny whirlwind figure disappearing into the darkness of the passage.

Mr Campion pulled himself together and went quietly up to the ballroom. He was mildly startled. Young ladies who open bureau drawers with paper-knives and run off with mysterious packages wrapped in green georgette handkerchiefs constitute a responsibility which cannot be altogether ignored.

He had plenty of fish to fry of his own, however, for he had not braved an evening in the same house with Lady Laradine for nothing. He looked in at the ballroom again and reflected that every woman he had ever met at a dinner table seemed to be present with her daughter, but of the little girl in the green dress there was no trace at all.

Lady Laradine saw him from the other side of the room and bore down upon him like a very small ship in very full sail and he ducked into the first doorway to avoid her, thereby discovering the thing he had sought so unobtrusively for the past hour.

A black velvet tent hung with gilt fringe and topped by a directoire eagle rose up, dark and impressive, in the centre of the high-ceilinged Georgian room. He wandered over to it and raised the flap.

The scene within was much as he had expected, and the sight of it gave him a thrill of satisfaction. One point in particular interested him immensely. A strong overhead light shone down upon a small ebony table which supported a red satin hand-cushion and a black crystal ball.

The man who smiled at him over an unimpeachable

shirt-front was unusual. This Cagliostro was not the sleek huckster with the twinkle and the swagger which the credulous public has come to expect in its seers, but a surprisingly large man with thin fluffy hair and prominent cold light eyes. His smile was secretive and not at all pleasant. He did not speak, but indicated the consultant's chair very slowly with a sweeping movement of a great fin-like hand.

Mr Campion would have accepted the invitation but he was frustrated. Lady Laradine pounced upon him from behind.

'Oh, *there* you are,' she said irritably. 'Well, I hope you've been hearing something entertaining for it's more than I have. Has anybody *any* conversation at all these days? What did Cagliostro tell you?'

Mr Campion was explaining meekly that he had had as yet no time to consult the psychometrist when he caught sight over his captor's shoulders of a slender little figure in a green dress. There was quite a little crowd in the ante-room and she did not notice him, but made straight for the tent and passed inside.

'Really!' Lady Laradine, who had known by instinct the precise moment when his attention had wandered and had spun round herself, was now looking at him with impolite amusement.

'My dear boy, a *child?*' she burst out in her tremendous voice. 'Well, it's an extraordinary thing to me, but I've noticed it over and over again. You clever men are absolutely devastated by immaturity, aren't you? Still, seventeen . . . Dear boy, is it wise?'

'Do you know who she is?' Campion got the inquiry in edgeways.

'Who she is?' echoed the old lady, her eyes crinkling. 'My good man, you don't mean to say you haven't even met? But how touchingly romantic! I thought you young people managed things very differently these days. Still, this is charming. Tell me more. You just looked at each other, I suppose? Dear me, this takes me back to the nineties.'

Campion regarded her helplessly. She was like some elderly yellow kitten, he thought suddenly, all fluff and wide smile.

'Who is she?' he repeated doggedly.

'Why, the child, of course,' said Lady Laradine infuriatingly. 'Little What's-her-name. Jennifer, isn't it? To be presented next year when there won't be such a crush. You know perfectly well who I mean. Don't stand there looking like a fish. Roberta's sister, Dorothea's youngest daughter. So pretty. Like some sort of flower, don't you think?'

'A daughter?' said Campion flatly. 'She lives here, then?'

'Of course she does. Where should she live but with her mother?' Her ladyship's eyebrows seemed in danger of disappearing altogether. 'A child of seventeen living alone? Whatever next! She's a charming little thing, although I've never had any patience with schoolchildren myself. Still, she's far too young for you. Put it out of your mind. Let me see, what was I going to tell you?'

This was a secret Mr Campion never learnt. Lady Laradine, who had hitherto accredited him with excellent manners, was deeply disappointed in him. He stared blankly at her for a moment and then, turning away abruptly, strode across the room, passing behind the tent, to the door half-hidden behind it which led out into the house.

Lady Laradine saw the top of the door open and close and assumed that her victim had passed through it, which was just the kind of silly mistake which long experience had taught Mr Campion that most people were wont to make.

The long evening went on according to the programme the hostess had arranged, but there were certain additions to it which were not on her schedule at all. At half-past one in the morning a weary and somewhat stiff Mr Campion made his way gingerly out of the concealing folds at the back of the psychometrist's tent and, slipping into the house, walked quietly down to the little study where he had first met the girl in green.

He went inside and sat down in a wing-chair in the darkest corner. Presently he heard her coming as he knew she would. Her dress brushed the step and he heard her quick intake of breath as she closed the door behind her and, crossing into his line of vision, flung herself down on her knees before the bureau drawer.

'I say,' said Mr Campion, 'I suppose you know what you're doing with that chap downstairs? I don't trust him myself.'

This time his interruption was greeted with interest if not respect. Jennifer Pendleton-Blake screamed and swung round, her eyes terrified. Even so, however, her words were unexpected.

'What do you know?' she demanded.

'Quite a lot.' Mr Campion rose stiffly to his feet. 'I've been standing on one foot, half smothered by dusty black velvet, for an hour and a half.'

The girl gaped at him and he had the grace to look ashamed.

'I've been listening,' he said. 'What did you give that fellow to – er – "psychomet?" I couldn't see. Letters?'

She nodded miserably.

Mr Campion coughed.

'I don't want to seem unduly inquisitive,' he said, 'but I'm out to help in any way I can. Who were they from?'

Jennifer Pendleton-Blake turned back to the drawer and turned over its contents. The nape of her neck was pink and her shoulders were quivering.

'I don't know,' she said helplessly. 'That's just it, *I don't know!*'

Mr Campion knelt down on the floor beside her and looked into the drawer, which contained as fine a collection of sentimental relics as ever he had set eyes upon. There were several little bundles of letters tied up with different coloured ribbons, a choice selection of dead flowers, a university scarf or two, and quite a quantity of chocolate box lids.

He glanced at the seventeen-year-old at his side and

surprised her looking half her age. Inspiration came to him.

'Jennifer,' he said sternly, 'these are not yours.'

'No,' she whispered, her lips trembling.

'Whose are they? Roberta's?'

'Yes.'

Mr Campion lent her the handkerchief out of his breast pocket.

'Let's discuss this,' he said cheerfully. 'I think I'm getting the hang of it. I'll tell you the story as I see it and you correct me when I go off the rails.'

Miss Pendleton-Blake rewarded him with a pathetic acquiescing sniff.

'I don't know who you are,' she said, 'but you seem all right. Anyway, things can't be worse.'

Mr Campion ignored the somewhat dubious compliment.

'When a young woman feels she's grown up, but has only just arrived at that eminence, she often finds herself at a temporary disadvantage,' he began with a certain amount of oracular tact. 'I mean, for instance, when she is faced with the exacting problem of finding something really interesting to take to a psychometrist I can sympathize with her difficulty.'

The young lady looked at him gratefully.

'That was just it,' she said. 'I hadn't anything belonging to anyone whom I really wanted to know something about and I did feel a bit out of it, young and flat, you know. I'm not even presented yet. So I suddenly thought of Roberta's drawer up here, where I knew she kept all Tommy's letters. I thought I'd just get them, hear the low-down on Tommy and put them back. I didn't dream that the fortune-teller would be such a beast.'

'He wouldn't give them back to you?'

'Why, no. It was most peculiar.' Jennifer's face was the complete picture of youthful reproach. 'I put the packet in an envelope and sealed it, as he told me to. He stuck the envelope under the crystal. He told me a lot of silly stuff that obviously wasn't true and then he gave me what I naturally thought was the envelope back. I didn't examine it there, but when I got up here again I found it was only this.'

She opened her green handkerchief and produced a wad of neatly folded newsprint.

Mr Campion regarded the package gravely and with distaste.

'You went back to him, naturally?' he said. 'I heard the whole of that interview. You had to wait your turn to see him, of course. It must have been a trying experience.'

'It was filthy,' said Jennifer violently. 'Did you hear him laugh at me and say I'd made a mistake? Then he congratulated me on my sister's engagement and said he'd be seeing me again. He meant me to realize that he knew all about everything, you see. It wasn't until just now, though, that I realized the frightful thing. Those letters weren't Tommy's. They must have been Bobby Dacre's, or one of her other silly undergrads. They're always writing stupid letters to her because she's so frightfully pretty. Cagliostro must have looked at the letters I gave him and saw that they were written to her and not signed by Tommy, who, as everybody knows, is her fiancé. Now he'll keep them and make a row. What shall I do?'

Mr Campion grinned.

'Hold on a minute,' he said. 'He can't do much, you know, not in this case, although I *can* conceive a situation in which his little conjuring trick might prove decidedly awkward. Who cares who has been writing to Roberta? Not Tommy.'

'Oh, no, not Tommy.' Jennifer was contemptuous. 'But it might be frightfully awkward if he went to Tommy's perfectly revolting uncle. He's a horror. He's just straining at the leash to make an objection to the engagement. Everybody knows that. If this filthy fortune-teller so much as approached him he'd make it an excuse. Besides, you know how frightfully prurient everybody over forty is.'

'Are they?' said Mr Campion, feeling the dangerous age was uncomfortably close.

'Oh, yes!' said Miss Pendleton-Blake. 'What shall I do?' she added after a pause. 'Try and buy them back before he goes?'

Mr Campion regarded her with affection.

'You're what my more vulgar friends would call a proper little mug, aren't you?' he said. 'Our pal Cagliostro isn't so dumb. He certainly knows how to pick his clients. Now look here, we will do that. We'll do just what you say. We'll try to buy them back. But we'll need witnesses and, as we don't want publicity, we'll want the right witnesses. Oates will have to leave his bed, and it serves him right. Look here, can we be certain of keeping Cagliostro here another hour?'

Jennifer glanced up at the sunburst clock over the mantel-shelf.

'Oh, no,' she said. 'He's due to leave in ten minutes or so now. Perhaps he'll just take the money quietly and give them back.'

'In view of a rather horrid little tale I heard the other day I think he'll take the money and *not* give them back,' he said. 'And if we don't have the right kind of witnesses there may be a row, which is not what we want at all.'

The girl in the green frock shivered.

'Who's going to keep him here, then?' she said. 'You don't know these entertainers. They'll never stay a second after their time is up. Is it so terribly important?'

'Terribly,' said Mr Campion.

'Then we're sunk.' There was a wail in the young voice. 'Nothing on heaven or earth can detain people like that.'

A beautiful idea came to Mr Campion.

'I know someone who could detain anything,' he murmured, and went off in search of Lady Laradine.

At four o'clock in the morning Superintendent Oates sat in a small room on the first floor of Mrs Pendleton-Blake's house and regarded Mr Campion with a certain thoughtfulness. He was contented to know that in a cab speeding through the quiet streets Cagliostro the Second sat sullen and re-signed between two unsympathetic and sleepy police officers.

Opposite the superintendent stood Mr Campion, looking very wide-awake and wearing an almost intelligent expression. Jennifer Pendleton-Blake was clinging to his arm, her eyes dancing.

'It *might* be him,' said the superintendent grudgingly and ungrammatically. 'His papers do show that he only came over from the States at the beginning of the month. Anyway, it was the fairest cop I ever saw. He played straight into our hands. Never having met this little lady before, he felt he was quite safe from any trap, I suppose. He was more astounded than afraid when we walked in on him. Well, we'll keep the publicity right down; it's easy in this sort of case. You played your part very cleverly, Miss.'

Jennifer smiled.

'He was exhausted when I got to him,' she said frankly. 'Edith Laradine had been with him for a whole hour, you know. She did the really clever thing by keeping him here. She's wonderful.'

The superintendent cocked an eye towards the door.

Through the heavy panels and down two flights of stairs the steady murmur of Lady Laradine's remarkable voice reached them faintly as she recounted her experience to her friend and hostess. Oates listened for a moment and shook his head like an airedale.

'Yes,' he said heavily. 'Yes, indeed. She is. Wonderful is the word.'

Jennifer laughed.

'You were pretty clever, weren't you, bless you,' she said, glancing up at Mr Campion.

'Him?' said the superintendent. '*Him?*'

Mr Campion remained affable and blandly uninformative until, good nights having been said, they taxied back to Campion's flat together for a nightcap. Then the superintendent's dignity gave out sufficiently to permit him to ask a direct question.

'Simple, my dear chap,' he said. 'Your police experts *are* wonderful.'

Oates made an unofficial remark.

'You come off it,' he said after a bit. 'You know and I know that the chances are a hundred to one on this Cagliostro fellow being the same man I was telling you about last week. We shan't be able to prove it, I don't suppose, but it's clear enough. How did you do it? Luck again?'

'Luck?' protested Mr Campion in pained astonishment. 'My good policeman, when you actually meet brilliant detective work don't let its unfamiliarity blind you to its merit. Luck indeed! It was pure deduction and intelligent investigation, backed up by old-fashioned listening at doors.'

'Yes, I know all that.' Oates was irritated in spite of his satisfaction. 'Once you decided to watch your man, the thing was child's play. You spotted his game at once. It was a clever one, mind you. He must have made a point of keeping all letters handed in to him and taking a look at them, giving back the uninteresting ones as soon as his client spotted his "mistake", as he called it. He had a dozen of those little fake packets ready, all shapes and sizes. You spotted that trick all right because you actually saw, or rather heard, him doing it, but what on earth made you suddenly decide to watch a man who was simply entertaining at some wretched party at which you happened to be?'

'I didn't happen to be at the party,' objected Mr Campion with feeling. 'I went there deliberately and at tremendous personal sacrifice in order to find him. I was looking for him.'

'Why?'

'Because you told me to, my dear chap.' Mr Campion leaned back in the taxicab and spoke with weary patience. 'Cagliostro is the only Society fortune-teller to visit these shores regularly every October. As soon as you told me that story the other day it was obvious that he was the man you wanted, providing your tale had any foundation in fact. I wanted to find out if it had, so I went and had a look at Cagliostro at work. Is that clear?'

'Yes,' said Oates hastily. 'Yes, old man. Don't get excited. Yes, I see that. But why a fortune-teller? I didn't mention a fortune-teller. The idea never entered my head.'

Mr Campion seemed to be at a loss, but suddenly he smiled.

'Oh, *that*,' he said. 'Of course. I forgot. You didn't see the significance of the maid's story, did you? She insisted that her mistress had definitely said "It's no use. It's written in ink. He saw it in ink." Now is it clear?'

The superintendent swore.

'You make me tired,' he said. 'I've never heard such nonsense in my life. That statement was plain idiotic.'

Campion nodded. 'I know,' he said. 'It was. But the maid wasn't idiotic. The maid was a sensible girl, a good witness; you said so yourself. That's why it occurred to me that she must have made a simple, ordinary little mistake, the kind of mistake a sensible person might make. Don't you see, Oates, what her mistress really said was "He saw it in *the* ink. It is written in *the* ink." '

Oates was silent. 'Even so I don't see – ' he began.

Mr Campion chuckled in the darkness.

'You don't patronize fortune-tellers. If you did you'd know that, while some of them look at cards or peer into crystals, others read secrets mirrored in a pool of black ink. When you told me that story I thought of fortune-tellers, and when I looked into Cagliostro's tent this evening the first thing I saw was a *black* crystal. Then I knew I was on the right track. The unpleasant little trick he tried to play on that adorable guffin, Jennifer, put him slap into my hands. There you are, sir, it's in the bag. When do I get my illuminated address?'

'Eh?' said Oates, and after a second or so of consideration began to laugh. 'I'll hand it to you,' he said. 'You get all the luck, but you have a sort of flair, I'll admit. You'll have to excuse the five thousand words.'

Mr Campion handed him his cigarette case.

'Not at all,' he said firmly. 'I want my reward. Either

the address or you take Lady Laradine round the Black Museum for me.'

Oates accepted the cigarette.

'I'll do the homework,' he said resignedly. 'After all, life's short.'

XI

The Meaning of the Act

'TRIVIAL, vulgar, pettifogging, puerile, footling. At times even dirty,' said Lance Feering, taking up his glass. 'I don't want to be hypercritical, old boy, but that's how I see this life of yours. It repels me. My stomach turns at it. I gag . . . You see what I mean?'

'The light is filtering through,' agreed Mr Albert Campion affably, as he flattened himself against the ornate tiles behind him. 'Criminology does not appeal to you to-night.'

They were in the famous bar of the Pantheon Hall of Varieties, more affectionately known as the Old Sobriety, in Rupert Street. It was almost the last of the great music-halls and, as usual, the small circular room with its wide window giving on to the auditorium was crowded. Lance was in form. He was demanding a considerable favour from his old friend and, since such was his temperament, the experience was making him truculent.

'Of course you batten on it, I know,' he continued vigorously. 'It's a mania with you. It's got into your blood like a bacillus. That's why I asked you to come along to-night to this ungodly hole.' He paused. 'I thought you'd like it,' he added, glancing anxiously under his thick brows at the tall thin figure beside him.

'Quite,' murmured Mr Campion, bending forward to look through the window across the dark stalls to the boxes beyond. 'He's still sitting up there.'

'So I should hope. There's still a turn to go before the

lady comes on, isn't there?' Lance set down his glass hastily
and took a look himself. 'Good Lord, we don't want to lose
him. Shall we go back?'

'No, I don't think so.' His companion surveyed the small
bent figure in the second tier box. 'He's all right. He seems
to be enjoying himself.'

'That's what I mean. That's why the whole thing is so
repellent,' Lance sounded querulous. 'Why shouldn't he
have a night or two on the tiles if he wants to? I shouldn't
have dreamed of stalking the poor old badger if Marguerite
hadn't been so insistent and so frightened. You haven't
met Marguerite, have you?'

'His daughter?'

'Yes.' Lance was unusually laconic. He sighed. 'A
beautiful woman frightened out of her wits can be very
demoralizing. She's got bone, Campion, exquisite bone.'

'I thought you designed stage sets?' remarked Mr
Campion unsympathetically. 'Still, we won't go into that.
Why is this poor bony female afraid?'

'Well, he's a distinguished bird, you know. He's a recluse,
a famous man, an Egyptologist of world renown, he's lived
like a bishop all his life, and now he's started sneaking out
of the house like an adolescent and trotting off to music-
halls alone, all up and down the country, performance
after performance. She thinks he's either up to something
or nuts. And I said "bone", not "bony". It's a question of
design.'

'Dr Clement Tiffin,' murmured Campion. 'He's everything you say, and yet why should that name make me
think of crossword puzzles?'

'It shouldn't.' Lance was irritated. 'It should make you
think of pyramids, incredibly decent and decaying clubs,
and the pavilion at Lord's. Anyway, don't go deducing
who he is; we know that. I've got you along here to help me
find out what he's up to. I mean, does the poor girl call in
an alienist, or resign herself to the fact that the poor old
boy at the age of seventy-seven has fallen for a beautiful
Egyptian hip-waggler?'

Mr Campion eyed him over the rim of his glasses.

'Is that your only problem?' he said. 'Because believe me, if you've had the impudence to get me out here simply for that...'

'Well, not quite,' Lance admitted hastily. 'Marguerite certainly isn't a fool, and she's got something pretty serious on her mind. I couldn't get much out of her, but she seems to think that the old man is in some sort of danger.'

'Spiritual or bang-on-the-head?'

'Oh, physical. No dream stuff. I told you Marguerite's got brains.'

'Brains and bone,' said Campion. 'Dear me, and a very fine seat on a horse, too, I shouldn't be surprised.'

'I rather resent that, old boy.' Lance was not smiling, and Campion, who knew him so well that his mercurial temperament was not the mystery it might well have been, suddenly perceived the situation. Lance was indulging in a phase of 'utter decency' and, since he invariably took colour from the people who happened to be interesting him at the moment, it followed as the night the day, that the Tiffins were of a very definite class and type.

'Marguerite is not the sort of girl who'd come roaring round after Papa herself?' he suggested.

'Good heavens, no!' said Lance, scandalized.

'Ah,' murmured Campion.

Lance was silent for a moment or so and finally decided to unbend.

'If you only knew old Tiffin, you'd see how remarkable it all is,' he said. 'He's so very much the – er – the top drawer, if you'll forgive the phrase. He's got a great brain, too. The idea of him sneaking out to see this blessed woman dance time after time in the most revolting little halls all over the place is incredible. He's not that sort of chap.'

He looked round the pleasant dirty little bar as if he had never seen it before, and Campion watched him with his eyes dancing behind his spectacles.

''Ullo, Bert.'

The salutation rang out across the room and, as soon as

he heard the familiar cracked Cockney, Campion became
aware of an impending social crisis.

'Cassy,' he said.

'Wot O! Cor, this is a bit of all right. 'Ow are yer,
chum?'

The crowd heaved and billowed, and a figure emerged
from it. He landed squarely before them, his small rodent's
face alight with bonhomie and gin. He was a little man,
narrow-chested and narrow-faced, with slit eyes and a
long, slender nose with a twitch to it. Sartorially he was
quite remarkable, for he wore a vivid blue suit. His mind
seemed to be running on clothes also, for he flicked Campion's shirt front with a grubby thumbnail.

'Washington's come 'ome, I see,' he said. 'Come and
'ave one. 'Oo's yer pal?'

Campion performed the introduction with misgiving.

'Lance, this is Mr Cassy Wild, a very old friend of
mine,' he said. 'Cassy, this is Mr Lancelot Feering, a
celebrity.'

If the final description was intended as a warning, Cassy
was in no mood to take it.

'Sir Lancelot. 'Strewth, that's a moniker to go to bed
with,' he said cheerfully. 'Named after an 'orse, mate?
No offence meant and none took, I 'ope. What is 'e, Bert?
A dick?'

Lance was eyeing him coldly. 'I'm afraid I don't follow
you,' he said with the half apologetic smile which contains
the deadliest insult.

'And that is lucky,' cut in Campion, with haste and
emphasis, as he trod delicately on one of Mr Wild's long
narrow shoes.

'Oh, I see.' The newcomer cocked an intelligent eye at
his friend and a long and meaning look was exchanged
between them.

'How's business?' inquired Campion.

A row of abominable teeth appeared for an instant
across the pallid waste of Mr Wild's ignoble face.

'Not so bad,' he said. 'I caught a shice and did a carpet

in the spring. Had to come to town without a coal. But a denar here and a denar there soon mounts up, you know, and I'm in clover. By the way, this is my monkery, so who's your party?'

'Myself, my friend, and our punter is an elderly and distinguished finger in Box B,' replied Campion without hesitation.

'Okay, Bert.' Mr Wild shook hands effusively. 'See you some other time. So long. It's a nice show. The palone in the Didikye turn is a knockout. Wot 'o.'

Lance conducted Campion back to their seats in silence.

'That was rather an extraordinary thing to do, wasn't it?' he muttered as they sat down. 'Surely there was no need to mention Dr Tiffin to your repulsive friend, was there?'

'Didn't you take to Cassy?' Campion seemed surprised. 'He's a dear chap. As a matter of fact, that was most considerate of him. This is his district, as he told us, and he did not want to embarrass any friend of mine with his professional attentions. Very thoughtful. Cassy has gentlemanly instincts, if they are not sartorially expressed.'

'Professional ...?' Lance twisted round in his seat. 'D'you mean to say that fellow was a thief?'

'A whizz-boy,' said Campion modestly, 'i.e., pickpocket. The most skilful practitioner in the country. Don't raise your voice, old man. Listen to the pretty accordion player.'

'Yes, but I say, Campion ...' Lance was positively blushing. 'You do know some most amazing people. Good Lord!'

'Marguerite wouldn't like him?' suggested Campion, and Lance did not deign to reply. He sat glowering, ill at ease and apprehensive, while every now and again he glanced up at the dark box above them where the bent figure of a little old man sat alone, watching the glittering stage with idle introspective eyes.

Campion lit a match to look at his programme.

'Charmian, Exotic Dancer of the Desert,' he read softly. 'She's due any minute now. Cassy said she was a knock-out, although he thought she was a gypsy. Still, he's no connoisseur. I wonder . . . Why *does* that name Tiffin remind me of crosswords?'

'It doesn't. Don't keep saying that. You're getting on my nerves.' Lance stirred uneasily in his chair. 'Thank heaven this chap's finishing. Here we are; number eight at last.'

The dusty red curtain had descended with a sweep of tarnished tassel and fringe, and the accordion player was taking his call. The old man in the box drew back a little and raised his white head expectantly. The orchestra played a fanfare and the curtain rose again, disclosing a semi-darkened stage.

Gradually the light grew stronger, and Campion, who had expected the usual pseudo-Eastern eurythmics, sat up. The dancer was standing in the centre of the stage, her arms at her sides. She was dressed in a long white tunic and an Egyptian headdress and collar. She was not particularly beautiful, and the profile, outlined against the dark hangings behind her, was strong rather than lovely. He glanced up at the box.

Dr Tiffin had moved forward and the light from the stage caught his face. There was something unexpected in his expression, a sternness, almost a dislike, and Campion, seeing it, suddenly remembered why his name had reminded him so strongly of crossword puzzles. His eyebrows rose and his lips pursed to a soundless whistle as he turned back to the stage.

The girl who was billed as 'Charmian' was no ordinary dancer. There was even something of the old-fashioned contortionist in her performance, yet she contrived to make her slow, unnatural movements peculiarly graceful, and, what was far more extraordinary, peculiarly Egyptian, or, more specifically, ancient Egyptian.

Campion sat with his eyes fixed upon her, and again and again the rows of painted figures on the mummy cases in the British Museum leapt to his mind. The dance continued to slow music, and Charmian held her audience. The strange thing about her was her lack of facial movement. Throughout her turn she might have been wearing a mask, yet her powers of expression were amazing. She danced with an urgency of meaning which was unmistakable, and it seemed to be this dumb striving towards communication which reached out over the footlights and forced attention.

The clientele of the Old Sobriety was an exacting audience, and it could scarcely be called highbrow, yet it sat up and watched, fascinated.

Lance appeared to be spellbound. He did not stir throughout the turn, but remained rigid, his dark eyes round and surprised.

'Good Lord,' he said, when at length the curtain descended upon her. 'Good Lord, how incredible! She's like a blessed papyrus. Hallo, what's the matter with you?'

Campion said nothing, but there was a startled expression on his face, and his eyes were raised to Box B. Lance followed his glance and an exclamation escaped him.

'Gone,' he said disgustedly. 'Slipped round the back, I suppose, while we were gaping at his girl friend. Well, I don't altogether blame him for his enthusiasm. She's an experience to watch.'

'Be quiet.' Campion was on his feet. 'Come on,' he murmured, and there was so much anxiety in his voice that the painter rose and followed him without a word.

Lance did not catch up with him as he hurried through the auditorium, and only reached his side as he sprinted down the dusty corridor behind the circle.

'I say, you can't butt in on him,' he protested in a flurry. 'He's not that kind of old boy. We can't, Campion. Marguerite would never forgive me.'

Campion flung off his restraining hand and opened the door of the box.

Dr Tiffin lay on the floor beside the chair from which he had fallen. He had crumpled up and slipped forward, and there was a thin dark streak among his white hairs.

They got him out of the theatre and into a taxi. It was not altogether a simple matter, for the old man was still

unconscious, but Lance was convinced that the absence of
any scandal was of paramount importance, and Campion,
for entirely different reasons, was disposed to agree.

'We'll get him home first and then find his own doctor,'
he said. 'He's all right. I think. His heart is sound, and
there's no fracture. He'll be all right in a day or so.'

'I don't understand it.' Lance was white with appre-
hension. 'When Marguerite said "danger" I thought she
was exaggerating. This is fantastic. He's only a fan of the
dancer's, as far as I know. No one can mind him looking at
her, surely, however attentive he is.'

Campion glanced up from his patient, whom he was
supporting in the back of the cab.

'That rather depends,' he said slowly. 'Look here,
Lance, I fancy we're on dangerous ground. I think you may
just have to wipe this incident clean out of your mind.
Forget it. Pretend it didn't happen.'

'What do you mean?'

Campion did not reply. Dr Tiffin had begun to stir, and
his voice, thick and slurred, startled them both. At first the
muttered words were indistinguishable, but as they leaned
forward anxiously a single phrase came out clearly in the
darkness.

'*Thine uncle bears thee gifts,*' said the Egyptologist distinctly. He repeated it again, and the extraordinary words
ceased to be ludicrous in that thin pedantic voice. '*Thine
uncle bears thee gifts.*'

'What?' Lance was shocked into the question. 'What
did you say, sir? What gifts?'

The old man did not answer. His head had fallen forward
and he went off into incoherent mutterings once more.

'Did you hear that, Campion?' Lance's own voice rose
to a squeak. 'It's turned his brain. What an extraordinary
thing to say. "Thine uncle . . ."'

'Hush,' said Campion gently. 'Hush, old boy. Forget it.
Here we are. Help me get him into the house.'

Miss Marguerite Tiffin turned out to be a pleasant
surprise to Campion. Lance's reactions had led him to

expect, if not the worst, something very near it, but he found, instead of the academic snob he had envisaged, a very sensible and charming young woman with a snub nose and a quick, shy smile. Moreover, for a girl who was not used to having her Papa brought home on a shutter, she was remarkably cool and quick on the uptake. It was only when the old man was safely in bed with his doctor in attendance that she betrayed any sign of strain.

'I'm tremendously grateful to you, Lance,' she said, 'but you do see now that I was right to interfere?'

'Good Lord, yes.' Lance was holding her hand far too long, and Campion was inclined to sympathize with him. 'All the same I'm still in the dark. The whole thing bewilders me. It seems to me to be an entirely meaningless attack on an inoffensive old gentleman who wasn't doing anyone any harm.'

Marguerite hesitated. She had round grey eyes, and at the moment they were intensely serious.

'Lance,' she said slowly, 'do you think you could go on thinking that, and then – then forget the whole thing utterly? Never mention it to daddy or to anyone else. I can rely on you to do that, can't I, Mr Campion?'

'Yes,' said Campion gravely. 'Yes, I think you can.'

Lance came away unwillingly after lengthy farewells.

'I do wish you wouldn't be so darned mysterious,' he grumbled, as they walked out of Bedford Square together. 'I'll do anything Marguerite asks me within reason, of course, but why the hush-hush? What's the matter with the old man? Has he got some well-known form of bats-in-the-belfry which I've not heard about? What was all that about his uncle? Damn it, are you or am I?'

Campion hailed a cab, but Lance drew back.

'Now where are we going?' he asked.

'Back to my flat.'

'What for?'

'Drink,' said Campion. 'If you must know, drinks, ginger biscuits, and I should rather think a visitor.'

By midnight Lance was beside himself with irritation.

'An impossible evening,' he declared. 'What infuriates me is your blessed calm. Hang it, I invited you to help me follow old Tiffin, and what happens? First you introduce me to a little sneak-thief who seems to regard you as some sort of favourite relative, then we find Tiffin biffed over the head and we take him home, where Marguerite behaves as though she was taking in the laundry and you back her up in treating the entire thing as nothing to write home about. Finally, we sit up here waiting for a caller. Whom do you expect?'

Campion pushed the decanter towards him.

'I haven't the faintest idea,' he said truthfully.

'You're potty.' The childish accusation seemed to relieve the artist and he refilled his glass. 'You haven't invited anyone and you don't know who is coming, but you've just got a psychic feeling that a visitor is imminent. Well, if I've got to sit up all night I may as well make something out of it. I'll lay you a hundred to one in shillings . . .'

He broke off abruptly. Out in the hall the electric bell had begun to ring authoritatively. An instant later Campion's man admitted without ceremony Superintendent Stanislaus Oates and a companion, and closed the door after them.

The two men stood on the threshold looking tall and official in the brightly lit room, and Campion rose to greet his old friend. The superintendent was cool. He was not hostile, but there was a formality in his manner which was not customary. After his first greeting he introduced the stranger with warning deference.

'This is Captain Smith, Mr Campion,' he said severely. 'He'd like a few words with you and Mr Feering about your activities to-night, if you don't mind. No, thank you, we won't drink.'

The little company sat down stiffly. Captain Smith was a restraining influence. He was a lean, brown man with a dry precision of manner which enhanced the natural austerity of his personality. The one obvious fact about him was that his name was not Smith and that his rank was understated. Lance, who fancied himself as a student of faces, was startled by the impersonal penetration of his blue eyes. He glanced at Campion and was relieved to see that, although grave, he did not seem surprised.

'I rather expected a visit from the police,' Campion remarked to Oates. 'You've seen Dr Tiffin, I suppose?'

'Yes.' Captain Smith answered quietly, before the superintendent could speak. 'Will you explain exactly why you went to the Pantheon Music-hall to-night, and why you were so peculiarly fortunate as to have been on the spot to render assistance as soon as it was needed?'

'Mr Feering can explain that better than I can,' Campion was beginning, when a second ring at the bell outside jolted everybody. No one spoke, and the two visitors turned slowly in their chairs to watch the door.

The manservant was some time in coming, and when at last he did appear he spoke dubiously.

'Mr Cassy Wild to see you, sir,' he said.

Lance stiffened. As an addition to this already somewhat sticky party the ebullient Cassy did not appeal to him. The same notion appeared to have occurred to Campion, he was relieved to see.

'Oh, ask him to wait,' he said hastily. 'Put him in the study.'

'Very good, sir.' As the man withdrew, Captain Smith swung round on Campion.

'A friend?'

'Yes. A very old one.'

'That's all right, sir.' The superintendent spoke deferentially. His grey face was impassive, but there was the hint of a twitch at the corners of his mouth. 'I know him.'

'I see. Then we'll go on. You were on the point of giving me an explanation, Mr Feering.'

Lance told his story frankly. He was a friend of Marguerite's, and she had confided to him that she was alarmed by her father's new habit of going off by himself after a lifetime of regular and studious habits. She had discovered that he had made a habit of watching every performance given by the dancer, Charmian, and that in order to do this he followed her all round the country, sometimes to the most disreputable little halls. To satisfy Marguerite, Lance had gone to the Pantheon to see the dancer for himself and to watch the old man's reactions to her. Since he did not feel like going alone, he asked his friend Mr Campion to accompany him.

Captain Smith listened to the recital with a perfectly impassive face, and when it was over he turned to Campion.

'Perhaps you would describe the incident as you saw it? Please don't omit anything.'

Campion told the story of finding the old man half unconscious in the box, and Lance corroborated it.

'After the turn we looked up and could not see him in the box, so we went to investigate. We found he was hurt and did what we could,' he repeated.

'You saw no one else in or near the box?'

'No.'

'You're quite sure of that? No one at all?'

'No one,' said Campion. 'Nor,' he continued firmly, 'did I see him speak to anyone at all during the whole time that I was in the hall. He was entirely alone throughout the performance. Whoever attacked him must have opened the door of the box during Charmian's act, delivered the blow and left immediately. Nothing was touched. His pockets were not rifled. It was a personal attack. Someone meant to put him out and no one but him.'

Captain Smith's heavy-lidded eyes flickered and he looked at Campion steadily.

'An attendant?' he suggested.

'No,' said Campion decisively. 'No, I don't think so. He was sitting up there in the box throughout the entire show, you see. Anyone could have noticed him. I don't see that it need have been an attendant. Anyone was at liberty to walk down that corridor. It might have been anyone in the entire audience.'

'That's the devil of it,' murmured Captain Smith, and for the first time a smile appeared upon his face. 'Well, thank you very much for putting up with this intrusion. I shan't bother you either any more to-night, Superintendent.'

'Very well, sir.'

Oates took the dismissal respectfully and rose as the younger man took his leave.

After he had gone the atmosphere seemed a little easier, and Campion had just persuaded Oates to take a nightcap when the manservant reappeared.

'It's that Mr Wild, sir,' he was beginning, but broke off abruptly when he saw Oates. 'I beg your pardon, sir. I heard the door and I thought both the gentlemen had gone.'

'In a moment,' said the superintendent, who was thawing visibly. 'I'll be gone in a moment. Let him cool his heels. I'm fond of you, Campion,' he continued as the man went out, 'and there's a lot I'd do for you, but some of your pals are beyond me. I just couldn't bring myself to take a drink with Cassy Wild.'

Campion shook his head. 'You don't appreciate him,' he said regretfully. 'You're too conservative. You expect everyone to have the same virtues. Cassy has *unusual* virtues. They are quite as numerous, if not more so, than most people's, but they're different.'

'Very likely,' Oates observed without enthusiasm, 'but I'd want my pockets sewed up and my shirt padlocked to my collar before I went for a walk with him. Still, I didn't come up here to talk about Cassy. It was a pity you couldn't give the captain what he was after. You might have made yourself really useful for once. However, if you saw no one you saw no one; that's all there is to it.'

Lance frowned. 'I seem to be out of this altogether,' he said bitterly. 'The entire business is getting more and more bewildering. Who was that chap Smith, anyway?'

The superintendent coughed. 'He's a very important officer, sir. I don't think we'll discuss him, if you don't mind. Just keep the whole matter under your hat, if you will. It was a chance in a thousand and it got missed. That's the long and the short of it. It can't be helped.'

He paused and glanced at Campion with a sly smile. No one spoke, and the superintendent's grin widened in spite of himself.

'I ought not to laugh,' he said, 'but I can't help it. It's not often Mr Smarty gets himself into something that he doesn't understand. Right under his nose, it was, and he couldn't see it for looking.'

Campion did not smile. He lay back in his chair, his eyes half closed behind his spectacles.

'Smith's a newcomer in the Special Branch, isn't he?' he said.

Oates choked, and his thin face grew a dusky red.

'Who said anything about the Special Branch?' he protested. 'I don't know what you're talking about. I don't understand you at all. It's time I went home. It must be one in the morning.'

Campion let him rise without demur, but spoke again before he had reached his greatcoat.

'When I first heard Dr Tiffin's name to-night it reminded me of crossword puzzles,' he remarked. 'I could not think of the connection until I happened to see his expression as he sat looking at that dancer. Then it came back to me. He was in Room 40 OB during the war, wasn't he?'

'What if he was?' Oates was flurried. 'Campion, for goodness sake stay out of this. It's not your cup of tea. It's not mine either. As it happened, you couldn't help. Let it rest like that. I can't discuss it with you. I daren't. It's not our show.'

'Quite so. All the same I find it interesting, and if I'm right I think I might be useful.' Lance had never heard Campion so gently obstinate. 'Sit down and listen to me. I'll tell you how my mind is working. I may be shinning up a gum-tree, and if I am you can tell me so, politely and in official language. Now look here, this is how I see it. Dr Tiffin happens to be a distinguished Egyptologist. His books on cuneiform and even earlier writings are famous. Also he was in Room 40 OB, the cipher decoding office, during the war. Those are two facts. Here are two more. To-night I heard that he has suddenly started to visit every performance given by a certain dancer and during her turn this evening he was knocked out, presumably by someone who did not want him to see the whole of that dance. That gives me furiously to think.'

'Don't.' Oates' advice was brief but heartfelt. 'Forget it.' Campion sat up.

'I think I would,' he said earnestly, 'but I saw that girl dance, and I think Lance here said the most enlightening thing about her show. When it was over he turned to me and said, "She's like a papyrus." She wasn't, of course, but I saw what he meant. She *was* like some of that picture-writing on the mummy cases. Now do you see what I'm getting at? Suppose that long, slow procession of poses of hers was like writing, Oates? Suppose she danced some sort of limited message? It would have to be limited, of course, because it would be in a sign language, and sign languages are limited.'

Oates was staring at him. Presently he swore softly.

'You're too bright,' he said. 'You'll blind yourself one of these days.'

Campion laughed. 'I thought so,' he murmured. 'It's fantastic, but not so fantastic that it couldn't be true ... "Thine uncle bears thee gifts." '

The final words, uttered casually, had an astonishing effect on the superintendent. The blood receded from his face and his jaw dropped.

'Where the devil did you get hold of that?' he demanded.

'Overheard it. Nothing clever about that,' Campion admitted modestly. 'Dr Tiffin was muttering it when we carried him home. That was the message, I suppose, or part of it. He must have been rather quicker on the uptake than his assailant expected. Quite an easy message, I should think. Most of the tombs have something of the sort among their lists of funeral offerings. The burning question, I take it, Oates, is ... *whose* uncle?'

The superintendent did not reply. He seemed to be hovering on the verge of a confidence, and the soft knock

on the door came as an unwelcome interruption. Campion
sighed with exasperation.

'Oh, come in,' he shouted.

The manservant entered with a dilapidated newspaper
parcel on a silver tray.

'Mr Wild has had to leave and wished me to give you
this, sir,' he said gravely. 'I was to tell you he didn't mind
waiting, but he took exception to the company you keep. I
happened to let fall that the superintendent was here, sir.'

'Blast his impudence!' said Oates, laughing. 'What's he
sent you? The fried fish supper you were going to share?'

Campion took the parcel and laid it on the arm of his
chair unopened.

'Isn't that the question?' he persisted, as the door closed.
'Whose uncle?'

Oates shrugged his shoulders. 'You know too much,' he
said. 'You'll get yourself in the Tower. It's all right to
muscle in on my job, but you get your fingers into the
espionage machine and you'll get 'em bitten off.'

'Espionage?' muttered Lance under his breath. 'Spy
hunting, by George!'

'Put it out of your mind, sir.' Oates made the admonition
firmly. 'You can see exactly what's happened. That dancer
has been under observation by our people for months. No
one at all suspicious seemed to have access to her, and they
could never get the link between her and an espionage
system which must exist. Then it occurred to someone at
Headquarters that she was transmitting instructions in this
peculiar way through her dancing. Dr Tiffin tried to
decode the messages and I think he had been very successful, but the thing he couldn't tell, of course, was who else
besides himself in each audience understood what she was
saying, and that was the vital thing. That was what our
people needed to know. To-night there might have been a
chance of finding out. No one thought the old gentleman
might be attacked, although his interest in the lady must
have looked highly suspicious to anybody in the know. If
such a thing had been foreseen, he'd have been watched

and we'd have found out something. Who ever attacked Dr Tiffin is the key man, you see. He's probably living quietly over here under his own name like a respectable citizen.'

'I still don't quite follow,' said Lance frankly. 'What would they do if they found him? Arrest him?'

'Arrest him?' Oates seemed scandalized. 'Oh, no sir, foreign agents are never arrested. They're watched. They're even supplied with certain fancy information if they're mugs enough to take it. No, no, he'd have been followed. He would lead us to this "uncle" who has the gifts, or the doings, whatever it is, and then *he* would be watched in his turn. Like that we'd uncover the entire network, you see. As I said, it was a chance in a thousand, but now it's gone. We'll never know who in all that audience was the other man who knew.'

Campion nodded gloomily. 'Yes,' he said. 'My hat, I wish I'd cottoned on to it a bit sooner.' As he spoke he took up the newspaper packet and unwrapped it idly. An old brown leather wallet flopped on to his knees, and Oates laughed.

'Lumme,' he said, 'Cassy's brought you a bone! I'll have to pull you in one of these days, Campion. You'll get into trouble, mixing with scum like that. What *is* the explanation of that, may I ask? It looks darned fishy to me, I don't mind telling you.'

'I haven't the faintest idea.' Campion seemed surprised himself, and he bent down to retrieve a sheet of his own notepaper from the library desk which had fallen to the ground with the wrapping.

'Cassy's a dear chap, but he can't write,' he observed as he glanced at the dreadful hieroglyphics spread out before him. ''Strewth!'

The final word was forced from him and he sprang up, the wallet clasped in his hand.

'Oates,' he said unsteadily, 'read that.'

Lance and the superintendent read the message together. Some of the slang was beyond the artist, but the general meaning was clear.

'Dear old sport,' it ran. 'Hoping this finds you as it leaves me, dry as a bone. I kept an eye on your punter in Box B partly because I wondered what you was up to I admit that. Well, I took sights of the finger who sloshed him. I did not interfere because I did not want to be mixt up in anything thank you, specially there, but I thought you'd like a memento of him so I took his number which I give you gratis. I have not took above ten bob from it, may I die if I lie, but the rest will give you the dope on him and where to find him. I wouldn't do this for anyone but an old pal, Bert, as you know, but you've always bin one to me. Give old Oates a wish on the kisser from me. Ta ta. You know who. C. Wild.'

Oates read the note through twice without speaking. Words seemed to have failed him. Finally he took the wallet which Campion held out to him, and his hand shook a little as he opened it and spread out its contents upon the coffee table. Some minutes later he looked up, and his expression was wondering.

'His name and address on two envelopes, a prescription from his doctor, and his driving licence,' he said. 'Cassy's word might not jail a man, but it'll get this one watched. He's in the bag. Campion, you frighten me. Something looks after you.'

Campion took up Mr Wild's note and put it carefully in his pocket.

'Care for my secret, Superintendent?' he inquired.

'I'd like your luck,' said Oates. 'Well, what is it? I'll buy it.'

'Take a drink with anyone,' said Mr Campion, 'and pick your pals where you find 'em.'

XII

A Matter of Form

'THE trouble with crime to-day,' remarked Superintendent Stanislaus Oates seriously, 'is that one almost gets too much of it, if you see what I mean.'

'Absolutely,' murmured his companion with solemn, not to say owlish, gravity. 'The word you're searching for is "common", isn't it?'

The two men were sitting in the far corner of the long old-fashioned upstairs bar of the Café Bohème. Times had changed it since the grand gilt and red plush naughtiness of its youth, but it was still the centre of the town, and as Mr Albert Campion, who was looking a trifle thinner and grimmer in these days, glanced across its smoke-festooned expanse, it seemed to him to present a picture of the times – children in uniform and bankers in mourning.

The superintendent snorted, and his long sad face took on an even more settled expression of gloom.

'There you are,' he said. 'Just because you're overworked making yourself useful in some high and mighty hush-hush way, you think you can sneer at an old copper who has his hands full with more civil crime in every month than he used to see in a year. I hate this new ruthlessness. There used to be a time when I saw myself as a sort of sportsman cop. I'd bait my line, fling it out and watch . . .'

'That's right,' said Campion, echoing his philosophic tone, 'and the sight of you gallantly throwing the little ones back used to bring tears to my eyes. It's no good, guv'nor. The sentimental, kindly old sleuth stuff doesn't become you. It's not convincing. Fisherman my foot! You always have looked like a leathery old tomcat sitting by a hole; about as sporting and about as gentle. I can see your whiskers twitching now. Where's the mouse this time?'

'Mouse be blowed,' objected the superintendent. 'That's

a fine sleek young rat. Look at him. I wonder what he's calling himself now?'

Campion turned his head to follow the policeman's eyes, which, for all his kindliness, were as cold and bleak as a North Sea rock.

A man stood drinking alone at the round bar not a dozen feet from them. He was in early middle age, and the superintendent's description of him was not inapt. He was well-dressed, well-fed, and surprisingly handsome in that peculiar way which derives rather from general well-being than from any particular distinction of feature. At the moment he exuded happiness, confidence, and self-satisfaction. He drank deeply and with pleasure, and his flushed cheeks and dancing eyes smiled back at him with affection from the mirror behind the bar. In that anxious gathering, with its underlying atmosphere of brittle excitement, his contentment was noticeable, and Superintendent Oates, for one, was irritated by it.

'Someone's lost something, I bet a shilling,' he said unpardonably.

The man at the bar recognized the voice, and turned round.

'Ah,' he said, revealing a deep and by no means unpleasant voice, though his accent was far too good to be true, 'the dear old inspector.'

'Superintendent,' rebuked the policeman stolidly. 'How are you, Smith? Or isn't that the name now?'

'Well, as a matter of fact it's not, oddly enough.' The stranger lounged forward with elaborate confidence and stood beaming before them. 'Like you, I've got promoted. The name is Rowley. Smith is so usual, don't you think? I mean anybody might be a Smith. Anthony Rowley is the new moniker, and I fancy it suits me.'

'What are you doing? Wooing?' put in Campion, amused in spite of himself

The superintendent who had never been sung to sleep either in childhood or at any other time by the tale of the famous frog, was mystified by the allusion.

'Oh, it's love, is it?' he said ungraciously. 'I thought perhaps it was merely drink or an unguarded Chubb.'

The man who had decided to call himself Anthony Rowley frowned.

'Vulgar, unkind, and not even accurate,' he said. 'Breams, not Chubbs, were my undoing. Or I theirs, of course. It depends on how you look at it. Dear me, I am inebriated, aren't I?'

'You are.' The superintendent's tone was dangerously avuncular. 'And if you can get such indecent happiness out of a double or two in these days, you have my profound respect.'

A fleeting glimmer of caution hovered in Mr Rowley's bright blue eyes, but his unnatural elation killed it all too soon.

'Well, as a matter of fact,' he repeated perilously, 'as a matter of fact, and not because you're a policeman, but because you're a dear old gentleman and I like you, as a matter of fact my glorious condition at this moment is caused neither by love nor alcohol, but by something very much better than either.'

The superintendent's heavy eyelids flickered.

'I'll buy it,' he said.

Rowley laughed and winked at Campion.

'Isn't he an old duck?' he said. 'A dear harmless, friendly old duck. He's taken a fancy to me and he just wants to know why I'm so happy.'

'That'll do, my lad. Not too much impudence, if I were you.' In spite of the protest, Oates still maintained his unnatural docility.

Rowley turned away. 'You almost break my heart,' he said over his shoulder. 'You almost spoil my celebration.' The final word appeared to attract him for he repeated it and suddenly wheeled round again. 'I'll tell you,' he said. 'Do you know why I've been treating myself like a long-lost son all the afternoon? Do you know why I keep giving myself little drinks and jolly encouraging smiles in the mirror?'

'I'd make a darned good guess.' Oates's earlier humour showed signs of returning. 'Either you've just made an ungodly fool of yourself again or you're just going to.'

'Wrong,' said Anthony Rowley triumphantly. 'Wrong. Prosaically wrong. Your mind leaps to material facts as usual. You wouldn't understand, so I shan't give you the whole low-down, but because you're an old acquaintance I'll let you in half-way. I'm gloriously happy because I have had a beautiful thought. This will be lost on you because, dear good chap though you are, you're not the sort of man who has really beautiful thoughts. Don't take offence and don't worry about it. You can't help it; you're just not that sort of person. You understand that don't you, sir?'

His final remark was addressed to Campion, who made no attempt to hide his smile.

'A beautiful thought,' Rowley repeated. 'A peach. A delicate masterpiece of exquisite construction. An epic gem. Or, if you prefer it, a fizzler. Excuse me, I must go and brood over it again.'

He drifted away, only a trifle uncertainly, and Oates looked after him with a dour and introspective eye.

'He'll never forgive himself when he sobers up, will he?' he said presently, and for the first time that afternoon a brief, satisfied smile passed over his face. 'Poor chap, I'm almost sorry for him. That's my sporting instinct again. So he's on to something, is he? I'll get the lads to look him up at once.'

Campion's pale eyes behind his horn-rimmed spectacles were kindly.

'I wonder what it was,' he remarked. 'He seemed delighted.'

'He seemed tight,' corrected Oates drily. 'He was a very different chap last time I saw him. Not nearly so chatty, believe me. He belongs to the type of crook I've no patience with at all. He's not even very good at his job. You heard him admit it just now. Damn it, he's almost proud of his incompetence. Bream safes, that's his line. No one else's safes, mark you; just Bream's. He served an apprenticeship with the firm when he was young, learnt just as much as he needed to know and no more, and now no Bream safe is proof against him.

'They say the modern crook has to be a specialist,' he added, 'but that lad overdoes it. It's rank incompetence in his case, and he's lazy. He gets on my nerves.'

'I think you're unreasonable.' Campion made the criticism mildly. 'A man with a trade mark like that must play right into your hands.'

'Ye-es. So he does.' Oates was strangely reluctant. 'So he does,' he repeated. 'In a way. Yet he's slippery. Once or twice he's pulled a very fast one and we haven't been able to collect sufficient evidence to prosecute. We've known he was our man, and we've brought him in, and then he's wriggled out again.'

'Infuriating chap,' murmured Campion. 'He had more brains than the average, I thought.'

The superintendent got up.

'That's half his trouble,' he said heavily. 'He doesn't use 'em, or doesn't use 'em all. However, he's done it this time. He's opened his heart to the wrong man. That's why I think I'll just get back for half an hour or so. After all, when the mouse puts his head out of the hole it's silly not to pounce. You don't mind, do you?'

'Not at all,' Mr Campion was polite but tickled. 'Our delinquents must be taught to be efficient at all costs.'

Left to himself, it occurred to Campion that he might as well take a little food, and with this in mind he went downstairs to the restaurant.

The big ugly room was full, as usual, with a fair sprinkling of people present whom nearly everybody else knew at least by sight. He nodded to young Lafcadio, the painter, avoided Mrs Beamish, waved to Lily O'Dell, and was just settling down to half a dozen oysters when he caught sight of young Green.

Brian Green, whom Campion had last seen at the Oxford and Cambridge match, was in the uniform of a private in His Majesty's Territorial Army, and he was alone. He was also visibly depressed, but, on meeting Campion's eye, he brightened a little and came lumbering over, six-foot-three of yellow-haired good temper.

'Not so hot,' he answered in reply to the inevitable question. 'I'm on the lights, you know, down in the country. This is the first day of leave.'

'Sounds all right to me,' said Campion, waving him into the chair opposite. 'Why the lonely state? Hasn't she turned up?'

Brian's smile vanished once more.

'Well, yes,' he began awkwardly as he dug a small pattern on the tablecloth with a fork. 'She came all right but – er – well, she's gone.'

There was a brief silence between them, since Campion could not think of any comment which could possibly be considered helpful. The boy's depression increased.

'You're so tied, aren't you?' he observed at last. 'When you're in the Army, I mean, you can't be on the spot.' There was a wistfulness on his good-natured freckled face which made his host feel suddenly old. 'Of course,' he continued seriously, 'she's very young.'

Mr Campion checked the impulse to inquire if the woman was out of the cradle, and did his best to look intelligently indulgent.

'I thought she would rather like the uniform,' the boy added naïvely, 'but apparently she's got bitten by the Ministry idea.'

'The Ministry? What Ministry?'

'Oh, I don't know. She did tell me. Some awfully important Ministry, she said. Apparently all the intellectual lads have crowded into Supply and Defence and Economic and whatnot – at least that's her idea – and that's what's taken her fancy at the moment. It sounded too like the Post Office to me, and I told her so. She didn't like that. She's known me so long, you see, that she hasn't any illusions about my brain power. Anyway, that was why she couldn't go on to a show with me to-night. She had a date with one of these intelligent lads.'

'She'll grow out of that,' said Campion with conviction.

'Do you think so?' Brian was pathetically eager. 'We've been running around together ever since we were at school. She's a wonderful girl. Dances like a dream. We used to get on marvellously before she got interested in brains.'

'My dear chap, they recover from that. It falls from them like a cloak.' Campion spoke with great earnestness. 'Meanwhile, if you'll allow me to prescribe for the evening, food.'

'Food? Do you think so? I rather thought . . .'

'Food,' insisted his host. 'As from one who knows. Vast quantities of beautiful food. Wait a moment, we'll consult George.'

Three days later Campion met Brian again. To be exact, it was not so much a meeting as an ambush. He came hurrying into his own flat with a brief couple of hours in which to get through a month's correspondence, only to discover two young people sitting in suspiciously nonchalant attitudes, one on either end of his settee. The girl had been crying, and there was a damp patch on Brian's khaki shoulder. The soldier got up.

'Oh, there you are,' he said with relief. 'I do hope you'll forgive us barging in on you like this, but you were the only person I could think of to come to in the circumstances. By the way, this is Susan. Miss Susan Chad; Mr Campion.'

Susan was a dear. As soon as Campion set eyes upon her he forgave Brian much of his youth and understood many of his problems. Changing fashions produce changing women, and years of progress and emancipation are thought to have altered the sex unrecognizably, but there is one type of girl who never differs. In tiger skins, crinolones, or A.T.S. uniform she remains herself, dear, desirable, and chuckle-headed as a coot.

Susan raised a small round face to Mr Campion's own with a sweet dignity which had forgotten to take into account the tear-drop on the edge of her cheekbone, and said with devastating humility:

'I've been so frightfully silly and just a little tiny bit dishonest. What would you advise?'

'If you could convince her it won't mean the Tower it would be something,' muttered Brian out of the corner of his mouth.

'The hopeless thing about it is that it wasn't really my fault,' the girl protested. 'It wouldn't be so bad, somehow, if I'd done anything. It was the man in the station cloak-room. I didn't even look, or at least hardly.'

'I blame the fellow for saddling you with the responsibility in the first place,' said Brian stolidly. 'That was an unheard-of imposition.'

'No, Brian. You mustn't say that.' Susan was very serious. 'No, you can't blame him. I wanted the responsibility, and I was very honoured by his confidence. That's why this is so absolutely awful. I simply daren't face him. I'd rather die.'

'It's a code,' said Campion, who had been listening for some time with his head on one side. 'My bet is that it's a code. You've lost the secret password and the figures don't add up.'

The girl blinked at him reproachfully.

'I don't know what it is,' she said. 'I haven't been so indiscreet as to look. It's all those seals which are going to cause the trouble.'

'Seals?' muttered Campion, taken off his guard. 'I give in. Mention a couple of whales and I fly screaming from the room.'

Brian smiled apologetically at Susan before he eyed his host sternly.

'Perhaps we'd better explain,' he suggested.

'Perhaps you had,' agreed Campion huffily. What's up?'

'I'll tell it, Brian,' the girl put in firmly. 'There's one side of it that you don't see, and that's the part which matters rather a lot from my point of view. Mr Campion, I admire Tony tremendously, and that makes all the difference, doesn't it?'

'Oh indubitably,' said Campion, allowing the fog to close over his head. 'Let's start from there.'

'I'd like to.' Susan was still quiet. 'Tony is in a frightfully important Ministry, Consolidation of Defence, I think; I can't quite remember. But anyway, he's way up in it, and he's terribly responsible and utterly overworked. Last time I saw him we were going to a show, but he was suddenly called out of town on something he couldn't tell me about, and we had to dash back to his place and collect some things. It was all desperately urgent and, as he didn't know when he would be back, he gave me a small attaché-case containing some very secret papers and made me promise to take care of it for him. I swore I would, of course, and he left me on my doorstep with the case.'

'Of very secret papers,' echoed Mr Campion stupidly.

'That's what he said, anyway,' she protested. 'Only, of course, it was more impressive than I've made it. I – I'm not impressive.'

'My dear girl, forgive me.' Mr Campion was contrite instantly. 'I was only assimilating the facts. I'm not too bright this afternoon. He gave you an attaché-case to mind and you've lost it. Is that right?'

'Oh, no,' Susan grew crimson at the suggestion. 'No, I've not lost it, thank heaven. It's not as bad as that.'

'Here, let me tell it.' Brian came forward protectively. 'Susan isn't quite the little wet she sounds. She believes in this chap, you see, and evidently he realizes the sort of kid she is, absolutely dependable, and thoroughly first-class. Anyway, he wanted to leave this attaché-case in perfectly safe hands for a day or so. It was late at night, on that same evening when I met you, as a matter of fact, and there was no chance of shoving it in a bank or in his office, so he gave it to Susan.' He hesitated and blushed. 'You may think that unlikely,' he went on stoutly, 'but I don't, knowing Susan.'

Campion accepted the rebuke meekly.

'Oh, rather not,' he said with what he trusted was convincing enthusiasm. 'That's as far as I've got. Where does the seal come in?'

'It was the seal which got broken. That's the trouble,' murmured Susan. 'The cloakroom man did it – or rather he stood over me while I did it. It was too impossibly awkward. Tell him, Brian.'

The young soldier sat down on the arm of the settee.

'It's a perfectly simple story,' he said. 'Susan kept the case that night and most of the next day, but then she got the wind up, as anyone might. You know how you keep shifting something terribly important. Wherever you put it, it never feels quite safe. Finally it got on her nerves, as it would on anybody's, and so, very reasonably, she thought she'd stick it in a station cloakroom. Well, that was all right, but she'd forgotten the I.R.A. scares and the new regulations at some of the stations, and when she got down to Waterloo or wherever it was, the fellow in the office asked her to open the thing. She objected rather guiltily and that made him awkward. You know how these things happen. Finally there was a bit of a row and people started to collect.'

Susan looked at Mr Campion appealingly. 'I didn't dare to hurry away with it. It would have looked so suspicious. It was terrible,' she said earnestly.

'I can well imagine it,' he agreed. 'So you opened it, of course? Bursting the lock, no doubt. What did you find inside?'

'A package,' cut in Brian. 'This is the difficult part. There was a squarish package inside simply plastered all over with official seals. Frankly, the long and the short of it was that Susan had to break these. When the fellow saw that there was only a great wedge of forms and things inside he apologized, but that didn't help. For nearly two days Susan has been in agony waiting for this chap to turn up. When he does she'll have to explain, and she's afraid that he may get in a frightful row since the seals are broken. It's a jam, isn't it?'

'Jam indeed,' consented Mr Campion cautiously. 'Er— if it isn't a foolish question, what exactly do you expect me to do?'

Susan looked at Brian, who had the grace to hesitate.

'It was I who thought of you,' he said at last. 'Susan

came to me because she – well, she regards me as a sort of brother, so she says.' He was blushing furiously, and Campion admired his chivalry. 'We thought that if the seals could be somehow ... replaced, I don't know how or who by, but ... well, you're mixed up with all sorts of authorities, aren't you?' His voice trailed away and his shoulders drooped dejectedly.

'It was a wild idea,' he muttered apologetically.

Campion had not the heart to agree with him as profoundly as he felt.

'Where is this incriminating bundle now?' he inquired.

Susan fished under the sofa on which she sat.

'I haven't dared to let it out of my sight since then,' she said pathetically. 'I wish I'd never seen it. I used to think I'd be pretty good at this sort of thing, responsibility and secrets and all that, but I'm not. I'm bad. I'm hopeless, I'd never take it on again.'

In the face of this humility, any criticism which Mr Campion might have felt inclined to offer was stifled at birth. He took the small attaché-case with becoming reverence and raised the lid. The package with the broken seals lay before him.

To do it justice, it was an impressive parcel with quite two pennyworth of red sealing wax plastered about it and a length of green tape as binding. As he stood holding it in his hands, with the eyes of the two young people upon him, inspiration came to him as if from some psychometric source.

'Oh, by the way,' he said, 'and in strictest confidence, of course, what is Tony's name? I'm afraid you'll have to tell me that.'

'Of course. I don't think that matters. You may even have heard of him.' Susan spoke with a pride which seemed a little hard on Brian. 'He's Anthony Rowley. *The* Anthony Rowley,' she added hopefully.

Mr Campion saved the parcel and his equanimity with an effort, and the girl who was watching him caught her breath.

'You *have* heard of him,' she said. 'Then you will do all you can for me, won't you?'

Campion set down the package. 'All I may,' he said seriously. 'Tell me did Mr Rowley put these seals on this himself?'

'Oh, no, I don't think so.' The idea was a new one to Susan, and she looked a little bewildered. 'He might have, of course,' she added presently. 'He was away some time when he went up to the study to fetch it. That's an official seal though, isn't it?'

Campion studied one of the blobs of wax. There was certainly the imprint of a lion and a crown upon it, but many medallions bear this device, certain sixpenny pieces amongst them. He glanced up.

'All this happened on Tuesday, did it?' he said. 'On the evening I met Brian?'

'Yes. That's why it's so frightfully urgent. Tony may come back any time now. It's going to be unbearable. I'd rather die than have to tell him.'

Brian put an arm round her shoulders.

'Trust Campion,' he said. 'It's quite possible that he knows some important bug who will take a personal interest in the whole case, Rowley and all. Can you think of anyone like that, guvnor?'

Campion ran an easing finger round the inside of his collar.

'Someone does come to mind,' he admitted. 'To deny that would be wrong. Yes, definitely, someone very important does come to mind.'

Forty minutes later Mr Campion and Superintendent Oates sat looking at each other across the desk in the policeman's solid old-fashioned office. The attaché-case lay open between them, and a pile of buff-coloured forms which had been in the sealed package now rested on the superintendent's blotter. Oates, never an emotional man, was wiping his eyes.

'You can find the girl whenever you want her, can you?' he inquired when he could trust his voice.

'Oh, yes. She's being given ice cream and faithful affection by the long-suffering Brian. They're waiting for me to do a spot of philanthropic lese-majesty, bless them. What are you going to do?'

The superintendent placed a pair of shabby pince-nez across his nose, and picked up one of the forms. He read it again until his feelings choked him.

'We'll have to have 'em both up together,' he decided. 'When I've got word that we've pulled the man in, you fetch the girl.'

'No mental cruelty,' warned Campion hastily. 'I don't know if I want to be a party to this at all.'

Oates blew his nose. 'The party is mine,' he said dryly. 'Don't worry about the girl. I shall treat her as if she were my own daughter ... exactly, the wretched little imbecile.'

Leaning forward, he pressed the buzzer on his desk.

He was in much the same mood a little after eight that evening when a sober, but still mercurial, Mr Gilbert Smith, alias Anthony Rowley, sat in the visitor's chair regarding him with the bland affability of one who feels completely at ease.

'Don't apologize,' murmured Mr Rowley when he felt that the silence had gone on long enough. 'I don't mind coming along to see you, even at this impossible hour. I told your Watch Committee in the bowler hats that I should only be too pleased to come with them to look you up. I like you. Nice little place you have here.'

Superintendent Oates glanced at Mr Campion, who sat in a corner on the other side of the room. It was a quiet, satisfied glance, the glance of one who savours a delicate wine before tasting.

'It's nice to see your friend, too,' added Mr Rowley with increasing geniality. 'It's pleasant to find you in such – forgive me – but such unexpectedly intelligent company. You may not believe it, but I find an evening like this very jolly. I am a man of few acquaintances and there's nothing I like better than a chat.'

'You surprise me,' said Oates with heavy politeness. 'I

should have thought you'd have had quite a busy life up at the Ministry. Let me see, you're in the Registration of Office Premises Department, arent you?'

It was a hit. A shade, fleeting as a cloud shadow in a high wind, passed over Mr Rowley's sleek and smiling countenance. His eyes wavered for an instant. However, when he spoke his voice was perfectly controlled.

'What a pity,' he said. 'What a frightful pity. You're confusing me with somebody else. I thought this was a personal call. I'm disappointed.'

'Are you? Not nearly as much as you're going to be, believe me. I've got a form here, quite a number of 'em in fact. Perhaps I'd better read one to you.'

He took a flimsy buff-coloured sheet from the pile before him.

'This is a masterpiece in a small way,' he began condescendingly. 'Anyway, it has all the incomprehensibility and stultifying dullness of the genuine product. The printing is minute, and I doubt if many people would take the trouble to wade through it. I see the address is "Controller, BQ/FT/359 (A) 43, Whitehall," but that has been struck out and "25 Calligan Way, Wembley," printed in. You've been evacuated, I suppose?'

'I don't quite follow you,' murmured Mr Rowley politely.

'No? Well, we'll come to that later,' said Oates inexorably. ' "*Dear Sir,— In compliance with the recent Order in Council, No. 5013287, Sec. 2 AB et seq., you are required to complete the following details concerning the office premises now occupied by you. As you are doubtless aware, it has become important for police and the other interested authorities to possess certain necessary information concerning office premises in vulnerable areas, in order that proper protection for goods and valuables may be ensured in all eventualities.*" '

He paused and looked over his glasses at the expressionless face before him.

'Bewilderingly ingenious,' he said. 'If there was an Order in Council No. 5013287 it would be even better.'

Mr Rowley yawned. 'I find it tedious,' he said frankly.

'I don't,' said Oates. 'It made me laugh. When I first read it I laughed till the tears ran down my face. It's the ultimate labour-saving device of all time. The preliminary questions are magnificently simple. "*Full Name of Occupier of Office. Address. Nature of Business. Number of Staff employed. Whether Night Watchman employed.*" I liked that. That delighted me. But toward the end it gets even better. After "*Number of floors, Number of rooms, Whether all rooms are accessible to a Fire Escape, How many doors between main stair-case and each room, if said doors are locked and if so what locks are used,*" we come to the fascinating question of safes. That is Sub-section C.4 B/F, I notice. Let me read you the headings. "*In which room is your safe? State type (wall or box, etc.). State make of safe. State number of safe. State approximate date when safe was fitted. State approximate size of safe over all.*" And finally, the ultimate pitch of consummate impudence, "*Are you in the habit of leaving valuables in safe overnight?*" '

Anthony Rowley shrugged his plump shoulders.

'I'm afraid I can't follow all that Government stuff,' he said. 'The only thing to do with an official form is to fill it in, not to try to understand it.'

'Exactly.' Oates was triumphant. 'That's the general view. That's the fine fat-headed affectation adopted by half the great British public. That's why a pernicious document of this sort is so dangerous. The man who composed this banked on the astounding fact that the chances are that a man who has spent a small fortune on protecting his property would yet direct his secretary to complete any-thing of this type without hesitation, so long as it was printed on cheap buff paper and arrived in an official envelope.'

'Very instructive,' agreed Mr Anthony Rowley lan-guidly, 'and to a psychologist probably entertaining, but I don't see the point of it myself.'

'Don't you?' said Oates. 'That's odd, because a number of these forms which I have here have already been filled in. They all come from smallish busy City firms, I notice;

each one of them clearly a carefully chosen victim of the enterprising person who persuaded some small crook printer to set up the document. I should have thought you'd have been very interested.'

'Me? My dear fellow, why me?'

The superintendent appeared to appreciate the performance, for a brief smile passed over his grey face as he took a small sheaf of the buff slips from the blotter.

'These are the forms which have been completed,' he observed. 'The rest are blanks. Do you know, it looks to me almost as though someone had been in a hurry, not to say in a funk, and has hastily collected everything connected with the Registration of Office Premises Department and packed it into a parcel for safety, after which he probably gave the parcel to some trustworthy and innocent person, some person who would never be suspected by the police, until his own premises should be safe from their attentions. I can imagine a man doing that on sobering up and remembering that he had opened his mouth far too wide when in conversation with a Superintendent of Police. Still, we'll let that pass. The interesting thing is that out of the twenty-seven forms which various misguided members of the public have been pleased to complete, nineteen have been scored across with blue pencil. The eight which remain have *one thing in common.*'

'Really?' Rowley still kept up his polite indifference. 'And what is that?'

'They each record that the firm in question possesses a Bream safe, together with every conceivable detail concerning it.' Oates made the announcement quietly, but all trace of his earlier sprightliness had vanished and his eyes were cold. 'As you were so kind as to tell me,' he added, 'it was a very beautiful idea, but unfortunately it didn't wash.'

There was a long pause, during which Mr Rowley looked thoughtfully into the future. Presently he smiled.

'You're so ingenious,' he said. 'I've been working out your theory, and it's been an education to me. Now I know why ever since last Tuesday your troop of Boy Scouts have been paying me such a lot of attention. They've taken a very thorough look at my flat, and they've escorted me wherever I've gone with touching fidelity. Naturally, they've been disappointed to find me living in blameless and rather boring innocence. I can understand your zeal and their exasperation. But weren't you taking a little too much for granted? My dear chap, you know as well as I do that you can't hope to pin those forms on me simply because eight of them refer to Bream safes.'

Oates did not answer him. Instead he glanced under his eyelashes at Mr Campion.

'I wonder if I could trouble you to ask little Miss Susan Chad to step in here, my dear boy?' he murmured with the fine display of old-world courtesy abominably overdone which he was apt to adopt at particularly enjoyable moments in his career.

Campion experienced a sneaking sympathy for Anthony Rowley. Just for an instant he saw the whites of the man's eyes.

'She's something of a fan of yours, I gather,' Oates observed mercilessly.

'Is she? Rare and intelligent woman,' murmured his visitor cautiously. 'The name is new to me. I shall enjoy meeting her.'

When Campion returned with Susan clinging nervously to his arm he found himself hoping, most improperly, that she would live up to the testimonial. Oates rose at her approach and so did his visitor, who turned to meet her squarely.

Had Susan been an experienced accomplice, one glance at his blank, inquiring face would have given her the clue she needed. Unfortunately, at any rate from Mr Rowley's point of view, Susan was hardly experienced in anything and her immediate reaction was disastrous.

'Oh, Tony,' she burst out eagerly, 'when did you get back?'

He did not respond at once, and she glanced down the

room, catching sight of the attaché-case on the superintendent's desk. A wave of colour spread over her face and she turned back to the man impulsively.

'Oh, have I got you in a frightful row by breaking the seals? I'm desperately sorry. I wouldn't have had it happen for worlds, but I couldn't help it. Honestly, Tony. I couldn't help it.'

She turned to Oates.

'Does it matter so frightfully? Nothing has been stolen, you see. The whole package is just exactly as he gave it to me. Everything is there.'

Mr Campion always held it to Mr Rowley's credit that in that moment of ruin he laughed.

'So true, my dear,' he said suddenly, holding out his hands to her. 'As you say, nothing has been stolen. That ought to make a lot of difference.'

Oates sighed with satisfaction.

'Then you admit . . . ?' he began.

'Wait a moment.' The man who called himself Anthony Rowley released Susan's hands, smiled at her faintly with an odd mixture of apology and regret, and wandered over towards the desk. 'I should like to make a brief statement,' he said.

Oates leant back in his chair.

'Oh, you would, would you?' he said. 'You've got a nerve.'

The crook shrugged his shoulders.

'I should like to make a statement,' he repeated.

In the circumstances there was nothing else for it, of course, and Oates gave way ungraciously.

'We'll hear it first and take the shorthand note afterwards,' he said. 'Fire away.'

Mr Rowley walked away from Susan, who had planted herself beside him.

'It's a sordid little tale of vulgar vanity,' he began. 'I met Miss Chad, who lives in a rather different circle from my own, about a fortnight ago, and in order to ingratiate myself with her I regret to have to say that I represented myself as having some sort of important Government post.'

'Tony!'

Susan's voice was small and horrified. He glanced at her briefly.

'I'm sorry, Beautiful,' he said, 'but this is a police station, and when in the hands of the law the truth has a nasty way of being the only touchstone.'

'Yes?' inquired Oates grimly. 'And so what?'

'So nothing,' continued Mr Rowley firmly. 'Nothing of importance, that is, save that she believed me. I acquired quite a lot of fake prestige from this subterfuge. It went down very much better than the true story of my activities, which as you know are not very glorious, would have done. After all, an out-of-work motor car salesman twice convicted for burglary is not the romantic figure that a budding diplomat, I might almost say a blooming diplomat, appears.'

'Tony,' said Susan again, and this time he did not look at her.

'All went well,' he continued clearly, 'until – er – chance took a hand. On Monday evening I took a cab in the vicinity of Westminster, and in it I found a large manilla envelope, left, no doubt, by a previous fare. In the envelope were these forms in which you are so interested. Quite frankly I didn't bother to read them. I hate small print, and anyway I can hardly read, you know. I merely saw that they looked official, so I hit on the idea of packing them into a distinguished-looking parcel and giving them to Miss Susan to mind. I'm afraid I misjudged her. I took it for granted that feminine curiosity would be too much for her and that she would be bound to open the package, thereby receiving ocular proof that I was the important person I had set myself up to be. What I did not realize was that she would be so conscientious as to take the whole matter to the authorities.'

'Tony, if this is true, I'll never speak to you again,' Susan was pale with rage and humiliation.

'If it isn't true, which seems more than probable, you'll hardly have the opportunity,' murmured the superintendent.

Mr Rowley sat down.

'How embarrassing one's more childish follies always are,' he remarked. 'Truth is so naked, isn't it?'

'Tony, you're making this up. It doesn't sound like you. Tell me you're making it up.' Susan went over to him as she spoke and, since he could not avoid her, he smiled into her face, albeit a trifle wryly.

'Life is full of vulgarity, my dear,' he said. 'Let this be an awful warning. One swallow doesn't make a summer and one portfolio, alas! doesn't make a Cabinet Minister.'

Susan gaped at him for a moment, and then disgraced herself.

'Oh, I hate you,' she said indistinctly. 'I think you're the meanest, most revolting little tick who ever lived. I never never want to see you again.'

Oates glanced anxiously at Mr Campion, who led her gently from the room. Mr Rowley remained where he was, blinking at the superintendent, who leant across the desk.

'I suppose you think you've been very clever?' he demanded.

'No. Prudent,' said Mr Rowley. 'Prudent, and, in my own way, almost a gentleman.'

'Prudent be damned!' exploded the superintendent unpardonably. 'If you think I'm going to believe any cock-and-bull story about you finding these things in a taxicab, you're mad.'

Mr Rowley permitted a brief smile to break through the somewhat unexpected expression of resignation which had settled on his face.

'You misjudge me,' he said. 'It's not what I expect you to believe, is it? It's what I know you can prove. Did you send anyone down to the address printed on the form?'

Oates did not answer. The chit from a plain clothes sergeant reporting briefly 'Accommodation Address:

Wise Guy in charge: no change to be got there in a million years' lay open on the desk before him.

Mr Rowley got up.

'I shall be hearing from you, no doubt,' he said gently, 'if it's only to pass the time of day. Meanwhile you'll want to confer with your legal advisers, won't you? I should like to congratulate you on that ingenious theory you put forward, but you see the facts were far more simple and far more degradingly human. The wiliest of us do silly things to impress a woman.'

Oates laughed briefly.

'The wiliest of us don't escape every time,' he said bitterly. 'You wait, my lad.'

'Oh, I shall,' Mr Rowley assured him. 'You know my address.'

Mr Campion stood on the pavement looking for a cab which carried Brian and Susan out into the darkness. Having witnessed the grateful eagerness with which Susan had accepted his sheltering arm, Campion was inclined to bet that the young warrior's last day of leave was liable to prove more satisfactory than his first.

He was just turning back to have a word with Oates when another figure loomed up out of the dark gateway. It was Mr Rowley, and he came up to Campion in the moonlight.

'You were with Oates at the café that night,' he said. 'Tell me, did I call him an old duck, by any chance?'

'Er – yes. Yes, I think you did.'

'Fool,' said Mr Rowley. 'Fool. I'm always doing it. It's bad luck. It's prophetic. The association of ideas. See what I mean?'

'No, I – I can't say I do, exactly.'

'Why, the rhyme,' said the man excitedly. 'Don't you remember the rhyme? It was the "fine fat duck who gobbled him up," wasn't it? Fancy calling a Superintendent of Police a duck, anyway.'

'Oh,' said Mr Campion as the light broke in upon him. 'The frog, you mean?'

The other sighed.

'The frog who would a-wooing go,' he murmured. 'Ah, well, but such a nice girl. Such a very nice girl and such a beautiful thought.'

They stood looking down the dark road.

'Heigh ho,' said Anthony Rowley.

XIII

The Danger Point

MR ALBERT CAMPION glanced round the dinner table with the very fashionable if somewhat disconcerting mirror top and wondered vaguely why he had been asked, and afterwards, a little wistfully, why he had come.

The Countess of Costigan and Dorn was the last of the great political hostesses, and she took the art seriously.

Sitting at the head of the preposterous table, she murmured witticisms in the ear of the bewildered American on her left in the fine old-fashioned manner born in the reign of the seventh Edward, although the decoration of the room, her gown, and her white coiffure belonged definitely to the day after tomorrow.

Mr Campion had accepted the invitation to 'a little informal dinner' because the great lady happened to be his godmother and he had never ceased to be grateful to her for a certain magnificent fiver which had descended upon him like manna upon the Israelites one hot and sticky half-term in the long-distant past.

At the moment he was a little exhausted. His neighbour, a florid woman in the late forties, talked with an unfailing energy which was paralysing, but he was relieved to discover that so long as he glanced at her intelligently from time to time he could let his mind wander in peace. He observed his fellow-guests with interest.

There were sixteen people present, and Campion, who knew his godmother well enough to realize that she never entertained without a specific object in view, began to suspect that her beloved Cause was in need of extra funds.

Money sat round the table, any amount of money if Campion was any judge. The bewildered American he recognized as a banker, and the lady next to him with the thin neck and the over-bright eyes was the wife of a chain-store proprietor as yet without a title.

Campion's glance flittered round the decorous throng until it came to rest upon a face he knew.

Geoffrey Painter-Dell was still in his late twenties and looked absurdly youthful in spite of a certain strained expression, which now sat upon his round, good-natured face. He caught sight of Campion suddenly, and immediately looked so alarmed that the other man was bewildered. His nod was more than merely cool and he turned away at once, leaving Campion startled and a little hurt, since he had known the boy well in the days before that promising youth had acquired the important if somewhat difficult position as Private and Confidential Secretary to one of the most picturesque and erratic personalities of the day, the aged and fabulously wealthy Lady (Cinderella) Lamartine.

That remarkable old woman, famed alike for her sensational gifts to charity, her indiscreet letters to the Press, and her two multi-millionaire husbands, was not present herself, but the fact that her secretary had put in an appearance indicated that the gathering had her blessing, and Campion suspected that his godmother's discreet cadging for the Cause was doing very well.

He returned to Painter-Dell, still puzzled by the young man's lack of friendliness, and caught him staring helplessly across the table. Campion followed his glance and thought he understood.

Miss Petronella Andrews, daughter of the famous Under-Secretary, sat smiling at her neighbour, the brilliant lights shining on her pale arms and on her honey-coloured hair; and that neighbour was Leo Seazon.

Campion remembered that there had been rumours of a budding romance between Geoffrey and Petronella, and he quite understood any anxiety the young man might exhibit.

The girl was charming. She was vivacious, modern, and if gossip was to be relied upon, something of a handful. At the moment she merely looked beautiful and youthfully provocative, and Campion wondered, without being in the least old-maidish, if she knew the type of man with whom she was dealing so light-heartedly.

Leo Seazon was bending forward, his distinguished iron-grey head inclined flatteringly towards her.

He was a mature figure, handsome in the way that was so fashionable in the last generation and has never ceased to be fascinating to a great number of women. He seemed to be putting himself to considerable trouble to be entertaining, and Campion raised his eyebrows. In his own somewhat peculiar rôle of Universal Uncle and amateur of crime he had in the past had several opportunities to study the interesting career of Mr Leo Seazon.

The man was a natural intriguer. He had a finger in every pie and a seat upon the most unlikely boards. His fortune was reputed to be either enormous or non-existent, although his collection of *objets d'art* was known to be considerable. He was a man who turned lightly from jade and water-colours to stocks and shares, from publicity to politics. He was also, at the moment, unmarried. It came back to Campion that he had last heard his name mentioned in connection with a certain foreign loan and it occurred to him then that Miss Andrews, and more especially Miss Andrews's family, might be very valuable allies to Mr Seazon, could the matter be arranged.

He glanced back at Geoffrey with amused compassion. The young man still looked harassed, but now that Campion's interest was thoroughly aroused and he cast a more discerning eye upon him, he saw that his expression had an element of fear in it. Campion was startled. Irritation, alarm, bewilderment at the hideous taste of

women in general, all these he could have understood;
but why fright?

*

It was the florid woman on his right who answered his
question, although he did not recognize it as an answer
at the time.

'That's the Andrews girl, isn't it?' she murmured,
bending a virulently red head towards him. 'If she were
my daughter I don't think I'd let her run about with that
round her little neck.'

Campion glanced at Petronella's pearls. As soon as
they were pointed out to him he wondered why he had
not noticed them before. It may have been that the face
above them was sufficiently eye-taking. Now that he did
see them, however, as they lay on her cream skin and fell
among the draped folds of her pale satin dress, they
impressed him.

The necklace consisted of a single string of carefully
graduated pearls, with a second and much larger string
arranged in scallops from the first so that a curious lace-
like effect was produced. It was very distinctive. Campion
had never seen anything quite like it before. It was such
a sensational piece that even in that opulent gathering
he took it to be an example of the decorative jewellery
still in fashion. The Andrewses were a wealthy family, but
not ridiculously so, and Petronella was very young.

'It looks very pretty to me,' he said casually.

'Pretty!' said the woman contemptuously, and he was
astonished to see that her small dark eyes were glistening.

It was not until afterwards that he remembered that
she was Mrs Adolph Ribbenstein, the wife of the jewel
king.

At the moment, however, the conversation was cut
short by his godmother, who swept the ladies upstairs to
her new white and claret drawing-room on the first floor.

Campion saw Geoffrey watch Petronella follow the
others, her white train rustling and the incredible necklace

gleaming warmly on her small neck. His eyes were dark and questioning.

Their host, who seemed to come to shaky life only when his wife went out, developed an unexpected flair for interminable political stories, and Campion was unable to get a word with Geoffrey. Moreover, he received the impression that the young man was avoiding him intentionally and his curiosity was piqued.

Seazon, on the other hand, was in excellent form, and although a certain irritation with the elder man might have been excusable in Geoffrey Painter-Dell, now that the girl had gone any interest he might have had in the man seemed to have evaporated entirely, a circumstance which Campion found very odd.

Geoffrey sat with his head bent, his long fingers drumming absent-mindedly on the mirror table, and when at last their host consented to move he was the first guest to rise.

Circumstances were against him, however. As the little party mounted the staircase a servant waylaid him, and when he did come into the drawing-room some minutes after the others he went over to his hostess, who was talking to Campion.

She listened to Geoffrey's worried excuses with gracious tolerance.

'My dear boy,' she said, 'Cinderella has always been difficult. Run along at once and see what she wants.'

Geoffrey grinned helplessly.

'She either wants me to draw up a scheme for a Parrots' Home or ring up the Prime Minister,' he said wearily.

The Countess of Costigan laughed.

'Then do it, my dear,' she murmured. 'She's a very powerful old lady. There aren't many of us left.'

She gave him her hand and as he went off turned to Campion with a little grimace.

'Poor boy,' she said. 'His soul isn't his own. Cinderella's very difficult.'

Campion smiled down at her. She was seventy, as keen-witted as a girl and quite as graceful.

'Cinderella?' he said. 'It's a queer name.'

His godmother raised her eyebrows.

'She adopted it when she was first married, out of compliment to her husband. He was a German prince,' she said acidly. 'That ought to give you the key to the woman. Still, she's absurdly wealthy, so we must forgive her, I suppose. Albert dear, do go over and talk to Mrs Hugget. That's the thin one in the green dress. Dear me, money doesn't mix well, does it? I asked you and the Andrews girl to grease the wheels a little. I knew you wouldn't mind. Thank you so much, my dear. The one in the green dress.'

Mr Campion went dutifully across the room and passed Geoffrey Painter-Dell as he did so. The young man had paused to speak to Petronella on his way out and had evidently had some little difficulty in detaching her from a resumed conversation with Leo Seazon.

Campion passed by just as the young man was taking his leave and could not help overhearing the last half-whispered words. 'Oh, don't play the fool, darling. For God's sake take the damned thing off.'

A moment later Geoffrey had gone and Miss Andrews was looking after him, angry colour in her cheeks and her eyes blazing. Seazon reclaimed her immediately and Mr Campion bore down on the lady in green.

The party broke up early. Petronella fluttered away on Seazon's arm and Campion hurried off to see the final curtain of a first night whose leading lady was an old friend of his. But he could not get the odd scrap of conversation which he had overheard out of his mind, and Geoffrey's disinclination to talk to him rankled.

He saw Petronella again as he walked down Bond Street the following afternoon. She was sitting beside Leo Seazon in the back of a grey limousine. They had passed in an instant, but Campion noticed that the girl was not smiling and that Leo was particularly elegant, a poem in spring suiting, in fact. He shook his head over them both, for he had liked the look of Petronella.

His thoughts returned to Geoffrey and his strange appeal to the girl which had annoyed her so unreasonably, but he could arrive at no satisfactory conclusion, and presently he shrugged his lean shoulders.

'Damn the young idiots,' he said.

*

He repeated the observation on the evening of the following day when Superintendent Stanislaus Oates, of the Central Branch of the C.I.D., dropped in to see him in that peculiarly casual fashion which invariably indicated that he had come to glean a little information.

The two men were very old friends, and when Oates was shown into the Piccadilly flat Campion did not bother to rise from his desk, but indicated the cocktail cabinet with his left hand while he added his neat signature to the letter he had been composing with his right.

The superintendent helped himself to a modest whisky and lowered his spare form into an easy chair.

'How I hate women,' he said feelingly.

'Really?' inquired his host politely. 'They haven't invaded the Yard yet, have they?'

'Good Lord, no!' Oates was scandalized. 'Ever heard of Lady Lamartine?'

'Cinderella? I have.'

'Seen her?'

'No.'

Oates sighed. 'Then you haven't the faintest idea,' he said. 'She has to be seen to be believed. I thought someone told me you knew that secretary of hers pretty well.'

'Geoffrey Painter-Dell.'

'That's the fellow. Know anything about him?'

'Not much, except that he's a nice lad. His elder brother, who died, was a great friend of mine.'

'I see.' The superintendent was cautious. 'You can't imagine him being mixed up with any funny business? Not even if there were thousands involved?'

'I certainly can't.' Campion laughed at the suggestion.

'Sorry to disappoint you, old boy, but the Painter-Dells are absolutely beyond suspicion. They're the blood-and-steel brigade, *sans peur et sans reproche* and all that. You're barking up the wrong tree. Geoffrey is as innocent as driven snow and about as excitable.'

Mr Oates seemed relieved. 'I practically told her ladyship that,' he said, shaking his close-cropped head. 'What a woman, Campion! What a woman! She's so darned important too; that's the devil of it. You can't say "Run along, Grannie, you're wasting the policeman's time." It's got to be "Yes, milady, no, milady I'll do what I can, milady" the whole time. It gives me the pip.'

He drank deeply and set down his glass. 'She's been at me all day,' he said.

Mr Campion made encouraging noises and presently his visitor continued.

'You were in the States in '31,' he said, 'and so you don't remember the Lamartine robbery. The house at Richmond was entered and nearly a hundred thousand quid's worth of jewellery was taken. It was her ladyship's own fault, largely. She had no business to have so much stuff, to my mind. No woman of eighty wants a load like that. Well, anyway, it was pinched, as she might have known it would be sooner or later. Fortunately we got most of it back and we put "Stones" Roberts away for seven years. It was clearly one of his efforts, and we just happened to find him before he'd unloaded the bulk of the stuff.'

He paused and Campion nodded comprehendingly.

'Were you in charge?'

'Yes. I was Chief Inspector then, and Sergeant Ralph and I cleaned the affair up as best we could. We didn't get all the stuff, though. There was a thing called La Chatelaine which we never did find. We put "Stones" through it, but he swore he'd never seen the thing, and we had to let it go. Well, I'd practically forgotten all about it when the old lady sent for me this morning. She made it pretty clear that I'd better come myself if I was

Police Commissioner, let alone a poor wretched Super, and the A.C. thought I'd better go. When I got there she was all set for me to arrest young Painter-Dell for knowing something about this Chatelaine thing, and I had an almighty job to convince her that she hadn't a thing on the poor chap. I had a talk with him finally, but he wasn't helpful.'

Campion grinned.

'You didn't think he would be, did you?'

Oates looked up and his sharp, intelligent eyes were serious.

'There was something funny about the boy,' he said.

Campion shook his head. 'I don't believe it. The old lady was too much for you.'

Still the superintendent did not smile.

'It was nothing *she* said,' he insisted. 'She simply convinced me that she wasn't quite all there. But when I talked to the lad I couldn't help wondering. He was so frightened, Campion.'

At the sound of the word Campion's mind jolted and he remembered Geoffrey's face at the other end of the mirror-topped table. Fear; that had been the inexplicable thing about his expression then.

The superintendent went on talking.

'Lady Lamartine sent for me because her maid told her that Painter-Dell had been asking about the ornament. The robbery took place a couple of years before he took up his appointment. He'd never seen the thing and had never asked about it before, but yesterday he seems to have put the maid through it, making her describe the jewel in detail. The maid told her mistress and her mistress sent for me. I explained that no one could base a charge on anything so slight, and to pacify her I saw the boy. I kid-gloved him, of course, but he was very angry, naturally. He handed in his resignation and the old lady wouldn't accept it. I apologized and so did she. There was a regular old-fashioned to-do, I can tell you. But all the same I didn't understand the boy. He was sullen and quiet, and in my opinion terrified. What d'you know about that?'

Campion was silent for some moments. 'La Chatelaine,' he said thoughtfully. 'It sounds familiar.'

Oates shrugged his shoulders. 'It's one of these fancy names some jewels get,' he explained. 'It's a necklace which is supposed to have belonged to one of the French queens, Catherine de Medici, I think. It's an unusual-looking thing, by the photographs. Like this.'

He got up and crossing to the desk, scribbled a design on the blotting-paper.

'There's a single string and then another joining it here and there, like lace, see?' he said.

'Dear me,' said Campion flatly. 'What are the stones?'

'Oh, pearls. Didn't I tell you? Perfectly matched pearls. The finest in the world, I believe. Interested?'

Campion sat staring in front of him, bewilderment settling over him like a mist. In his mind's eye he saw again Miss Petronella Andrews at his godmother's dining-table, and round her neck, falling into the soft satin folds at her breast, was, only too evidently, Lady Lamartine's La Chatelaine.

It was then that he repeated under his breath the observation he had made in Bond Street on the morning before.

The superintendent was talking again.

'It's a funny thing that this should come up now,' he was saying, 'because "Stones" Roberts came out a fortnight ago and we've lost sight of him. He didn't report last week and we haven't hauled him in yet. I always thought he knew something about those pearls, but we couldn't get a word out of him at the time. Well, I'll be getting along. If you say the Painter-Dell lad is above suspicion I'll believe you, but if you do happen to hear anything, pass it along, won't you?'

Campion came to himself with a start.

'I will, but don't rely on me,' he said lightly, and rose to escort his visitor to the door.

He did not put the extraordinary story out of his mind, however, but actually set out that night on a pilgrimage round fashionable London in search of a young lady whom the superintendent would have liked very much to meet. Campion's conscience insisted that he take this step. It had clearly been his duty to tell Oates all he knew and, since he had not, he felt in honour bound to do a certain amount of investigating on his own account. Petronella was not easy to find. She was neither dancing at the Berkeley nor dining at Claridge's. He looked in at the ballet and did not see her, and it was not until he remembered the Duchess of Monewden's Charity Ball at the Fitzrupert Hotel that he found her, looking like a truculent little ghost and dancing with Leo Seazon.

He caught sight of Geoffrey almost at the same moment and accosted him, demanding an introduction to Miss Andrews. Geoffrey Painter-Dell grew slowly crimson.

'I'm frightfully sorry, Campion,' he said awkwardly. 'I'm afraid I can't. We – er – we're not speaking. Terribly sorry. Got to rush now. Goodbye.'

He retreated in considerable disorder before Campion could murmur his apologies, and disappeared among the throng.

Campion was aware of a growing sense of uneasiness. He had been fond of Geoffrey's elder brother and was genuinely alarmed at the prospect of seeing the young man involved in any sort of mess. He looked about him and espied old Mrs De Goncourt, who was only too happy to introduce him to her niece. She took him by the arm and waddled happily across the floor with him, annihilated the frowning Mr Seazon with her magnificent smile, and pounced upon the girl.

'The cleverest man in London, my dear,' she said in a stage-whisper which would have carried across Drury Lane. 'There you are, Albert. Take the child away and dance with her. Ah, Mr Seazon, you look younger than I do. How on earth do you do it?'

Miss Andrews glanced up at Campion and, although her smile was charming, her grey-blue eyes were very much afraid. He suggested that they should dance, but she hung back.

'I'd like to, but –' she began and glanced nervously at her escort, who was doing his best to extricate himself from the clutches of his redoubtable contemporary.

Campion did not press the matter. He smiled down at the girl.

'I saw you at dinner the other night,' he said. 'We weren't introduced and I don't suppose you remember me. You're not wearing your beautiful pearls to-night.'

She stared at him, and every vestige of colour passed out of her face. For a dreadful moment he thought she was going to faint.

'Not very beautiful pearls, I'm afraid.' It was Seazon who spoke. He had escaped from Petronella's aunt and now stood, sleek and very angry, a little behind the girl. 'Miss Andrews was wearing a pretty little imitation trinket she did me the honour to accept from me. Now, unfortunately, it is broken. She will not wear it again. Shall we dance, my dear? It's a waltz.'

He had not been actually rude, but his entire manner had been coldly offensive and there was an old-fashioned element of proprietorship in his attitude towards the girl which Campion saw was resented even while she was grateful to him for his interference.

Campion went home depressed. He liked Geoffrey, had been prepared to like Petronella, and he disliked Mr Leo Seazon nearly as much as he disapproved of him, which was considerably. Moreover, the mystery of La Chatelaine was becoming acutely interesting.

*

He had business which took him to the other end of the town the following morning, so that he lunched at his club and returned to his flat a little after three o'clock. His man, who admitted him, mentioned that there were visitors in the study but did not remember their names, so that he went in entirely unprepared and unheralded.

Standing in the middle of his own Persian carpet, clasped in each other's arms with a reckless enthusiasm which could be neither disregarded nor misunderstood, were Petronella Andrews and Geoffrey Painter-Dell. They turned to him as he appeared, but neglected to relinquish hands. Petronella looked as though she had been crying and Geoffrey was still harassed in spite of a certain delirious satisfaction in the back of his eyes.

Campion surveyed them politely.

'How nice of you to call,' he said fatuously. 'Will you have cocktails?'

Petronella looked at him pathetically.

'Geoffrey says you can help,' she began. 'Somebody must do something. It's about those utterly filthy pearls.'

'Of course the whole thing is fantastic,' put in Geoffrey.

'Paralysing,' murmured Miss Andrews.

Campion restored order. 'Let's hear the worst,' he suggested.

Geoffrey looked at Petronella and she sniffed in an unladylike and wholly appealing way. She took a deep breath.

'I've got a flat of my own,' she began unexpectedly. 'It's in Memphis Mews, at the back of Belgrave Square. You see, I've always wanted to have a place of my own, and Mother stood up for me, and after a tremendous lot of trouble we persuaded Father. He said something awful would happen to me and of course he's right, and I am so sick over that. Still, I needn't go into that, need I?'

She gave Campion a starry if somewhat watery smile and he mentally congratulated Geoffrey on the possession of his family's celebrated good taste.

'It begins with the flat, does it?' he inquired.

'It begins with the burglary,' said Miss Andrews. 'My burglary – the one I had, I mean.'

Campion's lean and pleasant face invited further confidence and the girl perched herself on the edge of his desk and poured out her story, while Geoffrey hovered behind her with helpless but adoring anxiety.

'It was last Monday afternoon,' she said. 'The day of the dinner party. I was out and my maid let a man in who said he was an inspector from the electric light people. She left him in the big room I call my studio and went back to the kitchen. Then she heard a crash and hurried in, to find that he'd pulled my bureau out from the wall, caught the legs on the edge of the carpet, and spilt everything off it on to the floor. She was still scolding him when I came in and then he just fled. Margaret – that's the maid – rang up the electric light company and they said they hadn't sent anyone. That's how we knew he must have been a burglar.'

'I see. Did you tell the police?'

'No. He hadn't taken anything. How could I?'

Campion smiled. 'It's sometimes just as well,' he said. 'And then what happened?'

'Then I found the loose board,' said Miss Andrews calmly. 'I said I'd put the room straight if only Margaret would get some tea, and as I was doing it I found that one of the floorboards, which is usually under the bureau, had been sawn off at some time and put back again. It was very wobbly and I pulled it up. There was an old cigarette tin in the hole underneath and I took it out and put the board back. I thought the tin had been stuffed there to make the board fit, you see.

'It took us some time to get the place straight and then I had to dress. I didn't think of the tin again until I was just setting out. Margaret had gone home. I took a last look round, because I do like the place to look tidy when I come in, or it's so depressing, and I saw this dirty old tin on the edge of the carpet. I picked it up to throw it into the wastepaper-basket when I thought it felt heavier than it ought to have done, so I opened it. The pearls were inside in some cotton-wool.'

She paused and blushed.

'I suppose I ought not to have worn them,' she said,

'but I didn't dream they were valuable, and they looked so lovely against my frock. It was natural to try them on and then I hadn't the heart to take them off.'

Geoffrey coughed and his eyes sought Campion's appealingly.

'Yes, well, there you are,' he said. 'I suddenly looked across the table and there they were. I recognized them at once. They're the famous La Chatelaine. The rooms I spend my life in are littered with paintings and photographs of Lady Lamartine wearing them. I knew they'd been stolen and never recovered, and I was pretty nearly bowled over. I realized there'd been some mistake, of course, but I knew how Lady Lamartine felt about her necklace. She's a very – well – impulsive woman, you know, Campion, and I'm afraid I said all the wrong things when I did get a moment with Petronella.'

Miss Andrews turned to him with a wholly delightful gesture.

'You were sweet,' she said magnanimously. 'I was a pig. He just rushed up to me, Mr Campion, and said, "Where on earth did you get those things? Who gave them to you? Take them off at once." I thought he was being a bit possessive, you know, and I was rude. And then of course he had to go. What made it so much worse was that when he phoned me early next morning I was still angry. I refused to give him any information and I told him I didn't want to see him again, ever. When he rang up again after that, I was out. I didn't want to talk about the wretched things by that time, you see, naturally.'

A puzzled expression passed over Campion's face.

'Why was that?' he inquired.

'Because I'd lost them,' said Miss Andrews blissfully. 'I lost them that night, the night of the dinner party. They just went. They got warm, you know, as pearls do, and must have slipped off without my noticing it.

'I've been everywhere to look for them. Leo Seazon took me everywhere the next afternoon. We went to the Carado first, and then on to the Spinning Wheel Club in Bellair

Street, and even to the coffee-stall where a crowd of us had some awful tea about four in the morning, but of course nobody remembered seeing them. I daren't advertise and I daren't go to the police because Lady Lamartine is so unreasonable and so difficult, and Geoffrey being her secretary makes it so much worse. You know what she's like. She'll make a frightful scandal and think nothing of it. Daddy will never forgive me and it will be ghastly for Geoffrey. What on earth shall I do?'

Campion considered the problem. It was not an easy one. Lady Lamartine was indeed, as even Superintendent Oates was prepared to admit, a very difficult old woman.

'It's all those people,' Petronella continued. 'All those people at the dinner party and at the Carados afterwards. You see, everybody seems to have recognized the wretched things. Apparently they're famous. The story is bound to go back to Lady Lamartine eventually and, of course,' she added thoughtfully 'there is Leo Seazon.'

Campion avoided Geoffrey's eyes.

'Ah, yes, of course, Seazon,' he said casually. 'Why did you tell him about it in the first place?'

'I didn't,' said Miss Andrews. 'He told me. I had no idea what they were until he came out with it. I've met him two or three times lately and he was always very attentive and all that. When we discovered that he was going on to the Carados too, we decided to go together. He seemed quite amusing. He left us at the Spinning Wheel and I didn't think of him again until he phoned the next morning and asked if I could see him on "a private matter of great urgency" – you know how he talks. I told him to come along and when he arrived he started off by asking me in a fatherly fashion if I'd be a good girl and take La Chatelaine to the police.'

She took a deep breath.

'I was simply staggered, of course,' she said, throwing out a pair of small gloved hands, 'but he made me understand what he was talking about at last and I got rather frightened. He put it so badly and he would keep begging me to "do the sensible thing" and "own up".'

'You told him you'd lost the pearls?'

She nodded and her little diamond-shaped face grew grave.

'I'm afraid he didn't believe me,' she said. 'He didn't believe the story of the cigarette tin either, even when I showed him the loose board.'

Geoffrey made an inarticulate sound and she turned to him.

'Oh, he didn't actually say so, of course, darling,' she protested. 'He pretended to be very helpful. But he did let me see that he didn't really trust me. And now he's come out in the open. He spends hours exhorting me to "be wise", to "trust him", and not to "force him to do anything he'd hate to have to do".'

She looked directly at Campion and he saw that behind her flippancy there was genuine distress in her eyes.

'It's almost a sort of blackmail,' she said. 'I'm getting to loathe him. I can't move him off the doorstep and I daren't shoo him away in case he goes roaring round to Lady Lamartine. The trouble is I'm afraid he's stewing up to the point where he's going to make an offer to marry me and keep quiet. I can feel that in the wind. I think he rather fancies an alliance between the two families.'

Geoffrey snorted and Campion intervened.

'Don't you think that's a little old-fashioned and melo-dramatic?' he ventured gently.

Miss Andrews met his eyes with an unexpectedly forth-right glance.

'Leo Seazon is old-fashioned and melodramatic,' she said. 'He must be nearly seventy.'

Campion, who knew that debonair and conceited man to be but fifty-six, felt a sneaking sympathy for Leo Seazon. However, it was not of long duration. Geoffrey took the girl's hand.

'When Petronella rang me up to-day and poured out the whole story I was beside myself,' he said. 'Lady

Lamartine is on the war-path already. She's heard something. There was a Yard man down there yesterday asking
nervous questions. He practically apologized to me for
bringing up the subject, but I felt pretty guilty. What can
we do, Campion? What on earth can we do?'

Campion made no rash promises. The two young people
standing so forlornly in front of him touched his heart,
however. He gave them a cocktail and sent them away
with the assurance that he would do what he could.

Just before they left, Geoffrey turned to him wistfully.

'About this fellow Seazon,' he began diffidently. 'I can't
pitch him out yet on the street, can I?'

'My dear boy, no!' Campion was mildly scandalized.
'I'm afraid Mr Seazon must be placated at all costs. He's
the danger point, you see.'

Geoffrey nodded gloomily. 'The man's practically
ordered Petronella to go to the ballet with him to-night.'

'Then she must go,' said Mr Campion firmly. 'I'm
sorry, but it's imperative. The one thing we must avoid
at all costs is publicity, I take it? Mr Seazon has a devastating tongue.'

'Here, but I say ...!' Geoffrey protested in sudden
revolt. 'If we're going to accept that premise, Petronella
may have to marry the fellow if La Chatelaine doesn't
turn up.'

Campion's pale eyes were hidden behind his spectacles.

'Let us hope it doesn't come to that,' he said solemnly.
'Bless you, my children. Let me have your card, Miss
Andrews. I'll ring you in the morning.'

As soon as his visitors were safely off the premises,
Campion sat down at his desk and drew the telephone
towards him.

Superintendent Oates was even more helpful than usual.
His curiosity was piqued and he listened to the Memphis
Mews address with considerable interest.

'Yes,' he said, his voice sounding lazier than ever over
the wire, 'it does strike a note in my memory. That's the
place where "Stones" Roberts's girl lived. Her father was

a chauffeur, I remember. They've turned all that Mews into society flats now. What's the excitement?'

Campion did not answer him directly. Instead he put another question and once again the Superintendent was helpful.

'It's funny you should ask,' he said. 'I was just thinking about Roberts when you rang. One of our men reports that there's a fellow very like him acting as a waiter at the Spinning Wheel Club. He couldn't be quite sure and didn't want to frighten him. He wants Ralph or me to go down and identify him.'

'Fine.' Campion sounded relieved. 'That's a real bit of luck. Look here, Oates, do me a favour. Don't pull the man in, but have him tailed. I've got a very good reason for asking.'

Oates began to grumble.

'When is your lordship thinking of taking the humble police force into his confidence?' he demanded.

'Right away,' said Campion cheerfully. 'I'll come round. Oh, Stanislaus, heard from Lady Lamartine to-day?'

Mr Oates made a remark which the telephone department would have considered vulgar, and rang off.

*

Petronella Andrews was entertaining Mr Leo Seazon to tea when Mr Campion telephoned to her the following afternoon. She was paler than usual and there were definite signs of strain in her young face. It seemed to her that she had been entertaining Mr Seazon for several hundreds of years without respite.

He sat, grave and handsome, in the quilted armchair by the fireplace and regarded her with the half-reproachful, half-sympathetic expression which she had grown to hate. They had been talking, as usual, of La Chatelaine, of Mr Seazon's considerable fortune, and of the advisability of a young girl having a husband who could protect her in times of trouble.

Petronella had skilfully led the conversation away from the sentimental whenever it had appeared, but it had been growing steadily more and more apparent that his evasion could not last forever, and the telephone call came as a heaven-sent interruption.

Campion was very discreet on the wire.

'Miss Andrews,' he said, 'do you remember some earrings you lost? No, don't speak; I said earrings. You lost them when your flat was robbed and you told the police. You may not remember all this, but I want you to know it now. Will you come down to Scotland Yard at once and get them? Mr Seazon is with you, isn't he? Perhaps he'd bring you in his car, which our man reports is outside your door. Don't be alarmed. Just come along. Explain who you are when you arrive and you'll be taken straight up to Superintendent Oates. I shall be there. Goodbye.'

An excellent training by a mother of the old school had taught Petronella both self-possession and adroitness, and within half an hour the courtly Mr Seazon, who was not unadroit himself, was handing her gracefully out of his grey limousine in the courtyard of the ugliest building on the Embankment.

The square high-ceilinged room in which Superintendent Oates received them with the avuncular charm he kept for pretty ladies was already half-full of people. Petronella's heart leaped as she caught sight of Geoffrey sitting next to Mr Campion in a corner, and when he smiled as he rose to greet her she blushed very charmingly.

Mr Seazon, who observed the incident, did not seem so pleased.

Besides the superintendent there were two other officials present, a thin man in uniform with a box and a fat man in a brown suit with a portfolio. It was very impressive.

Mr. Oates beckoned the thin man, took the box, and smiled encouragingly at the pretty girl.

'Now, Miss,' he said.

'My – my earrings?' stammered Petronella.

Oates regarded her blandly.

'A clerical error,' he said magnificently. 'The necklace, I think. Now would you identify this, please?'

He opened the box with a flourish and took out the shimmering string of loveliness within. La Chatelaine hung over his stubby fingers and glistened like frozen tears in the grey and ugly room. Petronella took them and her face lit up.

'Oh, this is marvellous!' she said. 'Oh, bless you! Where did you find them?'

'One moment, Miss.' Oates turned to a plump and shining little man who had been sitting unnoticed on the other side of Mr Campion and who now came forward.

'Yes,' he said, taking the string delicately from the girl. 'Yes, definitely. I can identify them. This is La Chatelaine. It has been through our hands several times for restringing and so on. We attend to all Lady Lamartine's magnificent collection of jewellery. Dear me, I never thought we should see this in its present lovely state again. You are to be congratulated, superintendent. If these pearls had been separated it would have been a sin, a major sin.'

He dropped them back into the cotton-wool with a little gesture which was almost a caress.

Leo Seazon coughed. His face was expressionless but quite composed. He conveyed the impression of a man gallantly concealing a deep disappointment.

'Well, now are you satisfied, my dear?' he murmured. 'The necklace goes back to its – ah – rightful owner, I suppose?'

'I am taking the pearls to her ladyship to-night personally, sir,' said Oates. 'She'll be very glad to see them.'

'I have no doubt of that,' said Seazon drily and a little unpleasantly, but Petronella silenced him.

'How did you get them?' she demanded.

The superintendent smiled.

'Police methods,' he said airily, avoiding Campion's eyes. 'The crook who performed the robbery in the first place was arrested and sent to jail. That was nearly seven years ago. We recovered practically everything he had had his hands on except the pearls. He'd hidden those in a place we didn't think of searching, under a floorboard in his young lady's father's flat. He didn't even trust her and the family left while he was in jail, so that when he came out and went back for his swag, he found the place had been done up and turned into fashionable little residences. As soon as he was certain he was not being watched, he made an attempt to get into the flat by telling the maid there that he was from the electric light company, but he was disturbed and went off without finding out if his cache was still undiscovered. At this time he was working as a waiter at the Spinning Wheel Club in the West End and the same evening he saw a guest come in wearing the very necklace he was after.'

Oates paused and a laugh of pure relief escaped Petronella.

'And so he stole them again?' she said. 'Oh, how wonderful! Oh, Geoffrey!'

Leo Seazon watched the young man go over to her and his round dark eyes were not pleasant.

'Very interesting,' he said briefly. 'It'll make a delightful story. I must add it to my repertoire.'

There was a moment of silence. The young people stared at him in consternation and Petronella put out her hand.

'You wouldn't,' she said huskily. 'Oh, you wouldn't?'

He regarded her coldly.

'My dear child, I don't see why not,' he said drily and turned towards the door.

Campion rose.

'I say, don't go,' he murmured affably. 'Hear the rest of the story, since it interests you. Our Mr Roberts, the original crook, didn't steal La Chatelaine *in* the Spinning Wheel.'

Leo Seazon swung round slowly and Campion went on, still in the light and pleasant tone that his enemies disliked so much.

'Oh, no,' he said. 'Our Mr Roberts, Mr "Stones" Roberts, merely saw the jewels at the club. He followed them and found it impractical to attempt to recover them that night. He hung about long enough to see where they were hidden, however, and made his plans to steal them. Unfortunately for him he took so long reconnoitring that by the time he made his successful attempt last night he had a couple of policemen on his tail. They caught him just as he was coming out of the house with La Chatelaine in his pocket. It was a "fair cop", as he said himself. Does that improve the story, Mr Seazon?'

The handsome man with the distinguished iron-grey curls attempted to bluster, but his face was haggard.

'I don't understand your inference,' he began.

'Don't you?' said Campion. 'Oh, well, then, you're going to get a jolly surprise as well, because the house from which Mr Roberts took La Chatelaine last night was your house, Mr Seazon, and Mr Roberts, in the statement which he has made to the police, distinctly says that he followed you home after seeing you slip the necklace off Miss Andrews's shoulders as you were helping her off with her evening cloak in the Spinning Wheel. It may be a lie, as I see you are about to suggest, but he was coming out of your house when he was taken with the pearls on him and he has described the drawer in the desk in your study from which he says he took them.'

'Ridiculous! Why should I steal? I'm a rich man.' Mr Seazon's voice was not too steady.

Campion looked at Miss Andrews.

'There's a frightfully trite old saying about wealth not being able to buy one everything one wants,' he said. 'Well, there you are. I've said my piece. It's up to Miss Andrews to prosecute.'

Petronella turned a pale, horrified face from her erstwhile admirer.

'I won't. I won't, of course, if only he doesn't *talk*,' she said.

Campion held open the door to the retreating Leo Seazon.

'He won't, I'm sure,' he said clearly. 'But if he should, well, you can always change your mind, can't you? It remains at your discretion, my children.'

In the background Oates chuckled.

'Lay you six to four he don't send you two a wedding present,' he said.

FOR THE BEST IN PAPERBACKS, LOOK FOR THE

In every corner of the world, on every subject under the sun, Penguin represents quality and variety – the very best in publishing today.

For complete information about books available from Penguin – including Puffins, Penguin Classics and Arkana – and how to order them, write to us at the appropriate address below. Please note that for copyright reasons the selection of books varies from country to country.

In the United Kingdom: Please write to *Dept E.P., Penguin Books Ltd, Harmondsworth, Middlesex, UB7 0DA*.

If you have any difficulty in obtaining a title, please send your order with the correct money, plus ten per cent for postage and packaging, to *PO Box No 11, West Drayton, Middlesex*

In the United States: Please write to *Dept BA, Penguin, 299 Murray Hill Parkway, East Rutherford, New Jersey 07073*

In Canada: Please write to *Penguin Books Canada Ltd, 2801 John Street, Markham, Ontario L3R 1B4*

In Australia: Please write to the *Marketing Department, Penguin Books Australia Ltd, P.O. Box 257, Ringwood, Victoria 3134*

In New Zealand: Please write to the *Marketing Department, Penguin Books (NZ) Ltd, Private Bag, Takapuna, Auckland 9*

In India: Please write to *Penguin Overseas Ltd, 706 Eros Apartments, 56 Nehru Place, New Delhi, 110019*

In the Netherlands: Please write to *Penguin Books Netherlands B.V., Postbus 195, NL–1380AD Weesp*

In West Germany: Please write to *Penguin Books Ltd, Friedrichstrasse 10–12, D–6000 Frankfurt Main 1*

In Spain: Please write to *Longman Penguin España, Calle San Nicolas 15, E–28013 Madrid*

In Italy: Please write to *Penguin Italia s.r.l., Via Como 4, I-20096 Pioltello (Milano)*

In France: Please write to *Penguin Books Ltd, 39 Rue de Montmorency, F-75003 Paris*

In Japan: Please write to *Longman Penguin Japan Co Ltd, Yamaguchi Building, 2-12-9 Kanda Jimbocho, Chiyoda-Ku, Tokyo 101*

FOR THE BEST IN PAPERBACKS, LOOK FOR THE

PENGUIN CLASSIC CRIME

The Thin Man Dashiell Hammett

All it took was a little persuasion. Like four .32 bullets, a blonde, the newspapers, the cops and a junked-up hoodlum in his bedroom. Nick Charles, retired Trans-American Detective Agency Ace, was back in business!

The Case of the Late Pig Margery Allingham

Kepesake was the perfect village. Perfect for murder … Albert Campion had forgotten all about it until he was called back there to investigate a peculiarly distasteful death. The body was that of Pig Peters, the sadistic school bully of Campion's childhood, freshly killed five months after his own funeral…

The Moving Toyshop Edmund Crispin

Gervase Fen, Professor of English Language and Literature at Oxford, turns from don to detective to confront a bizarre and baffling mystery. 'A rococo classic. It has abundantly the pervasive charm of the genre' – H. R. F. Keating in *The Times*

The Wisdom of Father Brown G. K. Chesterton

Twelve delightful stories featuring the world's most beloved amateur sleuth. Here Father Brown's adventures take him from London to Cornwall, from Italy to France, involving him with bandits, treason, murder and curses.

Death at the President's Lodging Michael Innes

Dr Josiah Umpleby, President of St Anthony's College, has been found dead in his study, his body in a litter of ancient bones. 'In a class by himself among writers of detective fiction' – *The Times Literary Supplement*

A selection

More Work for the Undertaker

In a masterpiece of story-telling Margery Allingham sends her elegant and engaging detective, Albert Campion, into the extraordinary Palinode household where nobody is beyond suspicion. Campion goes on to discover poison-pen letters, a coffin cupboard, suicide and murder.

Sweet Danger

Here Albert Campion poses as the king of a tinpot Balkan state looking for his lost crown. *Sweet Danger* is perfectly crafted, full of surprising twists and turns. What starts as a light-hearted, slightly crazy wild-goose chase becomes something much more dangerous, nasty and sinister.

Death of a Ghost

John Sebastian Lafacadio, R.A., 'probably the greatest painter since Rembrandt' (according to himself), is dead. But his influence is not. When, some time after his death, his family assemble to view his eighth painting they are treated to a murder. Albert Campion is present and finds himself facing a long line-up of possible killers.

Look to the Lady

The Gyrth Chalice has been the sacred trust of the Gyrth family for centuries. Its beauty and antiquity make it unique – and quite irreplaceable. When its safety is threatened by a ring of wealthy and ruthless collectors, Campion springs to its defence. Enlisting the help of young Valentine Gyrth and a few other willing and unwilling associates, Campion embarks on a game that is dangerous – and possibly deadly.

Dancers in Mourning

Everybody fell under the spell of Jimmy Sutane, the charming and talented song-and-dance man. Everyone, that is, except the spiteful practical joker who put a pin in his stick of grease-paint. Nothing too deadly, but when Albert Campion is called in to investigate, people begin to die, and there's no shortage of suspects when the first victim's death is so convenient for so many.

FOR THE BEST IN PAPERBACKS, LOOK FOR THE 🐧

PENGUIN CLASSIC CRIME

The Thin Man Dashiell Hammett

All it took was a little persuasion. Like four .32 bullets, a blonde, the newspapers, the cops and a junked-up hoodlum in his bedroom. Nick Charles, retired Trans-American Detective Agency Ace, was back in business!

The Case of the Late Pig Margery Allingham

Kepesake was the perfect village. Perfect for murder … Albert Campion had forgotten all about it until he was called back there to investigate a peculiarly distasteful death. The body was that of Pig Peters, the sadistic school bully of Campion's childhood, freshly killed five months after his own funeral…

The Moving Toyshop Edmund Crispin

Gervase Fen, Professor of English Language and Literature at Oxford, turns from don to detective to confront a bizarre and baffling mystery. 'A rococo classic. It has abundantly the pervasive charm of the genre' – H. R. F. Keating in *The Times*

The Wisdom of Father Brown G. K. Chesterton

Twelve delightful stories featuring the world's most beloved amateur sleuth. Here Father Brown's adventures take him from London to Cornwall, from Italy to France, involving him with bandits, treason, murder and curses.

Death at the President's Lodging Michael Innes

Dr Josiah Umpleby, President of St Anthony's College, has been found dead in his study, his body in a litter of ancient bones. 'In a class by himself among writers of detective fiction' – *The Times Literary Supplement*

BY THE SAME AUTHOR

A selection

More Work for the Undertaker

In a masterpiece of story-telling Margery Allingham sends her elegant and engaging detective, Albert Campion, into the extraordinary Palinode household where nobody is beyond suspicion. Campion goes on to discover poison-pen letters, a coffin cupboard, suicide and murder.

Sweet Danger

Here Albert Campion poses as the king of a tinpot Balkan state looking for his lost crown. *Sweet Danger* is perfectly crafted, full of surprising twists and turns. What starts as a light-hearted, slightly crazy wild-goose chase becomes something much more dangerous, nasty and sinister.

Death of a Ghost

John Sebastian Lafacadio, R.A., 'probably the greatest painter since Rembrandt' (according to himself), is dead. But his influence is not. When, some time after his death, his family assemble to view his eighth painting they are treated to a murder. Albert Campion is present and finds himself facing a long line-up of possible killers.

Look to the Lady

The Gyrth Chalice has been the sacred trust of the Gyrth family for centuries. Its beauty and antiquity make it unique – and quite irreplaceable. When its safety is threatened by a ring of wealthy and ruthless collectors, Campion springs to its defence. Enlisting the help of young Valentine Gyrth and a few other willing and unwilling associates, Campion embarks on a game that is dangerous – and possibly deadly.

Dancers in Mourning

Everybody fell under the spell of Jimmy Sutane, the charming and talented song-and-dance man. Everyone, that is, except the spiteful practical joker who put a pin in his stick of grease-paint. Nothing too deadly, but when Albert Campion is called in to investigate, people begin to die, and there's no shortage of suspects when the first victim's death is so convenient for so many.